Wetland and Other Stories

Robin Ray

ALL THINGS
THAT MATTER
PRESS

Wetland and Other Stories

This is a work of fiction. Any resemblance to actual persons, living or dead, is purely coincidental.

ISBN 13: 9780989403221

Library of Congress Control Number: 2013945355

Cover design by All Things That Matter Press
Published in 2013 by All Things That Matter Press

To my immediate and extended families, and to Cary Terra for getting it right and setting me on the path to self discovery.

"At night when the streets of your cities and villages are silent and you think them deserted, they will throng with returning hosts that once filled and still love this beautiful land."

Chief Seattle

Table of Contents

Wetland 1
Car 20 85
Little Hammer 88
The Statue of the Crying Virgin Mary 108
My Farsi Boyfriend 115
Iron Maiden 131
The Road to Hanoi 194
A Walk in the Park with Mozart 213
The Family of Gabriel 242
Strung Out 250
Belltown 308

Wetland

Chapter I

By Way of Texas

It's just a few miles outside of Amarillo, Texas on a bright Sunday morning. The sky is clear. The temperature outside is a balmy 72 degrees. A white prison bus marked Amarillo Dept. Of Corrections is making its way up U.S. Route 60 towards Panhandle, Texas. A sign on the side of the road reads *Mama Lucy's Country Store and Restaurant - Best Dagnabbit Coffee In Panhandle, Texas.*

The bus exits U.S. 60 to a road just past the sign and, within minutes, pulls up into the dirt parking lot outside Mama Lucy's. Curious onlookers, most attired in their Sunday best, stop and stare as the young, pretty female, Deputy Karen Hollinger, rifle in hand, steps off the bus. She's followed by eight male inmates dressed in prisoner's chain-gang black and white. This group of eight is followed out by the older, rotund, Sheriff Arnold Baker, who's also carrying a rifle.

"Now," Baker tells the criminals, "this coffee and bathroom stop is outside of Corrections Protocol, but seeing since you boys did a good job cleaning up these highways over the past couple of days, and this being the Lord's day an' all, we think you folks deserve a break. Just don't screw it up."

As they walk single file into the restaurant, a little boy picks up a stone and throws it hard towards the group. Gordon Gabriel, an inmate in his 40's, catches it with his right hand, almost as if he'd seen it coming from a mile away.

"You keep on like that, boy," Gordon scolds the kid, "and you'll be in one of these suits in no time.

"I ain't like you," the boy protests.

Gordon smiles.

"Only time will tell."

Gordon throws the rock on the ground. The boy goes silent as the prisoners are escorted inside.

It's bustling with activity inside the truck stop'. The roomy establishment sports a mini-mart, a souvenir gift section, and a handful of one-armed bandits. The inmates file past the diners and head toward two booths in the back. Prisoners Nos. 1-4 sit in one booth and the other four sit in the last booth by the back wall. The deputy and sheriff occupy seats at a booth just across the aisle from the inmates, their hands never leaving the clutch of their state-issued rifles. A few seconds later a young waitress comes over to the inmates' booths carrying an armful of menus.

"Good morning, y'all," the waitress introduces herself. "My name's Deanna."

They all say hello. She hands each person a menu and removes the "Reserved" standee off each table.

"Anyone for coffee?" she asks.

"Oh yes," the pock-marked prisoner known as Dannemann grins. "I've been dying to sample some of that best dagnabbit coffee y'all got—according to y'all's billboard."

"And it is," Deanna curtsies. "Just y'all wait."

She turns to the sheriff and deputy.

"Sheriff Baker! Boy, you're a sight for sore eyes. Ain't seen you in what, like, two months?"

"Hey Sheila," Baker asks. "How's it going?"

"Fine. The newspapers had you for dead, what with that ticker 'an all."

"Yeah. Don't write me out the book yet."

The waitress turns to the deputy. "I don't think we've ever met before."

They shake hands. "Karen Hollinger," the deputy introduces herself. "Got transferred over from Houston recently."

"Well, nice to meet ya, Karen. Any friend of Baker's is a friend of mine. I'll be right back for y'all's order."

As she walks to the kitchen, Dannemann watches her, eyeing her curves with devilish intent.

"Shoot," he licks his lips. "I already know what I want."

"You just put a lid on it, you hear?" Hollinger berates him.

"I'm scared of you," he grumbles under his breath.

"What was that?" the deputy asks.

"Just leave them boys alone, Karen," the sheriff councils her. "They don't mean nothin'."

"I don't like the way this one stares at me," Hollinger admits.

"Stop being so paranoid."

He points to her rifle. "You got Ol' Jesse there keepin' you company."

Soon, Deanna returns pushing a cart containing three jugs of coffee, condiments, and wet naps. She places one jug on each table, reaches into her black apron and brings out a pencil and order pad.

"Y'all ready to order?" she asks.

The inmates all nod or say yes.

"Hey Sheriff," inmate Jervis asks, "what's the limit?"

"Six bucks each," he answers. "We're in a fiscal crisis, you know."

"Anything's better than that prison slop we get," the prisoner called Ozone laments.

The inmates order by numbers: No. 4, no onions, No. 3, No. 9, extra cheese. After taking their orders, Deanna turns to the sheriff's table.

"What about you two?" she asks.

"You know," the sheriff admits, "I ain't been feeling m'self lately. I'll just nurse this cup o' Joe I got."

"Okay," the waitress nods.

"I'll have a sesame bagel with cream cheese," Hollinger orders.

"Sure, no problem. Comin' right up."

Deanna grabs the serving cart and leaves for the kitchen.

"Mighty fine tart, that one," Dannemann states.

"Remember the sanctity of this day, brother," Gordon advises him.

"Oh, what the hell," Dannemann protests, "You're gonna preach to me?"

"They went out of their way to let us in here," Gordon schools him. "Hospitality like that isn't handed out often to people like us."

"Oh, man," Dannemann rolls his eyes. "I know what kinda pictures you got up on *your* wall."

Gordon shakes his head.

"You can never wash the oil out of the frying pan, can you?"

"Y'all keep it down over there," Hollinger warns them.

She turns to the sheriff.

"I still think this is a mistake."

"Yeah, I know," he relents. "I've done this before. A little kindness and some of these fellas change their lives around. Let me guess, you don't believe in change."

"That some of them can get their life together? I didn't just get this uniform yesterday."

"And I've seen people change. I try to be optimistic."

"Hey, Sheriff," the previously timid now suddenly loud prisoner named Bostick yells, "I gotta use the bathroom."

"Hold it until we get back," the deputy tells him.

"It's all right, Karen," the sheriff says. "I ain't feeling so good m'self. Think I might have to go, too." He turns to Bostick, "Let's go." The sheriff grabs his rifle, gets ups and walks with the prisoner up the aisle and out of sight around the corner to the restrooms.

"That motherfucker has the bladder of a mouse," Othello, the one-eyed inmate, says to no one in particular.

"Excuse you!" Hollinger admonishes him.

"Sorry, my bad."

Dannemann turns to the deputy, "You got to learn to relax, girl."

Hollinger tightens her grip on her rifle, grits her teeth, and stares down the inmate. "I ain't no girl. Get that through your thick skull."

"Don't mean no harm, sister. We're not level-one offenders, that's why we're the roadside cleanup crew."

"Well, don't give me no lip and everything will be all right."

Dannemann shakes his head.

"Man," he whispers to another inmate, "that's one tough cookie. Probably ain't been laid in weeks."

"What'd you say?" Hollinger asks.

Just then Deanna returns with their brunches on a serving cart and passes the plates out. The Sheriff and Bostick return from the bathroom just as the waitress is leaving. Within seconds everyone is face deep in their Southern-fried meals. Gordon is the last to touch his plate; he first says grace. The deputy notices this.

"You know," she wonders, "I know you from somewhere. You look familiar."

"I'm not from these parts."

"Gordon Gabriel … can't forget a name like that. Too biblical."

"I used to live in Nashville. Franklin, to be specific."

"Yep. That must be it. I used to go shopping in those malls down there. Must've seen you around."

"It's where all the country stars live."

"I know that. That's why I was there."

"You're a singer?"

"I tried to be. Played Bluebird Café and other places every week."

"And now here you are."

"And now here I am."

"Mmm-mmm," Dannemann interrupts. "This here breakfast is the best thing I ever tasted since Mary Lou sat on my face last Christmas."

"Mind your manners," Hollinger warns him.

"You grew up in a sewer, boy?" Gordon asks, rhetorically. Offended, Dannemann starts to rise.

"Y'all just simmer down now," the sheriff says trying to deflate their tempers. "We're in public." Dannemann sits down.

"He's the poster child for deviants," the stocky inmate they call Boris says aloud. "Don't mind him."

"You still sing?" Gordon asks Hollinger.

She shakes her head, "I got two boys now. That kinda life ain't for me no more."

"Oh. Well, maybe in your next life."

"I got no regrets."

Gordon rubs his stomach uncomfortably. "Hey Sheriff," he complains, "I think this food's too rich for me."

"Probably the oil," Baker believes. "They slather their bacon and sausages in it. That's what gives southern fried its mystic charm."

"Well, I think it's my turn for the can."

"Geez. Can't it wait?"

"Yeah, I guess." Gordon's bodily expression states otherwise. He has a slight grimace and is twisting in his seat. Hollinger notices his discomfort.

"I'll take him," she promises.

"God's grace on you, sister," Gordon tips his invisible hat and gets up.

The deputy grabs her rifle and escorts him to the men's room. The two walk around the corner and out of sight of their company and arrive at the narrow aisle that separates the kitchen from the two bathrooms. The door on the right closest to the Emergency Exit states Gents. The other door on the same side just across from the kitchen reads Gals. They walk down to the last door on the right. Gordon opens it and steps halfway in.

"Are you coming in?" he asks her.

"Of course," she answers.

Once inside, Hollinger looks around the bathroom quickly. She checks the stalls. They're all empty. Other than an older man relieving himself in one of the urinals, there's just the janitor's broom and mop cart in a corner.

"When did this place become unisex?" the man at the urinal asks.

Hollinger turns to Gordon. "I'll be right outside," she warns him. "No tricks."

After she exits, Gordon goes into one of the two stalls.

Back inside the restaurant, it's clear the inmates are enjoying their meals. Some of them are eating as if their plates would be confiscated any second.

"Anybody up for parole soon?" the sheriff asks.

"Two months for me," Dannemann states.

"I got six months," Boris admits.

"I still got a year," Bostick moans.

"Well, remember," Baker informs them, "all this road work counts towards good time. The warden takes notice of these things. I could—"

Suddenly, he stops talking. A bitter cold chill goes ripping through his body. Reaching into a pocket he brings out a small medicine bottle, opens it, pops a pill in his mouth, washes it down with coffee and returns the bottle to his pocket.

"You okay?" Jervis asks.

Baker nods. Just then the waitress comes over.

"You alright, Sheriff?" she asks.

"Yeah. I think my belt's too tight."

She turns to the inmates. "Will y'all be needin' anything else today?"

"How 'bout your phone number?" Dannemann requests.

"Hush up, boy," Baker warns. He turns to Deanna. "Go get the deputy. She's by the men's room. Tell her I'll replace her now cos it seems I gotta get there soon."

"Will do."

Before she leaves she plops the check down on the sheriff's table. He picks it up and looks at it.

"Bill ain't gonna give you a heart attack, is it, Sheriff?" Dannemann asks.

"Comes out of county road expense account."

About one minute later, the deputy comes over.

"Where's your prisoner?" he questions her.

"I left him in a stall."

Sheriff Baker grabs his rifle and gets up. "Okay."

The sheriff enters the tile-covered gents' room and peers under the last stall. He sees the legs of Gordon's black and white coveralls and shoes. Satisfied, he enters the stall next to Gordon's, pulls down his pants, and sits down to go to work. Noticing a local newspaper folded atop the toilet paper dispenser, he takes it and begins reading.

"Tax breaks for the rich," he reads. "That ain't nothin' new." He flips through a few more pages. "Who's this Constantine fella?" he continues. "He wants to be the next mayor of Amarillo. Ever heard of him, Gordon?"

Gordon doesn't answer. The sheriff peruses more of the paper. "I see the price of alfalfa is down. That's good. You know, it's one of the best plant fertilizers there is. Gonna be retiring soon. Me and the old lady got property right here in Carson County. Thinking 'bout growing berries, cherries and grapes. We might even open up a little roadside stand. How does Baker's Berries sound? Got a nice ring to it, don't it?"

Again, Gordon is silent. The sheriff knocks lightly on the panel separating them.

"Gordon?"

He bends down and peeks and he still sees black and white striped pants and prison-issued shoes. "Hey boy, you okay in there?" The sheriff pulls up his pants, buckles his belt, and exits his stall and knocks on the door to Gordon's stall.

"Hey son, why you so quiet?" There's no answer. "Gordon!" The sheriff is livid. He tries opening the door but it is locked from inside. He walks over to his previous stall, steps up on the toilet, peers over into Gordon's stall and sees ..."What in tarnation?"

There's no Gordon. What the sheriff does see is the broom and mop, both broken in half and placed on the toilet and clothed in black and white prison coveralls. The foot part of the is wearing shoes and the shirt is draped over the raised toilet seat. The sheriff jumps off his toilet and yells, "Goddamit."

He was just about to leave the bathroom when he hears a muffled bang coming from the window. Looking over, he sees the wind i batting against it. He tiptoes and reaches up to the window. It opens. Too high to see out of, he grabs the janitor's mop bucket, flips it over on the ground, and climbs on it. He peers out in the distance towards the sagebrush some 200 yards away and mumbles, "Give me strength." Gordon, wearing only white underpants and socks, is running into the brush.

Quickly, Baker exits the bathroom and rejoins his group, panting and nearly out of breath.

"What's the matter, Sheriff?" Hollinger asks. "Looks like you seen a ghost."

"Where's Gordon?" Dannemann asks.

Sheriff Baker finally catches his breath. "He's gone."

"What?" Deputy Hollinger can't believe her ears.

"Let's go," Baker commands the group. "Everybody out. We got us an escapee."

The deputy grabs her rifle and stands up. "Y'all heard the man. Single file. Out."

With the sheriff in the lead and the deputy in the rear, the group of nine walks out of the restaurant and into the prison bus. The sheriff closes its door, starts the engine, and drives around the back of Mama Lucy's towards the sagebrush area.

As the bus arrives, Baker realizes they can go no further because of some large rocks. The sheriff and deputy exit the bus and lock the door from outside. A few of the inmates protest. They try to open the windows and emergency exits, none of which budge.

"Y'all hold tight for a few minutes," Baker tells them. "This won't take long."

The two officers turn and head into the nearly six feet high brush amidst the protestations of the inmates. Karen is so fast she's leaves Baker behind. He stops a few times to catch his breath. Looking back, Karen sees him in distress and runs back.

"Hey Sheriff, you okay?"

Yeah, yeah," he groans. "I'll be fine. I ain't gonna keel over just yet. Just gotta stay away from all them chili and beans the old lady likes.

"Yeah, no shit. Well, why don't you just head back to the bus and wait for me. I'll be back with Gordon in no time.

The sheriff looks at her.

"Ain't nobody gonna say nothin'" she promises. "Them boys back there won't say a word after that breakfast treatin'."

"Are you sure it's okay?"

"Time's a wastin'."

"Then I'll be seeing y'all back at the bus."

The ailing lawman turns around and heads back to the bus. Karen takes off like a rabbit through the brush. Moments later, she comes upon a hedgy slope that leads downhill towards a raging ravine. At first she hesitates; the hill is extremely steep. Then she catches a glimpse of the soaking wet Gordon climbing out on the far side of the ravine.

She fires a shot at him. It misses, but it does catch his attention. He raises his left hand and flips her the bird. She starts scooting down the steep hill. Gordon takes off into the nearby forest. Finally, she arrives at the river. From a distance it seemed fairly rapid, but up close it's an absolute monster.

"Oh shit," she swears, shaking her head and staring at the white rapids. "Fuck it."

With her ever present rifle, she dives into the water. At first it seems like she would swim successfully across this 100'wide watery chasm, but suddenly a downed branch coming downstream slams into her. The impact makes her lose her grip on the rifle. She reaches after it, blood trickling down her face, but the river is too fast. She continued to the far side without it.

Arriving at the slippery, muddy bank, her legs get caught in a tangle of underwater vines. She struggles against them but it seems like nature will win this battle. Just then, she feels someone grab her arms and tug her out of the water.

Looking up, she sees Gordon. Reluctantly, she accepts his help and allows him to yank her out of the drink.

"This doesn't exonerate you," she scolds him, unhooking a pair of handcuffs from her belt. "You're under arrest."

"I'm not going back."

She reaches to cuff him. "Oh yes—"

Before she could finish her sentence, he grabs her, and turns her around.

"Let go of me."

Ignoring her protests, he twists her arm till she releases the cuffs. Slapping them on her, he forces her to her knees, picks up a vine from the ground, and ties it around her ankles. Gently, he lays her on her side in the clearing between the forest and ravine.

"You're gonna pay for this," she threatens him.

"When I was a kid," he tells her, "I wanted to be in the rodeo."

"Well, you missed your calling."

"Would've done better without y'all's intervention."

"Come on. Let me go. I'm a deputy of the law. The state frowns on this behavior."

"Sorry. No can do."

"I'm all cramped up."

"Another man wouldn't be so nice after being shot at."

"Make it easy on yourself, Gordon. You just added resisting arrest and assaulting an officer to your felony escape.

"I ain't a bad man, Karen. I've just done some bad things, is all. But I'm one with the lord now."

"That doesn't pardon you."

"Are you a believer, Karen? You read the bible?"

"Yeah. Untie me."

He doesn't honor her request. Instead, he kneels down beside her, wipes some of the ravine water from her face, places his hand on her head, and starts preaching.

"Revelation 21, 4: And God shall wipe away all the tears from their eyes, and there shall be no more death, sorrow, or crying, neither will there be pain, for the former things are passed away."

The deputy groans.

"Good. Now get me up."

He ignores her, stands up. "I've been called," he brags. "It's bigger than this. Goodbye, Karen." He backs away into the forest.

"Gordon! Dammit! You ain't no minister!"

She continues struggling against the vine but it's not budging. I can just hear mama's mouth now, she says to herself. I told you that kind of work ain't for women. She struggles again but it's in vain. "Dammit."

Chapter II

35 year old Vietnamese Phong and his Chinese fiancée, Violet, 29, enter their breezy one bedroom apartment located in a four story building on Capitol Hill near downtown Seattle. Phong is in a tuxedo and Violet, carrying a violin, is wearing a frilly white dress. Several

trophies and plaques adorn the walls. Phong removes his bowtie and walks over to the fridge in the kitchen.

"Good show, huh?" he smiles.

"Good for you," she nods, plopping down on a sofa. "At least you snagged a publisher."

"You want a beer?"

She flips on the TV by remote control and raises her feet on a hassock. "What I want is a recording contract."

"Are you kidding?" he asks, opening two bottles of Singha. "You've placed in the Paganini Competition, the Stradivarius International and the Benjamin Britten. Don't worry. They'll come calling soon."

"I'm just tired of waiting. At least the performance we gave today got *you* recognized. I just hope you remember us little people."

He walks over to her and hands her a beer. "You won't be forgotten."

***

Gordon, finally exiting the woods, sees a small horse farm about 100 yards away. On the side of the road just outside the farm is a small white sign with black letters that reads: Carson City, Texas.

Climbing over the wooden fence, he walks past two painted pintos, tells them 'shh' and continues to a clothesline strung between a tree and the barn.

He sees bed linens and women's clothes. Finally, he comes up a pair of Levi coveralls. He takes it down and tries it on. Just a few sizes too big it will, nevertheless, suffice.

Sneaking into the barn, he sees two pairs of galoshes and a pair of brown leather shoes. He tries the shoes on but they're too big. Grabbing a handful of hay, he stuffs it in each shoe. He tries them on; they feel comfortable enough to walk around in.

Sneaking out of the barn, he spots a car driving up to the house. He stoops, turns and hurries away toward the back of the farm where he disappears into the tall brushes some 200 feet away.

***

Gwen Pham, a 35 year old Vietnamese beauty, is jogging south on the sidewalk by the train tracks on Alaskan Way in Seattle's waterfront district. The world famous thoroughfare is a hubbub of activity and filled with tourists, street performers, vacationers, and food and souvenir vendors.

A few minutes later she enters her condo on First Avenue. It's a nice, relatively new, building with sweeping views of Puget Sound. She takes the elevator to the fifth floor. Six people in their 20's and 30's are standing outside of her unit. She looks at her watch.

"Omigosh," she apologizes. "Sorry folks. I lost track of the time. I actually didn't think anyone saw the Craigslist ad."

They tell her it's okay. She taps her analog watch but the second hand has stopped. "I guess this is for sale, too, if anyone can spare the battery."

One of the ladies from the group takes the watch and examines it while Gwen opens her door and props it open with a chair.

The condo is a typical one bedroom with high ceilings, huge windows, modern appliances, and shag carpeting. The only things slightly out of place are the dozens of price tags attached to almost every item in the room. Adorning the walls are framed pictures of Vietnamese fishing villages. Between the pictures hangs a blown up photo of Gwen with the jazz singer Nancy Wilson.

"Hopefully you'll find something you need," she tells her visitors. "I'll brew some coffee and tea."

Before exiting to the kitchen, she puts on some music on a portable CD player. Nancy Wilson sings 'Someone To Watch Over Me'. The potential customers start examining the items for sale: desk and floor lamps, an LCD TV, a stereo system, IPod, chairs, a computer and printer, two acoustic guitars, paintings, stuffed animals, cutlery, pants and shirts, music CDs and DVD movies.

Gwen re-enters with a tray of coffee, tea, saltines, some cups and condiments, and places them on a center table which also has a price tag dangling from it. The guests help themselves to refreshments. A customer picks up an untagged animal encyclopedia from a bookshelf.

"Is this for sale?" she asks.

"Yes," Gwen answers. "Everything must go."

"Did you have a run of hard luck?"

"I think it's the recession," Gwen explains. "Everyone's feeling the pinch."

"So you're going back home? I mean, like, to your parents?"

"Maybe. I don't know yet," Gwen sighs. "Just kinda need the cash right now."

"I'll give you ten bucks for this book," the woman says, holding out the cash.

Gwen nods and takes the money.

"Thanks for stopping by. I needed the cheer up."

"Sure. No problem. I'll give you my number and we can keep in touch."

"Sounds good."

Another woman in her late 30's stares at the pictures on the wall. She points to one in particular—a photo of an old Vietnamese man standing and rowing a *thuyen doc moc,* a dugout canoe, with a little girl sitting patiently at the bow.

"Where is this?" she asks.

"Quảng Ngãi province in Vietnam," Gwen answers.

The woman walks over and stares at the picture.

"It's gorgeous. Looks so peaceful."

"You can only imagine the atrocities that old man has seen in his life," the woman says.

On another wall, a man looks at the photo of Gwen with the singer.

"She looks familiar," he says to himself.

Gwen overhears him and walks over. "That's Nancy Wilson, the jazz singer."

"Is that's who we're listening to now?"

"Yeah. She's been my idol for years. Met her at Jazz Alley a while back. Great singer."

"Are you a singer, too?"

"I wish. I don't have the pipes. Cursed by my genes. It's a dream of mine, though. Who knows? Maybe in my next life."

***

Dustin, a nerdy, bespectacled 21 year old Vietnamese college senior, is sitting up in bed in his room in the basement of a two-story, seven bedroom room off-campus student house. A football game on TV can be heard just beyond his door.

Busy looking at pictures of nude male models on his new hi-tech video cell phone, one of his roommates, Shawn, suddenly opens the door and pokes his head in. Dustin rapidly turns off the photos and puts the phone in video mode through which he views his housemate.

"Hey Dustin," Shawn greets him.

"Sup, Shawn? They don't knock on the planet you're from?"

"Are you filming me with that thing?"

"Just got it. Two-way video conferencing phones. It was a buy one, get one free deal."

"Cool. Hey, just letting you know, you're missing the game, dude."

Dustin puts the phone away. Shawn tosses him a can of beer.

"Thanks. What's the score?"

"Seahawks 7, Colts 24."

"Figures."

"We got pizza and hot wings outside, dude. Come join us."

"Um, I have an exam in the morning."

"So? You got all night. It's only 4 p.m."

Sitting on the edge of Dustin's bed he says, "You know, Dustin, me and the boys like you, right?"

"Oh, here we go again."

"Well. It's true. You spend too much time by yourself, dude. Remember that chick next door who wanted to get with you last party? Well, she's over here now. She's asking for you. She didn't want to come in here because she didn't know how you felt."

"Tell her … tell her I feel fine."

"You're not being anti-social because everyone's American and you're Chinese, right?"

"Vietnamese."

"My bad. The boys like you, though. At least you're not stuck up like some of them other Asians who don't drink."

"I don't represent any Asians around here. I'm just me. But, seeing as you went out of your way looking out for me, the least I can do is return the favor." Shawn pats him on the leg and gets up. Dustin also hops off the bed.

"You're a good guy," Shawn believes, "But you need friends. Gotta start hanging out more. It's not good to stay alone all the time."

Dustin looks his roommate in the eyes. "So get me drunk."

***

Night had fallen over the Emerald City. Being Sunday meant that there were just a few more hours before the start of the rat race. Some still try to take advantage of their remaining weekend hours and squeeze out as much fun as humanly possible. It didn't matter that their hometown team lost to the Colts that day. If a club or bar is open, it would still see a little foot traffic.

The Pink Pussycat Lounge in North Seattle is like a seedy casino. Its black walls, ceiling and floor, and the various red lights and disco balls scream *sleaze*. There are several small tables strewn about where scantily clad waitresses take orders for munchies and non-alcoholic beverages. At one end of the large room is a stage with a silver pole in the middle. A very shapely, nearly naked woman in her early twenties is "engaged" with the pole as throbbing music blasts from wall speakers.

Gwen, sporting a long platinum wig and a shiny skintight red vinyl suit, is applying makeup at a mirror in the lounge's dressing room. A younger African-American dancer, Skylark, is in the room arranging items in a locker. She glances over at Gwen several times and sees she's nervous.

"Let me guess," Skylark asks, "this is your first time, right?"

Gwen tries to brush her off. "What do you think?" she replies sarcastically.

"I'm on your side, woman. Don't get testy with me." Skylark reaches into her locker and brings out a small bottle of gin. She hands it to Gwen.

"Sip on this. It'll calm your nerves."

Gwen takes the bottle. "Thanks."

"Where'd you get the suit?"

"Red on Broadway on Capitol Hill."

"Funky."

Gwen takes a healthy swig from the miniature bottle. "You know, this is a non-alcohol joint."

"The johns come in here drunk," Skylark assures her. "Why shouldn't we?" Skylark takes the now half-empty bottle of gin from Gwen and downs the rest.

Gwen studies herself in the mirror. "I hope I can do this."

"I don't think about them. I'm in my own world, like I'm on the beach in Tahiti or something."

"Yeah. I'll bet you've never been to Tahiti."

"I seen the pictures on the internet," Skylark alleges. "That's good enough for me."

The two share a nervous laugh. Gwen extends her hand.

"I'm Gwen."

"Skylark."

"Skylark? What kinda name is that?"

"Cute, huh? Gets me paid."

Just then, Mr. West, the rotund manager with combed-over hair, yellow sunglasses, and cheesy wide-lapel suit opens the backstage door.

"Hey, Gwen," he shouts, "show time."

Gwen sighs and nods.

"Okay."

"You okay, girl?" Mr. West inquires. "Looks like you just took a dive in a swarm of bees."

"Go easy on her," Skylark begs. "You know she's as nervous as a cat in a dog pound."

"Well," Mr. West suggests, "every dog has his day. You're up, Gwen," he says while leaving.

"Here I go."

"Break a leg, girl. Earn that cash, honey."

Gwen smiles nervously and exits. Seconds later, she hits the stage to throbbing techno. The catcalls begin. They're loud, streaming, and furious. A few patrons comment that they've never seen an Asian in there before. Some of the Asian businessmen in attendance offer to take her back to their hotel. She ignores them and, fueled by the swig of gin, begins gyrating to the music. Mr. West stands in the shadows and watches. With the light in her eyes, Gwen can barely see who's shouting. Nervous or not, she doesn't show it. Within minutes, she's working the pole like a pro.

The patrons simmer down. A few of them hand her $5 bills. Slowly, teasingly, she peels her red suit off to reveal a matching pair of skimpy panties and bra. A few more bills come in and she stuffs them in her panties. Now, salivating, the patrons wait for what comes next.

Suddenly, becoming self conscious, she looks over the faces of the strangers in the red-lit room. Thoughts of uncontrollable horror flood her mind. Mr. West watches in horror as Gwen picks up her red suit and flies off the stage to the dressing room. Stunned, some of the patrons boo as she exits.

Inside the dressing room, she hurriedly changes back into her "normal" self. The wig is off and she's putting on a pair of jeans and a sweater. Mr. West barges in. Smoke is bellowing from his nostrils like a bull in Pamplona.

"What happened out there?" he demands.

"Oh, Mr. West," Gwen asks, "give me a break. It's my first night."

"It's your last night!"

"What? Come on. Give me one more chance."

"You embarrassed me tonight. No dancer has ever fled the stage."

"I'm sorry. I just ... I don't know. I wasn't expecting ... some of those guys are Asians."

"So?"

"It's like stripping for my brothers or my uncles."

"Gwen, you stand to make a lot of money here because you're the only Asian girl I have and we get a lot of foreign Asian businessmen. You'll bring 'em in and bring 'em back. That's valuable to both of us. But you got to strip."

"So you're giving me another chance?"

"Yeah, but not tonight. The damage's been done and we got some other girls who already paid to work."

"So tomorrow?"

"The place has been rented for a private party tomorrow. Tuesday night?"

"Yeah. Thanks."

He takes out an envelope from his inner jacket pocket and gives it to her.

"This is an incentive. I'm counting on you, Gwen."

"Thanks, Mr. West. I won't let you down."

"Good."

***

Gwen walks east on Olive Way towards her condo downtown. She checks the time on a clock in a closed clothing store: 10:30p.m. Standing near a street light, she quickly counts the bills in the envelope Mr. West had given to her and nods. Fortune is smiling upon her.

***

Gordon watches as drivers zoom past, ignoring his hitchhiker's thumb. Walking up a rural Texas highway, lit mainly by the moon and the occasional firefly, he sees a structure about 200 feet from the road. Trumping through the thick grass, he comes upon an abandoned silo. He peers through the lower windows but it's too dark inside to see anything. Slowly, he opens the door.

"Hello?" he asks.

No one answers.

"Anyone here?"

Again, no answer. He walks into the grain elevator and looks around. Even in the darkness he discerns the outlines of bales of hay strewn all over. Fashioning a makeshift bed, he stretches out on it, folds his arms, and promptly falls asleep.

Chapter III

Amongst the debris and rats, a few of Seattle's homeless souls are scouring through the brushes of a homeless camp hoping to find that one last crumb of drug that may have slipped unnoticed out of someone's jittery hands the night before. This Monday morning, one of the scavengers, Andrew, a slight Vietnamese man about 30 years old, kicks through a pile of old boots but comes up shorthanded. When two police officers appear at the edge of the camp everyone, including Andrew, quickly depart in the other direction.

In the grain silo, Gordon wakes up suddenly when he hears a noise. At first he seems confused as to his whereabouts, then, realizing where he'd spent the night, breathes a sigh of relief.

Rising to his feet, he walks in the direction of the noise. He sees a broken-off handle from one of the cobwebbed power boxes lying on the floor and deduces this is what made the sound. He takes a quick look around the silo. Not much to see: a few skids, a corn sorter, and several large rusted cylinders adorned with cobwebs.

He goes outside and stretches in the warm morning sun. Looking around, there doesn't seem to be anyone for miles. He can see a rural road hundreds of feet away; in the other direction, it's acres of dry grass as far as the eye can see.

Walking towards the road he notices that, up ahead, there is a small stream running just along the side of it. Within minutes he's face deep in the shallow stream taking in as much of the cool water as he can. He perks up when he hears a truck coming up the road.

Standing near the ditch, he waves the old red pickup truck down. Joe Johnson, a farmer in his 40's and toting a truck full of red and green peppers, ripe tomatoes, and green beans, slows to a crawl.

"Howdy. Need a lift?" he asks, chewing tobacco stuffed in his gums.

"Sure."

Joe reaches over and unlocks the passenger side door. Gordon gets in.

Gordon glances quickly around the pickup as it made its way down the old road. A little on the unkempt side, there are business cards and assorted paperwork sticking out of the vents, visors, and center organizer with a small basket of large bright red tomatoes beside it. Joe notices Gordon looking at them.

"Go ahead. Help yourself."

"Thanks."

He takes one of the giant juicy tomatoes and bites into it.

"That there's an heirloom tomato," Joe informs him. "A Brandywine. Finest in all of Texas. What's your name? Oh, what happened to my manners? My name's Joe Johnson."

"Gordon."

They shake.

"Joe Johnson from 'Johnson Acres Farm—Freshness Delivered Daily. Where ya headed?"

"Just north."

"Well, I'm headed up to Spearman in Hansford County."

"How far is that from the state line?"

"Beats me."

"You ain't from around here, are you? You're out in the middle of the road with no vehicle."

"People don't stop and give rides anymore," Gordon grieves.

"Well, I don't blame 'em. What, with all these criminals running around an' all."

"Ain't you worried?"

"Nah." He lifts up his shirt to reveal the shiny silver 6-shooter tucked in his pants. "My best friends, Smith and Wesson, are always with me."

Gordon nods as the truck continues up the road.

***

Phong awakens in his bedroom and it only takes him a second to realize Violet isn't next to him. Walking into the living room, he sees a note on the table. Written in Violet's hand, the message is short and sweet:

"Didn't want to wake you. Have a good time composing."

***

The alarm has been buzzing in Dustin's room for some time. Finally waking, he slaps the sound off. Sitting up, he grabs his glasses from a bedside stand.

He stumbles over to a closet, turns the numbers on a combination lock and opens the door. His clothes are neatly arranged, almost as if he used a ruler to check the spacing between hangers. He grabs a pair of pants and a shirt and blows a kiss to the life-sized poster of a chiseled, near naked young man taped inside the closet door.

***

Gwen is at the front counter of a fitness club speaking to one of the managers. She is cancelling her membership. The manager gives her a form to sign and hands her a refund check.

Later, she's busy selling some gold earrings, bracelets, and rings in a neighborhood pawn shop. The broker offers her an appalling low price for her items. She refuses and takes them back. They argue back and forth, neither one willing to give way. When the broker ups the price, she finally relents and sells her jewelry.

An hour later, she's in a bookstore filling out an application. She continues to do the same at a vitamin store and, finally, a coffee shop.

Exiting the shop, she takes out a box of Djarum clove cigarettes from a pocket and lights one with a brass butane lighter. Then, looking up the half-crowded block, she sees a red-haired woman she knows coming her way. Immediately, she turns around and quickly walks away in the other direction. Turning a corner she runs into her friend Mina, a chubby woman in her late 20's.

"Gwen!"Mina opens.

"Hey, Mina."

"Long time, no see. How's it going?"

"I'm okay. Can't complain."

The two turn and continue walking up the block.

"People at work are worried about you, Gwen. We haven't heard from you since they let you go over a month ago."

"Yeah, I know. I'm sorry about that. I know you guys mean well but I don't want anybody feeling sorry for me."

"Are you working now?"

"Nah. Still looking. It's been rough. Aren't that many talent agencies in Seattle."

"At least you get unemployment insurance, right?"

"Actually, I don't."

"How come?"

"They denied me because I was fired with just cause."

"Just cause."

"Well, I did tell the boss off."

"I heard you threatened him."

"I wouldn't go as far as to say that."

"Everybody's talking about it even till now."

"They treat us like cattle and you stood up against it."

"Hey, I was told that's the American way."

"Well, look where the American way got you."

"Yeah."

"You know we're there for you, Gwen. If you need money, food, a ride somewhere ..."

Gwen stops walking and takes a puff off her Djarum.

"... a pack of cigs," Ma continues.

"These are clove cigs. Want one?"

"I'll pass. I thought you were a health nut."

"Right now I'm so stressed I'm surprised I'm not a crackhead. I'm to my breaking point. Plus, these flavored cigarettes are illegal now. May as well use 'em up."

Just then, the red haired woman Gwen had skirted moments before finally catches up. In her early 20's, Jillian, a casual beauty, is the kind of distraction that can cause an accident at a construction site just by passing by it.

"Ah. Finally caught up with you," she tells Gwen.

"Hey, Jillian," Gwen greets her. Mina, grumbling beneath her breath, doesn't greet the redhead. Jillian doesn't let her indifference stop her.

"Hi, Mina."

"Shouldn't you be at work?"Mina flatly suggests. Jillian, however, brushes it off.

"It's my day off."

"Yeah," Mina protests, "but because of you, Gwen has *all* her days off."

"Mina."Gwen yells at her friend.

"It's got nothing to do with me," Jillian explains. "Didn't you get fired for speaking out or something, like challenging the boss's policies?"

"They created a hostile enough environment to weed people out," Mina says, "so you can get full time. She just got caught up in their bathroom politics."

"And I'm to blame?"Jillian asks. "So is that what I'm the bad guy?"

Mina looks her over from head to foot.

"Out with the old, in with the new. I guess I'm next."

"Geez, you guys," Gwen interjects, "I'm fine, but I gotta go. I have a busy agenda today."

"Let's get some coffee before you go," Jillian requests.

Mina stares into her eyes.

"Hell no."

"I had some earlier," Gwen admits. "I'll talk to you girls later."

She starts walking away.

"Wait!"Mina shouts.

Gwen continues without stopping. Mina turns and gives Jillian a look that can melt an iceberg.

"Why do you hate me so much?"

"I don't hate you, Jillian. I just don't like the ground you walk on. Oops. I didn't just say that. I can see my head on the chopping block now.

"Don't vilify me. I'm not a snitch!"

"That's what she said," Mina mumbles before walking off.

Jillian stares at her chubby friend ambling away. "Bitch."

***

Rte. 160, Baca County, Southern Colorado. Evening has fallen. Rocky promontories dot the landscape. Geckos and woodchucks dart in and out of makeshift tunnels getting ready to bed down for the night. Barn owls are screeching eerily in the distance.

Gordon is riding shotgun in an 18 wheeler with a driver that had picked him up not too long ago. The driver, a burly bearded man in his 40's, has seen better days. The intolerable years of driving interstate has been abrasive to his face. He looks at Gordon.

"Where you headed to, partner?"

"Just north."

"To Denver?"

"Isn't that where you're headed?"

"I couldn't let my fellow man linger on the side of the road."

"He reaches to a box behind his seat, opens it, and brings out two beers, one of which he hands to Gordon."

"I'm good," the runaway inmate informs him.

"Suit yourself."

The trucker cracks his open and takes a deep swig while driving.

"Ahh," he belches. "Nothing like a good hit down the interstate."

"This ain't the interstate."

He reaches over and touches Gordon's leg.

"You're feisty, ain't ya!"

Gordon forcefully removes the driver's wayward hand.

"Hey, you got me all wrong, pal."

"Bullshit. You're the one was eyeing me back at that truck stop in Springfield. I know your type."

Gordon produces a Gideon's bible from his shirt pocket.

"I'm a man of the lord."

"Shoot. Could've fooled me."

The trucker reaches towards the drapes behind his seat and pulls them back to reveal a makeshift bedroom complete with TV, lamps and, of course, a bed.

"You're ready?" he asks.

Duly insulted, Gordon punches the trucker's face. He loses a little control on the truck, making it dip precariously near the ditch.

"You got me all wrong, motherfucker." Gordon yells.

The trucker wipes the blood from his lips.

"You fucking bitch."

He reaches down into a compartment in the seat on his left side and grabs a gun. Before he can fire off a shot, Gordon opens his own door and jumps out. With the truck traveling at nearly 60 miles an hour, Gordon ends up rolling off the road towards the grassy shoulder. The driver slams on his brakes, flings the Gideon's bible out of the opened passenger side door, then closes it and resumes driving.

Regaining composure, the slightly tattered and bruised Gordon gets up and walks back towards the road. When he sees his bible he walks over, picks it up, tucks it back in his pocket, and starts trekking up Rte. 160.

***

Andrew, along with several other homeless people, is standing in a queue on the streets outside the Seattle Gospel Mission in Pioneer Square waiting for an evening meal. Around them, on either side of the street, are scores of homeless people—some sleeping on cardboard boxes, others just milling about waiting for their ship to come in. Just blocks away are the ultra-expensive Seahawks and Mariners stadiums. The collective scene is a grave study in contrast and inequality, one the city has been looking to eradicate, without much success, for decades.

***

Phong, wearing headphones, is jogging near the basketball court in Anderson Park, a recreation area smack in the middle of Capitol Hill. He checks his watch, then stops. Reaching into a small carrier on his side, he brings out his cell phone and dials a number. It rings endlessly.

"Come on, Violet," he whispers. "Pick up."

Hanging up after the tenth ring, he jogs out of the park towards his home.

Entering his apartment, he flicks on the light.

"Violet? Are you home? Violet?"

He walks around the apartment and can clearly see she isn't there. He looks at his watch again.

"10 p.m. Probably went shopping with somebody from work," he convinces himself. "No biggie."

He goes over to the refrigerator, removes a bottle of beer, opens it, takes a long drink, and sets it down on a table. Walking to the bathroom, he runs the water, removes his sweaty clothes, and brings them to the hamper in the bedroom. He then walks over to the slatted double door closet and opens it. Reaching in, he takes down a pair of long pajama pants from a hanger. Suddenly, he realizes Violet's clothes and violin are gone.

"What the hell?"

He looks around the bedroom and then rifles through the bureau. It's half empty, completely bereft of any female attire.

"Dammit."

In the living room, he picks up his cell phone and dials Violet's number again. A voice message comes on: "Violet's not in right now.

Please leave a message after the beep and she'll get back to you as quickly as possible. Beep."

He leaves a message.

"Hey, Violet, you picked a bad time to bounce. Things are just starting to happen. Call me back."

He hangs up, walks over to the open bottle of beer, downs the rest in one gulp, then plops down on the couch. He takes out his phone again and punches in another number. A man picks up after a few rings.

"Hello?"

"Hey, Chan. It's Phong. Is your sister there?"

"No. I haven't seen her in weeks."

"Okay. If she shows up ask her to call me."

"Is something wrong?"

"No. Everything's fine. Just some misunderstanding."

"I know she's not at our parents' house because they've over here now."

"Thanks, Chan. I'll call you later. Maybe we can have a beer at the old watering hole. Bye."

Phong hangs up. He scratches his head. "Weird."

***

Jupiter Records, a music store on Broadway in Capitol Hill, has seen better days. There was a time when there were so many customers you needed at least four or five clerks at the registers to serve them. Now, pockets haven been tightened. The lone clerk in the store, Dustin, had been rendered almost impotent thanks to the proliferation of online music sites. Thankfully, some people preferred the scratchy sound of acetate.

As usual, he's busy arranging music CD's on a shelf. There are no customers in the store. The manager, a stretch pants wearing, multiple piercings hipster in his 20's, walks over to him.

"Hey, Dustin."

"Hey, Warren."

"You can go home early tonight."

"You serious?"

"Well, we practically didn't move any units all day. Of course, it's only Monday, but still."

"Sure. Okay. I can probably get some studying done."

"Thanks. I'll see you tomorrow evening."

Walking up Broadway on Capitol Hill, Dustin sees a good looking young man coming his way. He slows his roll and smiles at the stranger who summarily ignores him. Minutes later, he walks past a group of young gay men cutting up outside Dick's Burgers. He stops momentarily, eyes the giggling group, then continues walking. His cell phone rings. He looks at the number then answers it.

"Hi, mom ... School's fine ... yeah ... Tomorrow after classes? Sure, that's fine. Can't stay too long 'cause I work up here in the evening. Okay. I love you, too. Bye."

He hangs up the phone and notices, up the block, a woman selling a laptop computer. She has it displayed on a rickety stool. He goes over to her. It's Gwen.

"I wouldn't put that computer on that stool," he advises her. "Looks like it might fall."

She shrugs.

"Just trying to be helpful," he adds.

"Sorry, man. I've just been having a bad day. Can't take it out on anyone."

"That's okay. Umm, how much are you asking for that?"

"Four hundred."

"Whoa! Past my budget."

"You know what the pawnshops are offering? Forty or fifty bucks."

"They're crooks."

"'Cause they think it's old. I brought brand new two years ago."

He glances at her left hand. She has no wedding band.

"What's your name?" he asks.

"Gwen."

"They shake hands."

"I'm Dustin."

"Tiêng Viêt?"

"Huh?"

"I guess not. I was asking you if you're Vietnamese."

"I am, but I came here as a toddler. My parents didn't want me to have a hard time in this country so they emphasized English in the house. Not that they spoke it so well.

"Same here."

"You live around here?"

Not too far."

"I go to school in U-dub. I work at the record store down the street. Jupiter Vinyl?"

"Sorry. I don't have a record player."

"That's okay."

There is an awkward pause. Dustin breaks the silence.

"Do you want a hamburger or something from Dick's?"

"Nah. I'm not hungry."

"How 'bout a drink?"

"Persistent little fella, ain't you. How old are you?"

"Twenty one. Just made it, too."

She sizes him up. "I'll take a rain check, Dustin.

"Sure. No problem. See ya later."

"Bye."

He starts walking away. She calls him back. "Hey Dustin." She hands him a card with her number. "In case you ever feel like talking."

He glances at the card. "See ya 'round."

She watches as he disappears in the crowd.

Chapter IV

In the Realm of the Senses

The sun is rising on Canam Highway, Rte. 85, in northern Colorado. It's been day three since Gordon's escape and limbs are really beginning to feel it. All around him he sees the vast expanse of farmland. With neighbors nowhere near shouting distance, this is as rural as it comes.

Walking further north, he comes upon a green road sign with white lettering that reads: 'You are now leaving Colorado, The Centennial State. Cheyenne 7 miles, Casper 149 miles, Billings 378 miles.' A few minutes later, he passes a Welcome To Wyoming –The Equality State. Up ahead, he sees Rte. 223. He spots a small gas station off Rte. 223.

This gas station seems to have been stuck in a time warp. The two rusted gas pumps out front are at least 50 years old. The roads around the station are not paved and there's a confederate flag flapping in the early morning wind, dangling from a pole beneath the eaves of the store.

Walking around the back he sees a restroom with a large bronze cross riveted to the door. He tries the handle. Luckily, it's open. He enters. Moments later, feeling refreshed, he walks back to the front of the station and enters the store. He triggers the sound of a bell hanging on the door. There is, however, no one around to greet him. He walks over to a standee of road maps, picks up a large U.S. atlas and leafs through it. Suddenly, he hears a woman's voice speak to him.

"Where ya headed?"

Looking up, he sees the store's clerk standing behind the counter and walks over.

"I'm going north."

A dead ringer for Dolly Parton, the clerk has light blonde, heavily layered hair pinned at the top, loud extravagant makeup, huge boobs, and clothes so tight it's a surprise she can even breathe. Gordon notices the likeness right away.

"Anybody ever told you—?"

"Ah look like Dolly Parton?" she asks, rhetorically. "Yeah, ah know. Just wish ah had *her* money. Where ya off to, sugar? Been starin' at them maps a while."

"Well, I'm actually headed to Seattle."

"Up in Washington State? Well, my my, you're a long ways off. Why you wanna go up there for?"

"I heard work is good there. Just something new."

"Ah know the area. A good part of mah lahf was spent with my deadbeat ex-husband in Portland. He wasn't worth the dirt he walked on. Miserable drunk."

"Oh, that's too bad."

"Yep. Quieter down in these parts. I like the pace, you know what ah mean, honey?"

She eyes him a little further. He may have been dirty, but perhaps he was her kind of dirty.

"You married?" she asks.

"Nope."

"Well, maybe you should take a chance on a Southern gal. Our hospitality goes a long way, if you know what ah mean."

"And settle down in Cheyenne? Spend all day sitting out front at Grandma's Pickle Parlor pulling nettles out my legs? I don't think so. I have a higher purpose."

"Is that raht?"

He retrieves the bible from his pocket.

"One night," he claims, "in the middle of this horrific dream, I was called. It was the lord. He told me I have a gift; a gift of saving souls.

The clerk smiles broadly. "You can start with mine's."

"I think you're already a decent God-fearing woman. I can see that."

"Wouldn't mind a man like you keepin' me warm at naht, sugar."

"Um, as much as I'd like to oblige, I really have to go."

"You can't really be in that much of a rush 'cause you don't have a car."

"Been hitchhiking. It's working out fine. Suits mah disposition."

The clerk leaves the back of the counter and comes around to the front.

"Ah have a firm belief in the lord, too," she admits, momentarily touching the fabric of his shirt, "and ah can feel you're a good man.

Ah'm gonna help you out. Ah know you don't have any money, and ah don't have any to give, but ..." She walks over to a shelf. "...ah could offer you spiritual guidance. But, in your case, that'd be like teaching a pig to jump in shit. Excuse mah French."

She takes down a sturdy backpack and brings it over.

"Ah'm gonna set you on your way right and, hopefully, you'll remember me in your travels."

She proceeds to fill up the backpack with canned food, crackers, a can opener, packages of dried soup, potato chips, bottles of water, utensils, and a bowl.

He accepts the bulging gift. "I can't thank you enough." He slings it on his back.

"Whoa, it's heavy."

"What's your name, stranger?" The clerk asks.

"Gordon Gabriel."

"You can call me Angie."

"Well, Gordon," Angie continues, "if ever you come back again to South Greeley or Cheyenne or even Laramie County, look me up. Don't be a stranger."

"That's a promise." He smiles, tips his invisible hat, and exits.

"Nice fella," Angie says to herself. She picks up a hand mirror from the counter and looks at her reflection.

"Girl, you try too damn hard sometimes. Let them come to you." She slams the mirror down hard on the counter. It shatters.

***

Andrew is brutally awakened from a deep sleep in his makeshift tent by the sound of a glass bottle being smashed on the ground outside. Getting up, he sleepily opens the tent flap and sees an old man staggering past. His liquor bottle is in shards on the concrete. It's raining.

As the old man stumbles away, Andrew gets out of the tent and stretches. Located in the nook of a small closed-off pathway, it sits next to a highway bridge behind a string of factories south of the International District. The oft-trodden concrete and grass path is grossly littered. The nearby graffiti-covered wall beneath the bridge smells like piss. Hundreds of rain-soaked cigarette butts are scattered everywhere.

Walking down the path, he hops over an old decrepit fence, strolls past the factories, and heads up the street towards the Little Saigon district.

Andrew knocks on the back door of the Saigon Deli and waits. Seconds later, a woman appears and yells at him in Vietnamese. He yells back in the same language. She goes back inside and slams the door. About one minute later, she returns with a Styrofoam container of food and hands it to Andrew. She yells at him again. Throwing up one hand, he yells back, then simply walks away with the vittles.

In a park at the edge of Chinatown, Andrew is sitting on a bench beneath a veranda eating his breakfast of Vietnamese noodles, chicken and pork. Still raining, he can see the dark clouds hovering over the Seattle skyline. It's the typical Seattle rain, more a slight squeeze from the clouds as opposed to a torrential downpour. It's the kind of drizzle Andrew is used to.

***

Phong is meeting with Amir, a music publisher, in the living room of a modest hotel suite downtown. The drapes are partially open. There is a clear view of Puget Sound from this fourth floor room. Not too much light is coming in because of the rain. The two men are drinking coffee. There are dozens of papers and a handful of pens scattered between them on the table.

"Pardon the use of this hotel," Amir apologizes. "It won't be long till our offices are fully renovated."

"I don't mind," Phong admits. "A meeting's a meeting, as long as it's productive."

"This is some city you have," Amir muses. "Rains all the time."

"I actually hear it rains more in Atlanta."

"Well, better months of rain than drought, eh? I remember that time you and Violet played in the park and it started raining. People started leaving but you two just *had* to finish that Vivaldi. Pure troopers."

Phong sighs and gets up. "Excuse me." He walks over to the huge windows. Parting the blinds even further, he stares out at Puget Sound.

"You know Violet? She's gonna come back. Women are like that; very unpredictable. Sometimes they need space but don't want to hurt your feelings by admitting it. I know. I've been there."

"It's just so out of the blue."

"Don't remind me. I feel I'm the one to blame."

"It's got nothing to do with you, Amir. I don't know. She just wasn't happy."

"I remember the minute I offered you that contract after your performance Sunday. Violet looked at me like I was her enemy, like I was stealing something from her."

"I think you're reading too much into it. She's good at hiding things. She has a high threshold for pain."

"Perhaps we should do these contracts some other time."

Phong walks back over to the center table. "I've been waiting for this opportunity all my life." He sits down and grabs a pen. "Just show me where to sign."

***

Gwen walks out onto the street outside of the downtown DSHS office as she exits the building. Clutching several sheets of paper, she seems angry. The falling rain doesn't seem to bother her as much as what's on her mind. She looks at the papers in her hands, rips them in two, and throws the lot in a recycling receptacle. Storming down the street, she stops beneath an awning for reprieve from the rain. She takes out her cell phone and dials a number.

"Hello?"she begins.

The person on the other end utters some words not to Gwen's liking.

"What do you mean I'm overqualified?" she asks. "A job is a job if you can do it."

The speaker on the other end says a few more words then hangs up.

"Damn."

At that moment, a car passes too close to her on the curb. Its tires splash a goodly helping of rainwater her way. Quickly, she jumps backwards and avoids a full body shower.

"Jackass." Unfortunately, some water did splash her phone. Drying it off, she notices the lights on the number pads have gone out. She tries to turn the phone but it's apparent it has died.

"Lovely."

Angry, she stashes the phone in her pocket and takes out her packet of clove cigarettes.

***

Phong exits the Embassy Suites hotel and, responding to the mid-morning chill and falling rain, pulls up his collar. His cell phone rings. He answers it while seeking shelter nearby.

"Hi, Theresa," he says.

Theresa, a co-worker and friend of Violet, is sitting on a couch in the break room at her job. Two other employees are sitting at a table drinking coffee and watching TV.

"Hey, Phong," Theresa answers, "is Violet sick? I haven't seen her in days."

"That's why I'm calling you, actually. You're her best friend."

"You haven't seen her, either? She never called in sick here."

"I don't get it."

"Did you two have a fight?"

"That's just it. Every thing's perfect between us."

"I take it you called her family already."

"Yeah, I did. Called the police, too. They said it's too soon to get the dogs out."

"Oh, I wish I could help you, Phong. Keep me in touch if you hear anything."

"Okay, Theresa. Thanks. Bye."

"See ya. Try to keep your chin up."

***

Benaroya Hall on 2nd Ave in downtown Seattle, home of the Seattle Symphony, has a remarkable façade. Coupled with the landscape and cascading water fountain, the structure is a modern work of art. Phong walks up the wide inviting steps, enters the building and walks directly over to the receptionist in the main lobby.

"Hi," he greets her. "Is Seattle Symphony conducting auditions or trials this week or any time soon?"

"You'd have to check the trades. I know there's nothing coming up soon. In a few months maybe."

He takes out a picture of Violet from his pocket and shows it to the receptionist.

"Have you seen her?"

The receptionist takes a quick glance at the photo. "I don't know. A lot of people come through here. Sorry."

Just outside Benaroya Hall, sheltered by a covered bus stop, Phong is on his cell phone. In his hand is a list of local symphony orchestras: Lake Union Civic Orchestra, Puget Sound Symphony orchestra, Seattle Baroque Orchestra. Most of the organizations have a line drawn through them.

"Thanks, anyway." He hangs up, takes out a pen, and draws a line through the last entry. Crumpling the entire list, he pitches it into a recycling bin.

***

On any given day, the downtown shopping plaza that is Seattle's Westlake Center is typically crowded. Just up the block at the entrance to Pacific Place a woman is playing a violin. Standing beneath a tree, she's protected from the rain. Occasionally, a passerby would stop, listen, and throw a dollar in her violin case. Either it was her playing that got their attention or her looks.

Dressed in dark, multi-layered clothing, her hair is dyed in various hues of red and blue. All of this is complemented by jet black Dr. Marten boots, black fingerless fishnet gloves, black eyeliner and black lipstick. What's even more striking is that this girl is Asian. It's Violet, complete with spiked dog-collar secured by a small padlock. Mama's definitely got a brand new bag. Her playing, though, is as angelic as ever, but even curious onlookers were wondering just what kind of statement she was trying to make.

***

Evening has fallen. Dustin is sitting near the front of a Metro bus reading a technical manual. It's a little hard for him to concentrate because several kids are cutting up loudly in the back of the bus.

Half an hour later, standing outside his parents' small house in suburban Beacon Hill, he feels a nervous pang as he steels his nerves to enter.

***

Gwen is a bit nervous as she walks towards the Pink Pussycat. Passing a bar that has its doors wide open, she sees several patrons enjoying happy hour. Looking at her clock, she realizes she still has some minutes left before show time, and decides to take a detour inside before heading to the club.

***

Several cars shoot past Gordon as he's hitchhiking on Old Highway 87 in eastern Montana. He looks at the sky. Remnants of the daylight have given way to the calm stillness of the evening. He eyes a barn several hundred feet off the side of the road and thinks about spending the night there.

Suddenly, two gents in an old light blue, two door sedan pass him and stop about 100 feet ahead. He watches as the car reverses towards him.

A man in his early 30's riding shotgun winds his window down. Smoking a cigarette, he and the driver studies Gordon. The preacher eyes them back.

"Need a ride, mister?" the smoker asks.

"If y'all heading up north."

"Lodge Grass."

"Where's that?"

The passenger blows out a puff of smoke. "On the Crow Res."

"The What?"

The passenger points northward. "That way."

Gordon thinks for a moment. "Yeah, sure."

The passenger leaves the front seat and jumps in the back. Gordon takes the front and the car takes off.

Gordon takes a quick glimpse around the car. It looks like it has never been cleaned since it rolled off the lot 15, 20 years ago. "My name's Gordon," he introduces himself.

"My name's Tom," the driver claims. "That fool in the backseat is my brother, Gus."

"Hey," Gus protests.

"How y'all doing?" Gordon asks.

"Fine," Tom answers. "You're a long ways from nowhere, mister."

"Been on the road for a while," he admits.

"What are you?" Gus wonders. "One of them fellas crossing the country for charity?"

"No," Gordon insists, "but it is for a cause."

"So, you're on a mission?" Tom queries his passenger.

"Something like that."

"Well, ain't we got us a live one!" Gus hollers.

He offers Gordon a cigarette, but the ex-con shakes his head 'no'.

"Not my thing," he explains. "Um ... do you fellas know the lord?"

"Oh, shit." Tom barks. "He's a preacher, Gus. We got us a bonafide preacher."

"Sure," Gus submits. "We know the lord."

He takes out a revolver from his waistband and places its cold barrel along the side of Gordon's face.

"This here is Revelation," he tells the hitchhiker. "She can be your best friend, or she can be the last chapter of your life."

Tom also takes out a gun, a nickel-plated 1911 Colt, and shows it to Gordon. It's as beautiful as it is ominous to behold in person.

"This is Leviticus," Tom explains. "She lays down the law."

The brothers share a wicked laugh. Just then, Gordon reaches into his inner pocket which, of course, doesn't go unnoticed by the brothers.

"Hey," Tom yells. "No tricks." He turns momentarily to his brother. "Check him out, Gus."

Gus does a quick pat down of the surrendering Gordon and finds nothing but a small bible.

"He's clean." The brothers put their guns away.

"Um," Gordon requests, "if you fellas don't mind I'll get out here."

Gus, however, isn't trying to hear that. "In the middle of nowhere?" he asks. "Shucks, we couldn't do that, Mr. Gabriel."

"How do you know my name?"

"Show him, Tom," Gus tells his brother.

Tom turns to Gordon. "Open the glove compartment." He complies. A mess of old and new tissues, coins, maps, hand tools, and similar refuse falls out. He sees a folded newspaper and brings it out.

"Look on the bottom," Tom suggests.

On the front page near the bottom of the paper, Gordon sees a picture and report on the Bewlay Brothers, Gus and Tom, wanted for murder, bank robberies, statutory rape and kidnapping in Colorado, Arkansas, and Texas.

"We're bonafide stars back in them states," Gus beams.

"But we keep our nose to the news," Tom warns. "You can't be too careful. Seems like you been mentioned quite a few times, too, mister. Kinda had a feeling we'd run into you out here."

"You gonna turn me in for a reward?"

"Shoot. You know we can't be within 100 miles of any policeman."

"We got a better plan," Gus avows.

He reaches under Gordon's seat, pulls out a backpack, unzips it, pulls out a cellophane bag with something the shape of a small brick wrapped in foil inside it, and shows it to Gordon.

"Grade A primo shit."

"I don't use that stuff," Gordon insists.

"You ain't gonna touch none of it," Tom acknowledges. "You're gonna drop it off and collect the money up in Lodge Grass."

"Is that meth?"

Gus smacks the back of Gordon's head.

"Hey," the preacher yells.

"Don't say that out loud," Gus admonishes him.

"Out here," Tom explains, "they call it shabu. Remember that."

"Shabu," Gordon repeats.

"Boom," Gus whispers. "That's why you gotta be hush hush. Them cops got long range surveillance thingies. They can hide out in the bushes and hear you passing gas from a thousand yards."

"I ain't gonna ask you boys no questions," Gordon insists. "Before this whole thing gets crazy and out of hand, just let me off here."

"Oh," Gus protests, "it's too late for that shit. You've been rightly introduced to the Bewlay brothers. No turning back now."

Gordon rubs his face in defeat.

"Don't freak, man," Tom explains calmly. "It'll be simple. You don't even have to waste time counting the money. We've been working with these natives for a while. You can trust 'em."

"So do it yourself."

"Hey, numbskull," Gus screeches. "You forgot we're on the front page now?"

Gordon shakes his head. "Y'all got the wrong man. I'm with Jesus, now."

Gus is skeptical. "You're with Jesus, huh?"

"So you're not down?" Tom asks.

"This boy's tighter than a new harlot in a henhouse," Gus complains.

"It surprises me," Gordon explains, "how people like y'all like running this stuff from state to state. The prison time just ain't worth it."

"Motherfucker," Gus imagines, "you ain't no angel."

"Hey, Gordon?" his brother asks. "You know what we really like?"

Gus takes out his gun again. This time he cocks it and put the barrel to the back of Gordon's head. "Hunting."

"And we ain't talking about ducks and quails and shit," Gus clarifies.

"Big game," Tom adds.

"Real big game," Gus alleges.

Tom suddenly slams on the brakes then pulls over on the shoulder. Parking the vehicle, he runs over to the passenger side, opens the door, yanks Gordon out, and flings him on the ground towards the bushes.

Gordon slowly regains his composure after landing forcefully, his head still spinning from the whiplash.

"You got ten seconds till we come after your ass!" Tom notifies him.

Sensing the imminent danger, Gordon immediately gets up and takes off into the nearby woods.

***

Dustin is occupying a soft chair in the living room of his parents' house. He is perusing a photo album. His father, Minh, is sitting on a couch nearby watching the news on a large flat-screen TV. The room is comfortably lit with Vietnamese decorations adorning the walls and round paper lamps dangling from the ceiling.

Dustin's mother, Kim, comes from the kitchen carrying a tray of hot tea and Vietnamese egg rolls. She places them on the center table, pours herself a cup of tea, grabs one of the hors d'oeuvres, and plops down on the couch next to Minh. The two men help themselves to some refreshments.

"So you've been doing well in school?" Kim opens.

"Yeah," Dustin answers. "Can't complain. Classes can be tough, though."

"You call that tough?" Minh complains. "How about spending twelve hours every day in a steaming hot laundromat?"

Kim stamps her feet.

"Minh, he doesn't want to hear about that."

"It's okay, Ma," Dustin says.

Minh groans and clutches his chest.

Kim jumps up. "Minh?"

"I'll be okay," he promises. "Just get me a nitro."

Kim reaches into a nearby drawer, takes out a tiny bottle of nitroglycerin pills, and places one of the tiny white tablets beneath his tongue.

"Are you okay?" his son asks.

"Yeah. This has been happening more frequently these days."

"These nitro pills should do the trick," Kim adds.

"I just gotta lay off the salt," Minh explains. "Kinda hard with the way your mother cooks."

"And when the food has no taste you complain," Kim rants.

Minh groans. Kim sits back down, grabs an egg roll, and eats it almost savagely.

"Dustin," Kim turns to her son, "when you first got here, you said you had something to tell us."

"Well, I—"

"Hây da!" Minh yells suddenly, interrupting Dustin's planned speech. He is pointing to the TV.

"Kim, I'm telling you. The men of today have no spine. Look at all this on TV. All these poofs. You'd never see that in Ho Chi Minh City. It's a disgrace."

Both Kim and Dustin look at the TV news. It's a segment about gay marriage.

"Oh, Jesus," Minh explodes.

"So if you can't take it, turn it off," Kim insists.

She reaches for the remote on the center table, but Minh motions for her to forget about it.

"Just leave it be, Kim. A lot of those people are my customers. I have to learn their language, right?"

She leaves the remote just where it was.

Minh reaches into his shirt pocket, brings out a picture, and hands it to Dustin. The young man stares at it.

"That's Cam Le," Minh explains.

"Tan Dung's daughter?"

"All grown up, huh? Ready and available."

"Minh," Kim protests. "He'll find his own."

"When?"

Kim stamps her foot again.

"What's the rush? He's just finishing college."

Minh throws up his hands in disgust.

"Always in such a rush to get a progeny in the laundry pool," Kim notices. Minh rolls his eyes.

"I'm not getting any younger!"

"No, but you're just getting more difficult."

"I have heart troubles! You know that."

"So you shouldn't be shouting."

Dustin leaps to his feet. "I'm outta here. Every time I come over it's the same thing over and over and over. This is exactly why I don't come anymore."

"You've got some nerve," Minh growls.

Dustin walks to the door.

"I'll see you two later."

Kim gets up. "What about the money for school?" she asks her son.

"I'll get by."

"Don't be hasty, Dustin."

She turns to her husband. "Stop being a baby and give him the money."

"I never said I wasn't giving it," Minh snaps.

He reaches into his wallet, pulls out a thick wad of cash, walks over to Dustin and hands it to him. Reluctantly, the young man accepts the gift.

"Thanks." He gives his father a hug.

"I have some rough ways, Dustin," Minh acknowledges. "I know that. The way I grew up, there was no decoration of the words, no coloring of the tongue. Everyone was direct with each other. We truly had no time or patience back then. We were at war."

"Kindness was weakness," Dustin adds. "I understand."

"It makes you vulnerable, but it doesn't make you a bad man to want the best for yourself.

He hugs his son again.

"I love you, pop. I'll see you later."

He then gives his mother a hug and exits. Minh and Kim returns to the living room, sit down in the couch, and pour themselves some tea.

***

Gordon is running through the woods off Old Highway 87 in Montana as if a hellhound's on his trail. He leaps over vines, roots and stumps like an Olympic hurdler. The sun is setting, making it hard for him to navigate through this thickly wooded area.

He stops along a declining path to catch his breath against a towering pine tree. A shot echoes through the treetops, causing a flock of herons to take flight. Immediately, he begins running again. Seconds later, he trips over the jutting root of a half dead tree. The fall gives him an idea.

Looking around, he sees a vine snaking up and around a slender poplar. Using a sharp-edged stone, he chops the base of the vine till it is cut through. Then, untangling the thick vine from the tree, he strings it loosely across the foot-trod path and fastens it around the base of two pines.

Hiding behind a huge rotting stump near one of the pines, he sees Gus coming down the path with his gun is in his right hand and a bottle of beer in his left. He takes a swig.

"Come on out, motherfucker," Gus shouts.

He fires a shot in the air and continues running down the path. Seconds later, he runs between the pines. Gordon yanks the concealed vine taut, causing Gus to trip and tumble head over heels down the path. He loses his gun and beer bottle along the way.

Immediately, Gordon rushes up to him and, before Gus can move, knocks him out with an old rotten tree stump. Throwing the stump away, he drags Gus off the path into the woods then returns and picks up the gun. Lifting the bottle of beer, he throws it in the woods. A shot rings out from the top of the path's incline. Immediately, he starts running down the path and through the woods again.

***

Gwen and Skylark are in the Pink Pussycat dressing room preparing to go on stage. Gwen is clearly tipsy. Uncoordinated, she has a hard time donning her red skin tight suit. Skylark goes over to help her.

"Girl," Skylark cautions her, "you really overdid it tonight."

"As long as we got paid, I don't care."

Skylark gives her a drink of water from a Styrofoam cup.

"Don't let Mr. West see you like this," she warns her.

"I'll be okay. Look."

Gwen stands at attention and successfully touches her nose sobriety-test style.

"See?"

"Try this," Skylark suggests.

Standing straight, the ebony beauty hovers her right leg about two inches off the floor for several seconds. Gwen makes several attempts at the same feat, but she loses her balance every time.

"This is silly," Gwen moans.

Mr. West opens the door and sticks his head in.

"Showtime, girls."

He exits. Seconds later, he sticks his head back in.

"Skylark, give your friend some juice and get her sober, huh?"

Gwen sighs. "He's got a nose like a bloodhound."

***

Gordon is perched behind a large rock in the thick, almost impenetrable Montana woods, watching as Tom comes walking down a path with a gun in his hand. Taking aim with Gus' pistol, he clocks the gun, never letting Tom out of its sight. By now, Tom is frustrated.

"You can't get too far, motherfucker!"

As Tom walks past, Gordon pulls a vine near his feet. A loud *thunk,* then a rolling sound, emerges. Startled, Tom turns and looks up the path to see a huge wall of stones barreling down his way. He immediately starts sprinting, but the rocks are too fast. A few of them knock him off his feet and into the woods, causing him to lose his gun.

"What the fuck?"

Gordon comes up beside him with a stump in his hands.

"We's just playing," Tom pleads.

"Not tonight," Gordon shouts before knocking him out with the stump.

Minutes later, Gordon is back on Old Highway 87 adding the finishing touches to his work: tying the unconscious Bewlay Brothers back to back with vines. He sits them by the side of the road. Both of Tom's sneakers are off.

Gordon, now wearing Tom's sneakers, goes back to the car, takes out the newspaper and looks for a pen. After finding one near a floor mat, he circles the article about the brothers, scribbles a message across it, folds it so the article is noticeable, and sticks it in the vines strung across Tom's chest. He then drives away in the Bewlay mobile. Passing by the captured brothers, he glances at his scribbled note: Thou Shalt Not Kill, Leviticus 3:24.

***

Several young people, including Phong, are having a little evening barbeque in the backyard of an apartment building. Music is emanating from a stereo inside a unit. Cases of cold beer, tiki torches, and food are visible almost everywhere. Phong and his friend Adam are off to one side drinking and talking.

"Phong, you know how impulsive she is. She'll be back."

"Yeah, Adam. This was a first."

"I tried calling her myself but she's not picking up her phone."

"It's okay, Adam. I know everyone here's looking out for her."

Just then, an acquaintance of theirs, Tessa, came over. She has a shish kebab in one hand and a beer in the other.

"Hey Adam, Phong," she says.

"Hey, Tessa," they reply.

"Nice party," Phong smiles wistfully.

Tessa agrees. "We should do this more often. Fun, huh?"

"I like the tiki torches," Adam admits. Nice touch. Whose idea was that? Yours?"

"Luke's," she corrects him. "Actually, we came up with it together. Hey Phong, you know I saw the strangest thing today."

"What?"

"I was riding the bus to Capitol Hill this afternoon. I'm reading *The Stranger* and I just happened to look up when we went past Westlake Center . I could've sworn I saw Violet playing there."

Phong is taken aback.

"At Westlake Center?"

She nods.

"Right on the street with an open case."

"That couldn't be."

"I don't know," she shakes her head. "If it *was* her she sure changed her look: braided her hair, changed her clothes. She's all black, all emo now."

"I think the fumes from that bus got to you," Adam interjects."Violet hates goth. Remember that time you tried to drag her to see *My Chemical Romance* at the Paramount? She said she'd rather sleep in a snake pit."

"Could've been her," Tessa surmises. "You know how unpredictable she is."

"Will you excuse me?" Phong asks, then leaves the group.

Adam looks at Tessa and shakes his head.

"Now look what you did."

"What I did? You brought up some negative issue regarding Violet. You know how torn up he is right now."

"Eh, don't worry about it. He'll bounce back. Anybody who could stay with Violet that long's gotta have nerves of steel."

***

Gwen, dressed in her familiar red skintight outfit and white wig, emerges from the Pink Pussycat dressing room and takes a quick gander at the Tuesday night crowd. It's hard to see faces because the club is so dimly lit. Most of the lighting is reserved for the stage.

When she hears her intro, "Sunny" by Nancy Wilson, she climbs to the red lit poled arena and begins a slow dance. Lip-syncing to the sultry jazz tune, her flirtatiously risqué gyrations cause a few onlookers to stop talking and pay attention. Mr. West, standing off in one corner, is observing cautiously.

Slowly, she loosens each zipper of her suit one by one. Several men come up individually and hand her money; a few even give her business cards. Mr. West, his fingers crossed, is biting the insides of his mouth. Gwen not only dances with and around the pole, she practically makes love to it all the while never losing pace with the song.

Stripping to her black underwear, she dances a little more, does a seductive split and other simple acrobatic moves. More money and business cards come in. She takes a juice drink from a nearby table and pours it over her chest. Finally, she twists and gyrates as the song ends. Grabbing her red suit, money, and cards, she bows and heads back to the dressing area while the onlookers applaud her performance.

Once inside, she begins changing immediately into her regular clothes. Mr. West enters.

"Great show tonight," he compliments her. "Didn't know you can sing."

"I wasn't singing so you could hear. I actually sound like a frog."

"Ah. You're too modest."

"When I leave here, I'm gonna take something to give me amnesia so I won't remember any of this."

"It's called vodka. Works for me. But I tell ya, Gwen. This isn't the sordid profession it used to be. Its reputation's changed over the years. We're just ordinary folks entertaining ordinary folks. Nothing to be ashamed of."

"Ordinary folks."

"Why don't you stick around? Get a little more lettuce later."

"I'm feeling woozy. I wanna go home and lie down before I get sick."

"You want some Alka Seltzer or vegetable juice?"

"What I want is some rest right now."

"You sure?"

"Uh, huh."

"Okay. You're the boss. See ya tomorrow?"

"Yeah ... maybe."

Minutes later, she's walking home along Olive Way. The downtown street, usually busy in the day, now has a paucity of life, most of them up to no good. Normally well lit, a few of the streetlamps are out. As she crosses the street, a dark car with tinted windows stays along the side of her. Not stopping, she continues on, taking occasional glimpses at the car whose occupants can't be seen because of the tint.

Up ahead, she sees a pile of bricks near a construction site. Grabbing one, she recoils to throw it at the car. It suddenly goes zooming up the road, disappearing around a corner. She throws the brick back in the pile and continues home.

Not long after, she's lying in bed counting money.

"Hey, Gwen," she speaks to herself, "you did good tonight. Made the mortgage. Well, thank you Gwen. I try. Oh, don't mention it. I'm so glad to have you as a friend. Hey, no problem. It's the least I can do."

Laying the money off to one side, she dims the lamp on the bedside table and starts crying.

***

Phong, having drunk his weight in beer, is staggering up and down the streets, tripping over garbage cans and pylons. He nearly gets hit by a car. The driver flips him off but he's too drunk to notice.

He passes by several establishments and finally ends up in Pioneer Square. As he's about to sit down on a bench he sees, or thinks he sees, Violet across the street. His vision is hazed. He squints in her direction.

"Violet!"

Dressed in white, she turns like a ghost in slow motion and glides up the block towards Occidental Park plaza. He crosses the street and runs after her. She ducks into the park. Phong races into the park and sees nothing. She's gone.

"Violet!" He sits down on one of the benches, bends over and holds his head.

Chapter V

It is early in the morning. A few people are crisscrossing the historic cobblestone park on their way to work. A police officer enters, walks directly over to the man sleeping on a bench and raps his baton so loudly on the armrest that the sleeper awakens. It's Phong. He's and dazed and confused, but is not lost for words.

"What the hell?" he shouts.

"You can't sleep here," the officer warns him.

Phong looks around. He still has a hard time figuring out where he is. The cop notices this.

"You're in Occidental Park. Where do you live?"

"Capitol Hill," Phong answers. He looks at his watch. "Dammit."

"You need a taxi?"

"Yeah. I'll just walk over to First and flag one down."

Phong takes out his wallet and checks it to see if he has any cash. He does.

"Consider yourself lucky," the officer shakes his head.

"It won't happen again."

***

Gordon exits his car after parking it in the rest area just off I-90 near Bozeman, Montana. His is the only car in the lot on this cloudless morning. He looks briefly at the sun, enjoying some of its healing warmth upon his neck. Walking inside the rotunda, he reads the giant state map on a wall, and mentally calculates some times and distances. Using his index finger, he tracks a route, then walks towards the men's room.

Once inside, he washes his face and dries it with paper towels. He notices a cache of plastic garbage bags hanging over the side of the large trash receptacle and helps himself to a few.

Standing behind his stolen auto, he throws unneeded items from the trunk into the trash bags. Most of the items are junk: old blankets and throw pillows, a beat up guitar amplifier, a broken stereo, newspapers, wood pieces, a red shoebox, underwear, shirts and pants. He discards it all, except the shoebox, and closes the trunk.

Opening the passenger side door, he unlatches the glove box, takes out the two Bewlay Brothers' guns, places them in the shoebox, and tucks it under the passenger seat. Afterwards, he clears out more newspapers, empty bottles of beer, cigarette boxes, dirt, mattress fibers, the cellophane bag of meth, and a cell phone.

He picks up Gus' box of cigarettes from the mat in the back. It is still nearly full. He begins to discard it but changes his mind and pockets it. He also pockets the cell phone and throws everything out except the meth, which he flushes down the toilet.

***

The mid morning light is filtering through clouded windows in a dark dusty abandoned building. There are planks of woods, bricks, empty cans and broken bottles of beer everywhere. The tiny patter of city mice can be heard scurrying to and fro, darting in and out of holes in the walls.

Andrew's sleeping on a cardboard box under an old blanket in a corner when he is awakened by someone kicking his feet. He opens his eyes. Looking at the stranger, he sees an anorexic dark skinned drug addict.

"Hey," the stranger greets him, but Andrew's in no mood just then.

"Go away, man. Let me sleep."

"You know anybody?"

Andrew stares at the man again.

"I know somebody in Beacon Hill," he answers.

"Then, let's go," the man insists.

Andrew moans but gets up anyway. "How much you looking for?" he asks.

"An eight."

Just as Andrew started tightening his belt buckle, the stranger sucker-punches him in the face so hard he staggers, loses his footing on the dusty floor, and falls backwards. He glances at his assailant, "Asshole." He grabs a wooden plank and hurls it at him. The stranger instinctively throws up both arms and blocks its impact. He then picks Andrew up off the floor by the collar and punches him down again. Andrew reaches for another board but his attacker prevents it by forcefully rifling through his pockets. Andrew grabs a brick and swings it with precision. He hits the man's head so hard it flies off him.

Getting up to hit him one more time, the stranger suddenly grabs a plank and slams it into Andrew's left leg. A nail in the piece of wood goes right through his skin to the bone. He screams out in pain.

"Ahh! I don't have any money, you asshole."

"Then go fuck yourself," the stranger yells.

Minutes later, in the industrial area just outside the condemned facility, Andrew's hobbling with the plank still in his leg. Looking back, he sees the stranger isn't following. He kneels down and, with intense pain, yanks the plank from his leg. He lets out such a horrendous blood-curdling scream that startled black crows nearby disappear.

Rolling up his pants leg, he examines the bloody dark hole. Blood is pouring out. Looking around, he sees an old bandana in the wet grass on the side of the road and limps over to it. Wringing it dry, he ties it around his calf. The bleeding stops. He rolls his pants leg back down and limps off down the block.

***

Dustin is perusing adult videos in a University District video emporium. Of particular interest to him this midday are busty lasses and Asian she males. After a few minutes, he finds one he likes, Vicious Vietnamese Vixens, and heads over to the cashier to buy it.

Exiting the store, he places a dollar bill in the case of a violinist on University Way. It's Violet. He only listens briefly to her playing before taking off. Most passers-by ignore her; some do occasionally toss a quarter or two in her case. At least, in this part of town, she can blend in with the locals and not look so out of place as she did in Westlake Center.

***

Dustin is sitting on his bed watching Vicious Vixens on his TV. It fails to stir him. He uses his remote to fast forward to the good parts. After several forwards and plays he turns the DVD off, takes out a gay men's magazine from underneath his mattress, and lies down. Suddenly, there's a knock on the door. As he quickly hides the magazine under a pillow, his roommate Shawn walks in.

"Hey, dude," Shawn begins, "didn't know you were home."

"They cancelled my morning class."

"How come?"

"They had a flood in the labs."

"Oh. I want to borrow that physics encyclopedia of yours."

"Of course you do."

Dustin gets up, walks over to a stack of books in a corner, and brings out a big tome from the bottom.

"Yeah.," Shawn nods, reaching out his hand. "That's the one."

He takes the book. "Thanks."

"Yeah, no problem."

"Hey, Dustin, it's Wednesday, so you know what that means."

"Yeah. Hump day."

They fist bump." Celebrating tonight?" Shawn asks.

"My goodness," Dustin remarks, hands on his waist, "you guys use any excuse to party."

"Life is short, baby."

"Right. The last time you said that we ended up in that shitty tavern. It was so hot and stuffy, like somebody opened up a bar in a sauna in Calcutta. Stunk of onions."

"Oh, ye of little faith. We got some place better tonight. You'll see. My treat."

"Right. That's what you said the last time, too."

***

With the red shoebox tucked under his left arm, Gordon is counting a handful of cash as he stands outside a loan company on quiet Harrison Avenue in Butte, Montana. Satisfied with his bounty, he flips the empty shoebox into a street container nearby, gets into his car, and takes off.

About three hours later, he pulls up into a stall in the quiet, near empty parking lot of a Super 8 Motel in Coeur d'Alene, Idaho. Getting out, he surveys the area located in the middle of a lakefront community. The glittering downtown lights, including those of nearby Wild Waters Park, give this northern Idaho enclave a classically picturesque look.

With evening slowly creeping in, he's beginning to feel fatigued. Sporting new clothes, he enters the motel. Conservatively dressed, he's also shaved and had his hair cut. Donning a smart blazer, khaki slacks, button down shirt and dock shoes, he gives no hint of a man on the run.

He notices it's a nice cozy lobby. A fireplace is crackling with life in one corner and a large console TV broadcasting the news is on across the room. There's an elderly man putting envelops into several mail slots behind the counter. Gordon taps a little silver bell sitting on the desk. The clerk turns to greet him.

"Howdy."

"Good evening. Beautiful town you have here."

"Thanks. Been here all my life. Wouldn't trade it for another. You looking for a room?"

Gordon nods. The clerk reaches beneath the desk and brings out an index card and a pen.

"How many people?"

"Just me."

"Smoking or non-smoking?"

"Non-smoking."

"Can I see your driver's license?"

"Um," Gordon scratches his head. "That there's a problem. I went sight-seeing in one of those overlook passes in Montana but accidentally left my wallet in the men's room. I'd driven nearly halfway across the state before I realized I didn't have it. When I returned it was gone."

"Probably one of them damn truckers. They got such sticky fingers I'm surprised they can open their hands like this."

He illustrates what he means by spreading out his fingers.

"I only need the room for one night. I'm beat. Been driving for hours."

"You have any ID at all?"

"No, sir."

The clerk studies Gordon briefly. "Well, you look like a decent enough fella." He hands him the index card and a pen.

"Just fill out whatever information you can."

"Thanks."

"Where you from?"

"Texas."

"Long way from home."

"Yeah."

"You heading up to Silver Mountain? Maybe do a little skiing?"

"Actually, I'm headed to Seattle."

"Well, while you're in town, give the place a gander. Mighty fine resort even if'n I do say so m'self."

"Maybe I will. Thanks."

"That will be $54. Check out's at 11 a.m."

Gordon takes out his brand new leather wallet, takes out $60, and hands it to the clerk.

"Keep the change."

"Will do." The clerk takes a key off a rack and hands it to Gordon. "Room 20," he informs the traveler. "It's down by the end. It's nice and quiet and has a good view of the downtown lights."

"Thanks. I appreciate it." Gordon walks in, plops right down on the bed, and kicks his shoes off. Grabbing the remote, he puts the TV on and heads to the shower.

Minutes later, as he's drying himself walking out of the bathroom, the TV news catches his attention. According to the broadcaster, not only were the notorious Bewlay Brothers —whose crime spree had extended to Idaho—in custody, but their old light blue car was missing. They display a picture of the stolen car on screen. Gordon quickly dresses and exits the room.

Just feet from his car, Gordon hears tires on the gravel coming from the entrance of the motel. Turning to look, he sees a police car entering. The elderly clerk is standing out front. Quickly, Gordon jumps into his stolen vehicle, starts the engine, and takes off quietly and unnoticed through the lot's rear entrance.

***

Andrew is limping out of Harborview MC's ER entrance. Wearing a new set of clothes, he stops beneath an awning of a nearby building, rolls up his left sleeve and, using the light of a streetlamp, checks the integrity of the small bandage He then rolls up his left pants leg and checks the bandage on his left thigh. Taking a bottle of medicine out of his pocket, he pops it open and swallows two pills.

Minutes later, he knocks on the rear door of the Saigon Deli and waits for someone to answer. Still in pain, he shifts intermittently from side to side to lessen its intensity. When no one answers, he knocks again. Finally, when no one answers after his third attempt, he curses in Vietnamese and leaves.

Hobbling down Jackson Street smack in the middle of the International District, he looks around, hoping to see someone he might know. Then, passing Canton Alley, he stops. Something has caught his eye.

Walking into the poorly lit passageway, he sees a white plastic Chinese restaurant bag with a food container inside sitting atop a dumpster. He opens it to find a generous helping of beef lo mein. There are no utensils or napkins. The food is still warm and looks like it has never been touched. Quickly, he repackages it and hobbles out of the alley as fast as he could.

Seconds later, a drunken man carrying a napkin and fork stumbles into the alley and goes straight over to the dumpster. He looks around and in the dumpster but doesn't find what he's looking for. "Fuck."

***

Violet, wearing only a black knee-length t-shirt, is sitting on the bed in a poorly lit motel room having dinner for one. In front of her, on the bed, are containers of food from a Chinese restaurant. On the nightstand sits a large bottle of milky sake. All around the room she's lit several candles.

With almost every mouthful of food, she reaches over, grabs the bottle of sake and takes a swig. The TV is on a game show, but even though the volume is off, she watches it anyway. Having her fill of the meal, she gets up, with drunken difficulty, and places all the leftovers in the small refrigerator sitting on the chest of drawers.

Jumping back into bed, she sits in a lotus position and resumes watching the silent TV. Without taking her eyes off the screen, she pulls open the top drawer of the bedside stand and brings out a razor. Taking a deep breath, she draws the sharp stainless steel across her left forearm and screams, almost silently. The pain is unbearable. But as tears fill her eyes, she repeats this action till she's sliced her forearm four times, screaming with every effort. Finally, she looks at her arm. Blood is everywhere, dripping on the bed like a faucet. Instead of getting a bandage or washing it off, she simply lies down stares at the ridges in the ceiling.

***

Standing just outside of the Pink Pussycat Lounge, Dustin seems a restless. At times he paces back and forth; mostly he's checking his watch.

"Come on, you guys," he whispers to himself, "y'all said y'all'd be here by nine."

Just then, Skylark comes walking towards him from down the block. Drinking from a stainless steel flask, she approaches. "Hey, sugar," she asks. "You coming to the show?"

"Well, I was waiting for some buddies of mine but they're not here yet."

She pinches his face. "You're cute. I'll give you a lap dance for free."

"Oh, ah, maybe some other time."

"No time like the present, sugar. By the way, there's no cover charge tonight."

She gives him her flask. "If Mr. West sees me with this," she confesses, "he'd kill me." She opens the club's door and says, "Don't be a stranger, sweetie."

Dustin takes a whiff of the liquor in the flask and recoils from the strong odor. He stashes it behind a large potted plant next to the club and checks his watch again. "Oh, what the hell," he sighs.

He opens the lounge's door and enters. The first thing he notices is the blue lights rotating all around; makes the place look as if there's a police raid going on. To his right are machines for cigarettes and lottery tickets; on his left is a ticket booth, but it's unmanned.

Entering, he can hear the throbbing music more clearly. Around the tables are several men, and a handful of women watching the two half naked dancers up on stage. His friends, and Skylark, are nowhere in sight. A server dressed in barely-there clothes approaches him. "What are you having tonight?"

"Um. I ... um ... You serve alcohol here?"

"Sorry, sugar. State rules."

"I'll just have an orange juice, then."

"I'll be right back. Go find a seat."

She exits and Dustin takes a seat at the one empty table near the back. In the middle of the table sits a flameless scented candle in the shape of a breast and a drink menu which he promptly peruses. The server brings his juice.

"That'll be four dollars."

He gets out his wallet and pays her, giving her a one dollar tip. "Here you go."

"Thank you."

She leaves. The two dancers on stage also exit. Suddenly, the rotating blue lights in the room fade to black, leaving just the red onstage lights. The tables' flameless candles, red-lit exit signs, and a few patrons' cell phones help to illuminate the lounge.

The throbbing music dies down and segues into Nancy Wilson's smoky, velvety rendition of 'Save Your Love For Me.' Suddenly, there's a burst of applause and a cache of raucous whistles. Gwen, dressed in her usual silky red suit and white wig, takes the stage.

Dancing, gyrating, and otherwise slithering to the pulse of the song, Gwen's vocal and dance routine has everyone captivated, including Dustin who's pinned to his seat in the rear.

As her routine progresses and layers of clothes come off, he can feel his temperature rising as his heart beats faster. As usual, money and business cards flood the stage.

At the end of her performance, Gwen bows to the applause, grabs her things, and exits to the dressing room. To many, including Dustin, it was the most sensual thing they've ever seen in their lives. He was so transfixed, he didn't notice when the server returned to wait on him. She had to raise her voice over the drum and bass track currently playing.

"Would you like another juice?"

"Oh. Ah, sorry. Nah. I'm okay," he stuttered. "I was just leaving."

He gets up.

"Are you coming back?" she queries.

"Um, I don't know."

"How late are they open?"

"Generally, it's twenty four hours, but you know, if it slows down ain't much sense keeping the doors open."

"What's your name?"

"Felicity."

"That's a nice name for—"

"For?"

"Nothing," he bows his head. "I gotta go."

"Okay, Sugar. See ya later."

"Yeah. Maybe."

He exits the nudie bar and starts walking up the road. From the corner of his eye, he sees a sultry figure leaning up against the side door on the outside of the lounge smoking a cigarette. It's Gwen. He walks down a narrow path towards her. She's already dressed in her street clothes.

"Gwen," he shouts, approaching her.

She squints, barely making out his face by the light of the rear security lights.

"Hey. It's Dustin, right?"

"You remembered me."

"I ain't that old yet."

She offered him a pull on her clove cigarette but he refuses.

"Sold your computer?" he asks.

"Not yet."

He kicks up a little dirt with his feet, anxious to let the next words out of his mouth flow as smoothly as possible. "So this is what you do, huh?" he wonders.

"You saw the show?"

"Yeah. It was pretty good."

"That's all?"

"No. It was better than good."

"Relax, Dustin. Do I make you nervous?"

"Well, you know me; books, books, books."

"Wanna go for a drink or something to eat?"

"Um ... yeah, I wouldn't mind. You sure?"

"*Du'o'c*. Let me get my things. I'll be right back."

An hour later, the two of them are sitting at a cloth covered table in a large, brightly lit seafood restaurant in the International District. Several hot dishes, as well as glasses of white wine, are sitting invitingly on their table. Sparsely populated, the restaurant nevertheless exudes its own romantic charm.

"This is the first time I've been here," Dustin admits. "Pretty nice place."

"They have the best braised duck in Chinatown." She takes a bite of her food. "Delicious," she continues. "When I was growing up my favorite dish was *Muc Nhoi Thit,* stuffed squid. Wish I had it every week."

Dustin, she notices, is barely eating. He seems jittery, as if waiting for a professor to finish scoring his physics homework.

"Are you nervous?" she asks.

"Sorry."

He picks up his chopsticks and digs in. Gwen eyes him curiously.

"Don't get out much, do you?"

"It's just that ... you're really, really beautiful."

"Shit. Now it's my turn to blush."

"Sorry."

"You know what?" she suggests. "Have some more wine."

She lays down her chopsticks and raises her glass. Dustin follows suit.

"*Chúc sức khoẻ*. To good health."

"Live long and prosper."

Gwen smiles. "You're nerdy to the bone."

Dustin adjusts his eye glasses. "This must be the part where you say, 'Well, it's been real. See ya later.'"

"I was actually wondering if you wanted to rent a movie."

"A movie? Like, watch it at your house?"

"Kinda boring to watch 'em by yourself, no?"

"Yeah. I'm down."

Several minutes later, having had their fill for the night, Gwen and Dustin are leaving the eatery. Dustin stops short at the doorway.

"I gotta use the bathroom real quick."

"Go ahead."

He goes back inside the restaurant. Gwen, wearing her Pink Pussycat backpack, takes it off, removes a box of clove cigs and lights one. Just then, Andrew comes walking down the block. He still has a limp, though not as profound as before.

"Hey," he asks Gwen, "you got another one?"

Gwen studies the stranger momentarily, slightly perturbed that he's interrupted her reverie. "Yeah." She takes one out, lights it with hers, and hands it to him.

"Thanks."

He takes a drag and coughs.

"Clove cigarettes," she informs him.

"Never had this before. It's kinda spicy."

She motions to his leg. "What happened to you?"

"I tripped in the stupid sidewalk. Can you lend me a dollar?"

"Lend you? You mean donate."

She takes out a five dollar bill from her pocket and hands it to him. "You're lucky you're in pain," she adds.

"Thanks, lady."

He turns to leave, then stops and speaks without looking at her. "Watch out for the ghosts."

"What?" she asks. "What are you talking about? Ghosts?"

Andrew doesn't explain himself. He simply hobbles back down the block and out of sight. Dustin emerges from the restaurant.

"Sorry it took so long. They were cleaning out the bathroom."

"They have more characters in this town than a circus."

"Life in the big city," Dustin muses.

"I don't know what's sadder: the homeless who's lost their way, or the ones who don't give a damn."

"Huh?"

"There's a Blockbuster near my place. We can take a taxi."

"Sounds good."

The two walk to the edge of the sidewalk and wait, hoping a taxi will soon come along. Dustin looks up at the cloudless starry sky.

"You know," he starts, "it's funny. Mankind has been travelling back in time and seeing blueprints for years."

"What?"

"And we just didn't know it."

"What are you talking about?"

"Well, look at those stars."

She looks up.

"They died," he continues, "millions and millions of years ago, but we're just seeing them now. We're looking at the past. We're looking at ghosts."

Gwen is taken aback.

"Weird, huh?" Dustin asks.

"Eerie," she adds. "In more ways than one."

Almost an hour later, the two are in Gwen's apartment. Having sold many of her furnishings, the condo is now sparsely populated.

Save for a handful of floor lamps, a couch, the TV and stand, there's hardly anything left.

Dustin's on the couch watching Nagisa Oshima's sexually explicit 'In The Realm Of The Senses.' Gwen, wearing sweat pants and a t-shirt, walks over with two beers, one of which she gives to Dustin.

"Thanks."

She curls up next to him. "So what are you studying in school?"

"Environmental Anthropology."

"Sounds pretty self-explanatory."

"Sustainable living, forestry resources ..."

"Cool."

Gwen focuses on the movie. Dustin bites his lip.

"Doesn't stripping bother you?" he asks.

"At first, of course, but the nervousness whittles away. I don't think about those guys."

"You must get lots of business cards."

"Eh, I don't call any of 'em. That's not my thing. From my point of view, they're really like dogs in heat. Not my type."

"If I'd known my housemates weren't gonna show up, I wouldn't have been there."

She kisses his cheek. Now consciously nervous, he remains as still as a branch on a windless day.

"I've never seen this movie before. In the Realm of the Senses. Nice name, though."

She rubs his chest. He remains tense. She works her hand to his midriff. He takes a long swig of beer.

"You *are* tense," she musters.

"This is the part where I admit I'm a virgin."

"I figured that. You're easy to read." She kisses him full on his mouth.

Minutes later, they're under the covers in her bedroom. The window starts fogging up. Illuminated by the glow of the grinning moon, and the flickering ebb and flow of a flameless candle on the nearby nightstand, there would seem to be no more perfect end for the night.

Chapter VI

Silver Spikes and Tender Septums

Dustin and Gwen are sitting in the window of a Belltown Café eating breakfast. The eatery is slightly congested this Thursday morning. There are seats and tables outside the café, but none are occupied as there is a cloudy overcast.

Despite the grayness outside, there are stars in Dustin's eyes. He's practically radiating like a miner who's just uncovered the largest diamond known to man. Gwen, casually reading a newspaper, is too engrossed to notice Dustin's quiet excitement.

After breakfast, they go for a walk, hand in hand, down the street. Occasionally, they'd stop and gawk at some of the clothes on display in various boutiques. Walking just past Pike Place Market on 1st Ave, they arrive at an adult book store.

"Stay right here," Gwen tells her new friend.

"Where are you going?"

"It's a surprise."

She enters the store leaving Dustin outside to ponder her intention.

He starts pacing back and forth. The sky, he notices, isn't clearing up any. In fact, it seems to have grown darker in the short time he's been waiting. He watches as tourists in bright Hawaiian shirts go strolling past reading a map only to be accosted by a homeless man begging for money.

Just then, Gwen exits the store with a red bag in her hand.

"What's that?" Dustin asks.

"You'll see."

Minutes later, the two are sitting on Gwen's bed. She teasingly, slowly opens the red bag and brings out a pair of edible red underwear.

"Strawberry," she informs him.

"Is that for you?"

"Not exactly."

***

The devastating sounds of a thick leather belt slices through the air, finding its mark to a young boy's back. The 12 year old, being disciplined by his father in the living room of a small house, is screaming as he's running around trying to get away. The boy never looks at the man, but he can hear his thundering footsteps and the swishing of the belt. The man, a Vietnamese émigré, is shouting.

"Lazy … selfish … good for nothing … they made a mistake at the hospital. *Xin lỗi anh!* You didn't spring from my loins. Too good for laundry work? *Cài này là gì?* Too proud?!"

The boy makes a beeline dash towards the front door, pulls it open, and flies off down the street. The man doesn't pursue. He simply stands angrily on the porch and watches the 12 year old run as fast as his legs can take him.

The boy runs haphazardly across the street. The man gasps when he sees a car screeching to a halt just inches from the inattentive child.

***

Andrew wakes up in a cold sweat from his nightmare. He looks around. He's lying on a tarp beneath a tree deep in the woods, "The Jungle", as the greenbelt south of the International District is locally known.

He rolls up his left pants leg and looks at the bandage. Blood is soaking through. Leaving the tarp, he limps up a narrow path. The slippery grass and occasional stones, compounded by the pain in his leg, makes his journey all the more arduous. Stopping to swallow one of his pain pills, he ascends the steep hill and crosses a barrier which brings him to the sidewalk at the edge of the greenbelt.

Walking to an Asian Help Center in the ID, he climbs up the steps and knocks on the door. No one answers. He peeks in their windows, but no one's inside.

Hobbling to the rear entrance of the Saigon Deli, he knocks on the door. No one answers. Waiting a few moments, he knocks again. When he sees a police car cruise by, he leaves immediately.

He limps towards a bus shelter, stops and asks for monetary assistance from the few people there. Most of them ignore him. An old Asian woman raises her cane and shouts at him. Speaking Chinese, he doesn't understand her, but her angry face says it all. It was time to move on.

Minutes later, he's standing at the overpass near the top of Beacon Hill. From there, he can see the two downtown sports stadiums: Century Link Field and Safeco Field. He focuses downwards at the cars, at the steel girders, and at the continuing construction.

***

Phong, dressed in street clothes, stumbles out of his bed and heads to the bathroom. He's seen better days. Bags, from lack of true sleep, have grown under his eyes. He has stubble now. He splashes some water on his face and stares at the dead tired reflection in the mirror.

Sitting on the commode, he casually picks out *The Stranger Weekly* clustered in with other magazines in the rack on the bathroom floor. Flipping through the pages, he glances at the usual fare: clothing, record store, tattoo ads, theatre and movie announcements, restaurant reviews, and escort services. Towards the back of the *Weekly,* he notices, in the Classifieds, a listing that was circled with a marker.

His eyes light up. The ad reads: Violinist Wanted for Goth Metal/DarkWave Outfit. Must be open-minded. Call Blood.

Standing in his living room, looking out of the window, he dials a number. A man answers.

"Hello?"

"Hello?" Phong asks. "Is this Blood?"

"Yes."

"I saw in your ad you're looking for a violinist?"

"Violin, cello, any instrument, really. We're always looking."

"Did a girl name Violet Chang come by?"

"Yeah. I remember her."

"Do you know how I can reach her?"

"She has a cell phone."

"She isn't picking up."

"Dude, take that as a hint."

"I'm her fiancée."

"Can't help you, bro. I just place the ads for my friend Morpheus."

"Morpheus?"

"He doesn't have a phone and he won't be here till this afternoon. You'd have to come down here to see him."

"Where is here?"

"University Tattoo."

"Is that near the U district?"

"Yeah, it's on the Ave., right on the main drag. You can't miss it."

"Thanks."

Two hours later, Phong enters the brightly lit tattoo parlor. The walls are filled with sketches of various tattoos. The display cases are brimming with an arsenal of branding, scarification, and piercing jewelry. There is no one at the front counter. The faint buzzing of a tattoo gun can be heard coming from the rear.

Phong walks to the unmanned register. "Hello?"

"Just a minute," a man answers from one of the tattoo booths.

Phong continues perusing the pictures on the wall. Most of the themes are dark with common elements of devilry, twisted metal, tribalism and skulls.

A heavily pierced, ultra-tattooed young man sticks his out from one of the booths.

"Just give me a sec," he apologizes. "You can go through the books and see if there's anything you like."

"I'm actually looking for Morpheus," Phong insists. "You know, about Violet?"

Just then, a large strapping man enters the store. Wearing black and red leather clothes, he's similarly attired as the tattoo artist, including wearing flesh plugs the size of golf balls in his ear lobes.

"Hey, Morpheus," the artist shouts. "This gentleman's looking for you."

He sticks his head back in his tattoo booth. Morpheus walks over to Phong and examines his earlobes, eyebrows, septum and chin, prodding and twisting it as if he was picking out the juiciest apple in a supermarket. Phong, obviously intimidated, allows the man to probe as he saw fit.

"You would look good with a silver spike through your septum, maybe a spiraling black tribal all the up to the back of your ears."

Phong backs off casually.

"I'm actually looking for Violet Chang," he admits. "She auditioned for your band?"

"Well, it's not exactly a band. It's more of a burlesque collective."

"Burlesque collective?"

"Or cold wave Americana troop, if you prefer. Your buddy, Violet, loves the idea. To have so much talent cooped up in such a frail body."

Phong studies Morpheus with intense curiosity. He doesn't know what to think.

"She plays beautifully. You know, they say the violin is the devil's instrument." He leans in towards Phong and whispers in his ear. "Personally, I think she made a pact."

"Why do you say that?"

"Her playing is unearthly."

"Do you know where she is?"

"That all depends. What do you want her for?"

Phong goes into his pocket, produces a small velvet ring box, opens it and shows the ring to Morpheus.

"She's my fiancée."

"So why are you asking me? Seems like you two got a couple of things to work out."

"Exactly."

"She's been seen up the street. She's been to the Mercury Lounge."

"In Capitol Hill? I know the place. Thanks."

He starts to leave.

"You sure I can't interest you in a nose ring?" Morpheus asks.

"Maybe some other time."

***

Club Noc Noc is a dark, atmospheric club that sits smack in a sketchy part of downtown Seattle. It's a good thing they have bouncers because, on any given evening, the immediate area will be populated by drug sellers and abusers, the homeless, and other sordid characters.

Gordon is sitting at the bar in the lounge enjoying a Long Island ice tea. Lit by several chandeliers, the club has a cozy industrial vibe. New wave music is playing through the various speakers on the walls. Several booths are filled with happy hour teetotalers. There are a few empty stools near Gordon.

Across the room, he sees a woman sitting by herself. When she turns to look at him, he quickly zips his eyes away. He picks up a flyer on the bar and peruses it. He then signals for the bartender to bring him another drink. Glancing at the woman again, he sees she's bobbing her head to the music. The woman, Gwen's friend Mina, sees him looking at her. She gets up and walks over.

"Mind if I sit here?" she asks.

"I'd never turn down company."

Dressed mainly in black, she plops herself down in the chair next to his.

"I'm Mina."

"Gordon."

"Let me guess," she wonders, "you're not from around here, right?"

"It's *that* obvious?"

"I come here a lot. Sometimes I work the bar."

"Just got to Seattle this morning."

"Where are you from?"

"Texas."

"Long way from home. What do they drink in Texas, Gordon?"

"Whatever's wet."

Mina turns to the bartender. "Two black and tans," she orders.

The bartender nods and starts preparing the drinks. Gordon has never heard of those aperitifs.

"Black and tan?

"Guinness Stout on the bottom, the lighter Harp on top."

"You must party a lot."

"Only when I'm not paying for it."

Gordon smiles and taps his fingers on the bar. The pair of black and tans are brought over. He sips his. "Not bad."

"You got family here in Seattle?"

"Uh, uh."

"Friends?"

"No. My goodness. Are all you Seattle folks that 'right to the point'?"

"Just trying to be friendly. You seem like a nice enough guy."

"Oh, I'm not complaining. Usually, you see women too scared to approach men, especially down south."

"Well, it's different here up here. Must be something in the air, makes us more—"

"Aggressive?"

"Compulsive," she corrects him. "I'm just having fun, brother. You know, some people are living, others are just buying time."

Just then, her cell phone rings.

"Excuse me. I'm at Noc Noc," she tells the person on the other end. "Twenty minutes? Yeah, I'll be there."

"Gotta go?" Gordon asks.

"I'm like the designated driver for my friends."

"Yeah? You've been drinking, too."

She slides her black and tan over to Gordon.

"You can have this. I didn't touch it. The tab's on me, so don't worry about it."

"Are you coming back later?"

"I'll see what's doing."

She gets up. Gordon watches as she exits the club.

***

Several people, most in their 20's and all dressed in black, are hanging around outside the Mercury Lounge on Capitol Hill. Some are smoking, others just chatting up a storm. The bouncer, a large man also dressed in black, minus the goth getup, is standing guard outside. Phong approaches.

"How much to get in?"

"This is a private club."

"A private club? So how do I get in?"

"You have to be invited as a guest."

Phong wanted to ask, "So how'd the *first* one get in?" But he could see the bouncer didn't look like the joking kind. He studies the group of smokers outside and sighs. He knows none of them. Taking a picture of Violet out of his pocket, he shows it to the bouncer.

"You ever saw her? Is she here?"

The bouncer takes a gander at the photo and shakes his head. "Never saw her before."

Phong then walks over to the small group nearby and shows it to them. "Excuse me. Have you guys seen this girl?"

They all look it over and shake their heads. Suddenly, a woman behind him calls his name.

"Hey, Phong!"

He turns around and sees Mina. He's seen her before but can't place her name. "Where do I know you from?"

"I was Violet's roommate in Madison Park. You forgot already?"

"Oh, hey Mina. I haven't seen you in, what, two years?"

"At least."

He soaks her entire figure in. She's obviously larger that she was two years ago. "You sure have changed."

"You can say it. I'm fat."

"I'm talking about all this black and fishnet and zippers and black and eyeliner—"

"You like? It's the new me."

"Hey, Mina. Are you a member here?"

"Uh, huh."

"Sweet. I need to get in."

She looks him over. Clearly he's not attired for a goth hangout. "Not like that. There's a certain vibe to the place, you know?"

"Yeah. I see."

"I didn't know you and Violet were into the scene."

"See, that's the problem. We had a little falling out earlier this week. I couldn't find her, then I heard she hangs out here."

"Well, I actually wasn't going to hang out here tonight. I just came to give somebody a ride home. If I see Violet I'll send her out. Give me five minutes."

Mina waves 'Hi' to the bouncer and enters the club as Phong watches. The small crowd that had gathered outside also enters.

***

Gwen and Dustin are walking side by side around the sprawling grounds of the Seattle Center. Constructed to commemorate the 1962 World's Fair, it is a triumph of science and technology. Several buildings and theatres on its grounds are a testament to its continuing popularity.

As visitors mill about in all directions, Gwen and Dustin stop to watch the large water fountain in the middle of the park spewing like an exploding cannonball.

"I could live like this forever," Dustin muses.

"You'd drown in that fountain."

"I meant Seattle."

He turns to face her. "I love you."

Gwen backs away quickly as if she'd just been kicked in the gut. "Not so fast," she admonishes him.

"Why? What's the matter?"

"All this is moving kinda quick, don't you think?"

"You make me feel like a different person. I *am* a different person. I've never been this open to anyone."

"Let's just give this some time. There are a lot of things on my mind."

"Like what? Maybe I can help you."

"I don't know. I was thinking about heading back home."

"Where's that?

"Minnesota. I don't know, Dustin. My head is spinning. I can't think straight. Just need to clear my head." She looks at her watch. "I have to start heading to the lounge soon."

"Do you think about us, Gwen? You know, me and you?"

"Yeah. I mean … I guess."

"You think we can be a couple?"

"Oh, Jesus." She starts walking towards the sidewalk. Dustin follows closely.

"I have a lot of fun with you," he explains. "No one's ever treated me like this. You make me feel whole."

"How sweet."

"It's true."

She stops to face him. "Let's slow down, huh? My head is spinning." She turns and flags a taxi.

"Can I call you? Hey, I don't even have your number."

"My phone broke anyway."

"I have an extra one if you want. It's hi-tech."

"Yeah, um, okay."

A taxi pulls up beside them. She opens the rear door and turns to Dustin. "I'll see you later, okay?" She waves him goodbye and enters the car.

***

Mina and a tipsy friend exit the Mercury Lounge. Nearly dark outside, they rendezvous with Phong. He'd been patiently waiting on the bench of a bus stop nearby. Mina bows her head apologetically

"Violet wasn't in there. Sorry."

"That's okay. Maybe tomorrow."

"Yeah, tomorrow. You'll still need suitable attire to get in."

"Black on black?"

"Something like that."

***

Gordon's driving through the congested streets of the International District. People are walking about everywhere; some are on their way to somewhere else, others are just standing around in the park or on the corners. A few of Seattle's Finest cruise around often.

Driving up Jackson Street, he sees a young man sitting on a bench beneath the Jackson Street Bridge. It's Andrew and he is in coming down off a high. His legs are shaking back and forth and he appears a bit nervous. Gordon pulls his car up in front of Andrew and rolls the passenger side window down.

"Hey."

Andrew, caught up in his own high world, says nothing.

"Where are the motels around here?" Gordon asks.

Again, Andrew doesn't answer. Gordon parks his car nearby, gets out, and walks over to the otherwise out of it Vietnamese.

"Do you need help?"

Andrew replies in a whisperingly soft voice. "Don't bug me."

Gordon removes Gus Bewlay's box of cigarettes from his pocket and offers it to Andrew.

"You smoke?"

Andrew lifts up his head, stares at the box and nods. Gordon gives it to him.

"Here. You can keep it."

Grabbing the box, he pulls a cigarette out and lights it with his own torch. He takes a puff and nods his acceptance to Gordon.

"My name's Gordon."

Andrew takes his hand. "I'm Andrew. Are you looking?

"Looking for what?"

"Nothing."

Gordon twiddles his thumb, chews the inside of his mouth, and stares at Andrew. "Are you hungry?"

Andrew watches the stranger with curiosity. "You want to buy me some food?" he asks.

"You look like someone in need."

Andrew gets up and points at a Chinese restaurant just one block away. "They have good barbecue."

"Let's go."

They start walking down towards the eatery. Buddhist chants emanate from the outside speaker of a video store nearby. The ubiquitous smell of barbeque pork and roast duck fills the air. Gordon notices Andrew has a limp.

"What happened to you?"

"I got stabbed."

"That sucks. You can't be too careful in these big cities."

"Where are the motels around here?"

"You're not from Seattle?"

"I just got here."

"I know where they are. I'll show you."

Several minutes later, Gordon and Andrew enter the dark room of a motel a few miles south of downtown. Gordon puts on the light. They're both carrying little takeout boxes of Chinese food. The room has two beds, one nightstand, a chest of drawers with a TV on top and a fridge in the corner. Gordon puts his food on the chest and turns the TV on. He looks around the room.

"Well, I guess this is as good a place as any."

Andrew sits down on the edge of one of the beds and digs into his meal.

"Boy, you *were* hungry." Gordon remarks.

He stares as the famished young man tears into a juicy rib.

"I've been walking all day. You mind if I go freshen up?"

Andrew shrugs.

Gordon exits to the bathroom and closes the door. Removing a gold cross from his neck, the preacher hangs it on a hook over the mirror. He undresses and gets into the shower. As the warm refreshing water washes over his skin, he starts humming a tune. Then he shouts out to Andrew.

"If you want to crash here tonight, that's fine."

He resumes humming. Suddenly, he stops cold. His arms stiffen, then tremble. His head falls backwards and his entire body quivers from a mild seizure. Fifteen seconds later, his seizure stops abruptly.

Regaining consciousness, he steps out of the shower. His hands, he notices, are still shaking. He rubs them together and eventually, they stop quivering. He dries himself, stares at his eyes in the bathroom mirror and then looks at the dangling cross.

"Are you trying to tell me something?" He puts his cross back on and dons his clothes. Opening the bathroom door, he walks back into the main room.

His jaw nearly drops when he sees Andrew sitting naked on the edge of the bed. The only thing he has on is the bandage spiraled around his left leg. Gordon approaches him with curiosity. "Are you okay?"

"You have oil?"

"Oil? What for?"

"Isn't this what you wanted?"

"Not at all. I was just trying to help you out with some food and a place to rest."

Andrew jumps up and puts all his clothes, including his shoes, back on.

"Are you leaving?"

"Can you lend me twenty dollars?" Andrew asks.

"What for?"

"What do you think?"

"I'm trying to show you there's a different way," Gordon pleads. "A better way."

"You gonna give me the money or not?"

Gordon takes out wallet and reluctantly hands Andrew the money. "Am I gonna see you again?"

"Yeah," he nods.

Then he turns and exits.

Gordon shakes his head and plops down on the bed. He sees a wallet on the floor between the beds. Picking up, he examines its contents: Andrew's jail ID, a food stamps card, childhood photographs, some phone numbers, a Starbuck's gift card, and an old crinkled photo of the young man as a child. He places the wallet on the center table then removes the cross from around his neck and speaks to it.

"Is this the one?" he whispers. "Is he why you brought me this far?"

Closing his eyes, he inaudibly mumbles a prayer, puts the cross back around his neck, lies down and closes his eyes.

Chapter VII

Mina is pacing back and forth in front of the Capitol Hill clothing, consignment, and costume store Red Light, checking her wristwatch intermittently. As usual, the Bohemian street is filled with students and other natives. She stops pacing when she sees Phong approaching across the street. He is carrying a zippered leather folder.

"Hey, Phong," she scolds him. "You're cutting this kinda close."

"Sorry."

"They only give us 30 minute lunch breaks."

"I appreciate your time, Mina. I was on the phone and lost track of time. It's this music publisher I know. He's heading out of town today and needed to take some of my material with him.

She motions to the folder. "Is that what that is?"

"Yeah. I'm meeting him after this downtown."

"So let's get on with it."

Inside Red Light, Mina and Phong peruse the aisles. At times, Mina would pick out something black and zippered but Phong would cringe. At other items, he'd simply shrug. He also took a closer look at a rack of boots, all of which were used. As he's going through the items, he sees someone walk past the front of the store.

"Violet!" he shouts.

Like a jackrabbit, he leaps through the aisles, runs to the front door, throws it open and looks up and down the street. Amidst the sea of walkers and strollers, there's no Violet. Mina comes over.

"Phong..."

"I'm telling you," he insists, "it was her."

"I don't doubt you, Phong. She loves you. She'll come back."

He sighs. "I'm already halfway to giving up."

***

Dustin, toting a small gift bag, is standing on the street ringing the bell to Gwen's condo. There's no answer. When a tenant exits the building, he moves to one side, then catches the front door before it closes.

Taking the elevator to her floor, he rings the bell on her door and waits for a response. Receiving no answer, he knocks.

"Gwen, are you home?" he asks. "I took off classes to see you."

Waiting patiently, there's still no answer. He glances downwards, sees a piece of paper jutting from beneath the door. It reads: 'Dustin, I had fun and truly enjoyed your company but we can't see each other anymore. Bye. Gwen.'

"What the hell?" He knocks on the door again. "Gwen!" He tries to open the door but it's securely locked. "Dammit." Removing the gift bag from his wrist, he loops its rope handles over the doorknob. "Merry Christmas."

***

Gordon is driving up one of the back roads in the International District when he notices Andrew's unmistakable limp about a block away. He cruises alongside him with Andrew's wallet displayed.

"You forgot this."

Andrew looks briefly at the wallet, snatches it from Gordon's hand, and continues up the road. Gordon stays with him.

"Are you hungry?" Gordon asks.

"I just ate."

"You need a ride somewhere?"

"I'm fine."

"I was driving around downtown just now. I see they have a Gameworks. You wanna go?"

Andrew stops walking and turns to Gordon. "You wanna go to a casino?"

"Actually," Gordon counters, "I have a better idea."

Minutes later, Gordon and Andrew are standing and looking at the façade of St. Mark's Cathedral, a hilltop modernistic church adjacent to Volunteer Park in Capitol Hill. Gordon is smiling, but Andrew isn't.

"You're joking, right?" Andrew scowls. "What is this? A food kitchen?"

"But seek ye first the kingdom of God and his righteousness, and all these things shall be added unto you. Matthew 6:33."

Andrew makes a "get away from me" motion and starts walking away.

"Where are you going?" Gordon asks.

"Chinatown. You're crazy."

"I can help you."

Andrew ignores the preacher and keeps walking down the road. Gordon gnashes his teeth and cuffs both fists, glances at the cross atop the cathedral, then turns towards the disappearing Andrew.

"Hold up!"

About one hour later, the two are in a motel room south of the stadiums. Even though it's broad daylight, the room, lit sparsely by two incandescent lamps, is relatively dark. The windows and blinds have been drawn shut. It is as quiet as a mausoleum at midnight. The TV is on but the volume is off.

Gordon is planted firmly in a soft arm chair, sitting stoically with his arms folded, the flickering light of the TV illuminating his angry visage. Andrew, tweaking in the opposite corner in another chair, is wiping his dry mouth.

"Stop staring," he whispers without looking up at Gordon.

Gordon watches as the young man goes through his pockets intermittently as if looking for lost treasure. "Is this how you spend your days?" Gordon asks.

"Nothing else to do."

"I can think of at least 100 things."

"You're not a saint. You came from jail."

"Never said I was, but I'm trying to make amends."

"What's that?"

"I'm trying to do good. All souls can be saved, but saving you is like trying to drown a fish."

"I don't have a soul."

"Yeah, you do. Seems like it's tortured."

"I'm thirsty."

Gordon sighs, gets up, and grabs the complimentary motel cup sitting near the TV. Walking over to the fridge, he pulls it open. It's empty.

"Bathroom water?" he suggests.

"Wash the cup," Andrew insists.

Gordon enters the bathroom, runs the cold water and tastes it. "You're in luck. It's cold and clear. Rare in these places." He closes the bathroom door momentarily to urinate. Seconds later, he exits the bathroom with the cup full of water and sees a wide open front door and no Andrew in sight.

***

Amir is at Phong's front door carrying his usual briefcase. He knocks once and adjusts his tie. Phong opens the door. The music publisher's jaw drops. The young composer, usually attired conservatively, is dressed like an extra from a vampire film. His hair is spiked and dyed black. He's wearing a studded dog collar, black clothes, black eyeliner, black lipstick, and black Dr. Marten's boots. Amir is at a loss for words.

"Hey, Amir," Phong greets him. "Come on in."

Amir follows Phong into the living room. Just then, Mina, similarly attired in black, enters from the bathroom.

"Mina," Phong tells her, "this is Amir, my music publisher."

"How do you do?" Amir asks.

"Can't complain," she answers.

"You guys going to a costume party?"

"Nah," Phong insists. "We're actually going out to look for Violet."

"Dressed like that?"

"Do you know her?" Mina asks.

"Sure," Amir answers. "I don't get this get up, though."

"Part of the plan," Phong explains.

"Well, I'm sure there a wonderful story behind all this," Amir surmises, "but I'm running late. I've gotta be down at SeaTac in about an hour." He sees a zippered folder and other assorted sheets of music on Phong's piano and walks over to it. "Are these the scores?" he asks.

"Yes," Phong answers.

Amir opens the folder and examines the scores.

"These seem incomplete."

"I haven't had the time."

"Time is of the essence in this business, Phong. When a door like this opens you don't fall asleep."

"I know," he sighs. "I've been busy looking for Violet."

"I understand, but you don't have the luxury of time. As great a writer as you are, they are graduating thousands around the country every quarter. From here I'm headed to Frisco, then I'm off to the Netherlands. They're waiting, but I don't choose their deadlines."

"You made it seem like you could approach any record company before. I thought that's how you phrased it to me anyway."

"I work with and within their time schedules, budgets, and limitations. It's not up to me. Just a pawn here."

"You're killing me, man. You're killing me."

"I'm doing you a favor."

"Favor? I'm the writer. You guys just hover like vultures waiting to pick our bones clean!"

"What?"

"I'm falling apart, man. I'm losing my fucking mind."

"Calm down, Phong."

Phong rubs his hair. "I can't think about music right now."

"Suit yourself. Do you want to submit these scores or not?"

"Whatever, man."

Amir places the folder beneath his arm and walks towards the door. "I hope things work out for you. I'll be in Frisco if you need to keep in touch."

"I'm sorry," Phong apologizes. "Now is just not a good time."

"I'll see ya later."

Mina turns to Phong. "Geez! A little high strung, are we?"

"I think I'm losing my fucking mind. Look at me. I look like a Marilyn Manson groupie."

Mina pats him on the back. "There, there. It's all for a good cause."

***

Dustin's sitting on the semi-crowded Metro bus, watching warily as the sun turns its back on another uneventful day. He's up front near the driver. Taking out his cell phone, he dials a number but there's no answer. He sighs loudly. The driver looks at him from the corner of his eye.

Minutes later, Dustin is walking up the street with the cell phone pressed to his ear. "Hey Gwen, it's Dustin. When you get this message please call me back at your earliest convenience." He hangs up and shakes his head. "That was so fucking lame."

Standing outside the Pink Pussycat half an hour later, he takes a deep breath and walks in. He sees a waitress carrying a platter of drinks and walks over to her. "Is Gwen here tonight?"

"Check the back."

The club, he notices, is crowded even though it's a little early. 80's disco is pumping out of the speakers. Several rotating disco balls have been added to the cheesy retro décor. He wends his way through various frat boys, businessmen and stag party attendees. Finally, he arrives at the door to the dressing rooms and knocks on it. After a few seconds, Skylark sticks her head out.

"Oh. Hi."

"Hey. Is Gwen here?"

"Not tonight, sugar. You sticking around for the show, boo?"

"Nah. If you see her can you tell her I came by? I've been looking for her all day."

"Sure thing, honey."

"Oh." He removes a small folded piece of paper from his pocket and hands it to Skylark. "This is her new phone number."

"Phone number? She doesn't know it?"

"I left her a new phone as a gift earlier."

"Oh. Okay. I'll let her know if I see her."

Skylark shuts the door and walks over to a bureau in the middle of the dressing room. Gwen comes out from hiding behind a long locker's open door.

"Is he gone, Skylark?"

"He seems like a nice enough boy, Gwen. Why are you avoiding him?"

"I just don't want him to get hurt."

"Seeing as you're such a bad girl an' all." She gives Gwen the folded paper.

"It's your new phone's number."

She takes it. "Thanks. Early Christmas present. Still trying to figure out the damn thing. It's so complex."

"He seems like a really sweet and innocent kid."

"Yeah. He's got a good future. I'll just end up making him lose track."

"Well, Mother Theresa, I myself wouldn't mind a nice, decent, honest fella for a change."

"So you go out with him."

"Sounds like a plan, but I already got my plate full."

***

Phong and Mina enter the Mercury Lounge, or 'The Merc' as it's known, to the sound of music blasting from the ceiling speakers. A few people are on the dance floor. Most are in booths or at the bar. Phong immediately starts looking around the club. Mina stays at his side. "Do you see her?" he asks. "It's dark in here."

"No, but it's early still. Let's get a drink. They make 'em nice and strong here."

Phong notices everyone isn't dressed goth style with some in regular jeans and sweaters,.

"See?" he tells Mina. "You got me looking like Frank N. Furter for nothing."

"Relax. I think you look cool."

Hours later, the two still no sign of Violet. The crowd has grown much larger. People on the floor are dancing to an electronic hard-edge band on stage. Mina and Phong, drunk, are standing together holding up a wall. Phong staggers slightly; Mina seems to be holding her own.

"She's not here," Phong observes. "I'm going. It's late already."

"You need a ride? I gotta sober up a little."

"I'm a big boy. I can find my way." He stumbles through the crowd, exits the club and promptly vomits out his gin and tonics on the concrete in the Merc's parking lot.

Chapter VIII

It is early the next morning in the greenbelt south of the International District. There's very little sunlight filtering into this area known locally as "The Jungle." Heavily wooded, it serves as a perfect hiding spot for the homeless and drug addicted. In the past few years it's seen more than its share of homicides, an embarrassment the Seattle Police tries to squash by unannounced intermittent raids.

Andrew, coming down off a high, is kicking through some debris on the greenbelt floor when he suddenly hears a loud shriek. Looking up, he is startled to see a huge ghost fly towards, and then through him. In a nervous panic, he limps down a trail as quickly as possible. This fete is made all the more arduous by the assemblage of ghosts "attacking" from all directions.

Finally, one of the ghosts manages to jump on his back. He shouts and wriggles to free himself, but it's in vain. Then, in one swift movement, the ghost bites into his neck. He wakes up from the torrid nightmare.

In a cold sweat, he looks around the jungle. From his sitting position on the ground beneath a large sycamore, he sees nothing but trees. There is nary a ghost in sight. Taking a deep breath, he gets up. Suddenly, he hears footsteps coming towards him. Immediately, he begins to limp away, but is almost carelessly knocked down by the same scraggly man who'd planted the nail in his thigh a few days ago.

That man, running through the jungle at high speed, is being chased by two uniformed officers. With the cops on his heel, the man takes out a gun from his waist and flings it in the bushes. This action goes unseen by the police who eventually tackle him.

***

Mina pulls her car into the sparsely populated lot of the Merc's parking garage, parks and gets out. She's attired in "normal" clothes this morning. Walking towards the club she sees a man, almost totally covered by an old blanket, sleeping on a cardboard box near the entrance.

"Sir, you can't sleep here."

The man, however, doesn't stir. She walks closer.

"Sir."

Finally getting close to, she realizes it's Phong who is still in goth gear.

"Well, I'll be damned. Phong."

Finally, he stirs a little. She kneels down near him.

"You slept here all night?"

"What time is it?" he asks, his eyes squinting from the morning sun.

"It's eight o'clock."

"What day?"

"Shit, you're so out of it you don't even know? It's Saturday, man."

"Who are you?"

"Oh, stop it." She helps him to his feet.

"Hey, Mina, do me a favor, huh? Don't tell anyone you saw me like this."

"Why don't you come inside and freshen up? I'm doing cleanup work and some accounting stuff for the manager."

"Can you take me home now? I don't have any cab fare."

"Oh, um, yeah, I guess. Just give me a minute."

Just then, her cell phone rings.

"Hey, Gwen," she utters, "yeah, I'm up for it. I'll be at the club for about two hours. See you around noon? Bye."

She hangs up and turns to Phong. "That was Gwen, my friend from work. She wants to do brunch later. You're welcome to come."

"Right now my head is splitting. I'll see."

"Why'd you sleep out here last night? I thought you had a ride. I was waiting for you and you disappeared."

"To tell you the truth, I'm surprised I'm not waking up in Portland this morning."

"You drank that much?"

"I guess."

***

Gordon is kneeling penitently at the back of the St. Mark's Episcopal Cathedral. It's lit primarily by soft fluorescent lights, sunlight streaming in through the stained glass windows, and the votive candles near the altar. There's no service. He's the only person in the huge room. Reaching into his pocket, he removes the crinkled photo of Andrew and stares at it.

***

Dustin is lying in bed in his small room with his arms folded across his chest. Reaching down to the area on the left side, he brings up a photo-booth strip containing four black and white photos of him and Gwen. In three pictures they're making clown faces; in the bottom fourth she is planting a kiss on his cheek.

***

Andrew is congregating with a group of Vietnamese men in a parking lot behind a restaurant in Chinatown. Forming a circle, they're reminiscing about the past and making plans for the future. Suddenly, a police car pulls into the lot. Andrew jumps up and runs into the alley like a frightened raccoon.

Scant minutes later, an officer is going through Andrew's pockets one by one. Standing with his palms pressed high up against a wall, he's giving no resistance. The cop, finding no contraband or weapons, warns Andrew about showing his face in Chinatown ,especially while he's on duty. His spirit broken, Andrew limps out of the alley.

***

Phong, Mina, and Gwen are sitting in the outside patio of a Belltown café enjoying their brunch and sipping mimosas. Phong still looks a little grey around the gills, but at least he's been changed back to his normal self. Gwen scans the café.

"You know, I don't think I've ever been there," she admits.
"It's a blast," Mina insists.
"Why?' Phong doubts. "I don't see the allure."
"Probably not your cup of tea," Gwen observes.
Mina nods in agreement.
"Bury his heart in Benaroya Hall and he'd be fine."
"Kids who go fishing and listen to Mozart," Phong boasts, "don't grow up to be gangsters."
"You should put that on a bumper sticker," Mina suggests.
Gwen's cell phone ring. She turns to her friends. "Excuse me." She looks at the caller ID. It's Dustin. She turns it off and slips it in her pocket.
"Who?" Mina asks.
Gwen pockets the phone. "It's not important."
Phong and Mina can see from her expression that see she's clearly lying.

***

Gordon spent the better part of the day sightseeing. He'd driven over to Lake Union and watched the boats launch. Later, he drove across the floating bridge and lunched in downtown Bellevue. Now, with the evening fast approaching, he's sitting in a dive near the King Street train station nursing a screwdriver. It's his third and he's beginning to feel its effect. Every so often he'd swing around the barstool and look around the dive as if expecting company.

The bar itself is not a place to take someone on a date. The regulars, all locals, have seen better days. The small cache of men standing around the pool table are probably drug dealers. Most of these regulars look like they're between jobs; the others look like they're between prison sentences. Whenever someone walks past Gordon, he takes out the photo of Andrew, shows it to them, and asks if they recognize him. They just shake their heads 'no'.

Getting up, he staggers towards the men's room. There's a queue of about four men all waiting to enter.

A few minutes later, he is standing between two dumpsters in a nearby alley relieving himself. It's drizzling out, lessening his guilt now that nature's own sanitation system is in play. Unbeknownst to him, a homeless Vietnamese man is sitting in a narrow doorway a few feet away. Just as Gordon is finishing, the man speaks.

"Can you help me out?"

Gordon gets startled. "Shoot! I thought I was alone."

"I haven't eaten all day and I'm cold."

Gordon walks over to the man. "They have a Mission just around the corner."

"I can't stand in line."

"Why not?"

"My legs are no good."

Gordon studies the stranger momentarily then removes the photo of Andrew and shows it him. "You recognize him? His name is Andrew."

"He looks familiar."

"Do you know where he is?"

"I don't know. Maybe."

Gordon takes out his wallet and pulls out a $20 bill. "Are you sure?"

The stranger stretches out his hand. "He's in the jungle."

"The what?"

The man takes the money. "I'll show you. You have a car?"

***

Gwen enters the Pink Pussycat Lounge through the front door and greets a security guard. Walking into the main room, someone calls out to her from a dark corner.

"Gwen."

Turning around, she sees Dustin. He's been drinking. Walking into the light, she can see his eyes are red and his color is wan.

"I told you," she sighs, "it's over."

"How can that be?" he protests. "We were having fun."

"We're not right for each other, Dustin. That needs no more explanation. Goodbye."

She turns to leave but he grabs her arm. "Wait." he shouts.

She struggles free. "Let me go."

The security guard comes over and asks, "What's going on here?"

"It's okay," Gwen insists. "He was just leaving."

Dustin surveys the scene quickly and exits.

"Was he bothering you?" the guard asks.

"Schoolboy crush," she explains then walks off towards the dressing room.

***

They say the ghost of Princess Angeline, daughter of Chief Seattle, walks the streets of the evergreen city, keeping watch over her homeland. It is now Saturday night and perhaps she's watching over

Phong and Mina who enter The Merc for the 2nd night in a row. There's no danger in it, but Phong, fully attired in black again, feels a watcher at the gates of hell. The club, already half-packed, has a faint smell of brimstone and risk. Industrial music is emanating from the speakers.

They find a spot at the bar. Mina notices that Phong seems a bit nervous.

"Are you okay?"

"Yeah. I'm just worried I overdid it last night."

"Just go slowly."

She motions for the bartender to come over. "A light draft and an orange juice," she tells him.

The bartender goes to prepare the drinks.

"I'll be right back," she tells Phong.

She exits towards the back. Phong walks over to a jukebox in a corner and peruses its contents. Most of what he sees are heavy and dark wave recordings by bands such as Ministry, Skinny Puppy, Bella Morte, Dead Can Dance, and Rammstein. A goth girl standing next to him, who had been observing him for some time, finally says, "Would you believe it? No Joy Division. No Bauhaus."

"Too bad," Phong laments.

"You look familiar."

"This isn't exactly my hangout."

"Mine, either. It's just my release."

"Do you know Violet Chang?"

The goth girl shrugs. "What do they sound like?"

Phong removes the picture of Violet from his pocket and shows it to her.

"It's not a band."

"Oh, violin girl," the stranger realizes.

Phong's face lights up like a beacon.

"You've seen her?"

"Yeah. She's here tonight."

"Where is she?"

"Down in the House of Pain."

"Where's that?"

The goth girl points to the floor beneath them.

***

Gordon and the homeless Vietnamese man pull up in the rain on the side of the road outside The Jungle, the notorious greenbelt just off I-5 south of the International District. Exiting the car, they stand in the shadow of the giant rust-colored Pacific Medical Center across the street. In front of them is a wire fence with a gate in need of much repair. Gordon is a bit apprehensive. He could feel his heart beat a little faster.

"So this is The Jungle?"

"Yeah."

The homeless man starts walking towards the gate.

"How far do we have to go?" Gordon asks.

"Not far."

The preacher gazes deeply at the woods and feels a pall draw over him.

***

Skylark is sitting on a stool in front of the large wall-length mirror in the Pink Pussycat's dressing room. She's applying makeup and sneaking sips of liqueur from a tiny bottle on a ledge beneath the counter. "As Long As He Needs Me" by Nancy Wilson is flowing from speakers in the lounge. A cell phone rings in a locker behind her but she ignores it.

She smiles when she hears whistles and jubilant calls beyond the door. The cell phone keeps ringing. She continues applying makeup as the ringing persists. Finally, unable to stand another minute, she gets up, opens the locker, takes out Gwen's new the video phone, and answers it.

"Hey, Dustin."

It's raining heavily on the Aurora Avenue bridge. Dustin, soaked to the gills, is standing next to the railing beneath a crossbeam. He can see Skylark just as well as she can see him.

"Hi, Sky. Can I speak to Gwen?"

"Boy, this phone is funky. I feel like Dick Tracy. You gotta get me one."

"I will. Can I speak to Gwen?"

"Um, she's performing right now. I really shouldn't be answering her phone."

"Show her this."

"Show her what?"

Skylark, looking at the phone's bright screen, sees Dustin's phone heading towards a half empty bottle of Jack Daniels about twenty feet away. It's sitting on the pavement next to the aluminum railing that protects pedestrians from traffic. She sees the bottle being picked up. Next, she hears a deep swig being taken then sees the bottle being put back into place.

Seconds later, Dustin props his video phone up against the bottle, allowing it to aim towards the other railing—the one closer to the outside edge. Then, Skylark watches as Dustin climbs on top of the outer railing while holding onto a crossbeam for balance. He turns to face Lake Union. Skylark covers her mouth.

"Oh my God!"

Out in the lounge, the Nancy Wilson song is complete. A techno track comes on. Gwen enters the dressing room covered by a bath towel. Her red vinyl clothes are in her arms. Her hair is soaking wet.

"Gwen!"

"Why are you shouting my name like that?"

Skylark hands her the phone and. Gwen sees Dustin atop the railing.

"Is that Dustin? Damn fool. Is this live?"

"He just called."

"Where is he?"

"He didn't say. Sounds despondent, though."

They both stare intently at the video. Something about the area, the crossbeams, and the size of the width of the railings seem vaguely familiar. Soon, the location reveals itself.

"Aurora Bridge," they both scream.

"We should call 911," Skylark suggests.

"If he's that despondent he might jump."

They look at the phone again.

"See?" Gwen adds. "He's waiting for me."

"Lend me your phone," she asks Skylark. "I'm calling a friend of mine."

Phong is walking to the rear of the Mercury lounge when Mina approaches him. Nursing a glass of beer, he's a little tipsy and almost doesn't see her.

"Hey, Phong."

"Hey, Mina. I know where Violet is."

"Good, but I gotta go. Gwen is having an emergency and needs a ride right now."

"You go ahead. I'll be okay."

Mina leaves. Phong continues walking to the rear. At the back of the lounge, a large well-tattooed man with multiple piercings is standing guard by a narrow plain black door. Phong approaches him.

"Is this the House of Pain?"

The man looks him over carefully. "You've got the wrong place, mister."

"They said ..." he takes a sip of his beer. "My friend is a member here."

"No entry without a membership card."

Phong checks his pocket. "I don't have one."

"Then you're out of luck. Later."

Phong takes out his wallet, pulls out a $100 bill and hands it to the guard. "Will this card do?"

The guard takes the money and gives Phong a clipboard with a form on it to sign. "Disclaimer," the guard explains.

Phong grabs the pen dangling from a string tied to the clipboard signs the form. The guard then opens the little black door and turns to Phong. "I don't know you."

"Me, neither," Phong salutes then enters the House of Pain. The guard closes the door behind him.

***

Gwen is standing outside the nude bar smoking beneath an awning. She's tapping one foot nervously on the rain-soaked pavement. Mina pulls up. Gwen takes one last deep drag, flicks the butt away, and jumps in the car.

Minutes later, with the windshield wiper slapping back and forth, Mina and Gwen make their way across town toward their intended destination, the Aurora Bridge in Fremont just north of Seattle.

Mina glances at her friend. "Your boyfriend really has issues, huh?"

"He's just obsessed. And he's not my friend."

"He could be in the drink by now."

Gwen, holding her video phone on her lap, shows it to Mina. Dustin, she notices, is still clinging to the pole atop the bridge's railing.

"I'd better step on it," Mina warns herself.

***

Phong descends ominously into the darkness that is the House of Pain. Brimming with the scent of jasmine, the dungeon seems inspired by gothic themes. The area looks like it was decorated by the same man who did set design for Jean Cocteau's 1946 fantasy of the macabre masterpiece 'Belle et le Bete'.

Along the walls are metallic arms holding incandescent torches. Incense burners are producing thick clouds of smoke from large urns atop iron tripods. The obbligato chain-mail curtains dangle and obscure some of the passageways. Along the top of the walls, at various points, small speakers are playing industrial music.

As he walks through, he passes tiny rooms protected by thick black curtains. Peeking in the first room, he sees a naked man, his ankles shackled to the floor, with his face to the wall and his arms tied up. He is being beaten with a cat 'o nine tails by a woman dressed entirely in black. In the adjoining candle-lit room, a "Roman soldier" is nailing a man dressed like the messiah to a cross. In another room, he sees a man with several metal loops in his body hanging horizontally by chains to the ceiling.

In another jail-sized space, Phong spies a woman lying flat on her back on a slab of concrete. Naked, her arms and legs are tied with ropes to spikes in the ground. A dominatrix brands various symbols in her abdomen and thighs. On the wall surrounding the dominatrix are various tools of the trade: saws, pliers, pinchers, thumb presses, truncheons, cast iron branding implements, and a hot stove.

Shaking his head, Phong continues on. A few patrons pass by before he peeks in another room. There, he seems a near-naked man sitting on what looks an old wooden electric chair. His arms and legs are tied to 'ol smoky' and he is blindfolded. He recoils as his torturer creates one inch slices in his body with a kukri, a long knife with a curved blade similar to a machete. Phong had seen one like it before at the Seattle Asian Museum and its striking deadly design stayed with him forever.

Just then, a dominatrix approaches him. "Are you ready?" she asks.

"What? Me? Oh, I'm just looking for somebody."

"Aw, you're a virgin," she rubs his chin. "Didn't know this was your first time. I'll be gentle."

She touches his arm. He yanks it away. "I'm afraid you're mistaken."

"Then get out of here!" she commands him, but Phong stands his ground.

"Not till I find what I'm looking for." Quickly, he runs through the winding narrow passageways peeking in each little room till, finally, he sees who he's looking for.

He notices Violet lying prone on a table. Wearing only a bikini, her back and legs are exposed. A dominatrix is dripping hot wax from a candle on her exposed parts. "Stop it." he shouts. He grabs the dominatrix but she manages to kicks him away with her stiletto heels.

Along the walls are rows and rows of sharp metal implements. Grabbing a heavy cast metal set of sharp thongs, he swings it at the dominatrix. One of the sharp points gets buried in her forehead just above her left eye. She screams and falls to one corner in pain.

***

Walking through the dark jungle, Gordon and the homeless man notice someone resting on a tarp in a relatively dry area. When they get closer, they see it's Andrew. Gordon turns to his guide. "Thanks."

"No problem."

The homeless Vietnamese man takes off. Gordon turns to Andrew. "You're one hard dude to find."

What do you want?"

Gordon takes a swig from the fifth of whiskey in his hand, stoops near Andrew, and offers him the entire bottle. "Take a sip."

"I don't drink."

Gordon suddenly presses the bottle to Andrew's face but Andrew pushes him off.

"Oh," the ex-prisoner from Texas yells, "little prissy Miss Cunt. Is that what you are?"

"Get out of here, man."

"Do you know why I was in jail in Texas?"

"Leave me alone, man. This is my spot."

"Me and this acolyte, you know, choir boy, were going at it in the back of this church. Don't worry. He was legal, but we got caught by the pastor. What the hell was he doing there that night I don't know. But I worked for the church so he threatened to turn me in. And you know what happened? That lousy prick had a heart attack later that night. Just like that. So I burned the church to the ground, the whole fucking thing. The little runt turned me in, though, so they gave me two years in state. Jesus spoke to me the whole time I was there, kept giving me the same mission over and over and over: save a soul, get redeemed. So now, I'm gonna give you want you've been asking for."

He takes a long sip from his bottle.

***

As Mina and Gwen approach the Aurora Bridge, they can see Dustin still perched on the railing. It's a surprise he's no attention from the police or a pedestrian. Still raining heavily, they pull up near him. Mina throws on her flasher and they both jump out of the car. Gwen runs over to suicidal young man.

"Dustin."

"Don't come near me."

"Dustin, this is stupid. You're gonna fall. Come down from there."

"You don't care about me."

"Then why am I here, huh? For fun?"

"Go back to your club and make some money. That's all you know, isn't it?"

"You know what, Dustin? You're a fucking selfish prick, you know that? We've been through this shit. I'm not the one for you. I'm sorry things turned out this way, but you got to grow up. We were just having fun. This separation is all for you. Put that in your skull."

"You're a loser."

Mina comes over and touches Gwen's shoulder. "Don't be so hard on him," she whispers to her friend. "He's in pain."

"Y'all want a show?" Dustin warns. "I'll give you a show."

Carefully, and while maintaining his balance, he strips off layers and layers of clothes. The two ladies stare in amazement.

"Stop that, you jackass," Gwen admonishes him. "You're gonna get arrested."

"At this point," he shouts, "I don't give a shit."

"You're drunk," Mina tells him.

"You're the one who's drunk."

And with that, his last bit of clothes gets flung in the water a hundred feet below.

"Oh, Geez." Mina shakes her head. "I can't look."

"Ya'll ready to watch me take the plunge?"

"If you jump in then I'm jumping in, too," Gwen advises him.

"Bullshit," he spits.

"You are so special, Dustin," Gwen insists, "but you're too young to know that. I've been your age and so I understand what it's like to be in pain at that age. I know it can be unbearable, but things get better. I'm living proof."

Just then a police siren is heard in the distance. Dustin looks up, sees the fast approaching squad car, and starts crying. He turns to Gwen. "I only wanted to be with you."

"I know baby, I know," she tells him. "Come down."

***

Phong is holding Violet up as they walk through the dungeon. Suddenly, the dominatrix who he'd injured, runs up and hits him on the back with a large hammer. Yelling, he falls on his face. Violet manages to hold herself up against an adjacent wall.

The bleeding dominatrix straddles Phong then raises the hammer to bash his head in. Her actions are thwarted when Violet kicks her so hard she flies against the opposite wall, knocking her head against a large stone vase.

Walking with Violet up the stairs, they encounter the huge security guard. As he came down towards them, Phong whips out the curved kukri and holds it menacingly towards the guard. The guard backs away, surrendering space.

Upstairs in the Mercury Lounge, the patrons stop dancing and stare in awe as Violet helps Phong through and out of the club.

***

Gordon is struggling with Andrew on the tarp in The Jungle. He's making an attempt to take his and Andrew's pants off. Andrew is doing his best to fight back.

"Be still, motherfucker!" Gordon yells. "You said so yourself, 'Isn't this what you want?'"

"Get off me. Help!"

Gordon punches him in the mouth.

"Shut your fucking hole," the drunken assailant berates him.

Andrew manages to slide a few feet off the tarp towards the wet ground but Gordon stays with him. "You want drugs?" Gordon mocks. "Is that what it takes? I'll give you some drugs. Where's your fucking dealer?"

"Leave me alone."

"You fucking draw me in, made me go where I didn't want to, and now you're playing prissy? Get the fuck outta here. Take off your fucking pants."

They struggle. Andrew's left hand touches something on the ground beneath some leaves next to the tarp.

"You're fucking making this harder." Gordon yells. "Hold still."

Suddenly, a shot rings out. It echoes through the trees. Andrew watches, stunned as Gordon falls off him and backwards on the tarp.

A few minutes later, Andrew, finally making it out of the Jungle and up the steep slippery hill, is met at the top near the gate by two squad cars with their lights flashing. Four uniformed offers, taking cover behind their cars, have their guns pointed at him in the rain. Andrew raises his arms up. The gun is dangling from his right hand. Obeying their orders, he drops his weapon.

Epilogue

The Executioner's Son

"Once upon a time, about 2000 years ago, China had an empire known as the Xin Dynasty. It was ruled by Wang Mang, an emperor who was a shrewd politician but wasn't much loved by the peasantry. They claimed his tribunals were unfair as they tried and executed many enemies without proof of their crimes.

The emperor had a favorite executioner. His name was Yaotang Shi. He was his favorite because he carried out each order without fail and with the greatest devotion to loyalty and fulfillment.

Yaotang Shi had only one child, a boy. He was called Lidong because he was born at the start of winter. Lidong enjoyed a good life since he grew up around his imperial majesty. Soon, however, he began to learn at what expense his happiness was created.

On short trips alone he witnessed poverty, destitution, and hunger. He saw the emperor's men kill innocent villagers, including women and children. As his heart wept for these people, he secretly joined with the rebels to topple the empire which would not reason with them.

Unfortunately, Lidong and his men failed. They were caught, brought to justice, and sentenced for execution in the imperial courtyard. As it turned out, the executioner Yaotang Shi was given the task of removing the head of his own son.

And you know what he did?

Yaotang Shi believed that every single subject of the empire owed their lives through industry and loyalty to the emperor as he was their protector, and that was their destiny. And that included his own son.

Thus, in one clean stroke, Lidong was made headless.

Did Yaotang Shi feel remorse for what he had done? There was no remorse, for he kept his word to the emperor which allowed him to leave this world with his honor intact. And that was all he lived for."

Minh, lying weakly in bed in a hospital bed, has a machine monitoring his heart, an IV running through his veins, and oxygen being delivered via nasal cannula in his nostrils. He takes a deep breath and speaks again.

"But now, my own three sons have brought me shame. Phong, you are the eldest. You are your brothers' keeper. Andrew, you were wayward from the start. Dustin, you're not disrespectful like Andrew, but you're still a man and should know better."

Standing at the foot of his bed, dressed in orange county jail jumpsuits are Phong, Andrew, and Dustin. All three are in shackles. In the background, through the glass ICU door, two deputies stand guard. Kim is speaking to them.

"I fear you three," Minh continues, "like my life, is slipping away. And I'm to blame. Consider your lives as gifts. If you live it right, once is enough. Do well—that is your destiny. I urge you, as my last request: honor your mother. Look what she has done for you. It wasn't easy to get you three here. To live honorably is to know what you are doing is right and fair. I would like to leave with my honor intact. To you, my sons, this is my destiny."

Dustin, Andrew and Phong then watch solemnly as Minh closes his eyes for the last time.

Car 20

"Car 20. Pickup, Car 20."

Mahmud picked up his microphone and pressed the talk button. "This is Car 20."

"Scoot on over to the Nite's Inn Motel on Aurora," the dispatcher requested.

"What room?"

"She'll be waiting up front."

"Ten four."

He replaced the microphone, turned his car around and headed up to Aurora Avenue. He noticed they cleaned up the snow on the main drag, but there was still about an inch of the powdery stuff piled up on the sides of the road.

The legendary avenue had been changing lately. Ladies of the night weren't walking as much. Spanking new businesses were being built, displacing the sea of contraband that usually flooded the area. At least the recently fallen snow gave the area a softer, less harsh hue.

Mahmud checked the time on his watch: 1930 hours. He'd been on duty for only 90 minutes but only had two short fares so far. He hoped the slowness wasn't a harbinger for the rest of his shift.

Pulling into the motel, he immediately saw his fare; she was the only person standing by the manager's station. Conservatively dressed, he figured her to be about fifty-five years old. Noticing her left arm was in a cast and sling, he got out and helped her get into the back seat of the cab.

"Good evening," she greeted him as he returned to his seat.

"Hi," he responded.

He picked up his clipboard and pencil and started to write.

"Where are you headed?" he asked.

"The Safeway in Ballard," she answered. "Do you know the one?"

"Market Street."

"Yes. That one."

He left the motel and started driving towards the grocery store.

"Are you going to work?" he asked.

"Oh, no," she answered. "Just shopping."

Hmm. He thought it was a little odd she'd go that far out of her way to a shop especially since they'd be passing at least three supermarkets, but a fare's a fare. It wasn't his to question. His passenger, though, did get the sense he wondered.

"What's your name?" she asked.

"Mahmud."

"Where are you from, Mahmud?"

"Bangladesh."

"Oh! How nice! My name is Barbara."

"Hello, Barbara."

"I like that Safeway because I used to live around there and their pastry chef is the best."

"I see."

"You know, I used to drive."

"You gave it up?"

"Remember the real heavy snowfall three weeks ago?"

"Yes, ma'am."

"I was driving to the doctor's and I got broadsided by some kid who couldn't stop."

"Wow. And you broke your arm?"

"No. This wasn't from that. Both cars are totaled, though."

"You can't be too careful."

"I moved into that motel two weeks ago."

"Really? I heard it's not exactly the safest place in town."

"I didn't have a choice. That's what Social Service will pay for. I used to live in Ballard, like I'd told you before, but some rat chewed through the electrical wiring in my house. It got set on fire. I woke to the house in flames."

"Oh, no."

"Yeah. I only had time to grab my keys off the center table. By the time I got outside, half the house was gone."

"You're a lucky person."

"I guess. My neighbors were pretty helpful. A few days ago I left the motel to walk to a local donut shop. On the way back I slipped on an icy patch on the sidewalk. Would you believe I broke my arm?"

"Just like that?"

"Just like that."

"I hope your whole life wasn't so unlucky."

"There were bad and good times—same as everyone else. How was your life in Bangladesh?"

"Ah, well, you know… it's a poor country. Some towns have no running water. There are people living in slums. There's no sanitation. Seems like you spend your whole life just trying to get out."

"To come to America?"

"Actually, any place with opportunity. Doesn't matter. Libya, Saudi Arabia, Australia…"

Just then the dispatcher's voice came on over the speakers.

"What's your location, Car 20?"

Mahmud picked up his microphone.

"A few blocks from Market Street."

"Oh, okay. Never mind," the dispatcher said then hanged up.

Mahmud also cradled his mike. Seconds later, he pulled up to the entrance of the Safeway.

"What's the damage?" Barbara asked, taking bills from her purse.

"It's okay," Mahmud answered, smiling. "On the house."

"Are you sure?"

"Yes."

Barbara took a $10 bill and stuffed it in his pocket anyway. Seconds later, he got out to help her exit.

"You're a good driver," she congratulated him. "You don't have to feel sorry for me."

"I just think it's good when folks can help each other out. Doesn't always have to be about the almighty dollar."

"I'll need a cab in about an hour. Can you pick me up?"

"If I'm in town and not busy."

"I'll call them and ask specifically for you, Mahmud."

"Okay," he agreed, then got back into his taxi and took off.

It was chilly out that evening, but as he drove out of the parking lot, he realized it was the first time he'd smiled in ages.

Little Hammer

The Curator

It was dusk when a hostage situation was underway at a large six bedroom suburban home in the North Seattle neighborhood of Bitter Lake. A paranoid priest, Father Benedetto Rio, held his 11 year old daughter, Amelia, captive. Her mother, Catherine, had died last year of cancer, a disease that was devastating to the whole family. Two Seattle Police Department detectives working on a tip, Frank Tucker, svelte, golden haired, late 20's, and Michael LaTour, handsome, black, late 30's, had knocked on the door, but no one answered. Upon hearing a bang coming from inside the house, they drew their guns, circled the building carefully, then broke in—Frank through the front and Michael in the rear.

The smoky house was bathed in black and red lights and decorated in extreme gothic. There were lit candles, incense burners, shrouds and crucifixes everywhere. There was even an altar in the living room. On every wall was there were cryptic messages in Latin, handwritten with pig's blood. The interior looked more like a twisted Sistine Chapel than those of a house nestled comfortably in the 'burbs.

Frank entered the living room where Rio, dressed in a purple robe and alb, was sitting lotus-style on a wooden pew in the living room. He was holding a gun in both hands with the barrel pointed upward at his chin. Packets of heroin sat on a center table. Rio recognized Frank and relaxed his pistol.

"Welcome to paradise," Rio greeted him.

"Where's Amelia, Benny?" Frank queried, his service revolver trained firmly on him. "Where is she?"

"Such impertinence from a civil servant," Benny observed, sweat pouring down his brow. "Your lack of subtlety is most disturbing."

"Put down the gun," Frank ordered him.

Father Rio, however, didn't comply. "You know what's more depressing that a suicidal priest?" Rio asked. "A dead cop."

He lowered his gun and pointed it at Frank. Instinctively, Frank fired, hitting Rio once in the chest. He slumped over backwards on the pew while his gun fell to the floor. Frank walked over, picked up his gun, and checked his pulse. He had none.

Michael, entering the rear hallway bathed in a thick smoky haze, darted to one side upon hearing the shot.

"Frank?" he shouted. "Was that you?"

Then, from out of a bedroom between the two officers, Frank noticed a short girlish figure emerge. She was brandishing a firearm.

"Michael, she's got a gun," he shouted.

Impulsively, Michael glanced at her and fired. The girl flew backwards, slammed against a hallway bookcase, and fell supine to the floor. Approaching her, Michael kicked the gun away from her body. Frank picked it up.

"What have I done?" Michael asked. "It's Amelia."

He reached down and palpated her carotid artery. There was no pulse.

"Dammit it," Frank yelled, examining the pistol. "It's a BB gun."

"What?" Michael blurted. "A toy?"

"You didn't know," Frank replied. "It's too hazy in here. Too dark."

"Fuck," Michael yelled. "Why'd you shout like that? Now look what happened."

"I thought it was real," Frank explained. "Dammit. I was looking out for you!"

"You should've been looking out for her."

"Internal Affairs is gonna have a field day with this."

"Yeah," Michael agreed, "like I don't have enough trouble as it is."

Soon, other officers, the fire department and paramedics arrived. They set up crime scene tape, took lots of pictures, and confiscated the drugs which had the words "Little Hammer" stamped on the packages.

Later that evening, Michael, interrogated for reckless endangerment and dereliction of duty, had his gun and badge taken away by the police chief, pending further investigation. They concluded that he acted too rashly. Both he and Frank explained that the air was thick with smoke, but by the time assistance arrived, a lot of it had dissipated. Nevertheless, per protocol, the police chief insisted he had to let Michael go.

The next day, when Frank visited the coroner, he found out that the cause of the girl's death wasn't the bullet wound to her left shoulder, but a fractured cervical spine. Her neck was broken by the backward thrust and crash against the bookcase. The acute angle of the fracture indicated an accidental blow to the back of her neck.

Michael hung out at a cop bar that night with Frank. Frank told him about what he'd discovered and discussed it with the chief. The chief told him they won't pursue a criminal investigation, but they still needed to have a forensic hearing.

Michael didn't care. As far as he was concerned, the damage had been done and he'd had enough of the SPD. His only plan that night was to get *fubar*. It might take a fifth of Jack Daniels and a pair of boilermakers, but that was his idea.

Around midnight, Frank drove him home and helped him walk to his apartment. Placing his drunken ex-partner on the living room couch, he glanced around the room. It'd been a while since he was there. There were several medals and trophies in a bookcase. On the mantel, and attached to the walls, were pictures of Michael surrounded by the mayor, police commissioner, and a few local celebrities. Frank picked up a framed photo from a desk. It was a picture of him and Michael in fishing gear at a lake.

***

Two months later, Michael got hired by Central Protection, a private security guard agency. It was his first job since leaving the SPD. He'd thought about exiting Seattle altogether, since he had no family there, but he figured the Emerald City was just as cozy as any other, and since he already knew it like the back of his hands, why bother moving?

Central Protection sent him to the work at the Seattle Art Museum. They were having a Monet exhibit and needed extra security. That day, everything started smoothly. Patrons milled about peacefully studying the works of art while Michael and his partner, Mona Angelique, a shapely, athletic woman in her early thirties, looked for anything or anyone out of the ordinary.

Suddenly, three men with masks and guns stormed into the main gallery on Level 2 and ordered everyone not to move. After sealing the exits, they made one of the curators, Julia Somerset, an attractive, well dressed, French Creole siren in her forties, walk towards a room in the back. There, they forced her to open a safe containing deposits and donations in cash and bonds. Some of the patrons tried using their cell phone, but the gunmen made the docents line them up against one wall, effectively killing their chances of notifying anyone.

Scant minutes later, the robbers almost got away were it not for the quick actions of Mona and Michael. Mona, trained in Judo, wasn't so inclined to let them escape. Skillfully, she dispatched one robber with catlike and acrobatic skill. Michael immediately sided with her and knocked out the second robber, using self-defense kicks and punches he hadn't used in years. The third one with the money bag almost made it to the main entrance, but after a brief struggle, he was knocked down and captured by both Mona and Michael. A few minutes later, the patrons applauded when the police arrived to take the robbers away and collect statements. Mona and Mike's heroic efforts made TV, newspaper, and internet news and they were both given hefty bonuses by the museum.

One evening, Somerset asked her heroic guards out for a celebratory cocktail. Mona respectfully declined, but Michael accepted. He secretly hoped Mona would refuse because he'd come to notice how attractive his boss actually was, and the fact she didn't wear a marriage ring made her more appealing.

The first place she took him to was a martini lounge in Belltown. Sitting midway between two busy streets, it was a popular spot to see and be seen. After a few drinks, he realized she wasn't as stodgy as rumors painted her out to be, but a loose and somewhat life-enjoying individual. Over the next few days, they went out to different high brow bars around Seattle, usually on her dime. He did attempt to pay at times, but she always insisted in taking care of the tab, considering she either received discounts or they were complementary.

Inevitably, they ended up back at her house in Beaux Arts, an affluent village on the eastern shore of Lake Washington. Like the other homes, it was a pretty big place, boasting four bedrooms, a 20-seat theatre, a study, an exercise room, and a personal art gallery. Things were going well. The two were getting along like Raggedy Ann and Andy. His buddies back in the SPD would've been jealous.

One evening, Julia and Michael rendezvoused at an underground bar in Pioneer Square that made, so they claimed, the best martinis in America. Sitting at a corner table, Julia bought the first round. She had a Four Horsemen and Michael, a one-legged Flamingo.

"You know what's funny?" she asked him.

"No," he answered.

"There are many important works of art, mainly Van Gogh," she noted, "in various embassies in Seattle. All had been acquired illegally from the Art Underground."

"What's that?" he asked.

"It's a secretive network of art thieves who thrive on stealing art originally confiscated by the Nazis during WWII."

"And they're right here in Seattle?"

"Oh, they're everywhere. Imagine how big they must be, stretching from Germany, the Netherlands, northern Europe, through France, London and the U.S."

"A lot of it probably also ended up in South America since that's where a lot of Nazis went after the war."

"I wouldn't doubt it."

"Why would a reputable institution like an embassy buy stolen art?"

"Diplomatic immunity. Plus, there are international laws at work, makes their assets perfectly legal here in the U.S."

"I don't know. If I had a famous work of art on display that was stolen from the Nazis, wouldn't I run the risk of an heir claiming ownership through inheritance? I mean, the discovery of a painting by an artist like Van Gogh would be world news, no?"

"Possibly, but not if you make it known it's just a reproduction."

"Seems kind of odd, displaying possibly stolen art like that for the world to see."

"Exactly. Their arrogance knows no boundaries. That's where you come in."

Michael took a long sip of his martini.

"So what do you want me to do?" he asked.

"It's been my dream to make those art works available to the public again, not for just the few that enter those consulates, but for the world to enjoy. I want you to steal them and replace them with forgeries."

"Whoa! That sounds way out of my league, sister."

"I think you can do it."

"How am I supposed to break into those places? They're smack in the middle of downtown in huge buildings. You know, eyes everywhere."

"Not all. A few are in suburban locations."

Michael scratched his chin.

"I don't know," he groaned.

"It's simpler than you imagine," she claimed. "There are treaties at work that protect all parties involved."

"What do you mean? You'll just get 'em and put them in the museum with impunity?"

"Yep."

"Suppose somebody from the embassy happens to stumble across it?"

"And say what? This art was stolen from them. which they'd obtained illegally to begin with? Remember, what they have on display are *supposed* to be just replicas."

"Why don't you do it?"

Julia laughed. "I've seen how you move, Mike. You're very agile, almost catlike. You know the ins and outs of security. I think you'll do just fine."

Michael sighed. "This sounds crazy. Do you have inside information about all this?" he asked.

She nodded.

"How do you know about these thieves?" he asked.

She took a long swig of her martini, savored the taste, laid her glass down, and looked straight into Michael's eyes. "I used to be one of 'em," she admitted.

***

After spending another night with Julia, Michael returned to his own home. He found his apartment had been broken into and ransacked. Several items, including his medals and trophies, had been stolen. On his bathroom mirror, written with soap, were the words "Bang, you're dead."

Once the police left after getting his statement, he commenced putting his apartment together. Minutes later, there was a knock on his door. It was his landlord, Thurston Hatch.

"LaTour," the landlord began, "I hate to be the bearer of bad tidings."

He handed Michael a note. He glanced at it briefly.

"I'm being evicted?!"

"When you don't pay your rent," Hatch said, "that's what happens."

"I told you I needed time, man. You said it was okay."

"Don't shoot the manager, LaTour. If this was my place I'd let you stay. You've been a good tenant."

"Good tenant? My being here … just my presence alone keeps drugs out of this building."

"Yeah, well maybe the Nubian Tigers got pissed off about it."

"The who?"

"You know, those guys selling pure dope on the streets?"

"Never heard of 'em."

"And you're a cop. I thought you guys knew everything."

"That's why we rely on our good fellow citizens every once in a while."

"Well, what happened tonight?" Hatch asked, looking around the room. "This place is a train wreck."

"I've been out of town. Looks like a crime of opportunity."

"Too bad, but you know how it is with managers, man. Money talks."

"How long do I have?"

"Three days."

"Three days? What the fuck."

"I don't know, LaTour. It must be for their relatives. They've been looking for a place."

"I don't believe this."

"Yeah. Um, I'll see ya later, okay?"

After the manager left, Michael didn't resume cleaning up. There was no point. The walls looked like they were suddenly mocking him, laughing at his misfortune. Angry, he picked up a porcelain cup and threw it at the mantle. It broke into dozens of pieces.

The next day, Michael learned from Central Protection that his services were no longer needed at the museum because the exhibit was over and they'd downsized their security. They also informed him they had no other security positions at the moment.

He spent a few more days seeking employment. Unsuccessful, he finally told Julia about his failed efforts. She offered him to help him, but there was one little catch: she would give him shelter and a living allowance if he'd replace the embassy's art with forgeries. Reluctantly, he agreed.

He spent the next few days in pawn shops, an Army-Navy supply store, and a security warehouse buying and building new surveillance and anti-surveillance gadgets. He also purchased a ninja warrior uniform, entirely in black, which he later modified to have secret compartments.

One night, after finally studying some floor plans procured by Julia, he thought it was time to put her dream into action. Driving over to North Seattle, he parked his car a few houses down the street from the two-story Icelandic Embassy and donned his black body suit. It was a relatively dark and quiet night, illuminated by a half moon and the occasional street lamps. The nondescript consulate, sitting quietly near the Ballard Public Library, small businesses and various homes, was as plain as can be. It should be an easy mission, he thought, if only his heart wouldn't beat so damn fast.

The Consulate

Using grappling equipment, Michael quickly climbed to the roof of the embassy. Quietly, he removed the grill covering an air vent, crawled down a narrow passageway, and entered the janitor's closet through an access port in the ceiling. He used his devices to listen for sounds in the video room next to the closet. Satisfied it was vacant, he broke into the locked room and shut the security cameras down. He then quickly looked around the room for the security alarm controls, but soon realized they weren't there.

Sneaking into the main hall on the ground floor, he used a fist-sized machine to blow a huge puff of powder into the darkened room. Then, turning on his infrared eyewear, he saw white lasers crisscrossing the room. Stealthily, he stooped, sidled, hopped, ducked, flipped and slid past the beams of their state-of-the-art security system till he finally arrived at his destination: the Van Gogh painting 'Boy with Spade' up on a wall. Carefully, he took it down, opened the frame, and replaced the original art with a replica from his long pants pocket. Seconds later he put it all back up on the wall, stashed the original in his pocket, evaded the beams again, went back upstairs, turned the security cameras back on, and escaped out the same route he'd entered.

An hour later, he celebrated with Julia. Sitting together in her living room, they both drank champagne and studied the reframed painting lying on the center table.

"You did it," she gushed, toasting his glass.

"We did it," he corrected her.

"You're sure you weren't seen?"

"Not a soul out there tonight. I've never been so nervous in my life."

"If I was a betting woman," Julia avowed, "I'd say you've done this before."

"Breaking and entering's not my thing, Julia. SPD, remember?"

"Oh, yeah. Hey, wanna see something gorgeous tonight?"

"I'm game."

She took him to Fay Bainbridge Park, a scenic shoreline park on the northeast corner of Bainbridge Island, an affluent city in Puget Sound near Seattle. Even though accessible by car, a lot of citizens travel either by boat or ferry. From the park they had a clear and unobstructed view of the Cascade Mountains, Indianola and North Seattle. The Pacific Northwest night was typically cool and free of the murmurs of civilization. Aided by fine Napa Valley bubbly, they grew closer to each other. It was the perfect spot for love.

***

Next morning, Michael ran into his old partner, Frank Tucker, inside a Starbucks in downtown Seattle usually frequented by the police and staffers from the mayor's office. Frank was sitting at a small table reading the Seattle Times. Michael startled him when he playfully, unexpectedly, slapped the paper.

"Hey, partner," Michael greeted him. "Long time no see." They shook hands. Michael sat down.

"You've been hard to find," Frank admitted. "You lost your phone?"

"Nah," Michael apologized. "Just been kinda busy."

"Yeah, I know. You hooked up with that lady from the museum, right? Julia?"

"How'd you know?"

"Through your ex-partner, Mona."

"Mona, huh? You two are an item now?"

"Kinda, sorta."

"How'd you meet her?"

"I took her deposition over that attempted robbery."

"You work fast. Lucky you. Does she talk about me?"

"Not really. That business with the robbers was popular with her for a while, but after she got me in bed, you just became a sad memory."

"Yeah, right."

"Hey, Michael. We got a strange call this morning. You know that Consulate General of Iceland where they had that hold up two years ago?"

"Yeah. In Ballard. I remember."

"They found some powder-like residue all over the main lobby. They think they've been burglarized but they checked and nothing's been stolen."

"Powder residue? You mean like a toxin or something?"

"Uh, uh. Harmless. Probably makes the invisible security beams visible."

"So why did they called the SPD?"

"There was a glitch in their security, like it was shut down for a few minutes."

"Enough time to steal something."

"That's why they called us," Frank surmised. "They want me to look in on it 'cause I know the joint. Would've been better if you were along, too."

"Yeah," Michael shook his head, "my days of reading Miranda and gun slinging are over."

"That's what I'd told 'em. You'd be the best man for this job."

"Maybe some other time. Hey, you want to come over to the house for dinner?"

"Julia's house?"

"Yeah."

"Sounds like a date."

"Bring Mona."

"Will do."

The next day, Frank and Mona went over to Julia's house as promised. Mona brought a bottle of Australian Shiraz and Frank carried a box of bon-bons. The meal went well. Julia, trying out her new Italian cookbook, had prepared Tuscan prawns, Caprese salad, Penne Siciliana and chocolate mousse. All were pleasantly surprised. Mona suggested that Julia should think about cooking professionally, but she indicated she was busy enough with the museum.

Towards the end of the evening, Frank had to use the bathroom. While there, he happened to notice a piece of black cloth jutting out near the base of a narrow wall closet. The cloth was caught in the door. Thinking it was a black skirt or dress being ruined, he opened the door and discovered it wasn't a dress but a black ninja warrior suit.

"Must be for a costume party," he thought.

Then, looking up towards a shelf high in the closet, he saw a long ornate pewter box with unusually distinctive clasps. Curious, he brought it down, opened it, and saw a few pieces of surveillance equipment and other high tech gadgets. When there was a knock on the bathroom door, he quickly replaced the items, put the box back, and exited. Mona was standing outside the door.

"You okay?" she asked him. "Been in there a while."

"Maybe the Italian was too rich for me. You know, I'm low brow."

"I'll be right out." Mona entered the bathroom while Frank returned to his hosts.

***

Later that night, Michael tackled his second assignment for Julia: the Royal Norwegian Consulate in suburban Greenlake. As before, he donned his black suit and entered through the roof. He sneaked past a few rooms where the diplomatic attaché, his family and other Nordic citizens were asleep in their rooms on the second floor.

On the first floor in the main room, he successfully eluded their security cameras to replace the Van Gogh painting, 'Old Man with his Head in his Hands, At Eternity's Gate. While substituting the work of art, the brass hook slid out of the plasterboard wall and fell to the ground behind an arm chair. Moving the chair aside, he found the hook. Next to it, on the floor, was also a small plastic package he'd seen before. He picked it up. On its side were stamped the words "Little Hammer." Shoving it in his pocket, he put the Van Gogh replica in place and straightened out the furniture.

Suddenly, the attaché walked in the room and put on the light. Michael hid off to one side while the Norwegian went to his desk. Just then, the security alarms went off. The attaché looked up just in time to see Michael run upstairs. Instinctively, he reopened his desk, brought out a gun, and went after the black clad intruder.

Another man from a bedroom on the second floor appeared and, when he saw Michael, fired a shot. It missed. The ex-cop ran towards a window facing the street. The man fired again but his gun jammed. The attaché came up the stairs and also fired a shot. It missed and made a small hole in a window. Michael then thrust his entire body through that same window and landed on the lawn below. Quickly getting up, he ran down the street, jumped into his vehicle, and took off.

The next morning, he sat in the kitchen nursing his bruised and sprained left ankle. The kitchen TV was on a news channel. Julia walked in the room all dressed for work.

"I didn't hear you come in last night," she attested.

"Didn't want to wake you," he alleged.

"What happened to you?"

He slid the Van Gogh on the table towards her. "You're welcome," he shook his head.

She picked it up and looked it over. Her jaw dropped. "Oh my God!" she smiled. "You can see the traces of crayon. You know, there are seven known impressions of this work in museums and collections around the world—Amsterdam, Paris, Tehran—this is just amazing."

"Glad I can help."

She kissed him. He groaned from his ankle pain.

"Oh, sorry," she apologized. "You did this last night?"

"Why didn't you wait up for me?"

"I guess I had too much Shiraz."

"Well, it was the last time. I'm done."

"Why? We're not finished."

"Too dangerous. I almost got shot."

Just then, news came on the TV about a recent explosion in South Seattle. The home of a city council member was firebombed. No one was seriously hurt, but responsibility was being claimed via a flyer left at the scene by the new and unknown black militia group the Nubian Tigers.

"Nubian Tigers," Julia shook her head. "Every time you turn around there's a new group springing up somewhere. I've never heard of these guys. Sounds like a Black Panther offshoot."

"Could be," Michael admitted. "My apartment manager's heard of 'em, though. Looks like they're getting around."

"Okay, Michael," she kissed him again. "I gotta run. Oh, check the answering machine."

"Who is it?"

"Your buddy, Frank. He and Mona had a fight."

"Too bad. He does have a temper, especially if he's liquored up."

"He was looking for you to go out and throw back a few. Called all night."

"I hope you didn't answer it."

"No. I let him wonder. I'll see ya later."

"Bye."

***

Michael met up with Frank for lunch that afternoon at a pizza parlor in the University District. It was a bright sunny day, so they decided to eat outside in a park. They watched as students ambled by, as well as young marijuana peddlers, skateboarders, Asian tourists, and Bohemian types.

"This is why I love this city," Frank began. "All this color."

"Is that what it is?" Mike asked, sarcastically.

"You know, you're hard to reach these days."

"Sorry, man. I half-heard your messages. I had too much wine. Listen, I ain't no spring chicken like you."

"Yeah, right. I've seen you move. Hey, there was another break in last night."

"At the Norwegian Embassy. I heard. It was on the news."

"Nothing was taken 'cause their security guards chased the perp out."

"Seems like he wasted his time. Forensics will track him down."

"This guy was good. Left no prints. Gonna be hard. Hey, you ever heard of The Ring"?

"Uh, uh. What ring?"

"It's a drug cartel, supposedly from Europe."

"Europe? That's different."

"Yeah. Everybody's getting in the act."

"What are they pushing?"

"Heroin. Keep your ears open, huh? The more eyes on the street, the better."

"Will do."

***

Driving back to Julia's pad in Beaux Arts, Michael saw three dark sedans parked in front of her house. Parking half a block away, he got out of his car and walked towards her home. Suddenly six men, all similarly dressed in black suits, emerged. Michael hid behind a tree as they got into their vehicles, two to each car, and drove off.

Julia's front door, he noticed, was ajar. Slowing pushing it open, he realized the living room had been ransacked. Chairs and tables were overturned. Clothes were spilled out on the floor as closets were emptied. Desks and cupboards were pulled apart one by one. He checked each bedroom. The visitors' frantic search was also evident as clothes and boxes were overturned and scattered all over.

Michael called Julia using his cell phone.

"Hey, honey," she answered.

"You've been hit, Julia."

"What do you mean?"

"Six guys were in your house looking for something."

"They make a mess?"

"Is Bill Gates rich?"

"What'd they take?"

"I don't know. I can't tell. This place looks like it was interior decorated by an army of chimps. Who do you think they'd be?"

"I ... I really don't know."

"There are things you're not telling me, Julia. A bunch of well-dressed suits just don't go breaking into a house out of the blue in broad daylight like that, especially in an upscale neighborhood like Beaux Arts."

"I think it's the Art Underground."

"What are they looking for?"

"I can't talk right now. I'll see you in a little while. Don't call the police."

After he hung up, Michael started putting the house back together. He placed all the clothes in their respective place, straightened the furniture, and restocked the desks and shelves. He checked on his ninja suit in the master bathroom. It was intact, as was his surveillance tools on the shelf above. Two hours later, Julia arrived. They met in the living room as Michael was putting up a painting, a replica of Edvard Munch's "The Scream."

"That's one of the world's rare impressions of The Scream," she informed him, "copied from the original that was stolen during the '96 Olympics in Lillehammer, Norway."

"I remember that," Michael observed. "Pretty big news."

She quickly looked around the house. Some items were still out of place, mainly books and other small knickknacks.

"Mr. Holm was probably behind this," she guessed. "Looks like his work."

"Who's that?"

"The gentleman you met at the Norwegian Embassy."

"He's involved with the Art Underground?"

"In as deep as can be."

"The art world is as crooked as the drug world," Michael attested.

"Where ever there's money, there's corruption," Julia posited. "Same as anywhere, just like in the whiskey world; they would kill for a true 100 year old scotch."

"What were they looking for?"

"Missing reproductions, prints, impressions, plates, originals ... the embassies would never tell the authorities they've been robbed, but they'd notify the Underground. They're probably checking all their old associates. I was expecting this."

"That's why you need a bodyguard."

"Sorry to drag you into this, Mike. I thought they'd died down."

"Surprised you."

"I don't have the real Van Goghs here anymore. They're in the museum in a safe."

"Are they gonna come back?"

"I don't know. These guys are unpredictable. After they got involved with some cartel called The Ring, I wasn't interested.

"You know about The Ring?"

"Just that it's Nordic and they have a ship, a cutter. But I stay away from hard drugs. I see the news."

"Where's the ship docked?"

The Ring

When Michael was a child, he never played hide and seek. If the subject was ever broached, he'd somehow encourage his childhood friends to play his variation which was "hide and discover." He'd usually plant a toy or candy for them to find. The first one who'd discover his "plants" won.

That night, sneaking into the quiet shipyard near Fisherman's Terminal in No. Seattle, reminded him of the joy of discovery and the tenacity of the hunt. Dressed in his now familiar ninja suit, he snuck unto the pier. The seagulls were off somewhere sleeping, perhaps dreaming of an overturned tuna truck. The marina was lit mainly by the moon and lights emanating from poles on the docks and nearby buildings. A handful of guards were milling about on the slightly swaying docks, some smoking cigarettes, others hoping for the day when their loyalty and devotion to the Art Underground would pay off.

Tiptoeing up to the first lookout, Michael quietly subdued him with a stranglehold, putting him to sleep and laying him gently on the ground. Then, dragging him silently out of sight, he laid him peacefully beneath a large blue tarp.

Walking further out onto the dock, he saw a large white single-masted cargo ship. Attached to the top of her sail-less foremast was a Norwegian flag. Along her hull were the words in blue letters: NORDIC HOPE.

Climbing onto the vessel, he peered through the blinds in the forecastle and saw the attaché, Mr. Holm, and an assistant from the Norwegian embassy, sitting in the living quarters speaking with two of the men who were in Julia's house earlier. While the attaché was deep in conversation, his assistant was counting packets of Little Hammers in a fancy metal case.

The ex-officer heard a speedboat approaching from the sound. Instinctively, he dove for cover behind a large plastic tarp draped over a rain barrel. Peeking out, he saw Julia being led out of the speedboat by two of the earlier house intruders. At times she'd try to pull away from their clutches, but with her firmly in their grasp, she couldn't escape.

They walked her onto the Nordic Hope. Minutes later, the two guards from the speedboat emerged and went over to their similarly suited friends, still smoking cigarettes and talking on their cell phones. Slowly, Michael moved towards the boat and climbed in again.

Looking in the covered quarters, he saw Julia tied to a chair with a bandana tied around her mouth. Her bare feet were in a large tub of water. Electrical wires, sticking out of it, were attached to a crude machine on a chest of drawers next to Mr. Holm. It seemed that when the attaché asked her a question, and the answer wasn't to his satisfaction, he'd flip a switch on the machine. Sparks would fly out of the tub and Julia would wriggle and silently scream as her body shook and trembled with each unbearable jolt of electricity.

Michael tapped gently on the window. One of the guards came out to investigate. The ex-cop quickly and silently put him in a choke hold. After knocking him out and taking his gun, he dragged him into a large fish barrel on the dock and set it upright.

A few minutes later, the second guard and Mr. Holm's assistant emerged. Michael took out two of his ninja stars and threw it at the two men. Catching them both in the neck, they fell over unconscious. Leaping onto the boat, he took their guns, then ran inside the living area. Mr. Holm, caught by surprised, opened his mouth to scream, but was silenced when Michael pointed a gun at his nose.

"Don't move," he ordered him.

With his eyes trained on the attaché, he untied Julia and took her feet out of the tub. Still groggy, she was able to stand.

"Are you okay?" he asked her.

"I'll live."

He then turned to Mr. Holm. "Have a seat," he ordered. Reluctantly, the diplomat complied.

Michael gave one of the guns to Julia. "If he moves," he cautioned her, "shoot him."

She nodded and took the gun. Using the same ropes, Michael bound Mr. Holm to the chair, tied the bandana around his mouth then turned to Julia.

"What do they want with you?" he asked her.

"They were looking for you."

"Why?"

She pointed to his black uniform. "They saw that suit in the house," she admitted.

He grabbed the case of heroin. "We'd better get out of here," he warned.

As they were exiting, a shot whizzed by just passed their heads. Looking up, they saw the four remaining guards running towards them. Quickly, they jumped into the speedboat and started it up. A few more bullets flew in their direction, but they were able to speed off without getting shot.

Pulling up to a dock in Beaux Arts, they moored the boat. Frank Tucker entered the marina unseen. Drawing his gun, he leapt out from behind a sign, his pistol pointed at the two.

"Not so fast," he told them. They stopped walking.

"What's going on here, Frank?" Michael asked.

"First," he said, reaching for the silver case, "I'll take that."

Michael had no choice but to let it go. Frank placed it on the ground then used his left hand to search and confiscate all the guns he found on Michael and Julia.

"You guys were packing tonight," he remarked, stashing the guns in his pocket.

"What are you doing here, Frank?" Michael inquired.

"I got a little confession to make," his ex-partner smiled. "I work with Mr. Holm."

"Since when?"

"It's simple economics. They keep me on the payroll and I keep the heat off 'em."

He picked up the silver case. "With this I'm gonna make me a fortune," he bragged. "Mikey boy, remember when we rolled up on Fr. Rio based on a tip? Didn't you ever wonder where that tip came from? There wasn't any. Rio was one of our biggest dealers, but he became an erratic user, forgot his own agenda. Kept his finger in the till. He had to go."

"What about his daughter, asshole? She was innocent."

"Unfortunate collateral, Mike. Life sucks."

From out the corner of his eye, Michael saw the last four remaining guards sailing towards them. Momentarily distracted, Frank turned and waved to mark his position. Michael, ninja star already in hand, flipped it at his ex-partner. Catching him in the neck, Frank collapsed to the dock. Immediately, Mike picked up the silver case and Frank's gun, then he and Julia ran out of the dock towards a nearby marine warehouse.

The four guards quickly docked, drew their guns, and ran towards the warehouse. Opening its large steel door, they tried putting on the lights. The building, however, stayed dark. Beams of moonlight shined in through clearer spots in the frosted windows.

The guards split into two groups. With only slivers of light peering in to guide them, they carefully groped along the walls. Inevitably, the first group on the left accidentally kicked over a metal pail.

"Shit," the guard whispered.

Out of the darkness, a ninja star sliced the air and found its mark to the neck of the Guard. He fell unconscious. Anxious, his partner shot wildly in the near darkness at an assailant he couldn't see.

"Watch your aim," another yelled.

Unfortunately marking his position, he's also felled by a star that struck his shoulder.

"Come on out and fight like a man." A guard screamed.

"Suit yourself," Michael murmured.

The guard shot wildly. Suddenly, his gun was kicked out of his hand. Frantically, he punched wildly in the air but missed his mark. Michael dropkicked him to his chest. He flew backwards into a pile of wooden skids. Getting up, he caught a glimpse of Michael's silhouette and lunged at him. Michael sidestepped quickly, grabbed him, and flipped him to the ground.

Another assailant ran towards the commotion and threw a few punches and kicks which Michael parried off. Throwing a few kicks and punches of his own, Mike round housed him, making him stumble backwards. Undeterred, the attacker charged towards Michael who ran up a nearby wall, flipped backwards in the air, and on his way down kicked him in his face with such force it knocked him unconscious.

As Julia and Michael walked out of the warehouse, a shot rang out. Michael, hit on his left arm, reeled sideways and backwards. The gunman, Mr. Holm, standing about 50 feet away near a shed, raised his gun to shoot again, but he's suddenly shot dead by Julia.

***

Within minutes, both of the docks at Fisherman's Terminal and Beaux Arts became flooded with police officers, FBI, paramedics, the press, neighbors and casual onlookers. Nearly an hour later, Michael, his left arm in a sling, stood near the Nordic Hope as officers brought out several boxes as evidence. Julia stood next to him. Officer Hank Gray, carrying a large cardboard box, stopped in front of Michael.

"Hey, Hank," Michael asked, "is that the last of it?"

"You should go home and nurse that arm," Hank replied.

"Ah," he brushed it off. "It's just a nick."

"He thinks he's Superman," Julia smiled.

"Oh, before I forget," Hank stated, "congratulations."

"For what?" Mike wondered.

Hank looked at him with puzzlement. "I thought you heard?" he informed him. "IA finished their investigation. They concluded you did nothing wrong at Fr. Rio's house."

"All right," Michael said with a smile.

"You can come back ... if you want."

"I'll think about it."

"You should, Mike," Julia added. "You've been vindicated."

"Look at this, detective," Hank remarked, laying the box down and taking its top off.

They both looked at its content: reams of flyers advertising the black militant group Nubian Tigers as well as a printer with the flyer's master template still in it.

"The Tigers aren't real," Hank surmised. "Why would their flyers be on a ship like this? Their so-called campaign was created here."

"These émigrés look like they were trying to start a race war," Michael added. "Why?"

"I'll show you why," a second officer said, walking out of the forecastle with a wooden crate in his arms. Opening it, they saw a varied collection of Nazi emblems, stickers, crests, iron crosses, brass swastikas, flags, and other paraphernalia.

"I don't get this," Michael admitted.

"This boat was more than a modified fishing trawler," the second officer spoke. "It's more like neo-Nazi headquarters; discrete and hidden in plain sight."

"And if they stirred up enough anti-white sentiment," Hank added, "they'd have new recruits, more kids rallying against the 'black scourge.' In the meantime, they'd continue poisoning the inner city with cheap dope and firebombing officials. That's more folks to pass the blame on to."

"Well," Michael surmised, "I guess it backfired. They tried to create a threat but failed."

The officers continued removing evidence from the ship.

He turned to Julia. "I don't think you don't have to worry about the Underground anymore. Seems like they're out of business."

"Good," she sighed. "I was starting to miss my beauty sleep."

***

A few weeks later, the investigation into the Art Underground and their relation to the fabricated Nubian Tigers and Mr. Holm concluded. The U.S. provided solid evidence of Holm's illegal activities which staved off an international and Norwegian crisis. His six armed henchman, all with ties to the Art Underground, were federally tried and convicted for illegal trafficking of heroin and stolen art, and obstruction of justice, earning them several years in prison. Michael was officially vindicated in the death of Fr. Rio's daughter. The SPD asked him to come back, but he still hadn't decided. Life with Julia was going well and he thought it best not to rock the boat.

***

One day, Julia was walking around one of the museum's galleries studying the displays. A patron, a well-dressed woman in her 50's, walked over to her and briefly read her ID badge.

"I need some help," the patron requested.

"Sure thing," Julia agreed. "How can I help you?"

"Do they have any museums in this city with a secret Van Gogh collection?"

Julia turned and faced the patron. "Not to my knowledge," she answered. "Is that your favorite artist?"

"One of them," the patron stated. "I was told you're an expert on Van Gogh."

"Really? Who told you?"

"Oh, I don't know. A gentleman. He said you'd know."

"Sorry," Julia apologized. "I don't. What's his name?"

"He never did say. He did mention he's in the Art Underground, though."

Julia shook her head slightly and peered curiously at the unfamiliar patron.

"I'll keep an eye out."

"Okay. Take care," the stranger said.

Julia then watched as the middle aged woman turned, walked down the hall and out of sight.

The Statue of the Crying Virgin Mary

Oh, yes. There's nothing like the peaceful serenity of a country farm, the smell of pine—Mother Nature's own air freshener—caressing the air, and the wistful, almost ethereal, chirp of the song sparrow to fill one with contentment. Not that Chimmy noticed. It was his turn this morning to haul wood in from the back of the farmhouse, and he wasn't too happy. Having had too much to drink last night, he was practically tugging at invisible strings in an effort to stay upright.

His band mates were all passed out in various stages of undress in the living room, the kitchen, and first floor bedroom. A few girls had chosen to stay over after the party last night, but because everyone was too drunk to drive, the girls opted to sleep in the bedrooms upstairs. They thought it was the least their hosts could do. There would be no hanky-panky that night, just good old fashioned sleep.

After Chimm, brought a few logs in, he placed them in the fireplace and started a fire. The house was sorely in need of heat. There was no snow on the ground this December morning, but the crispy chill could use a little nip in the bud.

He looked around the living room. There was David "Jockey" Moore, their band's guitarist and camera operator at KING 5 News, stretched out on the couch and wearing a bright red tuxedo with a long tail. He had the wherewithal to call in sick last night because he knew he always ended up going too far with his partying.

In the kitchen, Chimmy could see Tim "Juggler" Wranitzsky, the bassist. Short, slightly round, but light-tempered, he was the comedian of the group. Chimmy hoped Juggler called in sick to his job at the Woodland Park Zoo because, since he was on probation, he didn't have that many sick days at his disposal.

Peering in the bedroom on the first floor, he spotted Art "Local" Yokel, drummer, passed out in bed. The other members of his indie-jazz band, Great Aesop's Ghost, sometimes felt guilty about leaning on Local for financial assistance because he was the biggest bread winner of the four. His job in IT at Amazon paid the bulk of the rent at the farm and some of the P.A. stored in their practice room in the basement. Local never let his friends forget, though, especially when it came to getting paid after a gig.

Thomas "Chimmy" Chan, the band's singer and keyboardist, went upstairs to check on the two overnight guests, Samantha and Vanessa. They were already awake. Samantha was in the shower and Vanessa was getting dressed. He, himself, didn't have to call in because, as a bartender at a night club near downtown Seattle, he had lots of time before work.

After everyone got up, they drove in separate cars to a local diner in Marysville, Washington. Just 35 miles north of Seattle, it's a vibrant and bustling town. As far as Chimmy was concerned, they were lucky to have a farm in which to live and concentrate on their music. In many ways it was a dream come true, but in some ways, it wasn't all it was cracked up to be.

The site of a former strawberry farm, it only included basic amenities—running water and electricity. There was no heat, no internet, no microwave, no dishwasher, and no air conditioning. That was one of the reasons they were able to get it cheaply; a fixer-upper that would challenge them more than the band's music itself.

After breakfast, Juggler dropped the girls off at their homes while Local and Jockey went food shopping. Chimmy went back to the farm to straighten things up a bit, including taking out the garbage and picking up laundry lying around the house. By the time he was done, the other three band members came home. After putting the groceries away, they all couldn't wait to get back to bed. Chimmy stayed up to take care of band business.

First, he mailed out a handful of demos to local and national record companies, then he made some requests to be interviewed by various trade magazines. He also mailed a few of the band's one EP, The Strawberry Chronicles, to different webzines and blogs. By the time he was done, the rest of the band had finally awakened. They were able to practice for about two hours before Chimmy had to go to work at the bar.

The next day, when everyone went to work, Chimmy drove around to area record shops to drop off some EP's to be sold on consignment. The physical CD market was dwindling, but as a marketing tool, it still had its merits. Some patrons of the arts preferred physical CD's over digital recordings because they either felt closer to the artists, or were attached to the idea of the physical music platform.

The whole idea and concept of marketing the band was a sore point with Great Aesop's Ghost, though. Jockey, Juggler and Local worked all day so their hands were tied. Chimmy was then left to do the bulk of the band's advertising and press. It created a rift which, at times, almost led to the band breaking up.

Local and Juggler were against the idea of the band acquiring a farmhouse. He thought if they saw each other too much it could lead to unnecessary friction. Jockey and Chimmy thought it'd give them freedom to work on their craft without distraction. Since they were all dedicated to making it work, they decided to give it a try. They found the farmhouse on Craigslist and had been living there for almost a year. The isolation almost drove Local crazy, but he's since grown used to it. His alternative was living with his parent's in Hunts Point, an alternative he preferred to relinquish.

When the weekend arrived, they attended a punk fest in Seattle where they rented a booth to sell their CD's, t-shirts, buttons, and stickers. All went, except Chimmy, because he'd worked the night before and wanted to get some sleep. The band made a few bucks, just enough for beer and gas. They were all still necessarily dependent on their day jobs to carry them through.

That night, they played a gig at The Mirkwood and Shire Café in Arlington. It all went well. There was a good turnout. Chimmy even made a new friend, a girl with pink hair named Fuchsia. After the show, the other band members stayed at the bar while Chimmy went back with his new friend to her house.

Fuchsia lived on a small alpaca farm in Arlington. For a fleeting moment, Chimmy thought he would move up to Arlington and live with Fuchsia and her two sons. He liked the quietude of Arlington, the almost Amish-like simplicity. Perhaps, he thought, he could even be an alpaca farmer, raise cria all day, and sell their fleece in the farmer's market. This, he thought, was as close to serenity as any man could get.

The next day he and fuchsia had a falling out over her concept of raising her boys. Very liberal, she allowed them to litter, make noise, jump around, break their never ending supply of toys, and eat whatever they wanted from the refrigerator. Chimmy bit his tongue; after all, the boys weren't his, but he knew living with them would be a disaster. Ultimately, he realized he had to simply drive away and never look back.

However, he was fond of the stone statute in her front yard. It was a replica of Michelangelo's David, Chimmy's favorite piece of art as a child. It was defaced and contained graffiti, thanks to the boys. The little devils also modified it by taping a narrow transparent tube up one leg. When they poured water in the distal opening, water would pour out the other end by the penis. They thought they were clever, as did Fuchsia. Chimmy thought the statue was imposing and commanded respect, thus their alteration was in poor taste. Still, it did inspire him to get back into collecting statues, so he decided right then to purchase one and take it back to Marysville.

He went to a gravestone, garden and monument dealer near Arlington. They had all types of granite, porcelain, terra cotta and plastic statues. He saw several garden angels, gnomes, animals and stone dragons. Some were palm sized, others nearly 6 ft tall. He didn't see any replicas of David, so he settled for a large painted alabaster statue of the Virgin Mary nearly five and a half feet tall. Normally costing $3000, it was on sale for half price because of a chip in her robe near the wood base.

When he brought it back to Marysville, his band mates thought he'd lost his mind. Hardly a religious person, Chimmy explained he was simply enamored with its symmetry and perfection. He wanted to place it in the front yard, but because it was so large, the others preferred it be displayed in the back. They put this to a vote. Chimmy lost 3 to 1. The backyard planters won.

They rolled the one ton statue approximately fifty feet to the rear of the farmhouse and stood it up. The weight of the structure was enough to test their mettle. All except Chimmy protested from the outset. They thought his money could've better been spent elsewhere, maybe used for additional pressings of their EP or more t-shirts. Chimmy berated them for spending their money on tattoos. Obviously reaching an impasse, they decided to let the matter rest.

The next few weeks was proving to me too stressful for all. Juggler seemed to have lost some interest in the band. He complained about the mistakes the others made on stage. Local wanted to play songs he'd written, but the others nixed them. Jockey met a girl at a gig and started spending more time with her and less time promoting the group. Chimmy yelled at the others for not showing up at a scheduled photo session for a regional weekly. Inevitably, they were bound to separate.

Local was the first band member to move out of the farm. He got an apartment in Shoreline and only saw the band for practices and shows. Jockey and his girlfriend, Katsumi, moved to Columbia City about a month later. Juggler was the third to leave. He moved into his friend's house in Greenwood because it was cheaper and closer to his job at the zoo. Everyone remained in the band, but none knew how long it would last.

Chimmy was furious at the others for leaving him alone with the farm. They suggested he place an ad for roommates. He did consider it, but the horror stories he'd read about roommates made him think deeply about it. The others did contribute a small financial sum to the upkeep of the farm every month because their equipment was still there, but it wasn't always enough. Also, as they were playing a lot less gigs than before, it also became apparent the farm would become just a memory.

There's nothing like the cattle prod of desperation to push a man towards inventiveness. Chimmy himself was beginning to feel that.

One day, while he was spraying off the statue, he had an idea. All he needed was a power drill, a few extra long carbide bits, a shovel, nails, screws, a small water pump, and yards and yards of thin, transparent tubing.

Purchasing the items off the internet, he finally set out to work on his creation. Working feverishly for the next few days, he tinkered with the alabaster statue in the back yard without interruption. When he was complete, he built a square wooden fence with a gate around the structure. Then he placed an ad in the local paper:

> *"Witness with your own eyes, see for yourself, the Statue of the Crying Virgin Mary. Behold and feel the natural tears of this immaculate and blessed event live in Marysville, WA. All donations accepted. Call 555-616-1234."*

He started receiving a few phone calls, but they were mainly skeptics and jokers. Eventually, visitors started coming. They would arrive at his farm where, once he hinted about his poverty, they would donate to his cause. He'd then lead them to the rear of the house and stand them by the gate. There, they saw the statue which seemed to have tears dripping from its eyes. For those who didn't pay at the outset, they were encouraged to donate to enter the gate and touch the statue to help defray the cost of maintaining the farm.

Naturally, visitors wondered how he created such a hoax. He told them, of course, it wasn't a hoax. He'd bought the alabaster statue, drove it to the farm, and months later it simply started crying. People would examine the statue, its wooden base, and the ground in the immediate area, but saw nothing that would make them believe it was a hoax.

Eventually, news of this 'Miracle in Marysville', as it was dubbed in the local papers, started getting around. Churches would plan field trips to the strawberry farm. Nuns, priests and ministers would come from miles around to study and sing its praises. Donations started pouring in. Chimmy couldn't have been happier. A lot of people, including the other members of Great Aesop's Ghost, remained skeptical. A crying statue? Absurd. It had to have been a Chimmy trick.

Detective Matt Reivers from the Marysville PD paid a visit to the farmhouse one day. He came to find out if there were any building code violations going on. Accompanied by Lynn Webb from the Dept of Public Safety, they did an impromptu inspection of the statue. They inspected the farmhouse, the front and back yard, the electrical and plumbing system, and the statue itself. Eventually, they were both satisfied. Since they found everything in order, they left the farm without leaving any fines or citations. Chimmy couldn't have been more thrilled. The inspection, he was sure, would aid in allowing him to get more visitors to the site.

One Sunday afternoon, a woman in her fifties with a cane paid a visit to the farm. Limping up the stairs to the front door, she rang the bell. Seconds later, Chimmy answered. She introduced herself as Karyn Montenegro from Vancouver, B.C. and claimed she traveled all the way down from Canada to see the miraculous statue. She'd heard it answered prayers and had healing powers. When he asked her if she had any ailments besides the limp, she said she also had acute lymphocytic leukemia. She also stated that because it was in its advanced stages, her prognosis was poor.

Chimmy invited her in for some tea. She accepted, but was really eager to see the statue. Minutes later, she accompanied him to the back yard where she stood transfixed before the life-sized structure. She was so awestruck, tears came to her eyes. Simply standing before the sculpture gave her a feeling she'd never felt before. Receiving permission from Chimmy, she approached the monument and, trembling slightly, touched its robe. Then, she reached up and caressed the tears flowing from the statue's eyes. Seconds later, she prostrated herself and kissed the ground near the base.

Sitting on the ground, she reached in her pocket and brought out a syringe filled with a yellow substance. Chimmy asked her what was in it. She said it was a medicine that would make all her agonizing and intolerable pain end forever. Sensing it would end her life, he ordered her to stop. She insisted it was her right to do as she pleased because she had now made peace with the blessed statue, was convinced of its power, and was now prepared to meet her maker.

As she prepared the needle and prayed silently, Chimmy continued to try to talk her out of her decision. He pleaded, but his words fell on deaf ears. Since she believed the doctors had done all they could, the only choice she had left was not to die in vain and make preparations for the next world.

Chimmy paced back and forth, sighing and fretting loudly, sweat pouring down his brow. How was he to explain this woman's death at his homestead? Would he bear the blame for her demise? Can he let this stranger end her life right there in his yard? Could he have done something to stop it? The questions kept swimming in his mind. Eventually, he came to a conclusion.

Running to the nearby shed, he grabbed a shovel, ran back to the statue, and began digging in the dirt behind it. Begging her to look, he pulled up one section of the thin transparent hose and showed it to her. He explained there was a water pump hidden in the shed which flooded a chamber inside the statue. When the chamber filled, water flowed upwards and out of a pinhole tunnel he'd created near the statue's eyes, creating the illusion of tears.

Karyn shook her head, yelled "No," and cried. She called Chimmy many names and wondered how he could trick people like that. He apologized over and over, but she was still livid. She threatened to tell the churches, police, newspapers or anyone who'd listen to her. Truly humiliated, she threw the syringe on the ground and started limping out of the farm.

Chimmy followed her with his head bowed in shame. Whatever should befall him, he thought he deserved. When she arrived at the front path, she stopped. Chimmy watched as she bowed her head then turned to face him. He was prepared for more of her vicious tirade, but she simply looked at him, her face bearing no traces of anger, and told him he did a good thing. Puzzled, he inquired what she meant. She said she had sold all her belongings in Vancouver, donated the money to a church, and was prepared to die. Going to see this miracle, she added, would've been like icing on a cake, the conclusion of a perfect life. But now, as she was leaving, she realized there was no design to her life. The choices she'd made, the roads she'd travelled, led her to this place. And although she was expecting answers, all the questions left to be asked was impetus enough to spur her forward. So, thanking her American host, she turned and left.

After she left, Chimmy stopped showing and allowing people to see the statue. He stopped pumping water into its hollow chambers. In fact, to make sure his irrigation system was never again initiated, he completely removed the tubing and restored the statue to normal. At times, the other band members and their visitors would look at the statue and swear it still cried. Chimmy had never seen it, but in the back of his mind, he always imagined, "What if?"

My Farsi Boyfriend

My name is Michael Leigh Benèt. Years ago I worked as a nurse at Group Health Central Hospital on Capitol Hill right here in sunny Seattle. It was a very stressful job, but it gave me innumerable chances to see mankind at its best, and worst, every single day. I got along well with my fellow employees, and as long as I didn't disrespect the doctors, my managers, the patients or their relatives, I could keep the paychecks rolling in.

In the three years I was there I met a few guys I was interested in dating. The first one was a dental assistant named David Lupine. David was tall and lanky, the kind of guy people called "string bean" or "tall drink of water." Because of his height, his pants never fit right. They were always too short. Those who got close to him called him "high waters." He didn't mind, though, because he was smart and always had a quick comeback.

David wasn't the type of guy who betrayed his gayness. You just couldn't tell. I thought he was kind of cute, but never told him because I wasn't sure what his position about that was. My gaydar wasn't fully developed as yet.

One day, a few of us were in the lunchroom and the subject about children came up. One worker said, "I don't have any now, but if I met a girl who'd give me five, I'd love her forever." David's response to that was, "Shut my mouth and gag me with a spoon. If that would happen to me, I'd castrate myself on the spot." I thought that was an odd comment, but I kept my thoughts to myself. The next time I saw him I did ask about it. He stated he didn't want kids and his boyfriend couldn't make him adopt any.

Boyfriend? He had a boyfriend? Wow, could've fooled me. He later explained it was his ex, but they were contemplating getting back together. He also asked me to keep all this to myself because he wasn't out but he felt I could be trusted.

The second guy I was interested in was an ARNP, an advanced registered nurse practitioner. His name was Tony Wong. Being an ARNP placed his at just one step below a doctor, but several steps higher than my pay grade. I got along well with Tony. He had a sense of humor that wavered between sarcastic and morose. The older nurses didn't care for his bedside manner at all, but he didn't care. The patients enjoyed his jocularity. He did bring smiles to the faces of those in pain or those hearing incredibly bad news for the first time.

Tony found out I was gay because I sometimes wore a pink triangle pin on my nursing scrubs. It was a tiny gold pin, not one so huge and obstructive that the managers would order you to take off. We had gotten into a conversation about the symbol of the pink triangle, Nazi Germany and their persecution of gay people, and it somehow became apparent that I wore the button not only as in solidarity, but also in identity.

I'd asked Tony out one day but he refused. He stated he was continuing his studies and didn't have time to go out. He also said he feared it could lead to something, so he thought it best to leave everything between us platonic. I didn't learn till later that he had an on again, off again boyfriend and was just trying not to hurt my feelings. Too late. Group Health, or Group Death as the natives called it, may be large, but it was like a small town, a gossip mill at best. If you had a secret, keep it to yourself and out of Group Death, otherwise you may as well spell it out in huge letters in the cafeteria.

One day there was a new class of nurse recruits in the hospital. I was hanging an IV in one of the rooms when they walked past the door. Fresh out of school, the six students were being oriented to their new jobs by a manager. Minutes later, while I was writing some notes at the nursing station, the manager walked over with one of the students.

"Michael," she began, "I'd like you to meet someone."

I looked up. A male nurse in his early 20's, with hair as black as midnight, stretched his hand out to mine.

"My name is Shapour Shirazi," he said.

"I'm Michael Benèt," I responded, shaking his hand.

"He'll be shadowing you today," the manager explained.

"Fine."

Shadowing me? Well, this was unexpected. I hoped Shapour couldn't tell my hands were trembling. Yes. He was that gorgeous. It seemed like he was chiseled from a block of Asgard marble and brought to life. Okay, that's a little extreme, but you get the picture. Have you ever had that feeling where you met someone and it seemed you got lightheaded, giddy and sweaty at the same time? Well, that was one of those times. Embarrassing, to say the least.

"I haven't oriented someone in a while, Shapour," I admitted to him, "so if you want, you can do some quick rounds with me."

"Okay," he nodded.

I showed Shapour where the nurses' lounge was as well as our med room, oxygen room, small central supply, fire extinguishers and exits, the disaster manual, and other items. He seemed very eager to learn. Asking very few questions, he was like a cool breeze following me around. A few of the staff members and patients did notice him and introduced themselves; I even think some of them blushed when he smiled at them.

After lunch, I showed him how the med dispensing machine worked. He was a pretty quick learner and it became obvious he was comfortable around me.

"Are you new to nursing?" I asked.

"Yes, sir," he answered. His accent, as well as the formality in his voice, betrayed his foreign upbringing.

"Gee, you're so formal," I remarked. "Where are you from?"

"Iran," he answered.

"Have you been here long?"

"I came to America five years ago."

"Your whole family?"

"Yes, sir. My parents, my sister and myself."

"You make me sound old, Shapour. 'Yes, sir'."

"Sorry."

"That's okay. I'm just playing."

I continued showing him how to use the med dispenser by punching codes in it and double checking to make sure the right patient's meds were being accessed. Central billing used to lecture us about this. It got tiring after a while.

"You're a good teacher, Mike," he smiled.

I nodded politely. If I could've bottled his smile and stuck it in a picture frame, it'd be hanging over my bed forever.

Unfortunately, Shapour, didn't spend the entire shift with me as he still had some paperwork to do in the educator's office. Before we split up he did say goodbye and that he'd see me again the next day. I couldn't wait.

That night, I couldn't stop thinking about him. I spent a good chunk of time on the internet looking up Iran, its people and culture. It's so funny to look at someone that looks as sweet and innocent as Shapour, and then see his leaders banging their fists and condemning the western world with pure vitriol. The dichotomy is startling; real, but startling. Shapour didn't look like those angry politicians and clerics at all. Clean shaven, his raven hair was almost to shoulder length. If he did have a mean streak, I guess he kept it well hidden.

The next day at work things went pretty smoothly. Again, I was given the task of orienting Shapour. Yay! He wore a different uniform that day. I normally wear light blue scrubs. He also did the same, not maroon like the day before. What did that mean? I was hoping it meant he'd noticed my colors and followed suit.

At lunch, we sat together, just the two of us. I looked around briefly for fellow workers but I didn't see anyone I knew.

"I want to learn more about your country," he commented at the table.

"What do you want to learn?" I asked.

"Everything. How cars are made, where newspapers are printed, your museums ... I want to see some western films. I saw a few in Europe but they were banned in Iran."

"You're very curious, huh?"

"Yes. You want to know a secret?"

"Go ahead."

"Your country is very open, no? You people have a lot of freedoms here. You can say what you want and do what you want."

"Well, within moderation. You speak English pretty well."

"My father's a businessman and did a lot of traveling. I'm not like the typical Persian boy who grew up in one small town. Iran has lots of restrictions, but my father was able to travel as a merchant to several European countries. I started learning English at a young age."

"Good for you."

"I saw a lot of things in Lisbon, Paris, and London. My eyes were open."

"Like what? What did you see?"

"Well, the way people lived … their openness. They were just free, not like they had a soldier looking over their shoulder all the time. You know what I mean?"

He suddenly reached over and touched my hand. My heart leaped.

"Yeah, I guess I do," I answered.

"I'll tell you more soon," he promised.

Later, as I was walking out to the parking lot to go home after work, I heard someone calling my name.

"Michael. Michael!"

Looking around, I saw Shapour walking quickly towards me.

"Hey Shapour," I greeted him. "What's up?"

"Are you busy this evening? Or right now?"

"Um, no, not really. I was gonna go home and change. I thought I might get some jogging in."

"Do you want company?"

Half an hour later, Shapour and I went jogging around a high school track near my house. The sun was on full blast. A few students were kicking a soccer ball around on the grassy field. A handful of joggers were also on the track

Because he wasn't prepared for jogging, Shapour had to wear one of my jogging shorts and t-shirts. They actually fit him well. I thought it'd swim on him considering he's a little bit smaller than me.

"You look nice in those," I told him. "Don't destroy 'em."

"I won't," he promised.

Minutes later, we took a break, sat in the bleachers and drank some water from our bottles.

"I learned some words in Farsi," I bragged.

"Oh, yeah? Like what?"

"*Um, salâm*."

"Hello."

"*Mo'afagh* bashed."

"Good luck."

"Wow, your language is hard. *Dastsuyi* man pore *màrmàhi ast*."

"My toilet is full of eels?" Shapour laughed. I blushed.

"It's my first time,' I admitted. "I know as much about Farsi as I do rocket science."

"They want to take my head in Iran."

"What?" Did I just hear what I'd thought I heard? They want to take your head?"

"Yeah. They don't like people like me back home."

"What do you mean? What's special about you?"

"Do you want to talk back to your house?" he asked.

"Okay," I answered. "Let's go."

Shapour and I were sitting on separate chairs in my living room. I was actually on the couch next to an unfinished jigsaw puzzle. We're both sipping beers. The news was on TV, but the volume was low.

"If I was to somehow end back up in Tehran right now I would be hanged."

"Why?" I wondered.

"I was born a Muslim, but I switched."

"You switched? What do you mean? Switched religions?"

"Well, something like that. That's called apostasy. It's punishable by death, according to the Koran."

"So you become a Christian?"

"I didn't become anything. I'm just a non-believer, I guess. Does that offend you?"

"Nah. You'd have to really go out of your way to offend me. After what we see all day at work?"

"It's really tough being an apostate in a country like mine's."

"They're pretty strict, huh?"

"Yeah. But not just that. I'm gay, too."

"Hmm. Double whammy."

"Yeah. They were looking for me."

"Who's looking for you?"

"The government."

"Here in America?"

"No. Back home. It's not easy. I did bring some shame to my family and I've been trying to make amends. My father knew it was best to get me out of Iran. I was lucky. He couldn't just forget about me like so many fathers do and leave me to there to burn. People do that all the time to save face, but all that traveling around we did in Europe opened our eyes."

"So everything's okay with your family?"

"Not the girls. My sister and mother still think it's an abomination—the gayness and apostasy. Needless to say, my relation with them is strained." He shrugs.

"Where do you live now?"

"I'm still with them, but everyone's so busy we hardly see each other. That's better for me."

"Well, at least your father's on your side."

"Not exactly. He's hoping I'll come around."

"Back to being a Muslim?"

"Back to both. I'm his only son so the burden of lineage is upon me."

"Heavy load to bear, my friend."

Shapour raised his bottle.

"A toast to those who didn't make it out alive."

"Hear ye," I added. "And a toast to freedom and new friendships and togetherness."

Suddenly, he got up, sat right next to me on the couch, and kissed me. It was long and meaningful and deep and absolutely unexpected. Seconds later, he came up for air.

"Did you know about me?" I asked.

"You glow like a neon lamp," he noticed.

"I do? I do not."

"Yeah. Read you like a book. I know you like me."

He kissed me again. "Yeah," I admitted. "You're kinda cool for a Farsi."

The next few weeks with Shapour were like a dream come true. Appreciative of American culture and the diversity of Seattle artisans, we spent a lot of time going out to "out of the way" ethnic restaurants and visiting local museums like the EMP, Seattle Art and the Wing Luke in the International District. We also went to a few movies at some local art houses. Other times, we simply gave hours to chilling at the Ballard Locks and other points of interest. He was quite the conversationalist once he got used to you. I probably learned more about Iranian life in those few weeks than I ever could in a lifetime.

The initial meeting with his family didn't go as well, however. His father, Davood, was cordial and respectful. The same couldn't be said for his sister, Chalipa, or his mother, Mozhdeh. It's not that they were as cold as ice, but you could tell there was no love lost between us.

One day, Shapour surprised me by inviting me to a picnic. It was to be held at Sunset Gardens, a local park in Ballard. Located on the beach, it was a popular spot for sun bathers and picnickers alike. When I got there that Saturday, I was met not just by him, but his family as well. It was to be our first meeting.

Davood shook my hand, told me his name, and asked how I was doing.

"Fine," I answered.

"So you're Michael?" his sister asked.

"You must be Chalipa."

I extended my hand. Reluctantly, she shook it.

"Are you Mozhdeh?" I asked his mother.

"You're pronouncing it wrong," she corrected me. "It's *Moe'sh'day*."

"Sorry," I apologized to her. "It's not a word I'm used to."

"As well you shouldn't," she responded.

Oh boy, I thought. I could see where this was going.

"Chalipa brought some traditional Iranian dishes," Davood explained.

"I hope you like it," she added. "Took me all morning."

"Whatever you brought, it'd be an honor to enjoy it."

Chalipa rolled her eyes. She was young, but flattery was obviously lost on her.

"One day I might open a Persian restaurant," she proudly asserted. "I've been told I make the best tabouli and *gheimeh bademjan* this side of Tehran."

"Good for you," I said.

Considering our differences, our meeting went rather well. I actually didn't think Shapour told his family about us, but considering how open he was, it was no secret. His sister and mother also clearly stated their position about his gayness and apostasy, but they also mentioned he'd be "back in the fold" once he met the right girl. Yeah. Good luck with that. Things continued going well with Shapour and me for the next few days till the ball dropped.

It was January 10. Iran was celebrating Bahman 22: Victory of the Iranian Revolution. Shapour decided to come to work that day dressed in cultural clothing. Over his typical scrubs he wore a green ankle-length cotton tunic called a *qaba*. Fastened at the waist with green ties, it almost looked like a long scrub top. He complemented his attire with matching cloth shoes and Dervish cap. The cap is basically a pointed rimless cloth cap with inscriptions on it. He was generally complimented on his attire. One employee, however, did take offense to it.

Joe Rizzo worked for several years as a transport aid at Group Health. He'd been disciplined a few times for wheeling elderly patients on gurneys too quickly, dropping patients off on the wrong floor from the recovery rooms, or telling the patients his personal problems. It was well known, especially since he spoke about it all the time, that he couldn't keep a girlfriend, often had problems with his landlord, was a heavy drinker and smoker, and never finished community college courses because of fights with the professors. From what is known about him, he did a two year stint in the army after high school, was dishonorably discharged, and spent the next couple of years after that sailing from job to job till he ended up at Group Health.

The other employees thought that Joe was just slow, but no one told him that to his face because he was six feet tall, weighed around 220 lbs, and was as strong as a wrestler. He did have a few friends looking out for him, though, and that's what got him saved from being fired.

On the day Shapour came to work in traditional attire, a lot of folks commented positively on his looks. The only holdout was Joe. When Shapour walked past him, Joe would whisper something anti-Muslim or something about terrorism or camel jockeys under his breath. Shapour told me about it a few times, but I just shrugged it off as the rants of an insecure loser.

I was in the supply closet looking for some generic aspirins, stool softeners and diabetic needles. I'd kept the door propped open because the heat in the tiny room was a little stifling. Joe knew I was good friends with Shapour, but he didn't know we were actually lovers. As I was filling my little cart, Joe came by.

"Hey Michael," he started. "How's it going?"

"Can't complain," I answered, continuing my supply quest.

"This country's going to the dogs, huh?" he wondered.

"What do you mean?" I asked.

"All these foreigners? Taking our jobs and women?"

Oh, oh. I knew where this type of dialogue was headed, so I thought it best to ignore it. Joe kept on, though.

"You know how many years I gave to this country? In the army?" he queried

"Two years, Joe." I was a little irritated already. "That's common knowledge."

"That's right. I'm a true blue born and bred American."

He points the small American flag tattooed on his left arm. "See that? These colors don't run."

"Looks good, Joe."

"I know you're friends with that new nurse, Ayatollah or whatever his name is, but we gotta do for ourselves in this country, you know? We gotta take care of our own."

I placed all the medical items in my cart, closed the supply room door, and turned to Joe.

"Listen Joseph," I told him, "if you have a problem with Shapour, just talk to him. You'll see he's not that bad. And he's not looking for a handout."

"I got his name stamped on the bottom of my jack boots."

"That's the worst fucking thing I've ever heard coming out of your mouth, Joe."

"Sorry, dude. That's how I feel."

"You wanna stand right here in front of me spewing this shit?" I was so heated I probably had steam blowing from my ears.

"Geez," he apologized. "Didn't know you felt that way."

Just then, Shapour came walking towards us from down the hall. Joe took a quick glance at him then took off.

"Something wrong?" Shapour asked, studying my expression intently.

"No," I answered, finally calming down. "It's okay. A lot of characters in Group Health."

"I've been getting compliments about my outfit."

I looked him in his eyes. It was the most meaningful thing to do at the time. "I love you," I said. He smiled.

"I love you, too." he smiled, patting my arm. "Where did that come from?"

"You make me whole," I admitted. "You just do. Oh, by the way, they squeezed my arm and got another shift out of me."

"For when?"

"Tonight. Somebody called in sick."

"I thought tonight we'd look at a Farsi movie."

Shapour was crestfallen. I didn't know he had something planned. "Being that today is your country's holiday," I offered. "I didn't think you'd mind. I thought you'd be hanging out with your family, anyway."

"Yeah, that's true," he admitted. "Some friends of theirs are coming over."

"Sounds like a party. I wish I could go."

"All the same. They're hardcore mosque dwellers. They're not as western as us. It was probably best if you didn't come."

"If I didn't—"

"They're not that understanding."

"Sounds like you want to hide me."

"Well, not hide you, but—"

"What? So you're embarrassed to be seen with me in front of your people?"

"Is that what I said? They wouldn't understand."

"You make it sound like my fault."

"It's our holiday. These people are traditional."

"Yeah. I get it. Lock Michael in the closet till this whole shebang is over."

"Oh, this is ridiculous!"

"Now I see what you think about me."

Shapour turned to leave. "Where are you going?" I ask. He waves me off.

"You sound impossible," he responds. "I'm letting you cool off."

"Oh, shit. I'm sorry, Shapour."

"Yeah, me, too."

I watched as he walked down the hall and out of site. Damn it. I lost my temper and blew up on the only man I loved. Note to self: learn to keep your anger in check. The next few days were also trying days between us because of a few things that happened to him.

In the first incident, he discovered a sticker of a burning World Trade Center on his locker in the employee lounge. It was a bitch to take off because its adhesive was unusually strong. Unfortunately, he had no one to blame and no one stepped forward to accept responsibility.

The next day, someone used a permanent marker to draw a few symbols on the plastic bag he kept his lunch in down in the employee lounge's refrigerator. It was a drawing of a crescent moon and star, symbols prevalent in the Muslim world. Next to it was another drawing of an equal sign and the devil. Again, no one took responsibility. Shapour did suspect it was Joe because of a brief encounter they had the next day.

Shapour was coming out of a patient's room reading a clipboard. He accidentally tripped and fell over a short metal cart that was suddenly thrust in front of him at the room's entrance. Looking up from the floor, he realized it was Joe and got up to confront him.

"You did that on purpose," he shouted.

"You need to look where you're going," Joe shot back.

"Just come out and say it, Joe. You don't want me here, right?"

"I don't care where you Arabs work."

"I'm not an Arab. I'm Persian."

"Same difference. A raghead's a raghead."

"I'm gonna report this."

Joe, suddenly turning as serious as a drill sergeant, walked straight up to Shapour. "Do whatever you want to me in here," he promised, "but just remember, outside is a whole different world."

Shapour watched as Joe stormed off in a huff. That evening, Shapour told me about his non-fateful encounter with Joe. He explained he was reluctant to report him because, from his experience, the majority never took the side of the lesser man. I reassured him America was a different kettle of fish, but he explained old habits are hard to break.

The next night, after getting home late from another double shift, I jumped right into the arms of my anxious couch. Always there, always comforting, nary a bad word was emitted by it. It was the best, non-accusatory friend a tired body could have. Suddenly, the phone rang. I looked at the caller ID. It was Shapour.

"Shapour," I began. "What's up?"

"I'm in the emergency room," he uttered weakly.

"In the ER? Working? Tonight?"

"No. I got jumped this evening."

"You did? By who? What happened?"

"Can you come to Harborview?"

"Yeah. Sure. Are you hurt?"

"I'll live."

Harborview Medical Center was only a ten minute drive away from my apartment. So, quickly gathering my keys, I dashed out of the house and headed towards the hospital.

There were several people, mostly indigent it seemed, sleeping in the ER's waiting room. I walked straight over to the receptionist.

"Hi," I greeted her. "I'm looking for Shapour Shirazi. He just called me from here a few minutes ago."

"Is he a patient?"

"Yes."

She looked through her ledger then finally saw his name. "He's in berth 4."

"Thanks. Where's that?"

She pointed towards a pair of double doors. "Through there."

"Thanks," I said.

It only took a few seconds to find berth 4. I wished I didn't. Sliding back the curtains, my stomach got filled with lumps. Shapour, lying on a narrow ER bed, had an IV in his left arm, a monitor on his right index finger, and bruises on his forehead, cheek and chin.

"Shapour," I shouted, running to give him a hug.

"Hey Mike," he greeted me with a kiss.

"What happened?"

"I guess your country isn't as tolerant as it seems."

"Who did this? Are you in pain?"

"I'm just sore right now. I'll be fine, though. Just a little shaken up."

"I'm so sorry," I affirmed. I felt so helpless.

"It was Joe Rizzo."

"He jumped you? That motherfucker."

"He never liked me. Always gave me bad vibes."

"Did you call the police?"

"Yeah. I gave them a statement earlier when my family was here."

"Are they still here?"

"Nah. They got tired when they saw I'd be okay. Plus, you know, they have to work in the morning."

"I'm sorry for doubting you, Shapour. I should've taken the threats more seriously."

"There's no way you could've known."

About two hours later, he was discharged. Instead of going to his own home he decided to come back to my place with me. I made him some tea. Within minutes, we were both fast asleep.

I took off from work the next day to take care of my paramour. We were sitting in a nook of my kitchen when he started talking about his days, mostly bad, in Tehran.

"I was bullied a lot," he admitted. "The other guys picked on me mercilessly. I couldn't wait to travel to Europe with my father. All they did was make life hell for me back home."

"I'm surprised you weren't suicidal."

"Of course I was. Those people … they're like simpletons, stuck in the dark ages. Made me rue the day I was born. You know what it's like to have no support? I ask you, how much hate can one man endure in his lifetime?"

"I guess ignorance is universal."

"Yeah, obviously."

"You know what?" I suggested, "We shouldn't live in fear. There are a couple of schools not far from here that teach self defense."

"I'm not a violent person."

"Neither am I. It couldn't hurt to check 'em out."

"You know, I studied capoiera in Tehran."

"What's that?

"It's martial arts, but it combines dancing with it. Very interesting."

"Were you good?"

"I never kept up with it because we moved a lot."

"Well, maybe you can pick it up again in the U.S."

"Yeah."

A few days later, after scouting different fighting institutions in the Seattle area, we began taking lessons in Tae Kwon Do from a *dojang*, a Korean martial arts school in Greenlake. In a relatively short time I felt stronger, more alert, and invincible. Besides learning how to kick and punch well, it also introduced us to meditation and discipline. The fighters on TV and kung fu movies sure made sparring look easy. In real life, though, that was a different story. We never learned how to walk on tree limbs or go flying through the air with swords. The instructor, a sixth degree black belt champion fighter, was as charming as a brick wall. Still, you had to overlook his overbearing ways to see the light at the end of the tunnel: gaining courage and strength to deal with your enemies.

In the meantime, Joe had been fired from work after spending a weekend in jail for assaulting Shapour. Still between jobs, Joe used to just walk around aimlessly in the city daring random pedestrians to engage him in a fight. He did have but a few friends at the local Army and Navy store that helped him out with food and money, but even they knew that their buddy had a few screws lose.

Late one evening, he was lying in wait for Shapour who was walking home from work with his backpack slung across his right shoulder. As he neared his house, Joe suddenly stepped in front of him from the bushes.

"You remember me?" he asked Shapour rhetorically.

"Aren't you supposed to be in jail?"

"Why? I didn't do anything to you."

"You jumped me."

"That wasn't me."

"What? You're crazy."

Insulted, Joe rushed Shapour and pushed him backwards. The gentleman from Iran stumbled but didn't fall; nevertheless, his backpack hit the ground.

"Stop it," he shouted.

"Stop it," Joe shouted back in a feminine way, mocking him with limp wrists.

Shapour started crossing the street to get away but Joe got in his way. Besides the two of them, there was no one else on the desolate street, and Joe intended to make the most of this opportunity.

"You still have your job, don't you?" he asked.

"What?" Shapour questioned him, puzzled.

"I can't find gainful employment because of you."

"You're the one who attacked me, asshole. It's your own damn fault."

Shapour should have run away from Joe, but somehow he felt that it'd be futile. Not only that, the unstable ex-employee could have a gun and be stupid enough to use it. It was best, he thought, to just try to reason with him.

"I don't want any trouble," he insisted. "I just want to go home. Is that okay?"

Joe suddenly pulled a police baton out of his back pocket and held it up for Shapour to see.

"What are you gonna do?" Shapour asked. "You're losing it."

Joe took a swing at him, but missed when Shapour dodged it.

"Stand still, fag boy," he shouted, swinging at him again but missing.

Suddenly, a patrol car came driving up casually. Joe, taking a quick glance at it, turned and ran off in the dark. The car pulled up alongside Shapour. The police officer winded his window down.

"Is everything okay?" he asked the Iranian.

"Yeah. I'm fine."

"Were you two fighting?"

"No. He's ... he works where I work. Just fooling around in the street, that's all."

"You live around here?"

Shapour pointed up the block.

"Right over there."

"Well, you just take it easy, okay?"

"Sure, officer."

When the squad car left, Shapour picked up his backpack and continued on home.

The next day, I was having coffee with Shapour in a cozy little cafe on Capitol Hill a few blocks away from Group Health. Something was bothering him. I asked, but he didn't want to tell me. We'd started spending less time taking Tae Kwon Do lessons because it was a little expensive and just made us sore. Also, its particular emphasis on leg exercises just seemed especially tiring. Eventually, Shapour did tell me about his meeting with Joe the night before

"You know why I don't run to the police?" he asked. "It's because they can't hold my hand forever. I've gotta stand up for myself, don't I?"

"Doesn't seem like Joe's letting up any time soon."

"Maybe we should've kept on with the Tae Kwon Do lessons."

"Maybe we should just buy guns."

"That's ridiculous."

"I'm just joking," I smiled. "My body just aches from all that kicking. Maybe I'll get a shiatsu deep muscle massage."

Shapour reached across the table and rubbed my face. "I'm not running scared anymore," he explained.

"You don't have to prove anything to me," I told him.

"Yeah. I know."

Two day later, Shapour saw Joe Rizzo in his neighborhood again. They didn't meet each other as Shapour had successfully avoided him. Still, tired of being everyone' punching bag, he continued his Tae Kwon Do lessons.

For the next few weeks I watched as he became more and more toned. The ripples in his arms and legs were becoming more pronounced. I was titillated and scared at the same time. His muscles were a joy to feel, but I feared if I crossed him he could break me in half like a twig. We still hung out and went to the movies as usual, and he slept in my house a few times. We were as close as we have ever been, but something was still troubling him. One night, he decided to put an end to the bullying once and for all.

He was walking home from work, his trusty backpack slung around his shoulder as usual. The street was eerily quiet. Just a few hundred yards to his house and he'd be home free. Suddenly, Joe jumped out from the nearby bushes with his baton in hand. He charged Shapour. Instinctively, Shapour sidestepped him, entangled Joe's legs with his own legs, and knocked him to the ground.

"You've been practicing," Joe admitted. "I'm still gonna fuck you up."

Getting up, he charged at him again. Shapour swung and delivered a roundhouse kick to his chest. He went flying backwards and landed on the sidewalk.

"You motherfucker," Joe yelled.

Getting up, he threw the baton at Shapour. It missed and landed deep in the hedges.

They started sparring with each other. Joe was large but he was surprisingly fast. Shapour blocked most of his punches. One punch did lucky and find its mark to his chin. He staggered backwards. His gums and bottom lip started bleeding. Joe lunged at him again. Shapour quickly sidestepped, kicked his knees, and knocked him to the ground. Then, flipping him over on his abdomen, he locked his tattooed arms behind his back and sat on his shoulder.

"Get off me," Joe shouted, his lips bleeding from scraping the sidewalk.

Shapour applied more pressure on Joe's locked arms. He screamed. "You're breaking my arms," he shouted, tears forming in his eyes.

"That's what you get," Shapour said. "I can take this further if you want."

"I'm ... I'm sorry, Shapour."

"Are you?"

Shapour twisted his arms again. He screamed. The pain was excruciating.

"I just want peace, you got that?" Shapour barked. "I didn't do anything to you. You failed in life but want to blame other people for it. Did I make you get fired? Did I kick you out of the army? Everything that happened to you was all your fault. Are you gonna man up and take responsibility or just keep jumping out of the bushes like a weak fucking predator? If you can't make up your mind, I'll be more than fucking happy to do it for you."

"No, Joe shouted. "I can't take no more."

"Are you sure?"

"Yeah. I'm sorry."

Shapour, still stinging from the brazen assault, finally let go. Joe started sobbing, a pathetic sight, lying prone in the middle of the street. Shapour shook his head, picked up his backpack, and walked away.

I saw Shapour for a few weeks after that. The stressors of working, and the incidents of bullying, had taken their toll. He said he'd needed some time to himself so we had a trial separation. At that time, his father secured a well paying job in Spokane and, as much as he didn't want to, Shapour went there with his family.

Those few months with Shapour were some of the best times I've had in my life. I learned a lot from him and I'm sure he learned a lot from me. I wanted to visit his country with him but, like everything else, it seemed best if was best if discovered slowly.

Iron Maiden

Chapter I

Don't Fear the Reaper

About twenty-five middle school kids are riding home joyously in a yellow school bus in small city Mill Creek, Washington. Situated 20 miles north of downtown Seattle, Mill Creek is reflective of America the Melting Pot. The vibrant youths, with faces of all different hues, shapes, and colors, interact favorably and without malice to each other. Like most kids, the students are involved in the usual round of after-school merrymaking: throwing spitballs, wrestling, pulling the girls' pigtails, and general clowning around.

Perry, an overalls-wearing, stalk-chewing, gap-toothed, suspiciously anorexic, frizzy golden-haired country boy in his mid 20's, is at the wheel. Looking in his rearview, he glances intermittently at one girl who doesn't seem to be involved with the others.

Sitting quietly with headphones on, this delicate, olive-skinned bespectacled maiden in a flower dress and long black curls is 13 year old Ingrid Werner. She is humming along softly to classical piano music while combing her rag doll's red hair. Pinned to Ingrid's chest is a large blue ribbon that reads: Heatherwood Middle School - 1st Prize Piano Competition.

Perry lets various groups of kids off at different stops until, finally, the last child left on the bus is Ingrid. When the youngster sees her street coming up, she quickly stuffs the doll and headphones in her knapsack, rises, and skips to the front of the moving bus. Perry zooms right past her street.

"Hey," Ingrid yells. "Where are you going, Perry? That was my block."

He turns and glares at her.

"Sit down. You'll get hurt."

"But that was my block. Turn back."

"Jus' relax now, girly. Yer ridin' with the best darn driver in town."

"You turn back now or I'll tell my father."

"Fuck 'im. Sit down! Everybody knows that crazy shopkeeper is out of touch."

"He is not."

"Shoot. Ingrid, both yer folks are so loopy they don't know baseball from brandy. Now siddown."

Frightened, Ingrid sits obediently. Perry turns onto a narrow dirt road. Ingrid leaps up and runs for the emergency exit window. Perry brakes, abandons his seat, and bounds towards the youngster who'd opened the window halfway. He grabs her arms.

"Oh, no, you don't."

"Get off," she screams. "Help. Somebody help me."

They struggle. Her glasses fly off.

"Go ahead and scream out yer pretty little lungs, Ingrid. Ah reckon ain't nobody gon' hear you way out here anyways."

Ingrid knees him violently in the groin. Recoiling in pain, he releases her. She races to the back door.

"Come back here, yer half-breed polecat."

Flipping the latch, Ingrid opens the back door, jumps off the bus, and heads into the woods. Perry gives chase.

Ingrid lopes through the thick woods as fast as she can. Perry follows singing, though he hobbles in anguish.

"Baby, don't the reaper ... baby, don't fear the reaper ..."

She clears the woods, sees a farm in the distance, and makes a mad dash for it. The farm, she notices, is abandoned. The farmhouse is old and severely weather-beaten. The animal pens are empty. The food and water troughs are bone dry. Spying an old axe, she picks it up, and holds it threateningly. Perry approaches cautiously.

"Stay away, you pervert," she yells.

"Tsk, tsk. Didn't your mama tell you never to use language like that?"

"Perry, you stay the hell away from me."

"And what you gonna do with that thing? Chop me some firewood?"

Perry strides towards her. She flings the rusty axe at him. It narrowly misses his head. She turns to run, but trips and falls over a bucket. Perry drops down over her and tries tearing her shirt off. Ingrid claws wildly at him. He slaps her.

"Be still, bitch. Christ. Yer like a fish outta water."

Groping the ground with her right hand, she feels the head of a flat rake beneath dried leaves. Grabbing its short handle, she brings it out forcefully and slams three of its four rusty tines into the left side of Perry's face. Screaming, he falls off her. Immediately, she gets up and bolts back towards the woods. Blinded by tears, she becomes entangled in a nest of vines. Struggling pitifully, she turns and sees Perry approaching with the rake in his hand and bloody hatred on his face.

"Stay away."

"You'll pay for this, girl."

Ingrid screams when Perry lunges towards her. Then, raising the rake to strike, his eyes roll backwards in his head. He falls silent on the shaken, frightened girl.

***

Young Ingrid's visage morphs into her own thirty-three year old face. Breathing heavily through her nostrils like a bull stabbed one too many times by a matador, she's perspiring and raw. Her emotions are raw. Those dark orbs moonlighting as eyes are raw.

And here she is, dancing in place in a courtyard twenty years later. Still beautiful despite the fury, in her dark leotards and short curly auburn hair, her femininity still manages to bust through. Her torso and arms are synchronized to music throbbing from loudspeakers off screen.

Soon, the other woman around her comes into view in this concrete empire. Like Ingrid, the twenty or so females are also dressed in leotards and completely in sync with Ingrid's movements. Some of the women are bald, some are fragile, and some are as hard as steel. An instructor is training the ladies. She's facing them, all of whom are moving to her verbal and physical cues. The back of her blue khaki jumpsuit says 'Washington Corrections Center for Women'. On both sides of the yard are heavily armed guards atop their perches.

"Could be worse," Ingrid thinks. "Could've been stuck in max for who knows how long. At least here in the minimum security wing we get regular exercise. The superintendent, Ms. Clausson, didn't approve me for work release, though. Just like a woman ... can't even trust me out on the street for a day. Still, I do get to wear these cool leotards. Beats prison greens any day. Don't know much about these other ladies. They might be killers for all I know. I try to keep to myself but, after nearly two years here, that's like an impossibility. I don't even know why I signed up for these classes. I guess it's just a way for me to forget where I am, or what put me here in the first place."

Hours later, the ladies are in the showers. It is a long cold windowless room without stalls, a wannabe slaughterhouse. The shower heads are about two feet apart. Ingrid is in one of them.

A burly corrections officer with a steamroller body and a face that can freeze a snarling pit bull in its tracks has a baton under one arm and is standing in the doorway watching the women intently. Next to her are white folded towels lying on a table.

Ingrid glances at the C.O. intermittently.

They call her Mistress, she thinks to herself. I call her Quasimodo, Hunchback of the Corrections Center. She's just as ugly. Wouldn't wanna spend five minutes alone with her. I've heard some horror stories from the ladies here. They say she makes Attila the Hun look like Mahatma Gandhi.

"Okay, chickies," Mistress yells. "Time's up. Turn off the water."

The inmates turn their showers off and walk obediently to Mistress who hands each of them a white towel. Ingrid, third in line, takes a towel and dries herself.

Behind her is her cellmate, a small delicate woman with short hair and a ghostly pallor. She calls herself Joey. Joey grabs a towel, but Mistress, keeping a firm grip on it, stares maniacally into the shivering inmate's eyes.

"P-please, Mistress," Joey stutters. "I'm ch-ch-chilly."

"What do you think this is, Club Med? You forgot where you are?"

Joey casts her eyes downward. "No, ma'am."

"Look at me."

Joey quickly looks up into Mistress' probing eyes and sees nothing but malice.

"C'mon, Mistress," Ingrid pleads. "Just give her the towel."

Mistress casts an evil glance at her. "Who asked your opinion?!"

"Look, she's ill. You want her to catch pneumonia?"

"I'm all right, Ingrid," Joey assures her.

Ingrid hands her towel to Joey. Mistress rips the towel from between them, throws it across the room, and turns to Joey. "You want the towel? Go get it."

Ingrid protests the callous treatment of Joey. "You son of a bitch."

The powerful C.O. suddenly grabs Ingrid's slender throat, making her gag. The other ladies stand aside, terrified they could be next. Mistress eyes her nemesis.

"I can squash you like a zit if I want to. You think you can challenge me? I'd been waiting for this moment a long time."

Ingrid's face turns beet red with exasperation. "Please ... Mistress ... I ... can't ... breathe."

Joey runs across the room, picks up the thrown towel, and returns to her Ingrid's side.

"Please, Mistress," Joey begs, "let her go. I did as you said."

The C.O. releases her victim. She slumps to the floor like a wet egg noodle. "You're a pathetic little worm. I'll see you both later."

She exits and Joey comforts tries her cellmate. The other ladies stand by, staring helplessly at the duo.

Later, Ingrid is lying on her cot in her prison cell, staring at the ceiling. There's a large black and blue area on her neck. She sees a roach scamper across the ceiling. If Mistress had a soul before coming here, she thinks, somewhere along the way it was robbed. Without a doubt she was an unwanted child. I didn't eat all day. How could I? Feels like every bone in my neck is splintered. That bitch is gonna push the wrong buttons one day, and I hope I'm around to see it. One person shouldn't have so much power.

***

It's late night in downtown Seattle. No place for a child, the usual coterie of prostitutes and pimps, drug dealers and addicts, are casually standing around, perhaps waiting for money to suddenly drop out of the sky. Ingrid, seductively dressed in a short red leather skirt, black patent leather boots, and a thin black leather jacket, is leaning against a concrete wall. Wearing a long red haired wig, she's smoking a cigarette.

Every night I spent out on the street, she thinks, could've been my last. I used to be a computer geek in some cheesy Internet firm. Imagine that. IT specialist. Yours truly. Did a lot of favors for the boss. One day, when no one was around, he got too friendly. I resisted and lost my job. They say I have a temper. Maybe I shouldn't have beat him up with the computer. Made it hard to get a new job. So what did I do? Went from the world's newest profession to the oldest in one month. What a gas. God, I can't even laugh. My throat hurts so much. Sometimes I wish I could just disappear into the woodwork. Sometimes I wish I could just crawl into a corner and die.

***

Back in the prison cell, Ingrid is lying on her side in the cot. Tears are in her eyes. She moves to a fetal position and starts thinking. I'm glad mom and dad don't know I'm here. This would definitely send them to an early grave. I haven't seen 'em in so long. When they see me I know they'll have lots of questions, like, "How come you're not married? Why are you so thin?" I'll make something up. I'll tell 'em I was in the Peace Corps in Afghanistan but I couldn't stomach the grubs. They'll believe anything.

Chapter II

Barbra Streisand is on a Hunger Strike

The next day, Ingrid and the other female inmates, under Mistress' watching eyes, are on their knees planting saplings. All are in prison greens. The noonday sun is at full blast, just hot enough to make the women pant like dogs.

One of the inmates, succumbing to heat exhaustion, passes out. Mistress, sitting comfortably in the shade drinking lemonade, looks the other way. Ingrid goes to the fallen woman's aide. Mistress turns and sees it.

"Hey, you," she yells. "Get back to work."

"This lady just passed out," Ingrid informs her. "She needs water."

"You must have cotton in your ears. I said back to work"

Ingrid, ignoring Mistress, takes out a handkerchief, pats the inmate's forehead, and helps her to stand. Mistress tightens her stare.

"I must be seeing things."

Ingrid takes the woman in her arms and brings her to Mistress who simply glares at her. "You on a suicide mission, Joan of Arc?"

"Have a heart, Mistress. Can't you see she's parched? We all are."

"Everybody will get water when I call break."

"We'll be dead by then."

"Did I bring you to this prison?"

Brazen as a fox, Ingrid grabs Ingrid's pitcher of lemonade and brings it to the inmate's lips. Before the seared woman could take two sips, Mistress knocks the pitcher out of Ingrid's hand. All of its contents splash out on the arid ground. Ingrid is, of course, astonished.

"You can't do this."

Mistress puts her hand on her hips like a circus strongman. "I just did."

Ingrid helps the stricken inmate sit in the shade. Ingrid turns to Mistress. "We're fucking thirsty and you're playing games?"

"Get back to work!"

"There are laws against this!"

"Oh, really? When you pass the bar, sue me. Right now, I can do what I want."

"You're lower than pond scum," Ingrid whispers.

"What did you say?" Mistress leaps to her feet and runs after Ingrid. Ingrid, younger and thinner, eludes the stocky overseer, but she doesn't give up so easily. "Come back here."

Ingrid dashes towards a fence. Too high to climb, it is also barbed at the top. Running further, she encounters fence after fence until, finally, she's cornered. Mistress, out of breath and waving her baton, closes in on her.

"The only way out of here," she pants, "is through me."

Like a possessed rhino, Ingrid charges Mistress, butting her in the stomach. The C.O. topples over, losing her baton. Ingrid picks up the stick and holds it ominously over Mistress' face. "You want more?" Ingrid yells. Mistress clutches her aching abdomen.

"Go ahead, tramp. Seal your fate. You'll be here forever. You'll be my pocket pussy the rest of your miserable life."

Ingrid continues staring at the downed C.O. then, surrendering, she grunts, throws the baton down, and walks away. Mistress smirks.

Two hours later, the inmates are eating goulash and talking among themselves in the mess hall while two workers clean up the serving area. Two C.O.'s are on opposite sides of the room. One of them is Mistress.

Ingrid is sitting at one of the long metallic tables. Not touching her so-called food, she's simply sitting on her hands staring at the swirling live glop in her soup bowl. She's black and blue all over. There's a cut over her right eye. Her left eye is black and swollen. Her cheeks are also bruised. Her bottom lip is split and has dried blood on it. There's a bandage on her yellowish, bluish chin. Mistress, noticing that Ingrid isn't eating, stomps over. The room goes eerily silent.

"What's the matter?" Mistress asks rhetorically. "This swill ain't good enough for ya?"

"I'm not hungry," the battered inmate answers without looking at the C.O.

"I'm not hungry," Mistress mocks her. She turns to the other inmates.

"Lookee here, ladies. Barbra Streisand is on a hunger strike."

She turns back to Ingrid. "You trying to be Mother Teresa in your next life? Oh, yeah. I forgot. Your mother's black, ain't she?"

Mistress turns to the food servers. "Hey. One order of ribs and collard greens over here. And make it snappy."

Ingrid looks at the C.O. "You've been in my files?!"

"Just pick up that spoon and dig in!"

Ingrid doesn't move a muscle. Mistress grabs the spoon, dips it in the lumpy gruel, grabs Ingrid's face, and tries to force the mush into her mouth. Ingrid clenches her teeth while fighting her off. Unfortunately, the C.O. isn't ready to give up so easily.

"Open up," she demands.

Ingrid, trying to push the C.O. off, keeps her teeth clamped.

"Open up, I say."

Another C.O, with a serious look on her face, marches over to Mistress. "Let her go," she requests bluntly.

Mistress stops forcing herself on Ingrid, turns, and stares at the other C.O. Her name is Samara, She's a bold black woman almost a head shorter than Mistress.

"Say what?" Mistress asks, astonished.

"You need to know when to turn it off sometimes, Mistress," Samara advises her. "What if Ms. Clausson walks in?"

"Fuck her. She's just a pencil pushing politician. I run this joint."

"You don't have it like that, Mistress."

"I don't? I've been supervising this cell block long before you sucked your first dick. Don't tell me what I can and can't do."

The two C.O.'s stare at each other, neither one backing down. Ingrid and the other inmates watch patiently as if a volcano was about to explode. The veins in Mistress' temples are bulging with anger as are the muscle's in the other C.O.'s fist.

Finally, Mistress gives in. She tosses the spoon on the table and walks away. Samara breathes a sigh of relief. Mistress stops in the aisle saying, "You just went to the top of my shit list."

Samara turns to Ingrid. "Are you okay?"

"Yeah."

"You wanna see the nurse?"

Ingrid shakes her head. "Why does she have so much power? Why do y'all let her push you around like that? What's so special about her?"

"Ms. Clausson is her cousin."

"That makes no difference."

"It does when Mistress has as much dirt as she does on her cousin."

That night, about twelve inmates are in a spacious rec room watching TV. Among them: Ingrid and her cellmate, Joey. One inmate is crouched quietly in a darkened corner completely oblivious to the world. The one C.O. in the room, an older woman, is nodding off intermittently in one of the long, comfortable couches. Joey is staring blankly into space.

"Six more months," she mutters.

Ingrid's concentration on the TV news program breaks.

"Huh? What'd you say?"

"Six more months," Joey reiterates. "That's when I get out."

"I thought you said you'd copped a three and a half to five."

"I did. I'm trying to work out a deal with Ms. Clausson."

"Shoot. If Ms. Clausson is anything like her crazy cousin, you're doomed."

"I know, but since you helped me get my GED, that makes it easier for me to get an early release. Thanks, by the way."

"No problem, Joey."

Joey notices the inmate crouching in the corner. "What's with Maria tonight?"

"Beats me," Ingrid answers. "This place is putting her through a lot of changes."

"What's she in for?"

"I don't know."

"I heard she sold her baby on the black market, but you know how ladies gossip."

"Really? Sad. You gotta be super desperate to do something like that."

"I don't believe it, though. I know her. She's got a good heart. I think her man abused her a lot. He forced her to take drugs."

"What a bastard."

Joey gets up.

"Where're you going?" Ingrid asks.

"I want to invite her over." Joey walks over to Maria. Seconds later, Joey suddenly screams, "Ingrid, come quick."

"No," Maria yells.

Ingrid leaps to her feet and runs over to Joey. The other inmates stop watching TV and look curiously in Joey's direction. Ingrid, approaching the crouched duo, sees what made Joey shout. Maria has a razor pressed against her left wrist. There's already blood dripping down her arm.

"Maria?" Joey asks. "What are you doing?

The suicidal woman, frightened and confused, backs herself deeper into a corner like a startled rat. "Leave me alone," she screams.

"Why, Maria?" Joey asks.

"I'm fuckin' tired of living."

"You have to hang in there, Maria," Ingrid insists. "We're all going crazy in this place."

Some inmates come over to watch the unfolding scene.

"I don't have no will no more," Maria acknowledges. "I just can't hold it together like you."

"Girl," Ingrid asserts, "I'm just like you; making shit up as I go along."

"I'm just so fuckin' tired of living, tired of this place, tired of Mistress."

Ingrid rubs the troubled woman's shoulder. "All of us are, Maria. Places like these are designed to break you down so you'd have the strength learn and grow and do the right thing. I know it sounds stupid, it even sounds corny to me, but I know once you accept that, it becomes easier to bear."

"I'm trying, Ingrid. I'm trying."

The ladies watch as Maria keeps the razor pressed to her wrist. Ingrid knows she must pour on the sympathy or risk losing a friend.

"Sometimes I wanna get to the top of the water tower," she admits, "and just take a flying leap, but I know there's life behind these stupid walls."

The older C.O., finally waking up, walks over to see what the commotion is all about.

"What the hell is going on here?" she asks.

The inmates spread out a bit. The C.O. sees the bleeding inmate. Maria stares back at her.

"Get back," she shouts, "or I swear, I'll—"

"Take it easy," the C.O. tells her, but Maria is still angry.

"I hate you damn pigs. You don't know whose side you're on."

"Give me the razor, Maria."

"No."

The C.O. runs to a wall phone and dials for help.

"Give me the razor, Maria," Ingrid requests softly.

"I didn't sell my baby," Maria swears. "I would never give my daughter away."

"I know, honey. I believe you. That's why it's important you hand over the blade so you can get out of here and get her back. She needs her mother."

After a tense pause, Maria relents and gives Ingrid the blade. They hug. Joey takes the blade from Ingrid and imparts it to the C.O. Maria starts crying. "I'm sorry," she moans. "I'm so sorry."

"Shh," Ingrid coos. "It's okay. It's all right."

"We're right by you, Maria," Joey affirms. The other inmates agree.

"They'll put me in isolation for this," Maria warns.

"I won't let them," Ingrid states, but Maria looks at her.

"You can't promise that."

Ingrid looks over at the C.O. with a questioning face. The C.O. shrugs then shakes her head, indicating Maria won't be isolated. Ingrid rubs Maria's shoulder again.

"Everything will be fine."

Chapter III

It's Our Home

Sitting in a community-donated piano booth the next morning, Ingrid is in the small plain chamber playing a Chopin etude on an upright piano. Her face already shows signs of healing from yesterday's beating. The piano, though old and slightly out of tune, sounds wonderful, nevertheless. She stops playing when there's a sudden loud rap on the door's large glass window.

It's Mistress, and she doesn't seem amused. "Open this door," she demands.

"I signed up for this room with Recreations. I still have an hour left."

"I said, open this door."

Ingrid takes a paper from the piano and slides it under the door. "This permission slip, signed by Ms. Clausson herself."

Mistress picks it up, gives it a cursory glance, and tears it to bits. "If you don't unlock this door right now, I'll shatter this glass and make you swallow the pieces."

"Sorry, Mistress. I have permission."

Mistress, fuming, leaves. Ingrid resumes practice. Suddenly, a steel chair crashes through the glass door and flies unto the piano. Ingrid screams, leaps back, and sees Mistress standing there with fire in her eyes and smoke practically blowing out her nose like a ridgewing dragon.

"What the hell, Mistress?"

"You're dead."

"Ms. Clausson's gonna hear about this."

"I'm pissing my drawers." Mistress reaches to the inside knob. Ingrid grabs her hand. The strong C.O. parries Ingrid off then unlocks and opens the door. Ingrid shoves the solid, stocky woman. They wrestle out to the hallway, at times slipping on the broken glass on the floor.

Ingrid knees Mistress in the belly. The burly woman hardly winces. She slaps Ingrid so hard that the waifish girl goes flying against a wall. She stumbles into the adjacent kitchen and quickly searches for an exit. The two inmates in the kitchen run out when they see Mistress enter.

Ingrid quickly checks the exit doors in the kitchen, but soon realizes they're all locked. Mistress runs up and throws her entire weight against the trapped inmate. Ingrid drops. The C.O. grabs her by the arms, drags her into the adjacent storage room, and drops her on the dusty floor in a corner.

The room looks like the basement of an urban tenement; dark and foreboding. Rats scurry about here and there. Water drips from the rusty overhead pipes. Bags of rice, flour, and grain are ripped open, their innards scattered all over. Pots, pans, and other utensils are strewn about carelessly in this poorly lit oversized closet. This isn't a storage room. It's a horror chamber with an odor of dread and the smell of neglect, like the dried up bowels of a rotting corpse.

Ingrid cowers before her assailant. "Please, Mistress. I beg you. Don't do this."

The malignant C.O. grabs a wooden broom and snaps it easily in half over her own thick muscular knee. "Scream if you like," she brags. "Won't do you no good down here."

She discards the straw end of the broom, spits on the handle, and rolls the drool-saturated end of the stick back and forth in her left palm. "Pull down your pants," she orders the inmate.

"No," Ingrid begs. "Please."

Mistress shakes her head and eyes her prey. "Suit yourself. Like I always say, the chase is more fun that the catch." She leans towards the cornered woman.

In the hall outside the storage room, the other inmates who'd gathered because of the commotion hear Ingrid let out a blood-curdling, "No."

Later that night after 'lights out', Mistress passes by the rec room and notices the TV is on. She stomps in angrily. There's no one in the darkened room.

"Now who the hell left this on?" she asks herself. She clicks it off then turns to leave. An inmate, her hands balled into fists, appears in the doorway.

"Put it back on," she tells Mistress.

"What the hell are you doing out of your cage?"

A second inmate walks over to the first and faces Mistress.

"It's not a cage, Mistress," she insists. "It's our home."

The C.O. scowls. "Who let y'all out?"

Two more inmates, Joey and Maria, come over and enter the room with the other two. Mistress backs up a little. "What the fuck?"

Soon, more inmates enter. Eventually, they slowly surround Mistress. Frightened, she pulls the whistle from around her neck and blows it hard.

"Guards. Guards," she blows again. The ladies close in. She yells, "guards, help."

Maria rips the whistle from Mistress' hands, blows into it once then throws it against a wall.

"What ... what do y'all want?" Mistress asks. "Don't hurt me. I'll give y'all anything you want."

"That's the best lie I've heard all day," an inmate says laughing.

"You ladies are making a mistake."

"The only mistake we've made," Joey alleges, "is letting you getting away with all that cruel shit. Now Ingrid's in the hospital because of you."

"I didn't do nothing. It was an accident."

Maria glares at the C.O. "You lying worthless whore."

"Help!"

The ladies pounce. They punch, kick, and pound the hapless C.O. like they were kneading dough for artisan bread. Mistress throws a few wild punches of her own, but none of them connect.

Chapter IV

Good Luck Hunting

Two weeks has passed since Ingrid's brutal beating by Mistress. She learned from the doctor things could've been worse. If her cracked ribs had pierced her lungs or aorta, she could've hemorrhaged and died. Luckily, she was tough, which helped her survive. Now, packing her clothes in a suitcase, she's about to be released.

Attired conservatively in light brown slacks and a white long sleeve shirt, most of the bruises on her face are gone. The swelling above her eyes and neck have also disappeared. Joey is sitting on her bed watching her pack.

"I'm jealous."

"I know," Ingrid frowns. "I'll miss you, Joey."

"I'll miss you, too."

C.O. Samara approaches the cell. "Still packing?" she asks. "Shoot, I woulda been ready since last night." Using her keys, she opens the cell.

"Hi, Samara. I'm still feeling kinda weak."

"Hey, consider yourself lucky. You're getting out with your senses intact. Look at Mistress. She's a vegetable. Barely alive. Can't even talk. Pisses herself like a baby every hour. That was some long flight of stairs she fell down."

The two inmates giggle.

"She asked for it," Ingrid avers.

"You should be happy," Samara points out. "I know she was your worst nightmare. I know I didn't stand up for you much, but do yourself a favor: stay out of places like these."

"Believe me, I'd rather have a tumor ripped out of my ovaries with a fork than come back." She closes her suitcase and grabs a bottle of pills off a shelf.

"Almost forget these. Got 'em from the infirmary."

Samara takes it and reads the bottle. "Numbutol? They let you keep these in a cell?"

"I was being discharged. They knew."

"I've heard about these," Samara warns. "Avoid liquor and whatnot when you take 'em. They say the side effects are weird."

She hands them back to Ingrid who places them in her suitcase.

"I just use them for these headaches."

"So what are you gonna do now?" Joey asks.

"I don't know. Get out of town, get a job. I've had it up to here with the streets."

"Will you write?"

"Sure. I taught you how to read, didn't I?"

"Ingrid, I ..."

"What's up?"

"Nothing."

"Stop hiding what you want to say, Joey. You'll constipate yourself emotionally. When you explode, those who love you the most will help you the least."

"I'm just gonna miss you, that's all."

The two ladies hug. Then, Joey suddenly kisses Ingrid on the lips. Surprised, Ingrid, nevertheless, accepts her cellmate's parting gift. The C.O. shakes her head.

"If you want," Samara suggests, "we can extend your visit."

Ingrid grabs her suitcase and heads to the open cell door. The C.O. grabs her arm as she walks pass. "Word on the street," Samara adds," is that john you fingered?"

"Sticky Icky the gadget freak?"

"Yeah. He's still out there in Tacoma looking for you."

"I'm not going anywhere near there anyway."

She walks out of the cell, stops and speaks with her back to the C.O.

"Well, you showing me out or not?"

***

A Greyhound bus is zooming up I-5 just south of Everett, Washington. It's a clear cloudless day with the temperature in the early 90's. The bus' A/C is malfunctioning. Most of the passengers are fanning themselves. At least two older ladies, in danger of passing out, are being assisted by several passengers.

Ingrid is sitting in the back with her window open. She sees heat waves rising from the road. A little boy starts bawling. Ingrid gets up and walks to the front of the bus. The driver is also perspiring.

"It's hot in this mother," she complains. "Can't you do something about the A/C? People are passing out back there."

"What can I do? Everything checked out fine this morning. I have to stay on schedule. If you want, you can get off right here and hitchhike."

"We're burning up and you're making jokes."

"Well, I'm burning up, too. There's fresh water in the faucet in the back."

"Ugh."

Ingrid returns to her seat and reads a newspaper she'd found. The little boy in the seat in front of hers jumps up and stares at her.

"Hello," he says.

"Hi," Ingrid greets him.

"Are you a model?"

"No. I'm just an average person."

"You look like a movie star. Can I marry you?"

Ingrid laughs.

"You're kinda young, aren't you? You have your whole life. By the time you get to marrying age, I'll be an old hag. You won't want me then."

"Yeah, you're right."

He sits down.

"Smart aleck," she whispers.

Ingrid looks out the window and sees a large hospital complex nestled serenely amidst a plethora of fancy trees and shrubs. The sign in the front reads "Swedish Medical Center, Mill Creek". She walks to the front of the bus.

"That's new," she tells the driver.

"Yeah. New expansion."

"Pretty big for this area."

"You must not be from around here."

"You could say I'm coming back home."

"Going to Everett?"

"Mill Creek."

"Where've you been?"

"Um, I've been busy."

"You know, this bus doesn't go into Mill Creek. You'll have to take a cab in Everett."

"In this heat? Driver, I'm so tired. I was in the hospital these past two weeks. Can you drop me off there?"

"It's not on my route. Don't you have someone you can call?"

"I don't even have a place to live."

They see a trio of hotels up ahead. "Maybe you can stay in one of those."

Ingrid looks at the facilities: a Motel 6, a Holiday Inn Express, and a La Quinta.

"Can you drop me off at the motel?"

The driver takes a deep breath.

"Okay. I'll do you a favor. Only because it's hot."

"Thank you."

"If you don't mind," the driver asks, "can you return to your seat 'til the bus stops?"

Ingrid makes her way to her seat and sits down. The driver grabs the next exit and swings the bus back towards the Motel 6. He passes a sign in the road ahead which reads 'Welcome to Mill Creek, Washington'. Ingrid reads it.

"About time," she tells herself.

Minutes later, she grabs her things and returns to the front of the bus as it pulls into the parking lot.

"Last time I was in Mill Creek," she tells the driver, "the pop. was only about twelve thousand. I'll bet it's grown a lot since then."

"Blame the Lynnwood mall. Brings a lot of settlers."

"Good, 'cause I need a job anyway."

"Good luck hunting."

After Ingrid disembarks, the bus takes off. Walking into the motel, she heads straight to the lobby's soda machine, buys a bottle of apple juice, presses it against her forehead, then opens and downs it in one gulp.

After paying the clerk, she went to her room, washed her face, and called a taxi.

An hour later, she's standing in front of a small white boarded-up house on Village Green Drive in Mill Creek. It looks obviously out of place on this quiet tree-lined street. The paint is chipped. The weeds in and around the front yard have grown to be nearly three feet tall in places. She looks at the aged mailbox. It reads: "The Werners".

Minutes later, she leaves the Snohomish County Sheriff's South Precinct. Her face has a grim pallor, as if she was the receiver of bad news. Several strangers glance at her, but she doesn't look any of them in the face.

Soon, she's at a graveyard staring at two adjacent gravesites. Above each grave sits a pink marble headstone bearing the epithets: Gertrude Werner, 1939-2011 and Howard E. Werner, 1937-2011.

Taking two roses from a bag in her hands, she plants one in the dirt above each mound, then puts a pebble on both headstones.

Strolling through a park near the center of town, she sees several couples, young and old, walking about hand in hand; kids running about, riding bikes, skateboarding and just hanging out listening to music on their headphones.

Further up a winding lane, she approaches an ice cream stand and studies its huge colorful menu. The vendor, a weather-beaten woman with a kind face in her fifties, comes to the serving window.

"Can I help you?"

"In a minute. Everything looks so good. It's been a while since I've had this luxury."

"Take your time."

"Hmm. I guess I'll have a Rocky Road."

"That'll be one dollar."

Minutes later Ingrid, with cone in hand, is looking in the window of a local toy store. She sees dolls of every nation on display and a price tag beneath them. She opens her pocket book, removes her wallet, and counts her money. A look of disappointment crosses her face.

Walking up the block a little more, she enters the Mills Music Store. Even though she'd never been in the shop before, it contents all looked familiar. Memories of after school piano lessons fill her mind. Against one wall, a handful of visitors are checking out sheet music. Several pianos and organs, new and used, are on display.

In the middle of the store is a brand new Yamaha baby grand. Instinctively, she walks over to it and caresses its smooth lid like it was a long lost love. Mrs. Epstein, the shop owner, marches over with a soft handkerchief in hand.

"That's eleven thousand," she gripes. "No pay, no play." She uses the cloth to wipe off Ingrid's fingerprints.

"I was just looking. Beautiful piano."

"Expensive piano."

Ingrid pulls out the bench and plops herself on it.

"Young lady," Mrs. Epstein brags, "this is a one of a kind. You can't ..."

She suddenly becomes speechless when Ingrid starts playing a section of the 3rd movement from Rachmaninoff's 2nd piano concerto. Her playing is so fluid, Mrs. Epstein's expression changes from anger to awe.

Mr. Epstein emerges from the back room and, like his wife and the other visitors, becomes transfixed by Ingrid's soulful performance. Soon, people who were walking outside the store enter when they heard the music. Standing around, Ingrid suddenly segues into her own piano rendition of Minnie Riperton's "Loving You."

Singing along, Ingrid lays each birdlike note in place. After the first chorus, she stops. The listeners applaud. Mrs. Epstein is so overwhelmed, tears well in her eyes.

"You're wonderful," she compliments the visitor. "What's your name?"

"Ingrid. Ingrid Werner."

Getting up, she grabs her small bag and turns to exit.

"Can't you stay a little longer?" Mrs. Epstein pleads.

"Sorry," she apologizes. "I have a lot of things to do today. See ya."

"Come back any time."

Minutes later, Ingrid sees a teenage video store employee is retrieving videotapes from a sidewalk deposit box just outside the store. Ingrid approaches him. "Hi. Are they hiring here?"

"Nope. Maybe in a couple of months."

"In a couple of months?"

"Things are tough all over."

"Thanks."

"No problem. See you around."

She walks across the street to an outside bistro where a waitress is wiping down a table. "Excuse me," she asks the waitress. "Are they hiring here?" The waitress shakes her head.

Speaking some moments afterwards to the manager of a dry cleaning establishment, she learns they don't require help of any kind. Walking towards a supermarket, the weary ex-con sees a maintenance man sweeping the walkway in front of the building. She asks him if there are any openings. He tells her no. Frustrated, she grabs his broom and starts sweeping anyway. The man takes it back and shoos her away.

Trudging down the street, she's beginning to feel tired and completely bereft of hope. She sees a "Help Wanted" sign in a pet shop window. Taking a deep breath, she walks into the store. Reaching for the door's handle, she looks into the window again and sees someone remove the "Help Wanted" sign. The sky suddenly darkens ominously.

Sitting on a park bench with pen in hand, she flips through the classified section of the Mill Creek News. She crosses out an entry, then another, then another, then another. Frustrated, she scratches holes in the newspaper, crumples it into a ball, and throws it on the grass. Mere seconds later, a park employee on a bicycle pulls up and orders her to pick up her mess.

Ingrid steps wearily into her room in Motel 6 and kicks off her shoes and flicks the air conditioner on. Lying in the bed, she twists herself in the covers and cries herself to sleep.

Chapter V

It's Getting Late

Sheriff Lee Thompson and his wife, Audrey, both in their late forties, are eating dinner in the kitchen of their small Mill Creek home on the outskirts of town. Size wise, they are akin to Jack Sprat and wife. One is skinny, the other not so much. The kitchen itself is decorated in fifties Americana, complete with red and white checkerboard tablecloth, place settings, and curtains. There's a third place-setting of Viennese pot roast and cannellini beans, but no one is sitting at it. Lee glances at the Felix the Cat wall clock above the stove.

"Where's Houston? His dinner's getting cold."

"He'll be down in a minute," Audrey guesses. "You know how teens are, can't break them away from a computer."

"Still, I don't like it when he's late."

"The guy's not exactly Road Runner."

"Please, Audrey. Stop saying that. He might be a little slow now, but he'll improve."

Audrey shrugs, picks up her bowl of lobster bisque soup, and takes a noisy sip. "This is good."

"You know," Lee observes, "we have spoons in the strainer."

"Don't make fun of me, Lee."

"And what happened to that grapefruit diet you're supposed to be on?"

"Are you gonna start with me tonight, Lee?"

"I'm still trying to figure out how you got to be so big. I close my eyes for one second and you turn into Free Willy overnight.

Audrey motions for her husband to shut his trap. He waves her off. She finishes her bisque. "This soup is good," she admits, stretching, "but I have to get some air."

Getting up, she leaves the table and goes outside through the kitchen door. Houston, their thin pimply-faced seventeen year old son with scraggly brown hair and glasses enters. He sees Audrey standing at the door.

"Where's mom?" he asks.

"Outside," Lee answers. "Sit down and eat."

"I'm not hungry."

"Your mother went through this trouble nuking this stuff."

"I'm not hungry."

"Then pack it in a box and ship it to the homeless."

Audrey reenters the kitchen. Lee takes his seat at the table. Audrey ladles out some more soup from a pot for herself then sits down at the table. She resumes eating. Houston also digs in.

A pressing silence falls between the three of them. It is interrupted solely by the chapping sounds Audrey produces. Lee takes a sip of wine.

"The Werner girl is back in town," he offers. "She dropped by the station today. Poor thing never visited their gravesite until now."

"It's tragic to lose both parents at once," Audrey admits.

"What Werner girl?" Houston asks. "How'd her parents die?"

"She was a friend of ours," Lee explains. "Her folks died in a car crash."

"Didn't she go to their funeral?" Houston wonders.

"Rumor had it she was in prison," Audrey states. "I don't know."

"That's what *your* bridge buddies say," Lee tells her. "Hey, aren't you and your girls looking for a coach for your little exercise club?"

"She's a coach?"

"She's in good shape. Maybe she can teach you guys some stuff. Plus, I think she needs the money."

"Where's she staying?"

"The Motel 6."

Audrey eyes her husband with suspicion, curious he would know so much about Ingrid's affairs.

***

Early the next morning, Ingrid is strolling towards her motel suite carrying a stack of newspapers. Thankfully, the heat wave that overpowered some parts of the Pacific Northwest has finally abated. Taking advantage of the cool weather, she'd gone jogging in a V-neck tee shirt and Bermuda shorts combo.

As she walks up the street, Marty Seligman, a short, balding man in his early forties wearing a gaudy pinstripe suit, pulls up alongside her in his black late model BMW.

"Hey," he asks, rolling his window down, "don't I know you?"

She studies him momentarily, then resumes her walk towards the motel. He cruises alongside her at an easy pace. "You're new in town, ain't you? Wanna lift?"

"No, thanks."

"The name's Marty. What do I call you?"

"You don't."

Ingrid approaches her motel room, places the papers by her feet, and looks for the keys in her pocket. She doesn't find them.

"Shoot," she curses.

Marty parks his car in the lot and ambles over.

"What's the matter?" he asks. "Lost your keys?"

"You're taking a big chance, you know that? I could call the police."

He casually leans on the wall right beside her and takes out his cell phone.

"I can call you one."

Shaking her head, she finally locates her keys in her bag. Removing them, she sticks one in the door. It clicks open. Just then Audrey pulls up in her station wagon.

"Hey, Marty," Audrey shouts, "getting acquainted with the new arrival already? That was fast."

Marty starts walking towards his car. Ingrid picks up her newspapers and studies Audrey, trying to determine if she knows her. Seconds later, Marty gets into his car and takes off. Audrey parks her auto and walks over to Ingrid. "Good morning," Audrey greets her.

"Do I know you?"

"You're Ingrid Werner, right? My name's Audrey Thompson. My husband, Lee, is the Sheriff. I've got a proposition for you."

"Sure. Come in."

They enter the motel room. The TV is already on a news channel. Ingrid sits on a bed and Audrey grabs an easy chair.

"What can I do for you?" Ingrid asks, turning the TV's volume down by remote control.

"My bridge club might be interested in a few exercise lessons, if that's okay with you."

"Maybe. I'm kinda between jobs right now anyway. Want a drink? I have apple juice."

"Sure."

Ingrid gets up and gets a bottle of juice for each of them.

"Thanks," Audrey nods. "So when can you start?"

"I have a few places to check out this morning. How about this afternoon? Is that too soon?"

"That's fine. We practice aerobics in the high school gym?

"High school?"

It's okay. The basketball team is playing off campus today and the school is pretty community friendly."

Later that afternoon, after filling in a few applications in local stores, Ingrid meets up with Audrey at Henry Jackson High School's indoor basketball court. Set up as an aerobics gym, there are four large padded gymnastics mats scattered on the polished floor. Several other pieces of gear such as step platforms, exercise balls, dumbbells, toning bars and rings are lying next to the mats. A radio blasting high energy dance music is on.

Audrey's three friends enter as Ingrid prepares her lesson. The ladies, ranging from curvy to overweight, walk over to the mat area.

"Ingrid," Audrey begins, "meet Corky, Lorin, and Kyle, the best bridge buddies money can buy."

The ladies shake hands. Ingrid places her hands on her hips.

"Shall we start?"

Within minutes, all five ladies are sweating, huffing, and puffing to Ingrid's rigorous training regimen. Corky attempts to give up, but Lorin's encouragement keeps her in the game. Kyle has a hard time keeping in tempo with the music. Ingrid teaches her simpler variations of the rhythmic movements. Audrey falls flat on her abdomen in the midst of pushups. Her friends gather around her and offer to help her but she insists on doing it herself. Lorin has difficulty kicking her legs up. She also often falls out of step with Ingrid's synchronized pace when her right leg develops a cramp.

Kyle, ripping the seat of her leotard open when she bends forward too deeply, gets angry when Corky laughs at her. Corky later nearly kills herself attempting a split. Eventually, the ladies get so worn out they simply fall flat on their backs. Ingrid turns the music down.

"See?" she informs them, wiping her brow. "It's harder than you think. Next time I'll go a little easier on you."

"Next time," Lorin warns, catching her breath, "just bring some body bags."

Hours later, Ingrid, toting a boombox, is climbing up the stairs to the porch of the Thompson household. Ringing the bell, she turns and takes a quick survey of the area. All is calm, blissfully calm. Seagulls are flying overhead in their honest search for donated vittles. The suburban homes, separated by quiet acreage, sit like a portrait in a jigsaw puzzle.

As she moved to ring the bell again, Lee suddenly opens the front door. He smiles broadly when he sees her. "Hey, Ingrid. Nice to see you again."

"Hey, Lee."

"What brings you over?"

She shows him the radio. "This is Audrey's. She let us use it for our aerobic sessions."

"Actually, it's Houston's. That's my son. Thanks." Lee takes the radio. Ingrid turns to leave.

"See ya later," she waves.

"Oh, wait," Lee interjects, "you wanna come inside, have some coffee or something? Don't worry. I don't bite."

"Uh, yeah, sure."

They walk in. "Have a seat," Lee tells her.

She nods and sits in an easy chair. Lee enters the kitchen to prepare the coffee. Ingrid takes a quick gander around the room. There are dozens of photographs of the Thompson family on the walls and on the mantel above the fireplace. The furniture, all beset with floral designs, betrays Audrey's ubiquitous touch. After a few minutes, Lee re-enters with two steaming cups of coffee.

"Thank you." She sips it. It's so hot it nearly burns her lips. "Ouch."

"Sorry," he apologizes. "Our microwave's new. I'm just getting used to the settings myself."

"Where's Audrey?"

"Out with her bridge buddies. Houston's somewhere cutting up with his friends."

"I'm jealous," she remarks.

"Of what?"

"Of people with homes like these. Like this. It's been a while since I've been ... domiciled."

"Where did you go when you left Mill Creek?"

She shrugs. "I traveled, you know, spread my wings. Went to school in Spokane. I just wanted to get out. After a while, I kinda settled in Seattle."

"What did you do in Seattle? I take it you never got married."

"Never had the time. Really, I mainly got into a lot of trouble."

"What kind of trouble?"

Ingrid places the coffee cup down. "I think I should go." She stands up. Lee does the same.

"I'm sorry. Did I say something wrong?"

"No, it's not you. Just that they are a lot of things on my mind. I'm okay.

"Do you need a ride back to the motel?"

"Hey, I never refused a police escort, even when I wanted to."

About a half hour later, the two are taking a leisurely stroll down Seattle Hill Road, one of the main drags through Mill Creek. Lee points out the new developments to Ingrid. She takes it all in stride.

"The place has changed a lot, huh?" she asks. "The Town Center, the library … all renovated. A lot of the restaurants are new, though. Demographics have changed a lot, too. A lot more Asians moved in because of Microsoft."

Ingrid sighs. "I missed this place."

They make a right on Village Green Drive.

"You know," she mentions, "when I was a kid, I had this stupid dream of being the first winner of the Tchaikovsky Piano competition from Mill Creek, Washington. I saw myself taking a bow on stage, and people are just applauding with all their might in all corners of the auditorium. I'd look over to my left and see my teacher with tears in her eyes."

"Do you still play?"

"When I get a chance. When I was growing up everything was centered around the golf course. Music was just a minor distraction. We definitely weren't one of the rich ones."

"Sounds like you had a run of bad luck. That's too bad. A pretty woman like you should have permanent company, you know what I mean?"

They walk past a jasmine tree in full bloom. Lee takes a deep breath. "Smell that? Jasmine. Nothing like it in the world."

"Yeah," Ingrid agrees. She checks her watch. "It's getting late."

"Self imposed curfew, huh?"

"I'm just a little tired. It's been a full day."

"Come on. Let's go."

Minutes later, Ingrid is rotating the key in her door. Lee is at her side. The door opens.

"Well, see you tomorrow or some other time," she promises. I'm worn out."

As she turns to walk in, Lee gently massages her shoulders. "You are tense," he notices.

Slowly, he works his way up her neck and massages behind her ears.

"L-Lee," she stutters.

He whispers in her ears. "When was the last time you were with a man?"

"I ..."

"Maybe I should go. Do you want me to go?"

"Audrey ..."

"Ancient history, Ingrid. It's become a marriage of convenience."

He releases her. "I think I should go."

"No, wait," she turns to face him. "I can't stand being alone."

Lee nods. "We'd better go in before we get noticed."

They enter the room, locking the door behind them. Like hormonal teens, they tear each other's clothes off. Within seconds they're naked in bed, writhing around like snakes in a pit of mice. Soon, the mirror over the bureau gets steamed over. The blanket slips to the floor. Ingrid moans nearly as loud as a freight train. Passionately, she digs her nails into Lee's back. Gasping, he arches upward and catches a glimpse of a faceless silhouette darting away from the window above the bed.

Chapter VI

Take It for a Spin

Ingrid is palpating fresh fruits at an outdoor greengrocer's stand the following morning. Bustling with activity, she seems overwhelmed by the varied selection at her disposal. One of the workers, Houston, comes over to assist her. "Can I help you?"

"Yes. I need a bag for these bananas."

He rips off a baggie from a roll to Ingrid's left and hands it to her.

"Thanks. I didn't see it there."

"You're new in town, ain't ya?"

She shakes her head. "Can't keep a secret in this town."

"Why'd you come here? This town sucks."

"It's not so bad."

"My name's Houston."

"Oh, *you're* Houston. I know your folks. Thanks for letting me use your radio."

"You're pretty."

"How old are you?"

"Seventeen and three fourths."

"Jailbait."

She continues shopping.

"Are you here with your husband?"

"You're beating around the bush, Houston. Why don't you just come out and ask me if I'm available?"

"Are you?"

"Slow down, Flash. You move too fast and you're way too young. No, I'm not married."

"Do you live here in town? Where are you staying?"

"Why should I tell you?"

"Because you want to."

She looks at him, completely taken aback by his forthrightness. "Motel 6. Why?"

"Just curious. How can you sleep in that blighted dump."

"Don't believe the rumors just because it's the cheapest. It can be a little noisy, though. In any case, I sleep like a rock. You could pull my hair out by the roots when I'm snoring and I won't feel it."

Just then, Lee drives by in his patrol car. Houston waves hello. Ingrid nods in acknowledgement. Lee drives off.

"Your father's a hard worker."

Houston rubs his chin. "When he wants to be."

Strolling through a small car dealership on Bothell Everett Highway in Mill Creek a few hours later, Ingrid is looking at a handful of used cars. She's wearing a frilly pink long sleeve shirt with padded shoulders, pleated black bellbottom pants, and flat black shoes. The salesman approaches. "Howdy, gorgeous," he greets her. "Looks like you're all ready for a Woodstock Festival." He commences playing air guitar. She groans. Seeing she's unimpressed, he kills the mime. "I'm just playing. My name's Marty Seligman, but you can call me Marty."

"Ingrid Werner."

"How can I help you this fine effervescent day?"

"I need something cheap that runs. And it can't be a gas guzzler."

"Well, let's see ... I've got a Chevette for two thousand."

"Too expensive."

"What are you looking to spend?"

"I don't know. I guess about seven hundred."

"Shoot. You might as well buy a skateboard."

"Har har. I just want something reliable. It's been a while since I've been behind the wheel."

"Tell you what. I'm fixing a 10 year old Volkswagen as we speak. It's in all right shape. Just needs a new windshield and a radiator. Come back tonight around eight or nine. I'll have it fixed by then."

"Tonight? Who looks at cars at night?"

"If you're rusty, you can take it for a spin without anyone noticing."

"I guess."

"Good. Follow me. I'll show you."

They walk to a different section where she sees a red Volkswagen, minus its windshield. Its body, though basically intact, has a dents throughout.

"You like?"

Ingrid peeks inside the windows. "At least it's clean. 8 o'clock, did you say?"

"Better make it nine. These German cars aren't all that easy to service."

At 9p.m., Ingrid enters Marty's used car emporium sipping bottled water. The lot is as quiet as a grave. A soft leather purse is tucked beneath her arm. She walks over to the Volkswagen. It looks like it hasn't been touched. The windshield is still out. An open toolbox is on the hood. Suddenly, she gets a sharp pain in her head.

"Man," she winces. "I hate these headaches." She checks her watch.

"C'mon, Marty. Where are you? Geez, my skull feels like it's gonna explode." She takes out the small brown bottle of Numbutol from her pocket, washes one down with the bottled water then returns it to her pocket. Turning to leave, she gasps as she's startled by Marty standing there. Eschewing his typical business suit, he's dressed casually in a black pants and light blue shirt.

"Evening, Ingrid."

"What are you? Walking on air?"

"Sorry. I thought you heard me."

"You didn't work on the car. I came out here for nothing."

"The car's not worth the headaches. It'll be too expensive in the long run. I have a Mercedes for you."

"Really? What's the catch?"

"Why does everybody think there's a catch? I swear, the public puts car salesmen just one notch above serial killer. Consider the car a loaner 'til you build up your finances. Come inside. I have some papers for you to sign."

"Where's the Mercedes?"

"This way."

Marty closes the toolbox and picks it up. Ingrid follows him to a distant part of the lot where she sees a fifteen year old gray Mercedes Benz in relatively good shape.

"Check it out," Marty tells her.

She opens the driver side door and checks the instrument panel, seats, ceiling lights and other areas. "Hmm," she admits. "Seems okay."

"It's better than okay. It's a dream machine."

He brings a set of keys out of his pocket and hands it to her. "Take it for a spin."

Ingrid bites her lip and accepts the keys.

"I'm glad we're doing this at night."

The two go for a quick ride around the lot then drive up and down a few local roads. Minutes later, Ingrid is sitting in a soft chair perusing a magazine in the dealership's main office. Marty is at his desk drawing up papers. The Mercedes Benz's keys are next to the toolbox on the desk. A sixties rock tune is playing softly from ceiling speakers..

"You always have customers in your office this late?" Ingrid says.

"Just the special ones. Relax. You look tense."

"I'm fine."

He abandons his paperwork, opens the bottom drawer of his desk, and produces a bottle of wine with two glasses.

"This," he promises, "will take some of the edge off."

"Um, maybe I shouldn't."

"You insult my friendship. I'm doing you a big favor. That car is worth a lot more than the sticker price." He opens the bottle, pours out two glasses, and brings one over to Ingrid.

"How many people give away cars for a song these days?" he asks.

She swirls her glass of wine. "Thanks, but just this one."

"Good. I like an appreciative customer."

They toast then drink. She coughs a little. "Strong," she notices.

He downs his in one gulp. "Swig it, "he suggests. "Won't burn as much."

Complying, she drinks the rest of hers. He refills both their glasses then returns to his seat.

"Are you feeling it yet?" he asks.

"I really shouldn't be doing this."

"I hope you don't think I'm forcing you."

She shakes her head and takes a sip. This time she doesn't cough.

"Better, huh?" Marty boasts.

"Yeah, but I'm sorry. I've gotta go."

She gets up. Marty rises and walks over to her. Listen, Ingrid. Don't play coy with me. I know your story. I know why girls like you come back here. You're not the first. You're in trouble."

She gets a burst of sarcasm. "Not only is he a salesman, he's also a psychic."

"Why else would you be here?" he asks. "You're experienced. You know the drill. Take care of me, and I'll take care of you."

She stares at him. "You're crazy. That's the liquor talking."

He picks up the keys to the Mercedes. "Do you want these or not?"

"Marty, do you want the truth? I just got out of jail, found out my folks are dead, can't find a job, can't afford an apartment, and can barely rub two nickels together, so stop trying to buy me."

"Easy, Ingrid. Easy. I'd love to take the blame, but none of that was my fault. Listen, Ingrid. I'm a gambling man. There's no shame in it. I'll bet you can't afford to get into *any* kind of trouble. You probably can't even get caught spitting on the sidewalk."

She takes a healthy swig of the wine and finishes the glass. "You don't know a thing about me.".

"I know that anybody starting over in life could use a little help."

She reaches for the bottle of wine. "Gimme that." Pouring herself a drink, she takes another long swig.

"You drink like a fish," he observes.

"This one's for the road," she extols.

Turning to leave, she suddenly staggers. Marty rushes to her assistance. He catches her just as she blacks out.

Hours later, Ingrid, completely naked, awakens groggily in the near darkness of the dealership's rear office.

"Oh, my head," she moans as she regains consciousness. Rising to her feet, she looks for her clothes.

"Where am I?" whispers. "Marty? Are you here?"

Accidentally stepping on clothes, she picks them up and dons the pants and shirt. They fit a little loosely but she's too woozy to care. Walking a little further, she sees Marty's supine silhouette on the floor.

"Marty?"

She kicks him gently. "Hey, sleepy head," she asks, "where'd you put my clothes?"

He doesn't answer or stir. "Come on," she coaxes. "Stop playing around. Where are my shoes and my purse?" Marty doesn't answer. She nudges him again. "Marty, you drunk nut." She gropes for the light switch on the wall, flicks it on, and immediately notices blood on her hands.

"What the hell?"

Then, whipping around, she sees Marty and gasps. Dressed in her clothes, he's covered in blood. His hands are clutched around a long stemmed screwdriver sticking out of his stomach. His eyes are wide open. Women's makeup is grotesquely applied to his shocked visage.

"Omigod, omigod, omigod," Ingrid keeps repeating.

She runs to an adjacent bathroom and washes her hands. Using wet paper towels, she wipes the blood off her clothes, flushes them down the toilet, then wets more paper towels, rushes back into the rear office, cleans the blood off the 'on and off' switch and other places she touched, and pockets the towel.

She sees her keys on the floor by her handbag next to Marty. Nervously grabbing the keys and purse, she backs up to the door knob, jiggles it open, and flushes the bloody paper towels in the bathroom.

Walking through the darkened dealership, she notices the toolbox on the desk is wide open. Accidentally, stubbing her toes on a wastepaper basket, she limps in pain to the front door.

Pulling the handle, she soon realizes it's locked. Looking around, she eyes a side exit, hobbles to it, and pushes the door open. Poking her head out, she looks left, right, and center, then sneaks out to the parking lot. She limps on the hard gravelly surface to the lot's exit. Stopping by the sidewalk, she looks up and down the Bothell Everett

Highway. A few cars zoom past. Just then, she sees a flash of lightning. Seconds later, there is a loud thunderclap. It starts raining.

Dipping her hands in her pocket, she's pleasantly surprised to find a set of car keys there. Hobbling quickly back through the lot, she spots the gray Mercedes. Without hesitation, she opens the door, gets in, starts the engine, and drives out of the lot. Minutes later, she parks the car a block away from the Motel 6, gets out, uses her shirt to wipe her fingerprints off the latch then hobbles to the motel.

Passing by a janitor's cart in a nook of the building, she takes a large garbage bag and heads to her room. Once inside, she quickly changes into her own dry clothes, stuffs Marty's wet ones in the bag, drapes a jacket over her head, and exits the motel.

She walks casually down a quiet block and sees a dumpster in an alley. The rain, she notices, has abated. Carefully tiptoeing into the alley, she drops the plastic bag into the smelly bin. An albino raccoon startles her when it suddenly leaps noisily out of the dumpster. She hotfoots it out of the alley. Coming back to her room, she breathes a sigh of relief. As she prepares for bed, she stands transfixed when she hears a police siren. Seconds later, it leaves. She walks to the fridge and grabs a bottle of water. Her hand has a slight nervous quake.

She opens the bottle, takes a swig, puts on the TV and jumps into bed. Seconds later, she's in dreamland.

Chapter VII

There are Better Choices

Ingrid is in the same position in bed as the night before. The morning sun is peeking in through the blinds. Blackbirds can be heard singing just outside the window. There's a knock on the door. Ingrid doesn't stir. The knocking is louder second time around. She wearily rolls over to one side.

"Just a minute."

Getting up, she goes to the bathroom, splashes water on her face and hands, gargles with mouthwash, walks back out to the main room, and opens the door. A man is standing there with his back to the entrance. He has a leather attaché case in his hand.

"Beautiful morning, isn't it, Miss Werner?" He turns and faces her.

Ingrid stares curiously at the gentleman. Conservatively attired, he almost has an air of Richard Chamberlain or James Bond sophistication.

"Who are you?" she asks.

"I'm James Levanon, realtor. Can I come in?"

"A realtor? Who sent you here?"

"Corky's my wife. She told me you might be interested in housing assistance."

"Yeah, I am."

"Today's your lucky day, Ms. Werner. But before we get down to brass tacks, you look like you can use a little caffeine."

"You read me like a book."

"You know, your parents, Howie and Gertie, were good friends of mine."

"You knew my folks?"

"Howie officiated at my son's bar mitzvah."

"He did? That's weird. I didn't know he could do that. Okay. Hold on." She goes back inside and closes the door. James paces back and forth, checking his watch a few times. She reemerges shortly with a full change of clothes.

"That was quick," James remarks.

"I'm a fast dresser."

He eyes her briefly from head to foot and notices she's wearing bedroom slippers instead of shoes.

"My corns are killing me today," she apologizes.

The two go for a walk on a relatively sparse downtown street. Ingrid is having a particularly hard time with the awkward slippers.

"It must be hard for an athletic aerobics person like you to walk comfortably in those."

Ingrid nods.

They walk into a coffee shop and take seats at a small table. Ingrid orders scrambled eggs and sausage. James orders a toasted sesame bagel with cream cheese. After the waitress leaves to place the order, James opens his attaché on the table and produces some legal papers.

"What's this?" Ingrid asks.

"You parents never had time to prepare a will. The house on Village Green Drive belongs to you because you're next of kin. Actually, you're the only kin. Have you seen it? It's boarded up now."

"Why is that?"

"Kids used to throw rocks through the windows and go in there and have sex parties. They trashed the placed, left cans and bottles everywhere."

He shows her some pictures of the vandalism. "Still, the house is actually livable," he concludes. "As the executor and trustee of your father's estate, I had the electric company turn the lights on yesterday."

"Why?"

"'Cause you came back to town. Seemed logical."

He hands her some legal papers. "Just sign these and take 'em with you to the Sheriff's Office. They'll un-board the house and maybe even probably help you fix it up. Oh, in case I forget …" He reaches into his pocket and gives her a key, "this is yours. I have another, but I need entry to do some structural maintenance."

She nods and takes the key. "Thanks for everything."

She moans slightly and grabs her head.

"Are you okay?" James asks.

"I don't know. I get these constant migraines. No matter what I try, they won't go away."

"I have this friend who's a clinical neuropsychologist over at Swedish. He also has a private practice. I'm sure he can recommend something." He writes down his number on the back of a business card and hands it to her. "He takes all kinds of insurance," he adds.

"Thanks. Will he be able to see me this week?"

"If I call him he can see you today."

"Cool."

She reads the name on back of the card. "Dr. Kasper Kovalyov?"

It's not too long before Ingrid is sitting in the office of Dr. Kasper Kovalyov's sterile, but comfortable office. Hundreds of books and several oil paintings adorn each wall. Lace curtains cover the large windows. Dr. Kovalyov, a Russian émigré in his late forties with matching salt and pepper hair and beard, is sitting at his desk scribbling notes on a legal pad as Ingrid dictates her story.

"I was born here thirty-four years ago. Everything was normal until I was 13."

"Go on," he tells her. "Don't be afraid. Everything you tell me stays between us. No one will know. Everything is confidential."

"Like confessing to a priest."

"Yes, but without all the Hail Mary's and Our Father penances."

"Well, when I was thirteen, I stabbed a man who tried to rape me."

"How tragic. Did he die?"

"I never saw him after that, so I guess yes. That was followed by five years of reform school, though."

"For killing a man in self defense?"

"For behavior not become of an adolescent. Actually, after that, I became belligerent. School was like poison to me. My grades plummeted. I got into trouble. You couldn't tell me anything because I shut the world out. They had to send me away."

"Too bad."

"Yeah. Takes its toll. I had a good job, but then things fell apart. Ended up working the streets. Got two to six in women's correctional.

They slapped me with a 3P charge: prostitution, possession, and pissing off an officer. Two bicycle cops surround me one night in the parking lot of a Chinese restaurant in the International District. An officer patted me down rudely. During the pat down, I thought the bastard was groping too far. I kneed him in the groin and socked him in the jaw. I gave him what he asked for."

***

Back in the clinical neuropsychologist's office, Kovalyov is trying to disguise his look of alarm. She notices it.

"Everybody prostitutes in one way or another," she insists. "Some people sell their humanity, some sell their hopes and dreams. I just sold what's between my legs. Ain't no shame in my game. You gotta do what you can to survive."

"There are better choices."

"Doctor, if everybody made the best choices you wouldn't be in business."

She takes a deep breath. "The reason I'm here," she continues, "is because I've been having these blackouts recently. They just come on suddenly."

"Are using illegal drugs?"

"No, just Numbutol for migraines."

"I'm sure your prison life was abusive; probably where your narcolepsy originated. It affects one in two thousand persons, but it is treatable. I can prescribe Methylphenidate. It usually works."

"Doc, it's not that I just fall asleep suddenly. Sometimes I wonder if I even walk in my sleep. I wake up and things have been moved around. I got a messed up life, huh?"

He looks at her paperwork on a clipboard. "Hm. Tell me about your childhood. How does it feel being Jewish and black?"

"How'm I supposed to feel? Mexicans and Filipinos are technically half-breeds. If they can handle it, so can I. Listen Doc, not to be rude, but I'm more concerned about this sleepwalking disorder."

"Sleepwalking is a typical parasomnia sleep disorder. However, it's not treatable. Just try to cut down on stimulants like alcohol."

Ingrid nods. Dr. Kovalyov peruses the notes in his legal pad. "I'll order a CAT scan for you."

"Doctor, you can order all the tests you want, but I can't pay for 'em. As it is I'm five minutes away from homeless. I do have my parent's house, but that'll take some time to fix."

"Hmm. If you want, and I know you don't know me that well, you can stay down at my cabin on Three Lakes. It's only about 15 miles northeast of here. You can stay there at least 'til they finish repairing your old house."

"I don't know."

"You'll like it. I call it Kasper's Retreat. It's nice. I sometimes let my clients use it for spiritual cleansing. It's okay. I'll take you down there one day."

She nods, but the doctor can still see the look of concern on her face.

Later that day, Ingrid, now in leotards, enters the empty high school basketball court and looks at the circular clock up on a wall above the bleachers. It reads 4:05. She struts like a member of the Seattle Storm to the middle of the court and picks up a basketball. Dribbling it like point guard Sue Bird, she cuts through an imaginary defense, jumps, and shoots. The ball swishes through the net. Someone claps. She turns and sees Audrey approaching.

"I didn't know you played," Audrey smiles. "I'm impressed."

"Where's everybody?"

"Didn't you hear?"

"Hear what?"

"Kyle's husband committed suicide yesterday."

"He did? Wow. She must be taking it hard."

"They weren't close, but she's in shock. Yeah. He's been suicidal before, but Marty was a closet transvestite."

"His name was Marty?"

"Yep. Unbelievable, ain't it?"

"Too bad."

"Would you believe he stabbed himself in the belly with a screwdriver? It's the strangest thing. Nothing like that's ever happened here. The poor guy was so confused. Took his Victoria's Secret to the grave. Anyway, I just wanted to tell you the girls are suspending classes until this affair's over."

Ingrid nods her understanding.

"I know it doesn't pay much," Audrey suggests, "but they always need help down at the Farmer's Market or Town Center."

"Right about now I'd scrub this floor with a toothbrush for cash."

About an hour later, Ingrid is plucking weeds out in the front yard of her old home while Lee and Houston remove the windows' large boards. Lee is up on a ladder with a crowbar; Houston is steadying it below, but his focus is more on Ingrid. He glances at her often. Suddenly losing his focus, he unconsciously releases his grip on the ladder. A strong gust of wind causes the ladder to wobble.

"Keep it steady, will ya?" Lee shouts.

Houston steadies the ladder but continues gazing at Ingrid. Seconds later, another gust of wind shakes the ladder. Lee nearly falls off. Looking down, he sees Houston's attention is elsewhere. "Dammit, Houston," he yells again. "Hold the ladder."

"Yes, sir."

The distracted teenager steadies the ladder.

"Looks like you boys are having all the fun," Ingrid snickers.

"Yeah, we are," Houston admits. "Wanna join us?"

"You just keep the ladder steady," his father warns.

Lee turns to Ingrid. "Won't be long now."

After working outside, the three enter the house and survey what's left of the Werners' possession. Most of the furniture has been damaged by vandalism. Every curtain is ripped to shreds. The floors and walls are so dusty or moldy that they seem to have a life of their own. Cobwebs hang in almost every visible corner. The large oak entertainment console against a wall is smashed in. Several large holes are in the walls.

"It's worse than I thought," Ingrid observes. "I'm glad the light works at least."

"They should've boarded it up sooner," Lee laments. "I apologize for this mess."

"What're you gonna do now?" Houston asks.

Ingrid shakes her head.

"I'll think of something. Maybe I'll list it with the realtor."

"You won't get a good price," Lee advises her. "It's in bad shape."

"I know. I can't afford to fix this," Ingrid moans. "I don't even know where to start." She places her hands on her hips, looks around the room again, and sighs deeply.

After going through the house and making a mental inventory, Lee and Houston decide it was time to leave. They walk out to the front steps. Ingrid stays on the porch.

"I'm sorry to leave so soon," Lee tells her, "but we're in the middle of an investigation, and I have to get Houston home before his mother throws a fit."

"No, she won't," the young man protests.

"Hush," his father orders him.

"See y'all later," Ingrid waves and breathes a heavy sigh and returns to the house.

Walking to the kitchen, she opens the refrigerator. As hot as a desert, it is also empty, save for an opened box of baking soda and severely old leftovers. "Ugh," she says wincing.

She eyes the small metal gray door to the fuse box sitting in a wall. Walking over, she pulls it open. Dust flies out. When the air clears, she flicks on the breakers that were off. The refrigerator purrs to life.

Walking into the cluttered master bedroom room, she walks over to an old chest of drawers. Rifling through her parents bureau, she finds a few old clothes, pens, and an old hair dryer. Opening the closet, she sees a cache of old ripped clothes dangling from hangers. There are several pairs of old shoes, some of them torn. Grabbing a chair, she brings it to the closet, stands on it, reaches up above a shelf, thrusts her hand into a small hole, and retrieves a black pouch. Jumping off the chair, she blows dust off the pouch, unzips it, and removes her vintage 2twenty year old red haired rag doll still in mint condition.

"Still here after all these years," she whispers. "I'll bet a classic like you must be worth a fortune now."

The large old chandelier in the ceiling falls suddenly, missing her by mere inches. She screams and jumps back, watching as it swings back and forth before her like an ominous pendulum.

"That was too close." Slowly, she backs out of the room and shuts the door.

Chapter VIII

This is Beautiful

Ingrid, in a greengrocer's apron, is using a squeeze bottle to mist the fruits on the stands in the Farmer's Market the next morning. Houston is down the aisle packing fruits from boxes into their respective places on the stands. Mainly, he's paying more attention to Ingrid than his work. Accidentally, he knocks a stack of oranges off their stand. Ingrid hikes over and helps him pick up the citrus fruits. An ear to ear smile develops on his embarrassed face.

"How do you like working here so far?" he asks.

"It's okay. At least it's not like some inner city jungle gym where you have to watch your back all the time."

"It can get a little rowdy sometimes."

Just then, her cell phone rings. "Excuse me," she tells Houston before walking just outside of the market.

"Hello. Oh, hey, doctor … about 4 O'clock ... uh, huh ... nah, it's too run down, good only for termites ... 4:30? Yeah. Bye. Thanks, doctor."

It is now 5p.m.. The rat race for some is finally over. The clock has been punched, the foreman saluted, and the engines revved. There's no going back once the gears of freedom have turned.

A car is making its way up the long, winding country boulevard that's 3 Lakes Road in Northern Snohomish County. Just northeast of downtown Mill Creek, the landscape is dotted by rural homes, tiny mom and pop stores, and a forest so dense only a cannonball could penetrate it.

Dr. Kovalyov is at the wheel. Ingrid is in the passenger seat fiddling with the radio. After tuning it a classic rock station, she stares down the desolate road.

"Wow. It's farther than I thought."

"Do you wish to go back?" he asks.

"No. I guess I can hang there for a while."

"Don't worry. If your phone dies, there's a phone there. The people are pretty friendly. Anyone of them would be glad to give you a ride back to Mill Creek."

"What are the three lakes in Three Lakes?"

"Panther Lake, Flowing Lake and Storm Lake."

"Cute."

"I knew that from a pamphlet. The cabin is at Panther Lake."

"They have panthers running around out there?"

"I don't know why they call it that."

"What about your wife?"

"Lorin? What about her?"

"Won't she mind, you know, you bringing me up here?"

"Don't worry. This is purely business. If I had no patients, she'd have no home."

Ingrid shrugs and continues listening to the radio. Minutes later, Dr. Kovalyov parks his BMW by the side of a wooden cottage nestled in the lushly picturesque forest near the lake. A few yards away sits an old wooden lean-to almost completely covered with vines.

The two walk towards the front of the cottage. Ingrid is carrying a small basket of fresh fruits and a suitcase. Laying the suitcase and fruits on the ground, she gazes at the wide, misty lake. "This is beautiful."

"Peaceful, isn't it?"

"Absolutely," she nods. "I could live out here forever."

"Jenna likes it, too."

"Who's that?"

She brings out her red haired doll and shows it to the doctor. "She was my only friend when I was growing up." She sits the doll on a chair on the porch.

"I'm a romantic myself," Kovalyov insists, "but I wouldn't wish isolation all year 'round."

"At least you have a car, so it's not so bad."

The doctor tries his key in the front door. Unfortunately, it is rusted shut and it won't budge. *"Chyort voz'mi,"* he shouts. "Let's check the back."

She picks up the basket of fruit and her suitcase and they walk towards the back entrance where, on the porch, she sees an old plastic chair, a shovel, a plastic pail, an old circular wooden wheel for a boat, and a plastic crate filled with boating supplies. She also sees a rope dangling from the back porch's ceiling and reaches for it.

"What's this?" she asks.

"Something I picked up in an antique store. Pull it."

She does. A delicate chime attached to it goes off. "Cute. Why is it on the back door?"

"Thick headed me. I forgot the front door doesn't open. It serves as a doorbell."

Nearly 15 miles away, Audrey, Corky, and Lorin are sitting at a bridge table with their friend, Kyle Seligman. There's a palpable pall over the room as misery floats like an unwanted ghost around them. Lorin turns to Kyle.

"Are you gonna bid?"

Kyle, though, is lost in thought. "Huh?"

Corky speaks up. "Are you going to bid?"

"I'm sorry, ladies," Kyle apologizes. "I don't feel like playing tonight." She lays her hand down. "Count me out."

"We can't play without you," Audrey insists.

"Come on, Kyle," Lorin agrees. "It'll keep your mind off Marty for a while."

"Oh, Lorin, he was a goddamn bum," Kyle explodes.

Stunned, the other ladies look at each other.

"They say he was one a cross dresser," Kyle muses. "Can you believe that? I married a freak? I don't know. Something fishy's going on."

She turns to Audrey. "Didn't your husband learn anything yet?"

"He's working on it."

"Well," Kyle pounds the table, "tell him to work harder."

"Don't boss me around because you can't please your husband."

"What?" Kyle shouts. She leaps to her feet, her eyes filled with rage.

"Sorry, Kyle," Audrey laments. "I didn't mean—"

"Get out." Kyle points to the door.

"Take it easy, Kyle," Lorin suggests. "Audrey didn't mean anything. The four of us have been together too long for this kind of petty squabbling."

Kyle, however, isn't trying to hear any of it. "Out. I want all of you outta my goddamn house."

"Kyle," Corky crows. "This ain't the time to lose your head."

Kyle turns and grabs a decorative Civil War saber from a display case in the living room and brandishes it menacingly at the group. "Out, goddamn it," she orders them. "Don't make me do something I'm gonna regret."

The ladies get the hint. They rise and walk towards the front door. Lorin turns around and looks at Kyle. "You need our help desperately, yet you chase us out like dogs. Some friend you are."

"Out."

"I'm sorry, Kyle," Audrey worries, "but you're losing it."

Kyle's eyes light up like a glowing ball of brimstone. "Hah. Look who's talking. Lady Macbeth. You've spent so much time up in the psych ward I'm surprised you don't have a fucking lifetime membership card."

"What?" Audrey asks. "I was there for eating problems."

Kyle points the sword at her. "Every summer? Bullshit. You're the one that's a card short of a full deck." She throws the sword. It whizzes past Lorin's face and embeds in the wall near the front door. Lorin screams.

"She's crazy," Corky. "Let's get out of here."

"Get lost, you traitors." She grabs an ashtray and flings it out the open door at the trio. It narrowly misses them as they go down the walkway.

Taking a deep breath, she walks to the entrance, looks down the block, and sees her pals driving away. She then gazes at the hallmarks of suburbia: manicured hedges, functional street lights, and foreign late model cars sitting on the quiet street.

Walking back into the kitchen, she takes a bottle of Chablis out of the refrigerator and pours herself a glass. She sits at the table and drinks it in one gulp. Then, staring at the playing cards, she wipes them and her glass off the table in one movement.

Chapter IX

I Can Believe That

The loud warbling of Canadian geese awakens Ingrid from her deep sleep in Kasper's Retreat the next morning. Getting up, she drapes a soft terry robe around her, staggers into the small living room and accidentally kicks over an empty wine bottle. She picks it up and throws it in a waste basket. Walking across the room, she sees her crumpled underclothes scattered on the bear rug in front of the fireplace and picks them up.

"This is odd," she whispers.

Walking to the bedroom, she tosses her underclothes on the bed then walks out to the back porch. She spots the doctor's car and walks over to discover it is empty.

"Dr. Kovalyov," she shouts. "Are you here? Kasper?"

She walks to the edge of the lake and shouts for him. Again, there's no answer.

She dips her toes in the cool blue water then pulls them out quickly when she discovers the water is freezing cold. Returning to the cabin, she makes a pot of coffee, puts on the radio in the living room, and goes back to the bedroom.

Changing into street clothes, she looks for her shoes in the room. Not seeing them, she opens the closet. Dr. Kovalyov, as blue as topaz, falls suddenly out of the closet. Ingrid screams and jumps back.

Nervously, she turns him over on his back. Gazing at his naked corpse, she sees he's wearing grotesque makeup. His red lipstick, pinkish rouge, and black eyeliner have been applied haphazardly. He is also wearing a cheap pair of pearl earrings. The doorbell rope, she notices, is fastened tightly around his neck. The chime is stuffed in his mouth and his face has been scratched.

She walks to the living room and starts pacing back and forth. She picks up the phone and starts dialing a number. It rings five times then she hangs up. Jittery, she sits down and turns the TV on. Then, jumping up, she punches herself on both thighs.

"Damn these blackouts," she screams. "Gonna get me back in prison."

She races out of the cottage, grabs the old shovel from the porch, and dashes into the woods. Noticing an empty patch of earth amidst a secluded bevy of hawthorns, she drives the shovel in the ground. The blade, she discovers, is dull. Undaunted, she continues digging.

Minutes later, sweating buckets, she walks backwards out of the cabin dragging the body now wrapped in a blanket. Glancing over her shoulder, she continues pulling the corpse along the cold earth.

She drops the swaddled émigré into the freshly made grave, grabs the shovel, and fills the hole. When she's done, she covers the grave with branches and leaves so it looks.

Over Kovalyov's quiet study in his office, Sheriff Lee Thompson is scribbling notes in a pad while Lorin is sitting in a chair reading notes in one of her husband's journals.

"This is so unlike him," she attests. "He's never disappeared before. He's barely leaves home except for conventions and meetings.

"Or last year's Boys Night Out," Lee adds.

"Yeah. Your annual male bonding sessions."

"I didn't go. I had to work. When did you last see him?"

"Yesterday morning. Last night I was at with the girls."

"Yeah. Audrey told me Kyle went off the deep end,"

"She snapped like a twig."

"She's okay now," Lee nods. "I visited her first thing this morning. She's getting meds for her nerves. Don't you go losing your head."

Lorin picks up the phone on Kovalyov's desk and dials a number. After a few rings she hangs up.

"Still can't reach him, huh?" Lee asks.

"I've been calling the cabin all morning. Either the line's dead or he's out on a boat."

"Maybe he forgot to recharge his cell phone. I do that sometimes."

"He usually tells me when he's going out on the lake so I won't worry."

"Nothing goes on up at Three Lakes. I can check it out later."

"Thanks. It'll be okay. I think I'll start taking aerobics classes again. It's a good release of my tension. Maybe I'll call Ingrid for a private lesson later."

"Since she's moving back to her old house, she'll be up to her neck in dust for the next few days."

"I can believe that," Lorin nods.

Across town, James Levanon, realtor and Corky's husband, is on Ingrid's porch ringing the bell. Next to him are two gallons of latex paint, some brushes, rags, a box of trash can liners, a roll of cellophane tape, and a small LED TV.

Getting no answer, he takes out a large ring of keys, searches through them, finds the one he's looking for, sticks it in the lock, pushes the door open, and pokes his head in the front door.

"Miss Werner?" he asks. "Ingrid? Are you home?"

Grabbing all the items by his feet on the porch, he walks in, sets them on the dusty carpet, and closes the door. From what he can surmise, few attempts have been made to render the house more livable. He shakes his head.

"A charming house gone to waste."

As he starts dusting off a table, the bell rings. Opening the front door, he sees Houston, dressed in overalls and a bandana head wrap, standing there.

"Hello, young man," James greets him.

"Hi. Where's Miss Werner?"

"That's what I'm trying to find out. She's elusive, that one."

"I was gonna help her clean up the place."

"I don't know where she is right now."

Houston studies the realtor curiously. "Don't I know you from somewhere?" he asks. "You look familiar."

"Audrey's your mother, right? She and my wife, Corky, are bridge partners."

"Oh, yeah. I think we've met."

"I'm the trustee of this estate. I've got some painting supplies in the car. Mind getting them?"

"No."

James hands Houston a set of keys. "There might me some stuff in the basement, too."

"This house has no basement, not a functional one, anyway."

"Really? How come?"

"A few of the homes here don't. This one was designed like the Sears and Roebuck pre-fab houses. They literally hauled this in on a long bed and planted it here in the fifties. It was cheap, pre-built in the factory. Just right for the post world war rebuilding economy. They're not bad. I lived in one for years."

"Seems like they hold up pretty good."

Minutes later, James and Houston are drawing sweat as they sweep the floors, repair furniture, repair and wash the walls, restring the lights, dust and tidy the rooms, stuff garbage into large trash bags, and straighten out the kitchen cabinets and cupboards.

They also dust the tables, place the broken TV outside for the refuse truck, tape the broken windows with clear cellophane, replace the blinds, and paint the walls.

That evening, they stop to survey their work. The exterior of the house glistens with a new coat of white paint. Smiling, they shake hands. James takes out his wallet, peels out a $100 bill, and hands it to Houston.

I wasn't expecting to be paid," Houston admits.

"I know. Just showing my gratitude."

Houston pockets the money. "Thanks. Wait 'til Ingrid sees her house now."

"Yeah, but the question is, where is she?"

Ingrid is struggling up 3 Lakes Road with her suitcase in hand. Stopping for a moment, she sees the lights of a handful of businesses up ahead. Taking a deep breath, she continues marching.

A few steps up the road, lightning suddenly flashes across the sky, followed by an ominous rumble. Seconds later, it rains. Racing to the side of the road, she stands beneath a wide Japanese elm. The rain pours down even harder.

Back in Three Lakes, Sheriff Lee pulls up next to Kovalyov's BMW by his cabin. The rain is still coming down in torrents. He opens the doctor's car and examines it, checking under the seat and glove compartment for clues.

Releasing the back seat, he rummages through the trunk. After finding a few medical textbooks, a quart of motor oil, and a can of brake fluid, he puts them all back and returns the back seat to its upright position.

Walking to the edge of the lake, he scans left and right hoping to catch a glimpse of the neuropsychologist. All he sees are the drops of rain dancing on the lake like a water ballet.

Noticing the sky is starting to grow dark, he walks back to his squad car and removes a flashlight from the glove box. Flicking it on, he walks to the front of the cabin and tries the door. It doesn't open. He walks around the back and tries the rear door. It opens. Going in, he looks in all the rooms for a clue. He moves the furniture, checks under the bed, examines the closet, and helps himself to an apple from the refrigerator.

Walking outside, he scrutinizes the surroundings. The rain, he notices, has let up a little. He searches the shrubbery and nearby woods, climbing over fallen branches and sliding on wet leaves in his quest for an answer. Finding no sign of Kovalyov, he returns to the cabin, lights up a cigarette on the front porch, and takes a puff.

About an hour later, and the rain finally abating, Ingrid approaches her old house. She's astonished to find it has been repainted. The hedges have also been neatly trimmed and all the windows fully repaired.

Stepping in her refurbished abode, she closes the front door, lays her suitcase down, and throws the light switch on. Her jaw drops when she notices everything is clean, polished, and in place. She touches the fabric of the sofa, smells it, and smiles. Much attention, she realizes, was paid not only to its cleaning but to its restoration as well. A decorative blanket is draped over its back.

After marveling at the living room, she checks out the kitchen, then bedroom. A look of satisfaction fills her face. Exhausted from her walk, she peels off her wet top layer of clothes, dries herself, and falls backward on the bed. The doorbell rings.

She gets up, grabs a shirt from the closet, and walks to the front door. Sheriff Thompson is standing there in full uniform.

"Hey, Lee," she greets him. "How's it going?

"Sorry to bother you, Miss Werner. Will you come with me to the station?"

"Why so formal? You can come in."

"It's serious business, Ingrid. It's better if you came down to the station with me."

"Right now?"

He nods.

"Shoot. This had better be good."

Down at the South Precinct, Ingrid is sitting at a table in a small plain room. Lee walks in alone with a ledger and pen and sits opposite her. She pours some water in a paper cup from a pitcher on the table and takes a sip.

"Do you know why you're here?" he asks.

"You already told me. They're doing an investigation."

"Forensics did a lot of overtime matching fingerprints over at Marty's lot the night of his suicide."

"Okay. So why am I here?"

"Just routine. We're questioning everybody who was in the dealership that day. They did a positive match of your prints."

"I was there. I was looking at a used car."

"Which one?"

"A Volkswagen. I forgot the year."

"Then what happened?"

"Nothing. I left empty-handed."

"You didn't return that night?"

"Nope."

"Good." He holds her hands. "I knew you couldn't be involved in that."

"So you believe me?"

"Yeah. You could've asked for a lawyer to back you up. It shows innocence." Sheriff Thompson's beeper starts buzzing on his side.

"Excuse me."

He unclips it and looks at the number."It's Forensics. I'll be right back with a few releases for you to sign, then you can go."

After he exits, Ingrid takes another drink of water. She looks around the room, stares at the one-way mirror in the wall, and gazes at the floor. Moments later, Lee returns with two plainclothes officers, one larger than the other, but both in their late twenties.

"I'm sorry, Miss Werner," Lee explains, "but you're under arrest for the murder of Marty Seligman."

"What?" Aghast, she jumps up.

"You have the right to remain silent. Everything you say can and will be used against you in a court of law. Do you understand your rights?"

"Lee, go fuck yourself."

Chapter X

They Don't Scare Me

Corky, Lorin, and Kyle are grocery shopping at the farmer's market the following morning. All three are toting baskets already half-filled with foodstuffs. Kyle appears to be in much better spirits that yesterday. Not moping, she seems to be enjoying her friends' company.

They separate momentarily, then eventually convene at the butcher's stand. The shoppe is relatively empty, a fact that's not lost on Kyle. "I should go shopping on Sundays more," she tells her friends. "Look how quiet it is."

"I second that," Lorin agrees.

"Hey, there's one less person on the streets," Corky observes.

"Yeah," Kyle nods. "I told you guys something was up with Ingrid. I felt it in my bones."

Lorin tugs at Kyle's love handles. "Kyle, I'm surprised you can feel anything at all through this padding."

Kyle pushes Lorin's hand away. "You should talk," she retorts.

"Ladies," Lorin admonishes them, "I'm trying to be optimistic because Kasper's not back yet."

"Hope for the best," Kyle consoles her.

Corky suddenly spots Audrey up the aisle and calls out to her. "Hey Audrey."

The sheriff's wife comes over to the group carrying a basket containing a few canned items. "Hello, girls."

Audrey turns to Kyle. "Feeling better, yet? No knife throwing acts today, right?"

She crosses her heart. "I promise."

"Good, 'cause if I wanted knives thrown at me I'd join the circus."

"So now we're back to square one," Corky notices. "No aerobics teacher."

"I think we'll do fine," Lorin believes. "At least we got the ball rolling."

Audrey nods. “Say amen to that.”

Just a few blocks away, Ingrid wishes she was out enjoying the crisp clear morning air instead of standing in a jail cell clutching the bars. But fate deals the cruelest hand, and this morning she drew short. With a faraway look is in her eyes, she slowly plods over to the cot and lies down. Familiar territory, a cruel sorority she’s been doomed to.

The entire day goes by slowly when there’s no company in your cell. The thoughts in your head have to sustain you. With this much time on your hands, and left to your own devices, you’re given a chance to reminisce about your entire life.

Ingrid remembers the times kids called her zebra because of her mixed parentage. She’d tried very hard to win the attention of a soccer player, but he simply looked through her like she wasn’t there. She remembers her sympathetic parents showering her with gifts for her birthday, or even when she had nothing to celebrate, trying their best to erase the prejudices she’d faced or the solitude she’d embraced.

She remembers the time she nearly drowned in a swimming pool when she was practicing laps with the middle school swim team. She thought the other students neglected her and were probably laughing as she went under. Her coach insisted she was right there trying to save her, but Ingrid didn’t believe it.

She remembers her friends at her jobs, the bosses she’d fought, her acquaintances, her few boyfriends, her mistakes, and her eventual fall from grace. She remembers police lights, being surrounded, her arraignment, her defense lawyers, and even a few judges’ faces.

She remembers her days at Washington Corrections Center for Women in Gig Harbor, the tired look of the guards, the smell of the cafeteria, the crudity of the courtyard, and the hardness of both the floors and some of the other captives.

The evening comes along slowly. Restless and antsy, she sits on her blanket on the floor doing a few sit ups. Sheriff Thompson arrives toting a large ring of keys in his hand.

“Evening, Ingrid,” he greets her.

She stops and glances at him. “You look kinda serious, Lee. They’re sending me back to Gig Harbor, huh?”

“No. Actually, you’re being R ‘n R’d.”

“What’s that?”

“Released on your own recognizance.”

“I am? What’s the catch?”

He opens the cell. She gets to her feet.“I played a few holes with the judge out on the course this evening. We talked. He approves your being on house arrest.”

"You're got friends in high places. Well, I'm glad."

"Ingrid, you have to understand. This is my job and my life. What we did before in that motel was a mistake."

"I'm not asking for special treatment, Lee. I guess I should be grateful I get to stay in my own house. Thanks to the judge."

"He was in a good mood. I kinda let him win. That, and a few glasses of eighteen year old scotch." He retrieves a black ankle monitor from his pocket, kneels down at her feet, and rolls up her right pants leg.

"What're you doing?" she asks.

"This won't hurt."

He places the thick black band around her ankle. "It's an electronic monitor. This is your husband from now on, sugar. The only way to divorce him is to chop your foot off."

"Thanks for the advice."

After fastening the monitor, he rolls her pants leg down and gets up. "It has a limited range of 100 feet. That means you can't leave your house once it's activated. We'll know right away."

"At least I'll be out of here. What about when I run out of food?"

"Our people will drop by with stuff. We won't let you starve."

An hour later, a small unmarked squad car pulls up in front of the Werner house. Seconds later, Lee exits the vehicle and opens the left rear door. Using his keys, he removes Ingrid's hand cuffs, assists her out of the car, closes the door, and escorts her to her house. Just then, a car full of rowdy teenagers rolls up the street. One of them, dressed in drag, sticks his head out the window.

"Hey, Ingrid," he yells. "I wanna be your prom queen. Let's go out tonight." He displays a bloodied doll in drag with a screwdriver stuck in its chest.

"I know who you boys are," Sheriff Lee warns.

The car screeches off. Lee turns to Ingrid. "I expect this sort of thing would happen."

She shrugs. "They don't scare me."

"Everything seems okay for now. Deputies will be patrolling frequently."

"Thanks for the tip."

"Come on, Ingrid. It's not so bad. Could be worse. Um, I hate to be the bearer of bad tidings, I gotta go."

"Yeah. Sure."

"I know this is hard for you."

"You think?"

He sits in a chair opposite hers. "Look, Ingrid. I was a natural born cut-up in elementary school. Hell, I was the truant officers' wet dream.

If there was a law to be broken, I made sure I did it. But, things caught up with me. I broke probation once too often, finally got my ass hauled away to White River Academy. That's a military school for boys in Utah. The teachers were drill sergeants, I swear. A lot one of them were screwed up, took out all their aggressions on us, so I know what it's like to be on both ends of the law. Believe me, I ain't no angel."

He gets up and walks to the door. "I enjoy your company, Ingrid. When this is over..."

She puts a finger to his lips. "Shh. Don't make any promises you can't keep."

He bows, turns and exits. She locks the door, goes back to the living room and tries removing the ankle monitor. It doesn't budge. Walking into the kitchen, she shuffles through a drawer by the sink, removes a long thin knife, and walks back to the living room.

Sitting down on the couch, she tries cutting the thick band which she soon realizes, is tougher than she thought. Angrily, she tosses the knife on the center table

Chapter XI

Beginner's Luck

Lorin is in her husband's private office the next morning going through his files hoping to find a clue to his disappearance. The doorbell rings. Lorin presses a buzzer on the wall and Sheriff Thompson enters.

"Morning, Lorin."

"Hi, Lee. He's still not here, and he's not at his mother's. I just talked to her."

"We had some divers check the lake, also. There was nothing there. We even had a dog checking the grounds. Nothing showed up. This is very odd. I hate to ask, Lorin, but I have to. Did he ever mention another woman?"

"I know my husband, Lee. I may not have his education, but I know what kind of man he is, and he's not a cheater. I know all the rumors. I married him so he could become an American citizen. He's in the Russian mafia and they came for him. He went back to his wife in St. Petersburg and he was too ashamed to tell me. He's a spy with the KGB. All lies."

"Sorry, Lorin. Just official business. Found anything in his journals?"

"He kept notes on patients, but those are confidential. I can't show them to you."

"Well, they may have a key to his disappearance, but that's up to you. I can get a warrant if you wish."

"I already looked them over. Just take them if you want."

She opens the bottom drawer of the desk and hands the sheriff two ledgers.

He thanks her, sits down in a chair, and scans the pages. Lorin stands idly by watching. The sheriff seems puzzled about one particular entry. "He treated you for depression?" he asks.

"You're on the wrong page."

"Sorry." He continues perusing the doctor's notes.

"It's under control now," she says.

"I didn't mean to pry, Lorin."

"That's okay. With all the nuts running around, I'm probably the sanest." She gets a cup of water from a cooler and sits down.

Lee, reading the notes more, half-whispers to himself, "Schizophrenia, nightmares and delusions, paranoia, coming to terms with the past, lodge, retreat. He mentions the retreat a lot."

"I know. I think it was his hiding spot. I don't remember him ever fishing there."

"Maybe I should have another look."

"You want company?'

Lee's squad car is making its way down 3 Lakes Road as winds blows heavily through the trees. Minutes later, they arrive at their destination. Lee parks his car next to the BMW again and they both exit.

"This is a dead end," Lee admits. "The place is empty."

"I figured as much," Lorin agrees, "but it's been a while since I've been here. Nice to see the old place again."

She walks to the edge of the lake. "I feel like going for a dip."

The sheriff also walks over to the lake. "I'd probably join you but I'll bet that water's ice cold."

"Tell me, Lee, honestly, what do you think happened to my husband?"

"Remember Nate Harrison a few years ago? His wife reported him missing, but he had just upped and left with no explanation? It happens."

"I hope it didn't happen to me."

Sheriff Thompson shakes his head. "You never know."

Standing there by the lake, they watch the reflection of the setting sun glistening off the surface of the lake. "Don't you ever wish you can bottle this?" Lorin asks.

Lee nods, then scratches his chin as if deep in thought. She notices it.

"Something on your mind?"

"Maybe. Are you ready to go?"

"Yeah."

"I'm gonna drop you home, but I might check around here again. Something's just not sitting right with me."

"Okay."

Ingrid, lying on her couch in her robe, is peeling an orange and watching a children's show on the flat screen TV James Levanon had donated. Bored, she changes the channel but come across one commercial after the next.

A children's ad for a dollhouse comes on. Suddenly remembering she'd left her own doll back at Kasper's retreat, she jumps up and she peeks out through the front window. The two plainclothes cops, she notices, are nodding off in their unmarked car.

Walking into the kitchen, she takes a roll of aluminum foil out of a cupboard. Raising her right foot up on the sink, she rips off a large swath of foil and wraps it around the monitor.

She then opens the back door, exits, and tiptoes quietly outside like a thief in the night. Seconds later, she becomes startled when the two plainclothes officers suddenly appear before her with their guns drawn.

"Dammit," she yells.

Don Scholl is the older of the two. Broad as a wrestler, he looks to be in no mood for games. Aaron Biondi, his younger, thinner partner, could almost pass for a nerd with his thick glasses and ill fitting clothes.

"Where are you going?" Don asks her.

"I was just getting some air."

"You should notify us," Aaron explains.

They holster their guns in their shoulder harnesses.

"I didn't think you'd allow me."

"You wanna stay out for a while?" Don asks.

"Geez," she queries, "now I need permission just to stretch my legs?"

Don stretches out his hand. "My name's Don. This here's Aaron."

"Nice to have such strong guardians." She crouches down and begins removing the aluminum foil wrapped around the monitor. While down there, she notices the large ring of keys dangling from Don's belt. She rises, crumples the foil, and hands it to Aaron.

"Damn thing doesn't work anyway," she laments.

Aaron smiles. "You do get points for trying."

"Hey," Ingrid asks, "can you boys keep a secret?"

"What are you talking about?" Don wonders.

"Y'all feel like throwing back a few?"

"We'll get suspended," Aaron says, "maybe even thrown off the force."

Don rolls his eyes. "It's not a big deal, man."

"Nobody would know except us," Ingrid promises.

"I'm game," Don smiles, rubbing his hands together.

Aaron, though, is not so sure. His nervousness is borne in his eyes and he wiggles his fingers nervously.

"Tell you, partner," Don says to him, "I drink, you watch. How does that work for you?"

"Whatever, man. Whatever you say."

"Good."

He turns to Ingrid. "So, what d'ya got?"

Minutes later, Ingrid and the two deputies are sitting around the center table in the living room playing a card game. There are empty and full cans of beer, and several boxes of opened and half eaten Chinese food on the table. All three already look like they've had a few. Aaron's face is flushed and he's loosened his shirt. Ingrid and Don seem more relaxed.

Ingrid flips a card, the Queen of Spades, on the table.

"Take that," she beams.

"Not bad," Don admits.

He covers her card with the King of Diamonds.

"You got a second pack stashed somewhere?" she asks.

He smiles. She pops open a can of beer and gives it to him.

"Beginner's luck," she explains. "You win."

Aaron lays his hand down. "I guess I'm out."

She opens a can of beer and hands it him. "Everybody's a winner at Ingrid's. You know what?" she asks. "I feel like dancing."

She gets up, walks to a shelf, puts on the radio and tunes it to a Top 40 dance music station, turns it up, and starts swaying to the beat. She looks at the deputies.

"You boys just gonna sit there?"

Don staggers over and dances with her. Aaron remains seated and drinks his beer.

"You're a good dancer," Don tells her.

"I've had lots of practice."

She eyes the keys dangling at his waist when he does a twirl. Walking to the center table, she opens a can of beer and offers it to him. "Go ahead. Drink up."

Slowing his dancing movements for a moment, he takes a long swig. Ingrid stares as he downs it.

"You guys look like honeymooners," Aaron teases.

Don suddenly grabs and kisses Ingrid. His partner's jaw drops. Ingrid struggles against the surly deputy but loses. When he finally releases her, Ingrid slaps his face. Astonished, he pushes her with such force that she's thrown to the sofa. She looks at him.

"Get out, you bastard."

"You know what you are?" he asks "You're a foul mouthed little hooker."

"Come on, Don," Aaron scolds his partner. "That's enough."

"Hell no. I ain't finished with her yet."

"What you gonna do?" Ingrid asks. "Kill me?"

Don un-holsters his gun and points it at right her forehead.

"No," he says. "That would be too easy."

Aaron holds his head. "This is getting out of hand."

Don motions to the radio. "Turn that shift off," he tells Aaron.

The young deputy complies.. His larger partner stares intently at Ingrid. "You think you're hot stuff, don't you?"

"Come on, Don," Aaron pleads. "Forget her. She ain't worth the trouble. You could screw up the rest of your life right here. Think about your kids, man. Think about your family."

Don ponders his buddy's words for a moment. They ricochet like a proton in his head.

"Yeah, you're right." He holsters his gun. Ingrid breathes a sigh of relief.

Suddenly, Don picks her up like a baby. She struggles but he doesn't turn her loose.

"Leave me alone," she begs. "Get away."

"Isn't this what you wanted?" he brags. "Huh? Who bought the drinks?"

He carries her towards the bedroom.

"You can't do this," she protests.

"Be still, dammit. And who you gonna tell? The cops?"

"Don," Aaron worries aloud, "this is really getting outta hand."

"Don't be a pussy all your life, John Boy. C'mon, help me with this vixen. She's like a beast."

Reluctantly, Aaron helps his buddy drag the protesting ex-con towards the bedroom. Suddenly, Ingrid kicks Aaron in the shins. He screams.

"You two should burn in hell," she hollers.

The two deputies slam Ingrid down on the bed. She tries to roll off but Don restrains her, then turns to his partner. "Find me some scarves or towels or something. This one's got a big mouth."

"You guys are so dead," she warns.

Like an obedient soldier, Aaron begins searching the room for strips of cloth. Ingrid spits in Don's face. He butts her head with his. It stuns her into semi-unconsciousness.

"Stop fucking with me," he shouts.

She moans. He turns to Aaron. "Hurry up!"

Aaron finds a handful of shirts and stockings and brings them over. "It's all I can find."

"Better than nothing," Don realizes. "Tie her up."

Aaron raises his eyebrows. "What?"

"Tie her up."

Like an obedient puppy, Aaron uses the stockings to tie her arms to opposite ends of the head posts. Then he uses the shirts to bind her ankles to the foot posts. Don grabs a bandana from Aaron's pocket and ties it around her mouth. Afterwards, he rips her shirt open. Aaron shakes his head and exits the room.

"Nice body you got there," Don whispers to her. "Must've made a lot of money in Seattle. Let's see what the rest of you looks like."

She struggles again. Don begins peeling her pants down, but stops at the knees because of the way she's tied. "Aaron, he yells. "Come in here."

Aaron enters but he doesn't look amused.

"Help me with this wench," Don orders him. "She's too damn feisty. And why'd you disappear, anyway? The party's over here."

Aaron removes the bind from her left ankle. Like a karate expert, she suddenly kicks Don in the face. He flies off the bed. Aaron restrains her leg. Don, bleeding from the mouth, gets up and peels her pants down to her right ankle. Aaron quickly rebinds her left leg to the bedpost while his partner wipes the blood from his mouth. Don snarls at Ingrid. "You're gonna pay for that, bitch." He loosens his collar and unbuttons his shirt.

Sheriff Thompson is, again, searching the woods behind the cabin. He's moving quickly because it's near dark and, in no time, he'd be searching in vain. There is a shovel on his left shoulder and a flashlight in his right hand. Assisted by a police dog, he has company in his quest.

Amidst the sound of the wind howling eerily through the treetops, he hears the canine barking up head. "What's the matter boy?" he asks. Following the barking, he sees the German Shepherd digging in the dirt. "Whoa," he tells the cur. "Stand aside."

Obediently, the dog stops digging. Thompson lays the flashlight on the ground and uses his shovel to remove a couple pounds of dirt. The dog starts barking again when they both see a hand protruding from the ground.

"Easy," he tells the dog. "Easy." The dog runs away.

Laying the shovel to one side, he removes more dirt off the buried body. Eventually, it becomes slowly discernible. Removing dirt from the head of the grave, he discovers the cold blue wrinkled body that was Kasper Kovalyov. He unhooks the walkie-talkie from his belt and dials in a frequency. "Dispatch, this is Sheriff Thompson. I need an ambulance. I've got a 214 down here at Three Lakes just off Panther Lake Drive."

After the dispatcher on the other end says "copy", he closes the transmitter. Seconds later, the German Shepherd comes galloping back with a rag doll in its mouth.

"What do you have there?' the sheriff asks.

The dog drops the doll on the earth. Lee picks it up and examines it. He then tweaks a frequency in his walkie-talkie. Don's walkie-talkie, sitting on the dresser, squelches and beeps. Aaron picks it up. Don eases off Ingrid.

"Come in," the young deputy speaks in the transmitter.

"Hey, Aaron, this is Lee. Whatever you do, don't let Miss Werner out of your sight."

"Copy that. Where are you, sheriff?"

"I'm out at Dr. Kovalyov's retreat in Three Lakes. I'll be there soon. Over."

Aaron turns off the device. Sweating profusely, he's as nervous as a crackhead at a piss test. Don is as cool as an Alaskan mountain spring.

"I think we went too far," Aaron groans.

"Relax," Don reassures him. "He's miles away. What he doesn't know won't hurt us."

Leaving Ingrid, he grabs his shorts from the floor and puts them on. "What are you waiting for, boy?" he tells his young partner. "Your turn."

"I … I don't know, Don," he stammers. "This is crazy."

"Are we partners or not? Didn't I cover your ass when you stomped on that Mexican in the back of the Alderwood Mall? You could be some greasy spic motherfucker's personal bitch in Clallam Bay right now. Think about it."

Aaron punches his own chest several times."I hate this shit." He unbuttons his shirt, keeping his eyes fixed on the flustered victim.

Chapter XII

Your Life is in Your Hands

James Levanon, nicely dressed with his long hair tied back, grabs his jacket from a wall closet in his house and heads to the front door. Corky, keys in hand, enters.

"Oh, hey Corky," he greets her. "I left some chicken strips in the fridge for you."

"Where are you going?"

"To the office. I have some papers to finalize."

"This time of night? Dressed like that?"

He shrugs.

"Where were *you* all night?"

"Just went for a walk, no biggie."

He kisses her on the cheek. "I'll see you later."

"Without that?" She points to his attaché case on the sofa.

"You're avoiding me," she guesses.

"Here we go again."

"Remember, James, how you used to say I was the best thing that ever happened to you?"

"You are."

"Bullshit. If I fell in a manhole you wouldn't shed a tear."

"This is ridiculous." He storms to the front door, opens it, and turns to face her. "Don't wait up for me."

"James, go to hell."

When he leaves Corky walks over and slams the door shut. She used such force that the strand of garlic hanging over the door falls. Marching to a shelf in the kitchen, she picks up a safe disguised as a soda can, unscrews its bottom, and empties the contents in her hand. Half a joint falls out. Screwing the bottom back on, she shelves the soda can, lights the joint, turns the stereo on medium, dim the lights, takes a toke, and dances by herself . The doorbell rings.

"Fiddlesticks." She snuffs out the joint and stashes it beneath a coaster, turns the music down low, puts the ceiling fan on high, puts the lights back on, straightens out her dress, and opens the door. Houston is standing there.

"Hey, Houston," she smiles. "Come in."

"Hi, Corky."

"Glad you can make it. Are you thirsty?"

"No, thanks."

She turns and pours herself a drink from a bottle of vodka sitting on a shelf.

"I heard you were out looking for me. I was at my buddy's."

He sniffs the air. "Mmm. Having a party? Where's James?"

"Who knows? Hey, Houston, I'm on my last joint."

She removes it from under the coaster and holds it out.

"You caught me at a bad time. I'm out."

"Yeah, but you know where to get this stuff."

"Maybe."

"So do me the favor, dammit, I'm fucking stressed."

"I'd have to go into Seattle," he groans. "It's kinda late."

"I can drive you."

"You're putting me in an awkward spot."

"Oh, never mind. I can't depend on nobody."

"Corky—"

She motions to the front door. "Go on. Get out. I wanna be by myself tonight."

***

Sheriff Lee is driving up 3 Lakes Road in the dark. Although his headlights are on, the sparse lighting in some sections of the road requires careful navigation. He comes to a screeching halt at a tree, a mountain hemlock nearly ten feet tall, sitting across his path. There's enough space to drive around it, but he knew his negligence could result in someone's accident later on.

Getting out of his car, he hikes to the evergreen coniferous and tries pulling it out of the way. Suddenly, he hears a loud creaking sound coming from the woods. Instinctively, he whips around and gazes into the thicket.

"Someone there?" he asks.

A gust of wind nearly blows his hat off. Continuing to look and listen intently, he hears nothing. He returns to the fallen tree and makes another attempt at pulling it out of the way. Just then, he hears a tapping, almost mechanical, noise coming from the woods. Ever vigilant, he walks to his car and removes the flashlight from the passenger seat. Drawing his gun, he begins tiptoeing slowly into the woods.

"Is anyone there?"

Creeping further, he steps on a shallow nest of twigs and drops a few inches into the ground. "What the hell?"

He shines his light at his feet to see where he'd tripped, then ahead where, suddenly, a life-side effigy of him drops out of a tree. Instinctively, he fires and hits it then realizes it's just a prank.

"Shit!"

The hanging effigy, dressed like a Rocky Horror extra, is wearing lingerie and gaudy makeup. Sewed to its chest is a sign which reads, "Bang! I'm Dead!"

"Damn kids," he moans. Returning to the road, he puts the caricature in his trunk, pulls the tree to a ditch, hops in his car, and drives off.

Back in Ingrid's bedroom, Aaron, topless, is zipping up his pants as Don carefully unties Ingrid's bonds. "Remember, girl," he warns her, "your life is in your hands."

He removes the bandana from her mouth. She has a blank stare on her face. Her body, duly maligned by the two, is worse for wear. Weakened by her protectors, all she could do was moan.

Don walks out of the room. Aaron stares at Ingrid, his face mixed with anxiety and confusion. Slowly, she climbs out of bed and pulls herself to an upright position. Walking out of the room, she stops at the door, turns and looks at Aaron who is now buttoning his shirt. When he sees she's looking at him, he casts his eyes downward. She exits to the bathroom and closes the door. He bites his lip.

"This is bad."

Don enters, walks over to his pal, and puts his arms around him.

"Aaron, I know her type," he whispers. "She won't talk. Too damned scared of going back in the hole on some technicality."

"What do you do? Make a habit of this? This sounds like it ain't your first time."

Don smirks. Aaron pushes his pal's arm off him and trudges stiffly out towards the living room.

"Where are you going?" Don asks.

"I'm going outside for some air, man. I think I'm gonna be sick."

He opens the front door and exits. Don shakes his head.

"Pussy."

In the kitchen, Aaron is filling water in a coffee brewer, desperately trying to control his hands which are shaking like leaves in a hurricane. He walks to the fridge, removes a can of beer and walks over to the sink. Opening it, he takes a swig, then pulls out his service revolver and badge and stares at them with disdain.

Back in the bedroom, Don sits idly in the room. After a moment, he gets up, walks to the bathroom and raps on the bathroom door.

"Hey," he shouts, "ain't you finished yet?"

Placing his ear to the door, he can hear Ingrid singing. Though faint, it sounds like "Home On The Range." He opens the door slightly and, from the slit, sees her immersed in a tub of water.

Opening the door wider, he sees the water is blood red. Ingrid's left arm is dangling to the floor. There's a gash on her wrist and a razor on the floor by her bloody arm.

"Oh, shit," Don squalls. "Aaron! Come quick!"

His young partner runs into the bathroom and over to the tub. Ingrid, half-alive, is still singing "Home On The Range", but her voice is monotone, almost robot-like.

"What the hell?" Aaron explodes, grabbing his head. "What the fuck."

"Help me with her," Don shouts.

"I can't believe this shit."

"Stop whining. You can't fall apart now, man."

Don leans over and puts his hands beneath her arms to lift her out. Ingrid suddenly reaches into his holster and whips out his gun. He lunges for it but she points it at him.

"Back off," she shouts.

"Shoot her," he yells at his partner.

Aaron fumbles for his service revolver. Ingrid shoots Don. As he falls, she quickly trains the gun at the other lawman. Too slow in removing his sidearm, he raises his hands. She climbs out with great difficulty, leaving a streak of blood across the tub.

"Easy, Ingrid," he stutters. "I'm on your side."

She stares at him. He can see her scope of sympathy has run out. He makes a move for his gun. She fires. He falls, collapsing like a house of cards. Ingrid stares at him.

"Spare the rod and spoil the child," she moans.

She drops the gun on the floor, removes the bandana from Don's pocket and ties it around her slashed wrist. Grabbing a beach towel off a rod, she wraps it around her body and staggers into the bedroom.

Dragging herself to the chest of drawers, she goes through it and brings out a pair of pants, a shirt, and the old hair dryer. After putting the clothes on, she plugs the dryer in an outlet by the bureau and flicks the switch. The dryer doesn't go on. She unplugs the dryer and staggers into the bathroom with it.

Stepping on the wet, blood soaked floor, she stares at the mirror. She plugs the dryer in an outlet in the vanity lights. Just then, the doorbell rings. She stops and listens. Seconds later, the bell rings again, followed by knocking on the door. Standing silently, she listens.

After almost one minute, and satisfied that her visitor has left, she flicks the 'on' button on the dryer. Suddenly, it sparks. The lights in the house go out and she drops the dryer.

"Of all the times," she whispers. Groping her way towards the living room, she hears a key jiggling in the front lock. Quickly, she grabs a poker near the fireplace.

Watching the lock intently, the front door opens. A man pokes his head in. Even by the light of the moon, she can see it's James.

"Miss Werner?" he asks. "Are you home?"

Quietly, she exits out the back door. James walks in and throws on the wall switch. The lights stay off. Even with slivers of moonlight streaking in the windows, the house is nearly pitch black. He looks up and down the block and sees the street lamps are lit and a few houses have their lights on.

"Hmmm," he wonders. "Must be a fuse."

Back in the house, he gropes through the darkness and bumps into something large.

"Oh. You scared me," he utters. "Ingrid? Is that you?"

Removing his lighter from a pocket, he ignites it. A flash of steel from a blade cuts through the air. He gasps as it strikes his left in his shoulder.

Screaming, he staggers backwards, then is stabbed again, this time in the chest. As he falls, the lights come on. The assailant, dressed head to toe in black, turns with his knife raised. Ingrid, standing by the fuse box, screams.

Sheriff Lee kicks in the front door, his gun already drawn. The assailant whips around and charges at him with the knife. Lee fires, and hits the intruder in the stomach. He hobbles over and falls flat on his face. Ingrid screams. The sheriff walks over and palpates James' neck. He's dead. Then, turning to the assailant, he flips him over on his back. Removing his black hood, he gasps when he realizes the intruder is his son, Houston.

"My God," he screams. "What have I done?" He raises Houston and cradles him in his arms. Blood seeps from the edge of Houston's mouth.

"This can't be happening," the astonished lawman moans.

"I don't understand," Ingrid says.

The boy coughs and opens his eyes weakly.

"Houston," his father cries, supporting his head. "Why? Why?"

He turns to Ingrid, "Call 911! Hurry."

She uses the phone in the kitchen to call for help. Houston looks at his father. "Remember the last Boys' Night Out ... last summer?" he asks him.

"Yeah."

***

James Levanon, Kasper Kovalyov, and Marty Seligman are sitting around a campfire deep in the woods getting drunk. Bottles of whiskey and beer are scattered throughout the site. Several tents are pitched in the background.

Levanon has a large beard and mustache. His hair is long and stringy with silver streaks and, even though it's nighttime, he's wearing a pair of dark aviator glasses. Marty, also bearded, has long which is tied in the back. Dr. Kovalyov has a red bandana around his neck and a cap on his head. Several tents are pitched in the background.

***

"All those guys," Houston continues, "Levanon, Dr. Kovalyov, and Seligman ... they ... they had their way with us boys."

"What?" the sheriff asks. "What are you saying?"

"They got drunk and took advantage that night."

"I didn't know what was going on," Houston admitted. "They must've put something in our food to make us drowsy. The men walked me out of the tent to a darkened area of the woods. I was scared, but I felt so helpless, like I couldn't fight. Maybe I'm just a wimp."

Sheriff Lee is stroking his son's hair. "Why didn't you tell me?"

"I couldn't tell you that. Plus, you were never around and those guys are your friends. You wouldn't believe me."

"I've always been there for you, Houston."

"I'm sorry, Pop."

They hear the siren of the fast approaching ambulance. Houston closes his eyes for the last time.

Ingrid, feeling as helpless as a lamb in a slaughterhouse, hangs her head.

Chapter XIII

Waiting for a Friend

Ingrid is in her new car on a pleasant afternoon driving out of town on a country highway. It's been two weeks since the assault and she has no plans of returning. All charges were dropped when they found out Houston was responsible, but fearing the inevitable backlash, thought it was best to leave.

Listening to soft music on the radio, she continues driving. She turns it up a little when a catchy tune comes on. In her own little world, she starts humming along to the song.

Her reverie is cruelly and brutally interrupted when a car comes flying out of the woods and smashes into hers. She skids off the road. Both vehicles go screeching and thrashing, metal and glass shattering wildly down a grassy embankment.

Shaken up, Ingrid crawls hazily out of her smashed car and onto the hill. Still in shock, she remains panting on the ground. She sees the legs of someone walking erratically, but quickly, towards her.

Looking up, she sees it's Audrey, and she's mad as hell. Blood is streaming down the heavyset woman's dour face. Her eyes are piercingly cold and empty.

"Audrey?" Ingrid yells weakly, her eyes temporarily blurry from the crash. "Is that you? What the hell are you doing? Are you crazy?"

Audrey kicks Ingrid in the face, causing her to go sprawling head over heels down the embankment, stopping against a nest of shrubbery. Audrey comes plodding towards her again.

"What's the matter with you?" Ingrid asks.

Her assailant pulls out a gun and aims it at her. Ingrid can see the woman's hand is trembling but her eyes are cold. "You think I'd let you get away with it?" Audrey screams.

Ingrid looks puzzled. "With what?"

"You ruined my life. My son's gone forever and my husband's never around. You talked Houston into blaming himself for those murders, you seducer, but I know it was you all along."

"What? You're drunk."

"Shut up." She kicks Ingrid causing her to go sprawling backwards.

"You're conniving," Audrey continues, "that's what you are. You got everybody in town thinking *I'm* crazy. Probably talked the school board into firing me, too, didn't ya? Didn't ya!? You bitch. You must give the best head this side of the Mississippi."

"Stop it, Audrey."

The sheriff's wife kneels down and puts the barrel of the gun to Ingrid's bleeding lips. "Open your damn mouth," she demands "Open it."

Ingrid stares at the gun. Audrey pulls the trigger. It doesn't fire. She pulls the trigger repeatedly, but the gun still doesn't fire.

Ingrid pushes the gun away and punches Audrey in the face. The stocky woman falls backwards. Ingrid grabs the fallen gun, gets up, and hurls it up the embankment. Audrey grabs a rock and throws it forcefully, clipping Ingrid's forehead. Blood comes trickling down.

Ingrid picks up a large stick. Audrey covers her face. Ingrid whacks her repeatedly about her arms.

"I'll kill you," Audrey promises.

"Not today, bitch."

"You go to hell."

The stick breaks. Ingrid throws the broken piece away and leaves Audrey on the grassy knoll.

"You know what, Audrey?" Ingrid tells her. "You're not worth going to jail over."

She staggers up the embankment. Audrey gets to her feet, picks up a large rock, raises it over her head, and charges Ingrid from the rear.

Ingrid bends down quickly, picks up the gun, turns the safety off, and fires at Audrey. Hitting her in the leg, she topples over and falls down the hill. Ingrid staggers over to her. "You forgot the safety, asshole."

Audrey raises a fist at her. "I'm not done with you yet, bitch. Just you wait."

Ingrid shakes her head, turns, and walks back to her car.

A few hours later, Ingrid is trudging up a nearly desolate road. Cars whiz past her. None stop. At times she stops and sticks out her thumbs. Some drivers honk their horns, but they just keep passing by. The sky starts turning dark.

Moments later, a rickety old chicken-transport pickup truck slows down. It's old and beat up and looks like it is being held together by staples and glue. Its muffler is creating sparks dragging on the concrete road. The driver, a man in his fifties with dark sunglasses, old blue overalls, John Deere baseball cap, and untrimmed beard, reaches over and opens the passenger side door.

"Wanna lift?" he asks.

Ingrid hesitates. Just the whiff of the truck is deterrent enough to warrant it.

"No, thanks," she lies. "I'm waiting for a friend."

Lightning flashes against the sky followed by roaring thunder.

"Lookee, missy. A storm's a-brewin'."

"Oh, no. I'm okay. I'm fine, seriously."

"Suit yerself."

He closes the door. It starts raining. She taps her fingers restlessly against her hips and stares at the sky. The driver starts to take off.

"Hey! Hold on," she beckons.

He brakes and reopens the door.

"Where ya going?" he asks, his old teeth punctuating a devious smile.

"Out of town. I don't care. East."

"What about your car?"

"Somebody'll pick it up. It was a loaner, anyway."

"Hop in."

The driver lights a cigarette, glances curiously at Ingrid, and offers her one. She accepts it as the truck takes off down the road. The odor of the chickens in the coops on the flatbed start getting to her.

"How can you stand the smell?"

"What smell?"

Her hands trembling, she removes the cigarette lighter and ignites her cigarette.

"What's the matter, girl?" he asks her. "Got a bad case ah nerves?"

She takes a puff. "This hasn't been my day."

"I can kinda tell."

She replaces the lighter in its socket.

"Yer sure shook up," the driver notices. "I hope it'll help ya relax."

"You got any Valium? That'll really help."

He takes out a bottle of Southern Comfort from his pocket. "This here is all ah got."

She stares at it.

"It's better'n nothin'," he adds.

She reaches for the bottle, glances at his face, and recoils when she sees three old deep scars on the left side of his face just above his beard.

He notices her being startled. "What's the matter?" he asks. "Looks like you jus' seen a ghost."

He taps her knees gently. "Jus' relax now, girly. Yer ridin' with the best darn driver in town." He smiles a gap-toothed smile.

The pickup truck continues on down the quiet, almost traffic-less highway and the driver starts humming a tune. "I'm singing in the rain, jus' singing in the rain ..."

The license plate reads "PERRY."

The Road to Hanoi

Kim called her son at his apartment that morning. Worried sick that her seventy-two year old father was really going off the deep end, she needed another voice to convince her he was ready for a nursing home. As it turned out, she couldn't reach her son Robert because, even though it was Saturday and he had no college classes, his roommate said he'd gone shopping.

It was rare for her to fret about her father, Thanh. He used to spend all his time playing board games at the Vietnamese Center with other folks. Now, he spent day and night working on a boat in the garage of her house.

Using his savings, she watched as he brought planks of wood, rope, hardware, large blue plastic barrels, electrical wires and two outboard motors to her home. She didn't mind her car being forced out into the street, but she was concerned his creation might sink.

Laboring day and night was familiar behavior for Nguyen Thanh Ngoc. Born in Hanoi in 1940, he was in his early twenties when the Vietnam War broke out. At that time, he was a police officer stationed in Haiphong, a coastal city about 60 miles away from his birthplace in northern Vietnam. As the fighting raged to the south in Da Nang and Saigon, he watched as the country changed overnight. Spared the misery of capture and imprisonment, he was nevertheless deeply affected by the conflict.

After the war, he worked tirelessly in the redevelopment of southern coastal cities such as Qui Nhon and Nha Trang. Coming face to face with the horrors of war not only destroyed the will, but poisoned the soul as well. He watched as fellow officers fell prey to the scourge of heroin addiction and swore not to succumb to it.

In 1977, when he was thirty-seven, he secured a passport and flew to Los Angeles with his wife, Cam, and daughter, Kim who was three years old. Working in maintenance while learning English, a friend told him about the burgeoning opportunities in Seattle and the growing sea of refugees there. So, packing his bags in 1981, he took a bus to the north and has lived in Seattle since.

He worked two jobs. The first was as a maintenance man for a business cleaning company and the other was as a writer for an Asian weekly. His second job didn't pay much, but it did help him develop a better grasp of the English language as writing bilingual poetry gave him great joy. He even published a few books. They mostly contained poems and stories reminiscent of growing up in a war torn land. It wasn't a subject he was particularly fond of, but it was what he knew best.

Cam passed away in 1990 around the same time Robert was born. After the funeral, Thanh became withdrawn. Whereas he used to be a staple at the Vietnamese Center, he was now just a plaque and a photo on the wall. He was encouraged by his daughter to move into her Central District house with her and her American husband, William Wilson. At first he rejected the idea. After what he'd been through, he wasn't comfortable with the notion of taking handouts and freebies. His pride just wouldn't allow it. Then, when he found out he'd actually be taking care of his newborn grandson while still being able to work at maintenance in the evenings, it became an entirely different matter. So while Kim taught grammar at a local middle school and William went off to work at an internet provider, Thanh moved into the spare bedroom in their furnished attic.

He officially retired in 2002 when he was sixty-two and Robert was twelve. The two had become very close. They went to the movies, zoo and aquarium together. Thanh bestowed his love of nature onto his grandson, introducing him to the Pacific Science Center and similar attractions around the Seattle area. When Robert went off to college in Spokane six years later, Thanh was saddened. Though consolable, he felt like he had lost a best friend. In the beginning, they communicated via letters, then e-mail, but as Robert's studies grew more intense, he wrote less and less.

Thanh was not the "sit on the porch, watch the world go by" kind of fellow. At five feet-five and 120 lbs, he was lively and energetic. If he didn't keep in motion, he felt he'd simply wither and die like a rose stranded in a desert. He'd take long walks to the central library to occupy his time. Sometimes he'd go to a movie by himself. He never gave Kim and William worry because it was apparent he was still enjoying life. Since he could drive and had a license, Kim let him borrow her car to visit places like the Washington Park Arboretum and Japanese Garden, Ballard Locks, and the Woodland Park Zoo.

It wasn't until he brought home the first plank that gave her pause. She asked him what it was for. He explained how he was building a pontoon. She was, naturally, taken aback. He showed her his drawings. She studied and showed them to William who stated, in essence, "Eh, let the old man do what he wants." In reality, William didn't want to get in the middle as it seemed like a father-daughter kind of affair.

For the next couple of months, Thanh labored on his boat in earnest. All the wood cutting was done at Home Depot since he lacked a power saw. And although he preferred working alone, he was amenable to assistance from his son-in-law.

The chevron shape of the base of the pontoon measured eight feet from port to starboard, twelve from bow to stern. Structured from pine, it resembled the deck of a sun room. Beneath it were eight barrels fastened by rope, four on the port side, the others starboard. The seven foot high cabin in the center of the platform was seven feet from port to starboard and eight feet bow to stern. There were three feet of space from the front of the cabin to the tip of the bow and one foot of space from the rear of the cabin to the edge of the stern.

The boat, nicknamed Grasshopper, contained twin 30hp solar powered engines. There was a cast iron fire pit anchored to the bow and one rear facing seat nailed to the stern. On top of the cabin on the slightly concaved roof sat two 100-watt 12-volt solar cells, each unit about the size of a suitcase. They were to be used to power the twin motors, a marine band radio, LED lights, and the 2.6 cubic foot refrigerator in the cabin. As a safeguard, some of the power was diverted to a backup battery. Using a trickle down supply, it would only be utilized at night when there was no sunlight.

The cabin contained acrylic windows on all four sides and in the starboard side door. The simple panel Thanh made contained a speedometer, an odometer, a battery charge meter, steering wheel, and the controllers for the outboards. The marine band radio sat on top of it next to a saucer-sized compass. To the middle and rear of the cabin was a chair, a sleeping bag and a blue plastic container with a white lid approximately four feet wide by three feet deep by three feet high. In it were a fishing pole, trawling net, bait, beef jerky, a first aid kit, waterproof matches, extra wood for the pit, filet knives, biodegradable toilet paper and soap, plates, pots and utensils.

Thanh's construction was interrupted when the family flew out to Spokane to visit Robert. As he was graduating from Gonzaga with a degree in journalism, it wasn't an event they wanted to miss. Thanh, though, had to be persuaded. He was so involved with his boat building that he hated to put it off even for one day.

As it turned out, Thanh had more fun visiting Spokane than he'd imagined. Believing it would be all academia, he brought along a notebook of his plans. His grandson, however, was so thrilled to see him and his parents again that he took them to the Northwest Museum of Arts and Culture, River Park Square, Manito Park, Riverfront Park Ice Palace, and other attractions.

After graduation, Robert returned to Seattle since he didn't have a job lined up anywhere. Kim and William were happy to have their son home with them again even though they knew it would only be for a short while. For the next few weeks, Robert left applications at several sites, including newspaper and magazine offices, and TV stations. He also left applications at Microsoft and Amazon just case they were hiring.

Because of his mother's urging, Robert made an attempt at persuading his grandfather from building the boat that, in her mind, would be a catastrophic failure. One afternoon, when he returned home from dining with a friend at a restaurant in the International District, he saw Thanh working in the garage. As the door was up, he walked in.

"Hey, grandpa," he greeted him. "What's cooking?"

"Hi, Robert. As you can see, I'm almost 100 percent finished."

The young man surveyed the craft. "Think it will work?" he asked.

"When I was in Hanoi," Thanh informed him, stopping work on the motors' electrical system, "I built many boats, sampans, for fishing. You know how we waterproofed them? Buffalo dung. The boats were made from bamboo and the seams were porous."

"How come this boat has no hull?"

"There is going to be one. I wanted to test its sea worthiness first."

"Sea worthiness? I thought you're just going out on a lake with it."

"Oh, I am. I'm just testing the strength of the motors. Would you like to take it for a test drive?"

"What? Me? Where?"

"Lake Washington."

Robert scratched his head. He was 100% percent behind his grandfather in all of his endeavors, but this was a bit more challenging than he was used to. "I don't know, grandpa. It makes me nervous."

"Okay, tell you what. At least help me get it down to the launch site. You don't have to get in. Can you at least do that?"

"Yeah, sure."

Around 2 p.m., the duo lifted the boat onto a trailer acquired by Thanh a week ago. Surprisingly, the boat itself wasn't that heavy. A fair estimate would place it at roughly 400 pounds. After hitching it to Robert's car, they drove it a few miles to the boat launch. Passersby's stared at the craft. Though none laughed or snickered, Robert thought he sensed derision.

"I think this is a bad idea. People are laughing."

"No, they're not," Thanh objected.

Pulling the car up to the edge of the launch, they got out, unhitched the boat, and pushed it to the edge of the lake.

"Are you sure?" Robert asked the old man. "You know how to swim, right?"

"Of course," he answered, putting on his life vest. "Are you going to take off or will you wait for me?"

"Take off?" Robert removed his cell phone. "I was going to take a video and throw it up on the internet."

"That's good," Thanh smiled. "Actually, that's a great idea. It'll allow me to look for irregularities like a list or a sway."

Together, they heaved and pushed and, in no time, had Grasshopper in the water. Watching her float, Thanh jumped for joy. Robert had never seen the old man so elated. Then Thanh, quickly hugging his grandson, ran and caught the boat before it sailed off. Leaping onto the stern, he walked into the cabin, sat down at the console, and activated the motors. Like silent jets, they sprung to life, thrusting the pontoon forward.

Thanh waved as the boat took off. To Robert's surprise, the Grasshopper was faster than he thought. Eyeing it through his camera lens, he saw his grandfather's boat slow down, speed up, bank left, bank right, do a complete circle, and maneuver between other boats. The twin hp motors were surprising fast. He guessed they topped off somewhere around 30 knots, pretty fast for electric motors.

After nearly an hour, Thanh returned to the shore. Robert had already turned off his cell phone because the battery was running low. As his grandfather pulled up, he walked over to greet him. Thanh turned off the power and walked off the boat. Together with his grandson, they pulled the boat onto the shore.

"How was it?" Robert asked.

"You tell me?" Thanh answered. "Does she look steady?"

"Yes. I'm surprised. How come those little motors have such power?"

"It's those plastic air barrels beneath the boat. They're very buoyant. Takes a lot of strain off the motors."

"I must say, that's the most impressive thing I've ever seen."

"Yeah. That's probably what they'll say in Hanoi."

"Huh? What do you mean?"

It was typical of Thanh to leave an idea hanging in search of a resolution. It used to frustrate Robert when he was a kid; he'd since grown used to it.

Thanh reached over and touched his grandson's shoulder. "I'm taking her to Hanoi."

"You mean—"

"Right. I'm sailing."

"What? On this? Across the Pacific?"

"That's right."

"Grandpa, that's like, 5000 miles."

"It's actually six thousand, eight hundred and twenty seven point eight miles, but who's counting?"

"This is insane."

"You mean I'm insane, right?"

"That's not what I said, grandpa."

Robert stopped for a moment, eyed his grandfather, and smiled. "Ah," he emitted. "You're just pulling my leg. Good one, grandpa. You had me fooled for a minute."

"Think what you want to think, Robert. Come on. Help me get the boat up on the trailer. I just remembered I have a doctor's appointment."

Over the next few days, Thanh created wooden ribs from the bow to the stern then attached a fiberglass hull to the skeleton. At the stern, it was 12 inches high, at the bow, 18 inches. Instead of using buffalo dung, he decided to be more modern and use boat sealant like he'd done to the bottom of the craft. He also painted the cabin white with blue sections to match the hull. After painting "Grasshopper" at the stern, he invited the family to the garage.

All four stood admiring the project. Robert was impressed, Kim was nervous, but William thought his step father did a good job.

"But what's this I hear about Hanoi?" Kim finally asked.

"Oh, he told you," Thanh lamented, eyeing his grandson.

"Is it true?" William asked.

"If you must know, yes."

"On this thing," Kim motioned to it.

"On this thing," Thanh concurred.

"I think you should think about it carefully, grandpa," Robert advised him. "Think about the potential for hurricanes and squalls. What about crests and wakes? The weather might not be in your favor."

"I'm not even worried about storms," Kim added. "There could be pirates. You know how the world is now. Pa, what do plan to do? Take weapons on board with you?"

"Of course not," he answered. "As long as you've known me, you know I'm a man of peace."

"I'm sorry for your past," William expressed, "but you must understand how dangerous this is and how much we care about you."

Thanh hung his head. The last thing he wanted to do was bring guilt to his family. He knew this moment would come and he just had to accept its consequential gravitas.

"I'm a fortunate man," Thanh explained. "I've been lucky, more lucky, than the thousands of people I grew up with. My friends died one by one at the hands of the Viet Cong. But the Viet Cong were not my enemies. We're from the same blood. We're simply brothers torn apart by the viscosity of war. Children shot on the beaches. Mothers betrayed like dogs in the rice fields. A whole generation growing up with no home and, possibly, no future. But I was given a chance. I survived. Why? Why me? Coming to America was a gift. Being able to tell my story so future generations would know and understand our pain is a gift. Being Vietnamese, and being Asian, makes me part of the sea. I was born there. It's where I belong, where I must travel, and where I must tell my story. It isn't so hard to understand."

Kim walked over to her father and hugged him. "You know,' she smiled, wiping away a tear, "you should've been a lecturer at the college. If it means so much to you Pa, go with my blessings."

"I guess I wish you good luck," William stated. "Have a wonderful trip. You should be back in, what, a month, right?"

"Something like that," Thanh responded.

"You mean *we'll* be back in about a month," Robert corrected.

"Huh?" Kim asked. "We?"

"I'm going," he admitted.

"What do you mean you're going?"

"I think it'll be a great experience."

"You want to come along?" Thanh asked his grandson.

"Sure, why not? I'm still unemployed. No one's hiring for the summer anyway."

"I think you should reconsider," William informed him. "That's a long time at sea."

"I think two heads are better than one," Robert insisted. "Plus, what a good start for a career in journalism. I can write about the whole trip and publish it later."

Kim shook her head. "I don't think I can hear anymore tonight. I'm going to lie down." Turning around, she exited the garage and walked back into the house.

"I hope you two think about this very carefully," William opined then went inside.

Robert rubbed his fingers along the hull, caressing it like a fair maiden.

"We'll need to add another seat in the back and another sleeping bag."

"You can have that one," Thanh admitted. "I don't sleep much anyway. Plus, someone has to stay up just in case."

"You're pretty brave, Grandpa. Most people would never attempt something like this."

"I think swimming from Florida to Cuba is more dangerous, but the lady tries it. I think climbing Mt. Everest has more risks, but people do it every day. The human body is stronger than you think."

"I hope so. How are we coming back home? Hopefully not the same way."

Thanh shrugged.

"We'll fly."

On the night before the trip, Robert visited his grandfather in his attic room. It'd been years since he'd seen it, but it was just like he remembered. It was neat and tidy with everything in its place. Entering the room, there was a twin bed to the right. Next to it was a chest of drawers. Across the room was a desk with a computer. Next to that sat a bookcase and a free standing closet. An octagonal window was built into the wall behind the desk.

Thanh was sitting at his desk making notes in his books. A map of the Pacific was stretched out next to the computer. Robert stood near the closet.

"How long do you think it'll take, Grandpa?"

"Fortune favors the patient," Thanh answered. "My guess? About fifteen days."

"Wow! That's a long time!"

"That boat has a top cruising speed of about 35 knots. At least we won't have to worry about fuel."

"What about food?"

"I've loaded up the carrier with beef jerky. Feel free to bring potato chips or pretzels or whatever you desire. I've already put drinking water in the fridge."

"Fifteen days. Won't we run out?"

"I'm going to teach you how to purify sea water."

Robert tried to remember everything he'd learned as a boy scout. If he needed to recall Survival 101, now was the time.

"What about the bathroom?" he asked.

"What about it? It's an adventure, Robert, not an excursion to London. I've packed biodegradable toilet paper and soap. For meals, there's a fire pit on the bow. It doesn't have to be sushi every day."

"So we'll be fishing then?"

"Of course. We're communing with the sea. This is a once in a lifetime chance. Think of the story you'll tell."

"Don't worry. I'm looking forward to it."

Early the next morning after loading last minute supplies into the boat, everyone jumped into William's car with the craft in tow. They drove north for two hours along Route 19 to Port Townsend. Thanh gazed wistfully at the scenery. The Pacific Northwest, a lush jungle in itself, brought back memories of his days in Vietnam. Kim was quiet most of the way. She didn't cry, but her face did betray a look of resignation. She just couldn't help thinking that perhaps she was saying goodbye to her father.

Picking up a few bottles of water in Port Townsend, they drove to Fort Worden State Park on the northern tip of the town. All four assisted with pushing Grasshopper onto the beach. Once she was in the water, Thanh and Robert hugged goodbye to Kim and William. Robert noticed his mother had tears in her eyes.

"I promise to be safe, mom," he whispered. "I won't let you down."

"I'm so scared for you," she admitted. "I can't sleep at night."

"I'm a strong man," he promised. "I'll look after Grandpa."

"You mean he'll look after you."

"Yes, mom. I'll see you in a few weeks."

"Hurry back."

Minutes later, Thanh and his grandson were adrift on the Salish Sea. Heading west along the Strait of Juan de Fuca, they waved as they passed the Dungeness National Wildlife Refuge, Port Angeles Airport, the Salt Creek Recreation Area, Clallam Bay, Shipwreck Point, and finally Neah Bay. After 75 miles, and two and half hours, they were face to face with the expansive, endless, magnificent Pacific Ocean.

Thanh had the foresight to build a few amenities into the craft. One of Robert's favorites was the solar-powered battery charger. With it, he was able to recharge his iPad, his sole means of entertainment. At least for the journey, he wasn't without his favorite musician, Beethoven. For the trip he loaded up all his symphonies, piano and violin sonatas, his piano concertos, chamber music, and other works. For variety, he also brought along the symphonies of Mahler, Bruckner, and Brahms and the tone poems of Richard Strauss and Franz Liszt. For all the time he had, he may as well have brought along Wagner's long operas, but he wasn't sure if Thanh would enjoy them. His grandfather loved classical music, but he believed opera was ruined by singing.

So far, everything looked promising. Thanh, sitting at the console steering the boat, was swaying his body lightly to the left and right. Either he was responding to the music in the cabin, or simply comforting himself. Robert sat in one of the rear facing seats looking out at the ocean. All the windows were opened.

"This is great," Robert admitted. "So this is how Columbus must've felt."

"I hardly think the Nina, Pinta or Santa Maria were this efficient," Thanh offered. "Think about being an oarsman. Stuck below deck, you can't see anything. It's just you and a hundred other sailors and the overseer with his whip yelling 'stroke.' Ah, I don't think I would've liked it."

Robert got up, walked into the cabin, opened the refrigerator, and took out one of the bottles of orange juice. Taking a quick inventory, he saw nine bottles of apple juice, twelve bottles of water, three packages of sliced cheese, two packages of sliced turkey breast, one packet of bacon, a container of eggs, and two gallons of milk.

"Looks like we're in good shape," he confessed.

"It's okay," Thanh admitted. "Tomorrow, I'll show you how to make fresh water from the sea. We may as well start because our supply is limited."

"Do you want me to take the wheel?"

"Okay. Come. I'll show you."

Thanh got up from the seat and Robert took it.

"You have to grab the throttle like this," his grandfather illustrated. "I've modified the motors so they work in tandem, off the same throttle and steered by the same wheel."

Robert tested it by speeding the boat up while holding the circular wheel straight.

"See?" Thanh explained. "We're about 30 knots right now."

The college graduate eased off the throttle.

"Yes," Thanh suggested. "Keep like this. We're cruising around 25 knots. Keep your eye on this compass." He pointed to the saucer-sized instrument anchored to the console. "Our heading right now is 26 degrees west. Try to keep it right on that mark."

"Aye, aye captain."

"I'm glad you came along, Robert. Not many people would do what you've done. I'm proud."

"You actually caught me at a good time."

"I think I'll lie down for an hour. I'm spent."

"Sure grandpa. Good ahead. I'll be fine."

"Don't let me sleep too long. I'll need to check the heading."

"Aye, aye sir."

"Wise guy."

Two hours later, Robert checked his watch. It was 9 p.m. He turned on the cabin's LED lights and looked at his grandfather. Not having the heart to awaken him, he kept his post at the wheel. According to the compass, he was right on course. Taking a break, he changed the music on his iPad and put on something more energetic. A big fan of metal, he put on some tunes by Godsmack, one of his favorite bands. He kept it low so as not to disturb Thanh. Looking to stretch his legs, he left his post and walked out to the bow. Spreading his arms, he let the sea breeze blow over him from all sides. Looking around, all he saw was ocean, miles and miles of it. Even though the sun was gone, he could see the moonlight glistening off the waves. Luckily, the sky was cloudless. At least there was no rain in the near future.

Returning to the wheel, he looked at the compass. It was headed directly as Thanh plotted. Staring at the marine band radio, he clicked it on. All he heard was static. He flicked on the roam button hoping it would latch onto a used frequency. When it found nothing, he turned it off. Opening the blue container behind him, he took out a beef jerky, removed its wrapper, and took a bite. Returning to his post, he resumed his control on the steering wheel.

The Pacific winds, floating through the cabin like wandering spirits, started to make his body shiver. Getting up, he closed all the windows. As it was late, he turned off the music on his iPad. Just then, his grandfather stirred and peered at his wrist watch.

"Wow," he yawned, 'that was a good rest."

"Hey, Grandpa," Robert greeted him. "Slept well?"

"Actually, I'm surprised I slept at all. That was my first time with the bag. It's pretty comfortable. Are we on track?'

"Everything looks fine."

"Good." He rose to his feet. "I've got to empty my bladder. When I come back I'll take the reins."

"Okay."

Walking to the stern, Thanh relieved himself over the side of the boat. Then, dipping his hands in the water, he splashed some of it on his face. Putting his hands on both motors, he pulled them off quickly because of the heat they emitted. He then returned to the cabin.

"Throttle down a little," he cautioned his grandson. "We don't want to burn the motors out."

Robert complied and brought the speed down to about five knots.

"Good," Thanh complimented him. "Why don't you get some shut eye? Tomorrow's gonna be our first full day out here and you'll need your strength."

"No problem." Relinquishing command, Robert stepped away from the console and walked towards the sleeping bag. He stared at it momentarily.

"What's the matter?" Thanh asked.

"I'm thinking about whether I should use the bathroom first."

His grandfather laughed.

"That's pretty funny. It's weird how we use these terms so casually. Bathroom, like there's one anywhere near here for miles."

"Well, you know what I mean."

"I know, Rob. Just having fun with you."

After Thanh took the controls, Robert did go to the bathroom. Minutes later, after splashing the brine on his face, he returned to the cabin, crawled into the sleeping bag and promptly went to sleep.

The following morning, Robert was awakened gently by the smell of cooked bacon wafting in through the cabin. Getting up, he noticed Thanh was not sitting at the wheel. In fact, the boat wasn't even moving. Looking towards the bow, he saw him. He was working at the fire pit, flipping bacon in a pan like a diner chef. At times, grimacing in pain, he'd stop and use both hands to grab the right side of his abdomen. Robert walked over.

"Morning, Grandpa. Are you all right?"

The old man quickly resumed cooking.

"Never better."

Eyeing Thanh with curiosity, Robert thought it best to let his prying mind wonder. "What time did you start the fire?"

"About an hour ago."

Robert watched as Thanh removed the pan from the pit and place three strips of bacon on two plates which also contained scrambled eggs.

"When I get married," Robert notified him, "I'm hiring you to cook for us."

"I don't think so. You couldn't afford me."

They both sat down on the bow and ate their breakfast.

"Did you start writing in your journal yet?" Thanh asked.

"In a little while, I will," he answered. "I'm just soaking in this whole experience."

"This brings back memories, doesn't it?"

"You mean during my boy scout days? Yeah, I remember."

"Oh," Thanh uttered. "I forgot the milk."

He began to stand but Robert motioned for him to sit. "I'll get it."

Rising, he got up, removed the milk from the fridge, grabbed two cups from the blue container, and brought them over. He poured a glass for his grandfather and one for himself, then returned the milk to the fridge. Seconds later, he rejoined Thanh. "Remember how you used to tell me about Vietnam?" Robert asked.

"Yeah. Depressing stories in the middle of the night."

"I actually remembered some of them. Back in college, I used a lot of our conversations as essays and papers for my classes."

"I'm glad you remembered me."

"Of course I did." Robert paused and stared at his eyes. A slight feeling of guilt seeped into his veins. "Did you think I forgot about you, grandpa?"

"Not at all. I know you're busy with school. Can't concern yourself with an old fool like me."

"I know you're just saying that. I thought about you all the time."

Thanh ate the rest of his bacon and eggs and washed it all down with the milk. Always the speedy eater, he practically never let his food get cold.

"I had a girlfriend," Robert revealed. "I thought it was a serious thing, too."

"What happened?"

"Well, you could say we just weren't compatible. We got along fine, but we just had different interests. There are no hard feelings between us. Things just didn't work out."

"When we're done here," Thanh promised, "I'll show you how to make the water. I have to start the engine, though. I don't want to waste time."

They sailed westward for the next few hours with Thanh at the wheel. Robert bided his time by reading an eBook on his iPad while sitting in one of the stern's chairs. A fan of biography, he dined on the history of Benjamin Franklin. At times, he'd read while lying on the sleeping bag, other times he'd stop and watch his grandfather manning the wheel. Intermittently, the old man would jot some notes down in his ledger. Robert gazed at the odometer in the console.

"How many miles have we traveled?"

Thanh picked up his notebook and handed it to his curious passenger.

"See the odometer? It says 687 miles, but in reality, it's probably closer to 600 nautical miles. We're on track."

Robert checked his watch. "It's close to 1p.m. I think I'm gonna wash my body."

"I'll have to stop," his grandfather said.

"No. Don't do that on account of me. I think if you slowed down to about five knots I can handle myself."

"Okay." Thanh throttled down to five knots.

"I'll be quick," Robert promised. "It's just that I'm feeling sticky."

"Okay. Don't forget the soap."

"Thanks."

Returning to the cabin, Robert stripped naked, fished the biodegradable soap out of the container, walked out to the stern, and jumped in the water. He held onto the boat with his left hand as he washed himself with his right. Thanh, seeing the difficulty his grandson was facing, stopped the motors.

"Take all the time you want," Thanh shouted.

Robert waved to his grandfather then let the boat go. Immediately, he started doing breast strokes in the water. "This is the craziest thing I've ever done," he screamed. "A shark can swim up and bite off my *watusi!*"

"Well then I suggest you hurry!" Thanh warned.

After Robert soaped and washed himself, he donned the same clothes. Unfortunately, because they made no provisions for clothing, they had to wear the same attire. When he was done, his grandfather showed him how to make fresh water.

First, they lit the starter logs and dropped it in the fire pit. Robert manned the wheel while Thanh rested and the logs grew hot. Half an hour later, Robert watched as Thanh dipped their ten liter aluminum pot in the ocean and filled it halfway with the brine. He then placed it on the grill above the pit. Grabbing a two liter Pyrex beaker, he placed it in the pot where the water level was only half the height of the transparent container. Then he placed the pot's transparent concave lid upside down over the pot. They both watched as the salt water boiled and condensation formed on the lid. Within minutes, the condensed, or salt free water, was dripping down into the beaker.

They filled an empty apple juice bottle with the water, then repeated the procedure. Over the next few hours, with Thanh at the wheel, Robert created four new bottles of fresh water and refrigerated them. It was a tedious undertaking, but effort necessity.

Later that evening as the boat continued westward, Thanh showed his grandson how to use the trawler. It was simple, really. The net, attached to a pole, was simply dragged in the water from the bow. The boat was slowed down to 15 knots as they risked missing their catch. Successfully, they pulled halibut, black cod, and Chinook salmon out of the water. Because the numbers caught were few, they also cast lines from the stern.

Setting the boat on autopilot, they sat together that night in the stern and angled deeply using their fishing rods. Robert, new to fishing, almost got pulled into the water by an incredibly strong yellowfin tuna that must've weighed at least twenty pounds. Reeling in the monster, they kept it in a plastic bag and hung it off the stern. Tomorrow, it would serve as breakfast and lunch, sushi style.

Over the next few days, things went well. A lot of the supplies were used up. In fact, the only foodstuffs left were a few beef jerkies and newly bottled water. Still miles from nowhere, they began to experience craving and hunger. They had bad luck with trawling. Surprisingly, they pulled nothing out of the water for nearly a hundred miles. Fishing from the stern wasn't that successful, either.

Extremely fatigued from the fish hunt one day, they turned off the motor and went to sleep.

They were awakened two hours later by a voice coming in over the marine radio. Getting up, Thanh grabbed the microphone. To his surprise, it was the Honolulu Coast Guard. As it turned out, Grasshopper was barely twenty nautical miles away from Hawaii. Stopping at Kahana Valley State Park in Hauula, they were greeted by curious spectators, some of whom took pictures. Robert took a lot of pictures. Eager to continue on their way, they didn't stay on land for long.

After a brief rest in a hotel, and with their clothes newly washed, they refilled their fridge with all kinds of sundries and set off a few hours later, back into the wild unknown.

From Hawaii, they made a rest stop at Johnson Atoll some 750 miles west of Hauula. That trip took a day and a half. The next place they stopped, Wake Island, took approximately two days to reach. There they had a slight run in with the United States Air Force near a base. They had to produce papers and show they were simply journeymen and meant no one any harm. Robert took a few pictures, but a lieutenant warned him if he didn't cease and desist, his cell phone would be confiscated. Complying, he stashed his device. Minutes later, they were back on their boat. At least they did manage to get a handful of water purification tables and a crate of MREs. Military slang for passable food.

Two days later, they stopped at Saipan in the Northern Mariana Islands just north of Guam. Fatigued from the sea, Robert convinced his grandfather to stay there overnight. A minor argument erupted between them because, to Robert, it seemed like Thanh was in a rush. His grandfather retorted by saying it was no rush, and if Robert didn't like his pace, he could have well remained in Seattle. Not looking to argue, they bought a hotel room and promptly fell asleep.

The next day, they boarded their little cruiser and set off once again. For the first time at sea, it rained. Thanh, manning the wheel, finally found out how difficult it was trying to keep a lightweight boat upright in heavy winds. Robert spent a lot of time bailing the water out while his grandfather steered. This went on for approximately four hours. With the waves lashing against the boat, it felt at times like it would capsize. At least they weren't arguing.

Later, after the storm passed, the two made peace with each other. Robert promised to take Thanh out to the restaurant of his choice. His grandfather promised to procure a 55 gallon tank, or larger, for him as a Christmas present.

By the end of the next day, they reached Santa Ana, a city on the northern tip of the Philippine Island of Luzon. Stopping briefly to stretch their legs in a park, they continued on to the Paracel Islands, or as the Chinese called it, Xisha Islands. Located in the South China Sea, where there were territorial disputes between Vietnam and China over its occupation. Robert learned from Thanh that the islands, now under the administration of the People's Republic of China, were known to the Vietnamese as Hoang Sa Islands. Not willing to incite the Chinese authorities, the duo decided to skip the islands altogether and continue on. Within thirty hours, they were finally in Vietnam.

As they neared the shore, they saw several fishing and transportation sampans, some large enough to carry twenty people comfortably, sailing to and from the coastline. The smaller ones were being moved by rowers standing in each boat's bow, the larger motor-driven crafts being navigated quietly though the shore were painted and outfitted to look like their wooden cousins.

Blending in with the other boats, Robert and Thanh docked at the Xuan Thuy National Park. Grateful they went undetected by authorities, they casually stepped out onto the windswept beach. Thanh, overcome with emotion, fell to his knees and hugged the earth. A handful of people walking by simply stared at him, but none made fun of him or ridiculed his presence.

"Are you happy now?" Robert asked him.

Thanh grabbed his grandson. "If only you knew. This is a triumph for me, not just because of the distance, but over time as well."

"Is this Hanoi?"

"No," Thanh answered. "We're about 60 miles east of it."

"How will we get there? What about Grasshopper?"

"Leave her for now. No one will take her. This park is pretty safe. It's been a haven for fishermen for years. The authorities don't even bother you here."

Minutes later, after getting their important items—the iPad, notebooks, cell phone, and other items—they took a taxi to Hanoi. They made a quick stop at Noi Bai International Airport. Thanh told Robert to remain with the driver while he went inside to purchase tickets back to Seattle.

By the time they arrived downtown, it was nearly 9 p.m. The vibrant city, with neon lights shining everywhere, resembled midtown Manhattan or even Las Vegas. Standing on Hang Bong Street just outside the Hanoi Old Centre Hotel, Thanh took in a deep breath.

"Do you smell that, Robert?" he asked.

"Yeah. Smells like roast duck."

"I meant the essence. Can you feel the spirit? It shoots right through me like Cupid's arrow."

Robert watched as pedestrians, staring at his ecstatic grandfather, continued on their way.

"I think we'd better get a room now."

"This air intoxicates me," Thanh confessed.

"Cool. Can you intoxicate inside?"

When they entered their room, Robert looked at his watch. "What time is it in Seattle?"

"I believe they're fourteen hours behind." Thanh glanced at his own watch. "Right now, it's 9:15p.m. That means in Seattle it's 7:15 a.m."

"Perfect. I can call mom before she goes to work." Using his cell phone, he dialed her number. Unfortunately, it didn't connect.

"You have to use a calling card," Thanh advised him.

Robert shook his head. "Man, with the advances we've made in telecommunications, you'd think a simple phone call would just go through."

"Why don't you see if the front desk has any phone cards? I think I'm gonna lie down."

"Good idea."

Scant minutes later, Robert secured himself a phone card from the desk clerk who, luckily, spoke English. Walking to a lobby phone, he carefully dialed the endless string of access numbers then dialed his mother's phone.

"Hello?" she answered.

"Hey, mom."

"Robert," she yelled. "My goodness. You had us worried."

"I'm fine. Grandpa is fine."

"Where are you?"

"Hanoi."

"Wow. I'd love to be there. You know, they're talking about you two on the news."

"Really?"

Typically, Robert shunned the spotlight. Still, an article in a weekly or a blurb in the Sunday news didn't seem so bad.

"Yes," Kim continued. "They talk about the storm you went through, all the islands you visited. People are rooting for you. I hope you took pictures."

"Yes, I did."

"Where's grandpa?"

"Upstairs."

"Listen, his doctor called us this week. He was never supposed to take that trip."

"Why not?"

Kim started crying. Robert became puzzled. "What's the matter, mom?"

"Robert, your grandfather has inoperable prostatic cancer."

"What? what are you saying?"

"It's metastasized to his bloodstream. Dr. Cairn didn't think he'd last this long."

"How come I didn't know? How come nobody told me?"

"I didn't know myself. Your grandfather kept it a secret from everyone. It's only now because he went sailing that they told me."

Robert grabbed his head. Its neurons seemed to be flying around the light pole of reason at blinding speeds. "Oh, mom. This is too much right now. I can't think straight."

"Maybe the doctor's wrong. Did you already buy two tickets to come back?"

"Grandpa took care of that."

"Are you sure? Ask him. There's probably only one."

"What do you mean?"

"I think he went to Hanoi to die."

Her son couldn't believe his ears. It was as if the world just stopped spinning. "I'm gonna go upstairs and check it out."

"Okay, Robert. I love you both. Be good."

"I love you mom. Tell Pop I said hi. I'll see you two in a while." Hanging up, he took the elevator to his room. Walking in, he saw his grandfather lying supine beneath the sheets.

"Hey grandpa," he whispered walking over to him. "Is there anything you want to tell me?"

The old man didn't answer.

"I know you and I had bad times," he continued, "but isn't that natural? I mean, families get into heated discussions, don't they?"

He stared at his grandfather again.

"Grandpa?"

Standing above him, he increased the light on the night table. His grandfather, once a vibrant man full of life, bursting at the seams with energy, was gone.

"Dammit," he moaned. Kneeling, he hugged his grandfather.

"Why didn't you tell me, you selfish bastard? Why didn't you?" He stared at the old man, his internal flame blown out. Painfully, he'd lost his best friend.

An hour later, the coroner came to pick up the body. Accompanied by a police constabulary and his deputy, they determined there was no wrongdoing. Going through Thanh's pockets, they found only one plane ticket. As it was made out to Robert for his return trip to Seattle, they gave it to him. He stared at it, then realized the old man finally achieved just what he wanted. No falling balloons, no brass fanfare, no honorary medal. He went out quietly, serenely like a northern star. Yes, he'd arrived. He'd reached his destination, his deferred dream finally realized.

A Walk in the Park with Mozart

December 4, 1791 – 9 p.m.

The famous German composer Wolfgang Amadeus Mozart, bloated and weakened from chronic emphysema and rheumatic fever, is lying on his deathbed surrounded by his wife Constanze, her sister Sophie and their seven year old son Karl. Lit candles are perched throughout the bedroom located in the apartment at Stadt 970, Rauhensteingasse, Kleines Kaiserhaus in Vienna. Mozart moans; Constanze holds his hand.

"I knew this day would come," the pale musician whispers.

"Don't say that, Wolfie," Constanze admonishes him. "Dr. Closset said you'll be fine in a few days then you can go back to composing again."

"Ach," Mozart protests. "He's a swindler. Constanze, we're in such debt."

"Things will get better. The publishers will come around. La Clemenza is doing well, as is Magic Flute—"

"You needn't worry about providing right now," Sophie chimes in.

A chill floods the room. The drapes and curtains bellow from the huge gust of wind.

"Did someone open a window?" Constanze asks.

"Not me," Karl responds.

A flash of blinding white light and fog appears in the corner of the room next to a window.

Constanze screams. Her sister gasps. A middle aged man, dressed completely in white, appears in the fog and stretches his right arm out towards Mozart. He motions to the ailing composer to take his hand even though he's standing about twenty feet away. Mozart raises his right arm out towards the stranger. A bright blue light emits from the man's right hand and covers the sickened genius.

"Wolfie," Constanze screams.

In a flash, both the man and Mozart suddenly vanish.

December 4, 2012 – 9 p.m.

In the middle of a large bedroom, partially decorated in 18th century Viennese, sits a large electronic contraption eerily resembling a huge gray beetle. Roughly the size of a minivan, several knobs, levers and gauges adorn its thick translucent glass door. To one side of metal and glass beetle sits a laptop on a stand. Beneath the stand sits several electronic components. A handful of cables protrude from the base of the machine and are attached to the modules near the computer.

Suddenly, the lights on the machine come to life. Emitting a whirring sound, a flash of light and fog fills the machine. Slowly, its door opens. Fog drips out. From out of the powdery mist the man in white, followed by Mozart, exits.

Mozart rubs his eyes. He is so shocked by the new sights that he stumbles backwards. Catching himself in the silvery dome, he hops backwards and stares at it.

"Gott in himmel," he shrieks.

"Herr Mozart," Bowen speaks. Astonished, Mozart looks up at the stranger than surveys the unfamiliar room

"Constanze," the confused composed shouts. "Karl?"

"They can't hear you," Bowen explains.

"Sprechen sie English? En Wien?"

"You are not in Vienna, Herr Mozart."

"What do you mean I'm not in Vienna? Where is Dr. Closset? Where is Constanze?"

"I assure you," Bowen admits, "everyone is okay."

"What contraption is this?" he asks pointing to the machine. "Where is this place?"

"You're in America, Herr Mozart."

"Well, you know my name, Mr ..."

"Henry Bowen."

Mozart tumbles on the carpet. Curious, he rubs it quickly, then glances over its surface. "An entire rug throughout the surface of the floor? Is this an asylum?"

"This is my home," Bowen informs him.

"Who paid you to play this trick on me? Was it Schikaneder? Or maybe some buffoonery from Constanze?"

"I brought you here."

Mozart, his brow furrowed deeply, walks over to a window and throws it open.

"If this was an asylum," Bowen continues, “that window would be locked, yes?"

Mozart stares out into the dark. He sees a few houses and well-trimmed hedges on an otherwise quiet suburban street; light posts dot the landscape. A lake, reflecting the soft light of the winter moon, is discernible in the distance

"Was I so ill I was brought somewhere without my knowledge?" Mozart wonders, rubbing his chin. "Nothing seems familiar. I am at a loss to explain this."

"You will soon learn, in time, everything that's transpired."

Mozart turns towards Bowen. "I've seen you" Mozart admits. "I was deathly ill in bed then ... then you arrived, like an angel." The composer's sudden realization he may be dead and in heaven fills him with awe. His lit appearance betrays this.

"I am not an angel," Bowen explains. "And this is not heaven."

"Then it is a trick, but one in which I will not participate in."

Mozart opens the bedroom door and walks out. Entering the living room, he takes a quick look around at the unfamiliar furnishings then heads to the front door. "This is clever." he tells Bowen. "Schikaneder far more creative than I give him credit for."

Then, Mozart opens the door and walks out to the porch. From there he looks up and down the street. Nothing in his sight is familiar; not the houses, cars, the curb, sidewalk, lights ,nor power lines. He scratches his head. "It just doesn't make sense," he whispers to himself. "Metal carriages on the streets."

"Constanze," he shouts. "Sophie? Karl? War ist du? Constanze?" Slowly realizing he's suddenly alone, he turns and walks back into the house, tears welling in his eyes?

"I don't appreciate this apothecary's trickery." he shouts at Bowen. "It seems so real."

Still confused, Mozart walks around the living room studying the accouterments. He touches the lamps, feels the mantle over the fireplace, takes a book off a shelf and leafs through it, then walks over to a piano he hadn't noticed before. He plays a few notes on a shiny black Steinway baby grand. "It is loud," Mozart admits. He then points to the keys. "The colours are backward." He stops playing, gets up and walks over to the stranger. "Herr Bowen," he begins. "Tell me the truth. Explain all of this."

"So you believe now that we're not in Vienna?"

"I've looked outside and nothing is familiar. Those metal carriages on the street?"

"Actually, you're half right," Bowen explains. "At one time all you'd see were carriages with horses, but they found a way to let you move the carriages without them."

"Just tell me where I am, Henry Bowen." Mozart demands. "These apparitions do my constitution ill."

"Today is December 4, 2012." Bowen gives the musical scribe some time to soak in the date. Mozart emits a slightly devious smile.

"I'll play along, Herr Bowen," Mozart avows. "Humor me if 221 years passed as you say."

"Well, Herr Mozart. It's nice to see you're so open-minded."

Mozart, touching his head, looks confused by the statement.

"Oh, I mean," Bowen clarifies, "your willingness to learn new ideas."

Mozart nods in agreement, then sits down on a sofa. Out of amazement, he lightly bounces up and down on the sofa and caresses its soft seat, arm and back like a child discovering a new toy. Bowen walks over to a large whiteboard on a wall and picks up a marker from a counter below it.

"Back in your time," he begins, "the lights in your homes, cathedrals and street were lit by candles and, later, gas."

"I noticed those," Mozart agrees, motioning to the various lights in the room. "I saw them outside, also."

"Exactly. Except an invention came along called electricity. It's a form of power."

"Power? Like coal for a locomotive?"

"Actually, yes, but it's not practical to burn coal in the homes because it also creates poisonous gases. So they created machines in the 18th century that made electricity." Bowen creates a sketch of a power generator on the whiteboard. He continues. "Over the past 200 years or so they've improved on its design—"

"Like the pianoforte," Mozart wonders.

"Man's quest for perfection and improvement knows no end, my friend. You might be surprised to know that the Stradivari and del Gesu violins from your time are still in use today."

"Hmm. They should be perfectly imperfect by now, yes?"

"On the contrary, they're held in high regards. Still the favorite of the best players in the world."

"Electricity ..."

"Fascinated by it, eh?" Bowen continues drawing on the board. "Electricity comes through every house and building through the walls."

"The walls?"

Bowen walks over to an outlet near the piano. "You can't touch it because it's dangerous, but this is where the power comes from."

"Fascinating."

"Yes. Walk with me." Bowen walks to the front door opens it. Mozart follows behind.

"See those cables there?" he asks pointing to the power lines.

"Cables?"

"Strung up overhead."

"Yes, I see them, like clothing lines."

"Right. Those are cables of electricity which brings power from the electrical building to all the homes and street lights here."

"This is the most realistic dream I've ever experienced. Such a poison that wafts through me."

"All industry has seen many changes, and this is in regards to law, science, invention, design—"

"Did the women change?" Mozart asks, winking more than a hint of licentiousness in his voice.

"They're exactly the same. Would you like some tea?"

"Ja. I'm glad to know they still have it."

Bowen closes the door and they walk into the kitchen. When the scientist puts the light on, Mozart gets startled.

"Your world is a scary one."

"In more ways than one." Bowen starts preparing hot tea in a coffee pot while the composer stares in wonder at the sink, stove and other utensils.

"Herr Bowen, the last thing I seem to remember is I was laying deathly ill in my chambers with my son, wife and her sister in attendance. They were somber, in tears. It was cold, but not snowing. I was bloated and pale, so weak I could barely move my body. Then ... this. This fantastic change bestowed upon me. This ... asylum."

"Electricity, as I was explaining before, has had various uses these past 200 years. Not only is it used to power lamps, but also all modern machines as it is a clean and reliable source. Behold." Bowen opens the refrigerator. Mozart's eyes light up.

"I still don't understand this wizardry."

"This is a refrigerator. Its use is in the preservation of foodstuffs."

Timidly, Mozart sticks his hand in. "It's cold." He shudders.

"Behold the power of electricity, Herr Mozart."

The composer studies the fridge's meager contents: tubs of spreadable cheese, cold cuts, milk, orange juice, some fruits, eggs and a few other sundries that befit a bachelor.

"Such wonder." Mozart smiles. "If Constanze could see this."

Bowen takes out two apples. He hands one to the studious Mozart, bites into his then closes the refrigerator's door. Mozart smells his first then, reluctantly, takes a bite.

"It *is* an apple."

"Oh yes, my sir. As real as the leaves on the trees."

"This is a very strange event, indeed. I don't feel like I'm under a spell, yet I remember my life slipping from me. I was weak and shriveling."

"The machine which brought you here reassembles its occupant through time and space to its basic cellular level."

"I don't understand."

"It's the basic tiniest structure of all living things. The machine transports, and in so doing, heals."

"Are there many machines like this? Is this how modern transportation is done?"

"No," Bowen answers. "I created it. It's the only one, as far as I know. It's quite a new invention, really. One I'm sure the government would love to own. I am surprised that it actually worked."

"If this be the future," Mozart surmises, "then I should like to meet my progeny."

"They wouldn't believe you are who you say you are."

"Why not? Show them the machine."

"It could get in the wrong hands, not to mention it's still under refinement, and the government can instantly make all my years of research and development null and void because it lacks regulation. That's what I fear the most." He takes the heated pot of water off the stove, pours two cups of tea and offers one to Mozart.

"Danke, Herr Bowen."

"You're welcome."

"I saw lager in this machine," Mozart hints, motioning to the fridge.

Bowen removes a bottle of beer, opens it, and gives it to Mozart. The thirsty composer downs it in one gulp.

"It is cold."

"A lot of surprises, Herr Mozart?"

"Ja. It was good. Tastes quite familiar." He reads its label.

"Stella Artois."

"From Belgium."

Mozart contemplates that for a moment. "Belgium?" he asks.

"The Netherlands?"

"Oh yes. I know."

"Antwerp. Brussels."

"I've toured there with father and Nanerl."

"Your sister."

"So you know. Tell me, who is the emperor of Germany now?"

"They don't use emperors anymore."

"No?"

"There are still kingdoms in the world but Germany is no longer one of them. The leader, a chancellor, is elected by the people."

"I see."

"Their leader is actually Angela Merkel."

"Merkel."

"A woman, yes?"

"Is this what time has wrought?"

"Here in America the leader is, well, he's a Negro."

"Like the pianoforte's keys reversed. The German leader has been reversed. Your future, up has become down, left become right."

"Um, you can say that. Yes."

"And electricity."

"Electricity." Bowen takes out another, opens it and gives it to Mozart. "These are the finest beers. It would serve you well to drink it slowly."

"Patience has never coincided with the best of my virtues."

"There's more where that came from. Help yourself." Mozart nods.

"Were there other travelers?"

"I had tested on animals. They transported well."

"Sir, I'm no animal," Mozart protested.

"No," Bowen reassures him, "but you are the first soul through it."

"I feel privileged."

Bowen gazes at him, not knowing if he's appreciative or being sarcastic. Still, tired from working all day, he stretches and yawns. Mozart finishes his beer and helps himself to a third. He offers one to Bowen, but he passes. The two walk back into the living room.

"Are you tired?" the composer wonders.

"A little," the scientist explains. "I've spent many sleepless nights working on this machine. It was actually built by my brother. He's since died so I continued working on his design. You, of all people, would understand the need to stay up night after night working on a score until it was complete."

"So you know about me?"

"The world remembers you still this day, Herr Mozart."

Mozart flops back down into the comfortable couch. Bowen walks over to the TV and turns it on.

"This'll give you taste of how far mankind's progressed," he explains.

As soon as the TV comes roaring to life, Mozart screams and jumps up.

"What's the matter?" Bowen asks.

His question falls on deaf ears as the thoroughly shocked composer drops his near-empty beer bottle and goes screaming and flying out the front door. Bowen takes off after him. "Herr Mozart!"

Mozart, still immensely confused, dashes down the suburban street.

"Constanze," he screams. But there was reply, no solace from his absent wife. He continues yelling in unintelligible German as Bowen follows behind.

"I'm sorry," Bowen shouts.

Mozart, panicking and tearful, keeps running haphazardly through the quiet streets. Still barefooted, he accidentally stubs his right big toe on a protruding slab of concrete. "Ach," he screams, not stopping to nurse his bleeding toe.

This action finally catches the eyes of a squad car out on patrol. At an intersection, their lights and a warning siren flashes. The car stops. The first policeman, Officer Kane, exits the vehicle. Mozart continues running.

"Mozart," the approaching scientist yells.

The second policeman, Officer Hobbes, gets out of the vehicle and motions to Bowen. "Stay where you are," he shouts. Bowen complies.

After a short chase, Kane tackles Mozart. They struggle in the hedges. The officer stands Mozart up. Urine has soaked through his nightgown. He walks him towards his vehicle. "What is your name?" he asks the crying composer.

Mozart, still deeply in shock, is unable to answer.

"He's with me, officer," Bowen explains.

“What’s your friend’s name?”

“Wolfgang. He doesn’t have his ID, I’m afraid.”

"Can I see your ID, sir?" Hobbes asks Bowen.

The scientist produces his wallet, takes out his driver's license and hands it to him.

"Dr. Henry Bowen," Hobbes reads. "Where do you work?"

"U-dub Department of Physics," he answers.

"Does this gentleman work with you?"

"Yes, sir," Bowen lies. "He's my assistant."

"He's had a bit too much to drink tonight," Kane suggests.

"How much have you had tonight, sir?" he asks Mozart. The stricken composer is still too teary eyed to answer.

"What's your last name?" he asks him. Again, the solemn composer gives no answer.

"Maybe a night downtown might loosen your tongue," Hobbes warns him.

"I'm also a trained in medicine," Bowen adds quickly. "He's only just learned of a family tragedy. Obviously it’s been too much to bear."

"Tell your friend to stand right here," Kane tells Bowen.

The scientist walks over to Mozart, consoles him, and bandages his bleeding toe with a handkerchief while the two officers walk a few feet away to talk.

"Why is this happening to me?" Mozart asks the scientist, tears still in his eyes.

"You're in shock," Bowen answers. "It could happen to anyone if they went through what you did."

"I don't understand that ...vision in your house. That box ... those people."

Bowen rises and looks directly into Mozart's eyes.

"This is not witchcraft or wizardry, Mozart. It's called television. It's in everyone's home."

"I have to get back to Vienna," Mozart realizes. "I've surely gone mad."

Just then the two officers re-approached. "We won't book him tonight, Dr. Bowen," Hobbes explains. "Just get him some coffee and some sleep and keep him off the street."

"Thank you, officer," Bowen states. "It won't happen again."

The two policemen return to their car. Bowen overhears one of the officers say, "Another lovers' spat gone wrong," just before they enter their vehicle and take off.

In the house, Bowen gives Mozart a red velvet robe. The much fatigued composer takes off his German nightgown, dons the robe, and lies down on the sofa to sleep. Bowen covers him with a soft blanket then heads to the kitchen. He stops up the sink, runs the hot water, and leaves the nightgown in it to soak. He then gets himself a beer from the fridge, takes a few sips, sits down in the living room recliner, and falls quickly asleep.

The next morning, Mozart awakens by the chill of the frost coming in from the front door. Crows, whippoorwills and robins sing their tunes outside as Bowen enters with some newspapers tucked under his arms. He closes the door behind him, lays the papers on the center table, and heads towards the kitchen.

"Good morning," he greets the former child prodigy. "Is your foot still in pain?"

"Ach, you taunt me," Mozart claims. "It's my head that is swollen. I hear a timpani."

"Do you still think this is a dream?"

"I-I don't know what to think."

"Do you drink coffee, Mozart?"

"Danke," he nods.

Bowen brings out two cups of coffee. Mozart sits up, takes a cup, and drinks from it. Bowen sits down in the recliner. Mozart touches his new unfamiliar robe.

"Your gown was soiled," he explains.

"Why am I here, Bowen?" Mozart asks.

"I thought you'd be an interesting subject to study.

Mozart points to the TV. "Show me electricity again."

"Television," the scientist corrects him. Instead of walking over to the television, Bowen turns it on with a nearby remote control. Mozart's eyes light up. Bowen hands him the remote which he studies intensely.

"It's a remote control," he explains, but Mozart seems puzzled.

"Simply speaking," Bowen continues, "it also works by electricity. In a technical sense, anyway."

Mozart barely listens as he's completely enthralled by the electronic device.

"See here," Bowen says, taking the remote. "You can view different things." He demonstrates by changing channels via the remote.

"Try it," he smiles, giving the remote back to Mozart.

Mozart flips through a few channels, laughing like a giddy child. He spends roughly two minutes on each station. "Is this television also in Germany?" he asks.

"Yes," Bowen answers. "It's worldwide. Everything you see here is worldwide. And if you think things are complicated, wait until I introduce you to the internet."

"The internet?"

"Once again," Bowen explains, "some of those wires your saw outside transmits information here, and we can also use it to send our own information. I'll show you later."

Mozart flips through a few more channels."Such a variety of knowledge," he admits. He turns to an arts channel. A pianist is playing a sonata. He studies it intently. "I don't understand this music," he admits. "No timing. Complete disregard of the metronome. So loud and violent."

Bowen recognizes the piece. It is Beethoven's 'Hammerklavier' sonata.

"That's of the later sonatas by Beethoven," he informs the composer.

"I've met him briefly," Mozart states. "Very talented young man."

"He single-handedly changed music. He brought it from the classical era to the romantic."

"Romantic? What do you mean? My music has no romance?"

"It's just a heading, a term. Rigid form and structure went to the wayside, somewhat. You would've been one of its main proponents, I wager."

"You know the date of my death." Mozart suddenly realizes.

"Mozart, I—"

The anxious composer jumps to his feet."You must tell me," he shouts, Bowen shakes his head.

"Don't you wonder why I brought you here?"

Mozart stares intensely at his host then walks over to the front door and opens it. He takes a deep breath of the crisp wintry air, turns around and faces Bowen. "I don't want to know," he states, suddenly changing his mind. "I may hasten it."

"I thought you'd be an interesting study," Bowen admits.

"Why?"

"There's some debate about if you were autistic."

"What is that?"

"It's a mental condition a few people have."

"Like insanity?"

Bowen gets up, walks over to a shelf and takes a large dictionary from it.

"Not exactly," he explains. "Some autistic people are geniuses, staying up night after night so enrapt in their arts. Some have trouble functioning in society and find it difficult to maintain friendships. Some do have all of their senses but find noise or lights intolerable to bear."

Mozart thinks about this summary for a moment. "Doesn't seem important," Mozart admits, "to go through all this trouble."

"Yes, I know," Bowen agrees. "Even though you're the first, you're an accident."

"Accident?"

"I actually wasn't expecting my time machine to work."

"So I'm your experiment?"

"Yes, well, something like that."

"Then I wish to go back immediately."

"I'll explain a little more about the machine," Bowen states. "True, it is powered by electricity, but there's another component in it called a battery. The battery also generates power. When the machine is used, the battery's power gets drained. It takes almost 24 hours to be recharged."

Mozart looks addled.

"To be powerful enough to make the machine work," Bowen explains.

"So I'm here for a day?"

"Yes. May as well make the best of it."

"In that case," Mozart suggests, "I'd like to visit your town."

"Thank you, composer," Bowen nods. "I'm glad you've accepted what is."

"It is what it is," the composer admits.

Several minutes later, Mozart is singing one of his opera arias, 'Notte e giorno faticar' from Don Giovanni, in the shower. The sensation of warm water steadily flowing over his body indoors is a feeling unknown to him and a luxury surely to be enjoyed solely by kings.

"Wunderbar," he shouts. Bowen, however, doesn't hear him as he's busy in the laundry room loading dirty clothes into the washer.

Minutes later Mozart emerges from the bathroom wearing some clothes loaned by Bowen: blue jeans, shirt, and a purple hooded University of Washington sweater.

"Herr Bowen?" he asks, entering the living room. He sees no one. Walking into the kitchen, he opens the fridge, rifle through its contents, and brings out a block of Swiss cheese. Placing in on the kitchen counter he draws a knife and cleaves a piece for himself. Bowen enters from the back room.

"Ready to see the city?" he asks the hungry composer.

"How does this look?" Mozart responds, modeling his new 20th century attire.

"It's a little big, but it looks okay. Ready to go?"

The two walk down the quiet suburban streets as cars drive past. Mozart is taken back by their rumbling, humming, wheels grinding on the asphalt sound. Intermittently, he'd look at each car, studying its passengers intensely."Is electricity responsible for this?" he wonders aloud.

"Remember the battery I was talking about before? The unit that stores electrical power? All cars have them."

"Cars. I see. Are there no more horses?"

"Of course, but they're kept mostly on farms. These days they're used for sport, like racing."

"Smelly beasts, they are."

"Would you like to ride in a car?"

"I think I must."

"I have one, but where we're going is walking distance. It won't be necessary."

"I don't mind. I find a good walk in the morning prepares me well for a day of creating."

"You're extraordinary. Your body of work, the operas, symphonies, piano and violin concertos, serenades—"

"Women," he laughs, adding to his exploits.

"You're lighthearted."

Mozart suddenly gets an idea."When I return, I'd like to go back at an earlier time."

"What do you mean?"

"When you brought me I was ill in bed."

"Yes."

"Was I dying?"

Bowen stops walking. Mozart stops with him."You were very ill," Bowen answers.

"So much unfinished business," he admits. "I've not prepared for my family like I should. I need to go back earlier, maybe a year or two, to fix my financial problems."

"You can't," Bowen explains.

"Why?"

Bowen quickly looks through the nearby hedges, breaks off a long thin branch, and shows it to Mozart. "This branch represents time," he begins, "from beginning to end. In this case, the moment you left Vienna to the moment you return." He bends the branch into a circle.

"The machine works in a closed loop," he continues. "The beginning and end occurs at the same time and place. I am able to insert myself at that one small dent in time. My place is kept because the machine has stopped due to lack of power. The battery takes 24 hours to recharge, but that dent in time is never lost."

"I don't understand your theories."

"Okay." He looks around and sees a low hanging branch jutting from a tree.

"Walk with me," he beckons to Mozart. He follows.

"Once upon a time we had a famous scientist. His name was Albert Einstein. In the early part of this century, around 1915, he explained that time is flexible."

"Time is flexible? I don't ..."

Bowen grabs the branch. "Time can be bent like this," he demonstrates by bending the branch.

"Time can be bent," Mozart repeats, uncertain of what the scientist means.

"Yes. It can be measured with the new fancy elaborate instruments. Have you ever seen a tornado or whirlpool?"

"No, but I'm aware of their existence. Powerful enough to lift horses in the air."

"Exactly. They spin fiercely. When they spin they pull objects into its core as if trying to reach its center. Einstein has shown that the sun and earth are a part of a larger universal whirlpool that's spinning towards a center. That very pull, away from a straight line, is what creates a bend in time. The theory is if you can bend time you can move along the timeline, the timeline of earth and life and existence, at will."

"Is that your machine?"

"Yes. I haven't told anyone because the government would just use it for wars."

"Wars."

"They take the most innovative inventions and use it in catastrophic ways to gain the upper hand: the catapult, the firearm, nuclear energy ... gets twisted by bureaucracy."

"I see."

"Mankind, I believe, is inherently good, but somehow always finds the time for evil. Why? I don't know." He bends the branch down without breaking it. "And the reason you have to return at the same place and time you left is this. " He lets the branch recoil back to its original place.

"Nature is absolute."

Once again, Mozart looks puzzled.

"Aristotle said nature abhors a vacuum," Bowen elucidates. "Nature hates a space which cannot exist. A nothingness. Aristotle was right. Empty spaces go against the laws of physics and science."

"Interesting." Mozart nods, rubbing his chin.

"All the space we see and feel around us is actually being occupied by something. In my time machine's loop system, the beginning and end of the journey of travel has to meet."

"I think I understand."

"Good. Let's have some lunch," Bowen suggests. "I'm hungry."

The two continue walking towards the center of the village.

It is mid-morning in the cozy hamlet of downtown Magnolia, a suburb of Seattle. The postman merrily drags his cart up the street as nannies pushing strollers with their tiny charges walk past. Joggers run to and fro as dog walkers and businessmen stroll hither and yon.

Bowen and Mozart are sitting at an outside table drinking coffee. For a December, the temperature is a balmy 60 degrees. Clouds fill half the sky. Birds are perched on several lines scattered through the downtown area. Buses and cars pass by while people stop at traffic lights or ride bicycles intermittently. Bowen glances at Mozart. He notices some trepidation and confusion in the composer's eyes.

"Is this too much scenery for you?" he asks him.

"It reminds me of Vienna," he admits, "just different. The excitement is the same. The noises are, of course, much more varied."

"Would you prefer a quieter place?"

"No. It's good."

While the two go over their menus, a car pulls up near them containing two teenagers. The passenger, a female of about 18, gets out and walks into the cafe as her partner sits in the idling car. His choice of music, modern rock, sounds caustic to Mozart's ears. He cuffs them half shut.

"What kind of music is that?" he asks Bowen.

"Sounds like rock," he answers.

"Rock?"

"Rock is short for rock 'n roll. They use instruments unfamiliar to you. Electric guitars. I'll show you later."

"Electric?" Mozart shakes his head. "It's that what music has become?"

"Not all. People actually love it, though. You'll see."

Mozart finally orders from his menu.

“Eggs and orange juice,” he tells the waitress.

“How do you want your eggs?”

“Hen’s eggs,” he bursts out laughing. The waitress, however, isn’t amused.

“We’ll take two Spanish omelet’s, wheat toast and orange juice,” Bowen interrupts. The waitress nods, scoops up both menus, and returns inside the cafe.

Mozart starts rubbing his eyes which have begun watering.

“Something disturbing you?” Bowen asks.

“No,” Mozart answers. “I think maybe it’s a little bright.”

Bowen looks up and down the block quickly and sees a gas station convenience store across the street. He gets up.“I’ll be right back,” he explains before dashing across the street. A few seconds later he returns with a newspaper and a pair of sunglasses. He hands the shades to Mozart.

“Try these on,” he tells him. Mozart complies. Smiling, he stands up and looks at his reflection in the cafe’s glass wall.

“I’m modern,” he utters.

“Yeah,” Bowen agrees. “You’re 20th century.”

Soon, the waitress brings them both their breakfast. They sit and enjoy it. Mozart spends good chunk of time perusing the Seattle Times. Bowen is mesmerized just watching the tunesmith absorb modernity at breakneck speed. Minutes later, when the waitress drops the check off on the table, Bowen takes out his wallet and hands Mozart his debit card.

“That’s how we pay for things,” he informs him. “It’s a debit card.”

Mozart bends it a few times. Bowen quickly takes it back before Mozart snaps it in two.

“Be careful, Herr Mozart,” he warns him. “It can break, and then I won’t be able to use it.”

“Do they not use currency anymore?”

Bowen takes out some money from his wallet and hands it to Mozart. "Yes, they do. I just don't use it that often. The card is used ... I keep my money in a bank. That one down there, as a matter of fact," he points to a nearby Wells Fargo location. "There's a machine in all of these stores that's connected through those wires to the bank," he illustrates, pointing to the cables strung up across the light poles. "The machines then can communicate to each other that way."

The waitress arrives, takes the card and check, and returns to the cafe.

"She'll just take the money she needs to pay for the food from my bank through her machine. Clever, huh?"

"More like mystifying," Mozart states. "Never in my dreams can I have imagined this."

"Let's go for ride. You'll see a lot more."

Several minutes later, Bowen is driving Mozart towards downtown Seattle. The composer is both thrilled and scared at the same time. The structures and developments fascinate him as they whiz past. He is also confounded by the innards of the car, namely the soft seats, the plethora of lights and switches in the vehicle, the glove box which he opens and closes a few times, the speakers in the door and dashboard and the air conditioner which he raises and lowers often.

"This is like your time machine," he shouts.

"Well, it's fast, though not quite like that. The time machine has a section that accelerates just past the speed of light."

"The speed of light?"

"When you see sunlight in the morning, it takes a little while for that light to hit your eyes. It's actually been measured. It's the speed of light. Very, very fast. One hundred and eight six thousand miles per second. Very, very fast."

"I have nothing in which to reference that, sir," Mozart admits, sounding a little dismayed but altogether confused. Bowen points to the speedometer in his car.

"See this gauge?" he asks him. "It says that this car is moving at forty miles per hour. The speed of light would be this same car driving about thirteen million times as fast."

"The only thing fast approaching is a headache," Mozart extols, holding his head. Bowen, sensing the composer's distress, puts on the classical music station. The adagio from Brahms's Symphony No. 2 is playing.

"How is this possible?" Mozart asks, listening to the sultry tones of the NY Philharmonic.

"This is actually easy to explain if you'll grasp the concept."

"Just tell me."

"Have you ever stood at the edge of a forest or a deep precipice and shouted your name?"

"Yes."

"And you heard your name being shouted back?"

"Is that an echo?"

"Exactly. A long echo. Mankind found a way to capture that echo. You can play back the sound whenever you wanted. They created machines that could capture that echo; it's called a recording and has been refined over the years, and allows you to play back the captured recording when you feel like it."

"Like this symphony?" he asks, motioning to the radio.

"Exactly. The recording itself is not in this car. There's a building that has the recording. We can hear it because of the radio."

"What's radio?"

"It's a way of sending and receiving sound waves through the air."

"I see."

"It's more complex than that. Understand I'm just simplifying it."

"I see."

"Is this all too much at once, Mozart?"

"Is there more? Anymore and my head will surely burst."

"I think that's enough for now."

Minutes later they drive towards the heart of the city. Still undergoing construction, there are huge cranes in a few places. The sound of jackhammers can be heard as well as the screech of emergency sirens, unintelligible voices, traffic signals, the random horns, and smoke belching from worn engines.

"So this is your Vienna?" Mozart asks.

"Yes, it is," Bowen admits. "Noisy, isn't it?"

"How do the people live here?"

"What do you mean? With the noise?"

"Yes."

He looks up and down the street. People of all colours, flavors, shapes, sizes and accouterments mill about here and there.

"Some of those can't be human," Mozart wonders. "Their hair styles are odd."

"Welcome to America, Herr Mozart. Times have changed considerably. But I'll show you something."

They pull into the rooftop parking lot of the city's giant Guitar Center store. Walking into the shop, they are greeted by a salesclerk. Out of formality, Mozart nods. The clerk smiles. Bowen enters through the turnstile which gives the composer a little difficulty.

"Why is this here?" he asks, pointing to it.

"To prevent theft, you know," Bowen explains. "Keeps the ruffians at bay."

When they enter the first room, Mozart is astonished. Never in his life had he ever seen such a huge display of guitars and other instruments. Some were on stands on the floor; the majority was dangling from hooks on the walls. Several amplifiers, keyboards, and music books on stands were scattered throughout the huge front room. He can see people scattered throughout the store either speaking to each other or perched at individual instruments.

"There were a few music stores in Vienna," Mozart informs him. "They sold instruments created by the Stradivari and Guarneri family, harpsichords by Donat and Romer—illustrious builders all."

"Today those would be worth a fortune."

"Would they?"

"Yes. Um, excuse me, Mozart," Bowen tells him. "I have to go to the men's' room, the toilette. I'll be back in a few minutes."

Mozart watches as the physicist walks towards the back area out of sight. Unbeknownst to Mozart, Bowen didn't go to the bathroom. Instead, he's studying the composer from a distance. Just then, another sales clerk approaches Mozart.

"Can I help you?" he asks him.

"What are these things?"

"What things?"

"These things ... there," he asks, pointing to a stack of amps.

The sales clerk looks curiously at Mozart as if he just came from Mars. "That's a guitar amplifier," he answers.

"What does it do?"

The clerk studies Mozart again. "You really don't know, do you?"

"They don't have those in Vienna, or Salzburg, or Mannheim."

"I'll show you." The clerk takes an electric guitar off a stand, straps it on, and plugs it into the amp. He plays some notes and a few chords. Mozart cuffs his ears.

"It is too loud," he shouts. The clerk stops playing.

"Sorry," he apologizes. He hands the guitar to Mozart. "Wanna try?"

"Nein," he answers. "Where are your harpsichords?"

The clerk points to the nearby keyboards room.

"In there."

"Danke."

Mozart walks away from the clerk and enters the keyboard room. Like the other room, it is filled with all sorts of instruments including microphones, speakers and music software. People are standing in front of display instruments, speaking to clerks behind a counter, or playing a few floor models.

Mozart walks over to one of the display instrument, an electronic keyboard. He runs his fingers over the keys but nothing happens. A clerk approaches him.

"Hello," the clerk opens. "I'm Alex. Can I help you?"

"This instrument produces no sound," Mozart insists.

The clerk reaches behind the instrument and throws a switch. Several lights on the keyboard spring to life.

"Try it now."

Mozart plays a few notes. It produces piano sounds. "Curious." he admits. "It is like a piano, but a little heavier." He continues playing.

"Do you wanna see what it's got?" the clerk asks. Mozart stops playing and looks quizzically at him.

"It's got different sounds," the clerk explains. He illustrates by pressing a button on the front of the keyboard.

"Try this."

Mozart plays a few notes. The sound of an organ is produced. It startles him. "This cannot be," he says. "This sounds like the organ at St. Stephen's Cathedral."

"You're not from around here, are you?" the clerk asks dryly, not expecting a response.

"I've never seen such-such, I have no words to explain myself!"

"Just go easy," Alex advises him.

Mozart plays the organ a little bit more. It goes without saying that his playing his impressive. Within a few minutes a relatively small crowd of salespeople and customers had gathered in the keyboard room to watch and hear his impromptu performance. Filled with fancy flourishes, dazzling arpeggios and seemingly impossible scales, he concludes to a rousing hand of applause.

"You're quite good," Alex tells him. Other people also congratulate the performer then resumed whatever they were doing.

"What's your name?" he asks stretching out his hand.

"Mozart," he replies. "Wolfgang Amadeus Mozart."

"Yeah, sure. No ... seriously."

"I'm the son of Leopold and Ana Maria Mozart of Salzburg."

"Whatever, man. You're still a good player. If you need anything just ask."

The clerk abruptly walks away to help another customer. Bowen enters the keyboard room and approaches Mozart. "Finding everything okay?"

"Your people are rude."

"They're not my people."

"They're lacking in class and temperament just the same."

"Do you want to look around a little bit more?"

"When I was in Vienna I used to walk to clear my head. It never actually worked but it was the attempt that satisfied me."

"Do you want to go for a walk now?"

"I appreciate the invitation."

Mozart is eating an ice cream and Bowen a popsicle as they walk downtown along busy Eastlake Avenue. Mozart is wearing his sunglasses. Bowen points out the different and varied landmarks along the way. He points out the Space Needle, the various hotels and towers, the plethora of nightclubs, cafes, restaurants and clothing stores, and the convention center in the heart of the city. Eventually, they make their way through Westlake Center and end up at the historic Pike Place Market where Bowen buys them both a pan pizza and sodas. They walk towards an overpass.

"When I was in Vienna," Mozart begins, "the city was under great development. His Imperial Majesty, King Leopold II, had taken over from his brother, Joseph II. They introduced a sewer system. Palaces were being expanded upon wherein you could fit another city in them."

"Do you see that airplane flying overhead?" Bowen asks, pointing to one high up above.

"What is it?"

"It's an airplane. It's like a car with wings. Popular route of travel these days."

Mozart takes off his sunglasses and peers at the flying machine. "I think I can hear it, too. Do you have one?" he asks.

"No," Bowen laughs. "They're expensive. They're only used for traveling far distances, not for a local jaunt into town. I'm afraid all my money went into building the time machine."

"How long did it take?"

"There were several prototypes ... models. I started building them about 30 years ago. It was just a hobby, but as it came closer and closer to reality, I focused all my energy, time and money building it. I think I've lost friends and companionship because of it. Such is life."

"So you're not married?"

"My friend, I'm married to the machine. Unfortunately, it's my life. I wish I was like you, so prolific, so steadfast in your discipline. How long did it take you to complete an opera or a mass?"

"They were all different; some a little more complicated than others. Don Giovanni took a few months, I think. La Clemenza de Tito and Die Zauberflote about the same."

"It's unfair that such talent should lie upon the crest of one man. Why was this gift not divided amongst your peers?"

"It was not without sacrifices, Herr Bowen. I have suffered headaches no man should be made to bear. I've endured a poverty no beggar would envy."

"That's unfortunate because you've given the world so much."

"I am pleased. It pleases me when they show appreciation."

Bowen looks to his left and sees a photographer sitting next to man-sized standees of the Space Needle, Elvis Presley and a tyrannosaurus rex. He approaches the entrepreneur?

"How much for each photo?" he asks.

"Three dollars," the man answers.

"We'll do the Space Needle pix."

The photographer nods and gets up to prepare for the shoot.

"Herr Mozart," Bowen calls out to his time traveling partner. "Come."

Mozart complies and walks over to Bowen. The photographer positions the two on either side of the standee, takes a few snaps and hands the photos to them. Bowen gives him a $10 bill. Mozart studies one of the photos. Like everything he's seen on his travel, he's astonished.

"This is me," he shouts in glee.

"This is photography," Bowen explains. "It was invented around 1840 by a Frenchman named Louis Daguerre. He was a chemist, I believe."

"In some areas of the world you could be burned for heresy just for this," Mozart suggests. "The fat pompous minister would sit on his throne, scoff at you, and throw you in a dungeon to rot for witchcraft. Make a pact with the devil, did you? Off with your head."

"Ignorance is the enemy of curiosity, Mozart. Mankind would stagnate, remain in the dark ages when pestilence and plagues ruled the land if we didn't seek out a greater experience and knowledge."

"This is what I've been telling my father," the composer agrees. "When I made changes to the music, made it more, how should I say, stirring, they rejected it. This was the masons, the Emperor, Schikaneder, even Haydn. I grew so tired or constructing the same passages, the same tempos, the same variations on a theme, not that they were the same, but to the untrained ear they were. Whenever I tried to expand past the sameness they rejected the notion. Ach! Music was being taken to new heights in, of all places, Turkey, but there was a fear the Turks would usurp all that was European in Hungary. It seemed as if I had resorted to simply repeating myself. My life was stripped from me. I was stripped bare."

"You have quite the imagination."

"I have the skill of attracting trouble. I've often thought the gallows worker saved a noose for me."

"But you were you well loved in your time, no?"

"All men have enemies. I had a few."

"Salieri? Your fellow composer?"

"Salieri lacks a certain gift, the gift of melody. But I don't mean him. I mean the creditors to whom I owe many florins."

"Did your wife help you?"

"Constanze stays with me. She's very good, that Weber. Father never approved, but she's a good woman. I'm a difficult man."

"I think you know what you want and that makes you very strong."

Some moments of silence pass as both visually soak in the hustle and bustle of the market. Mozart yawns.

"You're tired," Bowen notices. "I'll take you to my place of employment. You can rest along the way."

Bowen pulls into a parking garage near the University of Washington. Mozart is fast asleep in the passenger seat. He awakens him and they both begin walking towards the sprawling compass.

It is now mid-afternoon. There is still a cloudy overcast. Students are walking about, some carrying backpacks, some on skateboards. Half of them are on cell phones and it seems a good portion is also using headphones. Walking past students laying on the various fields, they enter the Physics-Astronomy Building.

"Were you educated here?" Mozart asks Bowen.

"Partially. I received my doctorate in physics from Washington State University." He points eastward.

"It's about 400 miles that way. I teach it here, though. This is the University of Washington. I'll show you my office." He leads Mozart through the halls, past several symposiums, and into the building's huge basement laboratory.

"Gott in himmel," Mozart whispers as they walk side by side throughout the cavernous interior filled with all types of machines, technical artwork and elaborate mobiles dangling from the ceiling.

Bowen introduces him to a few faculty members and students. Intermittently, he'd motion to the composer to not touch anything. Mozart, for the most part, was caught up in his own world for he had found a metallic structure the size of an elevator which played musical notes.

Bowen walks over to him. "This is the Hildebrandt Generator," he explains. "It's a musical instrument whose tones are produced by light."

He illustrates its fascinating design by producing a small flashlight from his jacket and turning it one. When he flashed its light on one of the Hildebrandt panels, it would chime like a bell. Each panel produced a different tone. Mozart is taken aback by the structure, its glimmering light flashing in his eyes.

"Not only does it respond to light," Bowen explains, "it also responds to color."

He illustrates this by turning a dial on his penlight which changed its light beam from a bright white to a fluorescent green. When he shines it on the Generator, a tone like a violin is emitted. "Now watch this," he tells Mozart as he flicks a switch on a projector nearby.

As the projector flashes different colours of the spectrum unto the machine, it responds by playing music that sounds like a symphony. Mozart is stunned.

"Are there no musicians involved?"

"No. It's pretty nice, huh?"

"Impressive. Which music is this?"

"Beethoven's 6th symphony. Pastoral."

"What year was this written?"

"I'm not sure. Maybe around 1805."

"I'd be fifty-one years old when he wrote this. The styles have changed immensely."

"Blame Beethoven."

"Had I no influence at that time?"

"Times and tastes change, Mozart."

"Did I become the kappelmeister to the emperor? I'm sure my fortunes would have been vastly improved by then. How many children did I have? Twenty?" he laughs.

"I'm sure you must agree that to truly appreciate life one must experience the joy of discovery."

"Then I agree. Don't tell me."

"It's always for the best."

After the visit in the lab, Bowen showed the curious pianist several other attractions including a large sundial, a giant pendulum, more research labs, and finally, the stunning planetarium in all its fully illuminated glory.

After eating dinner in an Italian restaurant near University Way, they walk into a record store. "Here in the 20th century," Bowen begins, "there are many ways to acquire music." He picks up a used album, takes the vinyl out and shows it to Mozart. "This is an album of rock music, for instance." He picks up another album from a different bin. "This is jazz music. It was invented around 1915, 1920. Still very popular today."

Something catches the corner of Mozart's eye and he walks over to it. It is a live album of Mozart's opera "Idomeneo" featuring Luciano Pavarotti. The composer is floored.

"I'd like to hear this," he shouts to Bowen. Embarrassed, the physicist motions for him to keep his voice down. But still excited, Mozart ignores him and runs to a clerk behind the counter.

"Play this," he commands him. The clerk is naturally taken aback.

"Umm, you have to buy it first."

"How many florins?" Mozart asks.

"How many what?" the clerk queries.

Bowen walks over. "Do you have this on CD?" he questions him.

"Aisle 6. All the classical is right there."

Bowen takes Mozart's elbow and walks him over to Aisle 6. Looking though the racks they don't find "Idomeneo", but several other CD's capture Mozart's eyes, including recordings of his operas "Don Giovanni", "Le Nozze di Figaro" and "Cosi fan Tutte." They also see some recordings of his concertos, symphonies, masses, string quartets, piano and violin sonatas, and requiems.

"I want them all," the tunesmith beams, grinning from ear to ear.

"Are you joking?" Bowen objects. "That's about three or four hundred dollars in your hand right now."

"I don't know how much that is and I don't care."

"You don't even know what they sound like. You might hate them. Just get one for now."

Disappointed, Mozart looks over the CD's and finally decides on a recording of "Don Giovanni." They place the other CD's back and return to the front counter clerk.

After Bowen pays for it, he opens it and gives the first CD to the clerk who puts it in the store's stereo. The overture begins. Mozart smiles and closes his eyes. Unconsciously, he starts directing the music. Every so often he'd hum along and make semi-audible comments such as "more tutti here", "slower, slower...", "forte!" or "presto adagio!"

"How does it sound?" Bowen asks interrupting his reverie.

"Which orchestra is this?"

Bowen picks up the CD and reads the credits in the back.

"Berlin Philharmonic. Herbert von Karajan conducting. I understand he's a bit of a Mozart scholar. Or should I say, a bit of a *your* scholar."

"The orchestra is much larger," Mozart notices. "How many violins in each section? Is that sixteen?"

"You can hear that?" Bowen wonders.

"So dense. It's like a forest. There must be at least sixty or seventy musicians there. They've expanded the brass section. The oboes and woodwinds have also been changed. The instruments sound bigger."

"Do you like it?"

"It's different."

Bowen, suddenly remembering something, peers at his watch. "We have to go," he tells Mozart. "Don't want to be late."

Mozart squints at him. "Late for what?"

Bowen whispers in his ear.

"Wunderbar, " Mozart exclaims.

Mozart and Bowen are walking towards the entrance of Benaroya Hall, the city's main symphony space. In the middle of the cascading staircase is a miniature rainforest complete with waterfall. Beset on all sides of the entrance are various statues. The huge posters dangling in the front advertise the hall's current program, a Mostly Mozart Festival.

"I said you weren't forgotten," the physicist informs him.

"So I see."

The two stand in line in the lobby waiting to purchase tickets. Mozart can barely hide his excitement. He twiddles his thumbs, hums a tune and dances lightly in place. His actions are noticed by the couple behind him.

"Seems like you're excited," the man tells him.

"I should be conducting," Mozart explains.

"Oh, are you a conductor?"

"I'm—"

"I've seen his programs before," the man interrupts. "He's one of the best interpreters of Mozart in the world."

"Better than me?" Mozart asks him.

Just then Bowen taps the overzealous composer on his shoulder. "Give me your hand. You have to get stamped."

"Was ist das?" he asks.

The clerk in the booth next to the ticket seller stamps a small picture of a treble clef on Mozart's right wrist.

"It's so you can drink," Bowen tells him.

"Of course I can drink," the puzzled musician clarifies.

"Come on, Mozart. Let's go to the beer garden."

Mozart is standing at the counter of the Wolfgang Puck restaurant in the main lobby of the hall. Bowen is off to one side speaking to two friends.

"Who is Wolfgang Puck?" Mozart asks a clerk.

"He's the chef. The owner of this place."

"My name is Wolfgang, too."

"Wonderful. What'll you have?"

"Ich verstehe nicht," Mozart replies, not understanding the clerk.

"Do. You. Want. Some. Thing. To. Drink?" she asks rudely.

"Anything with wine," he answers.

"Can I see your I. D.?"

Mozart looks puzzled.

"Your driver's license. A photo I. D. Anything."

"I don't drive." He shows her his wrist.

"I still need your I. D. Sorry. Restaurant rules."

The composer gnashes his teeth. He can feel his blood pressure rising.

The clerk turns, pours a glass of cold water, and hands it to Mozart. "On the house."

He takes a sip. "It's not wine."

"Next customer," she yells to the patron behind him.

Annoyed, Mozart storms off.

Bowen and Mozart are sitting in the theatre as seats start filling up. Mozart is drinking wine. He raises his glass to scientific host.

"Thanks for this."

"You're welcome, Mozart."

"Herr Bowen, I can tell you with certainty that, even though items may change, machines become more advanced, and cities continually grow, there is no absence of the discourtesy mankind will bestow upon each other."

"Inherent in us all," Bowen agrees.

Soon after, the lights dim. The conductor walks out onstage to roaring applause. He greets the first violinist. Then, taking his place at the podium, commences the strains of Mozart's Symphony No. 40 in G Minor.

Some two hours later, the two are driving back towards Bowen's house. "Did you enjoy yourself?" he asks Mozart.

"Yes. It was very exhausting. However, I must admit, I'm not ready for your world."

"I thought you'd be fascinated by all the new technology."

"I fear it's too much all at once. My sanity would slip away by several leagues at once."

Bowen glances at the clock in the dashboard. "It's almost time," he remarks.

"Time for what?" Mozart wonders. "Not another attraction."

"No," Bowen explains, "the branch is snapping back into place. The two ends of our time travel will be meeting again. It'll be time for you to return."

"And if I stayed?"

"Okay. I'll try to explain this simply. When I brought you here I created an interruption in the time and space continuum. I interrupted the natural flow of events. The bad thing about that is I created an unpredictable scenario. Can you, for instance, be younger than your own grandson? No, but in essence, that's what I've done. Such a shift could have dire consequences. That's why they need to be avoided."

"Okay," Mozart states although the reluctance in his voices betrays his disappointment.

The two are standing in front of the time machine. Bowen has changed into his white transmission suit and Mozart in his original bedclothes. The composer begins rubbing his legs. He's clearly nervous. Bowen continues making adjustments on the computer.

"Is it working?" Mozart asks.

"Almost there," Bowen explains. "Looks like everything's coming online."

"This has been a wonderful experience, Herr Bowen."

They shake hands. Mozart pats him on the back.

"You are a true brother," he comments.

"I wish you could take something back with you, Mozart," Bowen apologizes, "but for continuity sake, and to prevent a disruption in the transfer, everything has to be exactly as they were."

"I understand, I think."

"I'll forever treasure my memory of you," Bowen smiles showing Mozart the photo from Pike Place Market. Just then, several lights begin flashing on the machine. "It's time."

Bowen presses a button on the machine and its door opens. A thick cloud of cold fog rolls out. Bowen motions to Mozart to enter. As he does, Bowen follows behind and shuts the door. A whirring noise and a blinding flash of light erupt from the machine.

December 4, 1791 – 9 p.m.

The famous German composer Wolfgang Amadeus Mozart, bloated and weakened from chronic emphysema and rheumatic fever, is lying on his deathbed surrounded by his wife Constanze, her sister Sophie and their seven year old son Karl. Lit candles are perched throughout the bedroom located at the apartment at Stadt 970, Rauhensteingasse, Kleines Kaiserhaus in Vienna. Mozart moans; Constanze hold his hand.

Suddenly, a flash of blinding white light and fog appears in the corner of the room next to a window. Constanze screams. Her sister gasps.

A middle aged man, dressed completely in white, appears in the fog and stretches his right arm out towards Mozart. He motions to the ailing composer to take his hand even though he's standing about twenty feet away. Mozart raises his right arm out towards the stranger. A bright blue light suddenly emits from the man's right hand and covers the sickened genius

"Wolfie," Constanze screams.

The man in white disappears with the fog. All parties in the room are astonished by the vision. Karl walks over to the area where the fog was to investigate. He finds nothing. Mozart, lying firmly in bed and weakened from disease, is smiling.

"Why are you happy?" Constanze asks him.

"I have been to a world," he whispers weakly, "which you shall never see."

She feels his forehead. "You're as hot as the sun." She looks at Karl. "Please bring your father a basin of water and a towel."

Karl races off to do as his mother requested.

"You are special," Sophie tells the music writer. "For with my own eyes I saw an angel just now."

"That was no angel," Mozart explains.

"Who was that, Wolfie?" Constanze asks. "Was that God?"

"No," he explains. "Just a man from the future. A very wise man. I spent some time with him."

The two ladies look at each other with puzzlement etched on their faces. They turn and resume monitoring the weak composer.

"I think we've all been inflicted with whatever ails our dear Wolfgang," Sophie admits.

"Yes," Constanze agrees. "We'd better not tell a soul lest we get thrown into an asylum."

Mozart coughs weakly. Karl returns with the bowl of water. Constanze soaks the towel in it, wrings the water out, and places the towel on his brow.

"Was I a good provider?" he asks.

"Not was, but are, Wolfie," Constanze reassures him. Sophie takes his hand.

"You shouldn't worry so much."

Just then she notices the treble clef stamped in his right wrist. She and Constanze gasp.

"Where did this come from?" Sophie asks.

Mozart coughs again. Too weak to answer, he simply closes his eyes. At that moment, a strong gust of wind blows the window open. Constanze walks over to close it. As she does, she looks outside. In the distance she sees a ball of white light shimmer like a child's brand new playing marble. Then, she watches as it spirals further and further away in the distance and suddenly disappears.

The Family of Gabriel

I've had some unusual assignments for the local weekly newspaper I freelance for, but the one where the editor asked me to do an in-depth report on the Family of Gabriel takes the biscuit. I suspected the editor was running out of stories, but after spending some time with the Family, I thought he was just playing a cruel joke on me.

When I talk about the Family, I'm not referring to a man, his wife, their children, and an outing at Disneyworld. This was actually a group of friends and family members, all of them white as far as I could see, and all ranging from lower to middle class. From the last report I heard, they numbered something like 100 to 200 people. A religion-based group, they had their own church called the Church of the Bleeding Cross in rural Lake Ketchum, just 60 miles north of Seattle in Snohomish County.

I asked my editor what, exactly, did he want me to find out. He said they were mysterious and controversial, and the reports or rumors of their brutality and depravity needed to be revealed. Brutality? Depraved? Who were they brutal against? Their children? Their animals? Themselves? That's what he wanted me to find out. I'd initially objected because the last depraved thing I saw, Hideshi Hino's underground film 'Flower of Flesh and Blood', gave me nightmares, and I wasn't ready to re-up on that experience. After convincing me it may really just be rumors, I decided to give it a shot. It's not like I had an inbox filled with assignments.

The day I set out to investigate them, I had butterflies in my stomach. Actually, it was more like genetically-modified Monarchs with stinger attachments. A friend of mine warned me not to go because she heard it could be life-changing. I reassured her I had my head screwed on pretty tight, I hoped, so I shouldn't be easily swayed. I packed a few belongings in a backpack and headed out to the church.

When I got to Lake Ketchum, I asked the locals outside of an auto and marine store if they knew where the church was since it wasn't listed anywhere. Everyone said no. A young couple with multiple tattoos and piercings said they knew where its general location was and drew me some directions on a piece of paper. Following their arrows and signs, I drove down a few winding rural lanes, some of them unpaved. Finally, through the woods, I saw a church in the distance. Situated next to a secluded farmhouse, it was a perfect hideaway.

Parking my car on the side of the road, I walked the narrow path to the church. Attached to the front of it was a plaque containing a cross dripping blood. I should've taken this as a "keep away" sign, but I went inside anyway. Seeming much larger in its interior, it looked like a typical church. There were pews, stained glass windows, an altar with pulpit, a large urn of sticks in front of the altar, two sections of devotional candles, and other items.

The only people in the building were two young men in their twenties sitting in the pews talking. They didn't seem like they were praying so I walked over to introduce myself.

"Hey, fellas," I began. "I'm guessing this is the Church of the Bleeding Cross?"

"You got it," the first one with wiry brown hair said.

"Who are you?" the second one asked.

"My name's Justin van der Mey. I'm from Seattle." I shook their hands.

"I'm Caleb," the first man introduced him.

"I'm Ezekiel," the second man with long black hair uttered.

"How are you gentlemen?" I asked.

"Couldn't be better," Ezekiel nodded.

"Are you two brothers?" I queried. "It's not often you hear names like that."

"We're brothers of the spirit, not of the flesh," Ezekiel informed me. "A lot of folks around here are."

"I see. You two belong to this church?"

"Yep," Caleb answered. "So what brings you way out here to no man's land?"

"I write for a Seattle weekly. I'm on assignment."

"Assignment?" Ezekiel asked. "What kind of assignment."

"There are rumors circulating about the, um, well, I've heard ... ah, I'll just come out with it. The followers of this church teach pain as a means of redemption?"

"That's not true," Ezekiel affirms. "What people don't understand, they vilify."

"So there's no torture going on here?"

Both men laugh.

I watched them with curiosity. Something just didn't seem right. Perhaps it was their effortless laughter or their quick denial of the truth. I thought maybe I should press further. "I think you guys are holding out on me," I offered. "My editor has reliable sources that's never steered him wrong."

"Let me see your hand," Caleb asked.

"Huh?" I asked. "My hand? Why?"

"I thought you were a reporter," he speculated. "Where's your curiosity?"

Reluctantly, I stretched out my right hand.

"Is this the hand you write with, he asked?"

"Yes."

"Then let me see your left."

I stretched it out.

"What do you want to do? Read my fortune?"

I should have seen this coming. He grabbed my hand and placed it palm up on the back of a pew. Ezekiel whipped out a hammer and long thick nail from his pocket and, in one swift movement, drove the nail through my hand, fastening it to the bench.

I screamed as blood gushed out then grabbed my left wrist with my right hand to try and numb the pain. The men simply stood and watched as I writhed in agony.

"You bastards," I yelled. "What the hell."

"Watch your language in the house of the lord," Caleb admonished me.

"Pull it out," I screamed. "Pull it out."

Ezekiel complied and removed the nail. "You guys are crazy," I cursed, holding my hand against my stomach.

"Welcome to the Church of the Bleeding Cross," Caleb stated. "Hope you enjoy your stay."

I got up and started walking down the aisle.

"I'm going to the police with this," I threatened.

"Go ahead," Ezekiel insisted. "But they're with us."

"And you won't get your story," Caleb bragged.

I left the church, walked to the car, removed some tissues from a holder, and sopped up the blood. I started the car but then I looked at the church and the farmhouse next to the church and thought about going back to Seattle with no story. I wasn't sure how badly the editor needed this article, but if there was a good chance I'd be the one exposing the Family, I'd have a shot as a full-fledged writer. That meant a steady income, vacations, the whole nine. I took a deep breath, turned off the car, got out and walked to the house.

Knocking on the door, I was met by a woman with a kind face in her thirties. She was wearing a pastel no frills dress and wore a matching headscarf. "Can I help you?" she asked.

I held up my bloody left hand.

"Oh, I see," she stated. "Okay. Come in. Have a seat."

Sitting in a chair in the living room, I watched as two young children sat on the floor watching TV. The boy had bandages completely wrapped around both feet. The girl had her left arm in a sling.

"Hi," I greeted them.

"Hello," they said.

"What happened to you guys?" I asked.

"Nothing," the girl answered.

"Nothing?" I asked. "You're both bandaged up."

Just then, their mother returned from the kitchen with first aid supplies. "They're fine, Mr …"

"Van der Mey. Justin Van der Mey," I told her.

"My name's Serah. This here's Eli and Esther. Now, hold out your hand," she requested.

I did as she asked. Pieces of tissue had already stuck to the wound.

"Hold still," she advised.

Taking my hand, she poured alcohol on it. I screamed so loudly I saw stars.

"Don't you have an anesthetic or something that doesn't burn?"

"Not around here," she answered.

"Then how about a pain reliever?"

"Those are forbidden."

"What? That's ridiculous."

"I know your type," she informed me. "City slickers, think they know it all, think your way of life is the best because you're so advanced with your technology and your space flights. Around here, redemption is king. Sharing the spirit of the divine one rises above all."

Yeah, whatever, I thought. Another customer missing from the loony bid.

"You're more than welcome to join in one of our services," she told me. "That's how you learn. How about tomorrow after breakfast?"

"In the church next door?"

"Of course. Where are you staying?"

"Nowhere," I answered, the pain in my hand finally subsiding.

"You can stay here if you want. Don't worry. I won't charge you anything. It's my way of apologizing."

"Yeah, I guess," I stated. "Thanks for the offer."

"No problem. It's almost dinner time. Why don't you freshen up and we'll eat. You actually came at a good time. We're celebrating tonight."

"Celebrating what?"

"One of our members will be experiencing ascension tomorrow."

"What's that?"

"You'll see."

"Okay. Where's the bathroom?"

She pointed to the hall. "Down there to the right."

I got up, went to the bathroom, and took a nice long shower. Afterwards, I joined them for dinner. It was a splendid feast of stuffed baked lamb, green bean casserole, creamy garlic mashed potatoes with onion gravy, curried zucchini soup, and Southern lemon meringue pie. Surprisingly, despite there being many adults in attendance, there was no wine, beer or any other liquor. I did ask about it, but Serah notified me since liquor dulled the senses, it was forbidden.

Several of Serah's friends were also in attendance. There was Nathan and Nicholas, the twins with their wives, Abigail and Janna. Jacob and his wife, Gihon, a name she told me meaning valley of grace. Melchiah, Candace, Peter and Rachel from neighboring North Stanwood, and David and his new bride, Diana, from nearby Camano Island.

The women, I noticed, were all dressed the same. They all wore pastel dresses with matching head scarves. The men wore simple black slacks and white shirts. Sitting there in my jeans and t-shirt, I obviously felt out of place. They understood, though, considering the circumstances, and they were all friendly and open about their church.

During dinner, I got the sense that a man named Melchiah was their unofficial leader. When he spoke, everyone kept quiet. When he made a suggestion, they all agreed. I soon learned from Serah that it was Melchiah who was achieving ascension in the morning and, in the Family of Gabriel, it was the most honorable and respected position to be in.

Ascension, according to the dinner guests, meant he'd be closer to the spirit. He'd be one of the few to walk side by side with Gabriel. In essence, he'd be raised to a new position over his fellow man. How was he to achieve all of this? She promised I would see the next day.

I slept in a guest room in the farmhouse but had initially stayed up most of the night writing about the day's events and thinking about the ascension. I hoped I was prepared for it. Nathan told me it was nothing like I'd ever seen before. Abigail swore it'd open my eyes to a whole new world. David explained the ideology behind the Family of Gabriel.

Gabriel, he said, was an angel, or archangel as some believed. As an agent of the Lord, he was given the task of punishing the sinful or delivering the holy and worthy to heaven. Gabriel, himself, was also known for self flagellation and fasting as a response to man's lack of devotion or inhumanity. As the Family's patron saint, he was their beacon in a world of despair.

One thing I did notice, which was peculiar, was the dinner guests themselves. Abigail, Gihon and Peter all walked with a limp. Jacob's voice was slurred. There was a scar on his left cheek. I thought perhaps that had something to do with it. The twins were missing a few fingers on their left hand. Peter was most interested in my left hand and showed me his. There was a hole right through it where I could see Serah in the background. Bizarre. I don't know if this was a freak show or a nightmare come to life, but I didn't have the guts to ask why everyone was damaged.

The next morning, I ate breakfast with Serah and her kids. I asked her what happened to their father and she told me he ascended last year. Ascended? Yes. He experienced ascension and died shortly afterwards. I asked her what killed him. She said he was called. When pressed, she gave no further explanation.

Around 10 a.m., the church was packed with worshippers. A lot of the faithful, I noticed, were limping. Some wore slings like Esther, others had eye patches or sat in wheelchairs with their legs in braces or wrapped in a cast. The priest walked to the speaker's stand, picked up a trumpet from beneath the podium, and blasted out a note. Replacing it, he led them through one prayer of Our Father. Afterwards, he preached a little, recited a homily, and read a few chapters from the Book of Ezra.

Melchiah, who was sitting up front, approached the altar and knelt when the priest called his name. The parishioners applauded. Caleb and Ezekiel, now wearing priestly robes, approached Melchiah from the left and right and removed his robe. The kneeling supplicant, now wearing just a loincloth, kept his head bowed.

"One of our brothers has been called," the priest bellowed. The audience applauded. "Such acts of divinity are rare in today's society. Mankind deserves more. We quest for power, our ambitions are boundless, we taint the soil with our callous greed and our pretensions of sincerity, but it is us who are fooled. We have turned our back on his divine majesty. Today, one among us will reignite those flames and illuminate the path to Gabriel's merciful glory." The congregation exploded with raucous applause. Some even whistled like they were at a ball game.

"Brother Melchiah," the priest asked him, "are you prepared to lead the way?"

"Yes," the prostrate believer responded.

"Brother Melchiah," the priest continued, "I need to know if you are sincere in your ascension today."

"I'm sincere," he shouted at the top of his lungs.

"Brother Melchiah, are you ready to be borne on the wings of Gabriel to see the divine truth?"

"Yes. I'm ready."

The worshippers started stomping their feet methodically. The priest nodded to Caleb and Ezekiel. They nodded in response and walked over to a small cauldron that was sitting on a bed of hot coals in a nook near the altar. They picked it up, brought it over to Melchiah, and poured the steaming hot liquid on his back. He screamed. The congregation stomped louder.

The priest took a glowing hot brand from the hot coals and pressed it to Melchiah's back. He screamed again. Members of the audience lined up in the aisle, grabbed a stick from the urn near the front of the altar, and struck the bleeding blistering man while the priest poured hot water on his feet.

Minutes later, the priest returned to the altar and everyone took a seat.

"Finally," he remarked, "the last rite of ascension." He motioned to Caleb and Ezekiel who walked over with a device that looked like a giant stapler. "Though we all experience pain in our day to day lives to remind us of our frailty, today one of us will know what it feels like to never experience the end of our torment."

He motioned to his assistants. Caleb walked over to Melchiah and held the two parts of a giant thumb-sized rivet on the top and bottom of his right foot. Ezekiel used the giant stapler device to force the rivets together, joining them in the middle of the screaming man's foot. They repeat edthe same thing with his left foot.

"Now, my brother," the priest extolled, "you will know what it is like to walk with the flames of Etna every waking day."

After a while, I couldn't take it anymore. I felt my nerves twitching, my blood boiling, and my temperature rising. I jumped up and screamed.

"What the hell does any of this have to do with religion?"

Everyone stopped and looked at me, my veins bulging out of my neck like a weight lifter at a meet.

"This man has chosen ascension today," the priest enlightened me. "No jurisdiction, no mortal laws or ordinances holds sway over these proceedings. This, all of these people, all of our worship, is protected by *your* own constitution. This is *our* way of life."

"You people are insane," I screamed. "This can't be happening."

"Do what you wish with this information," he told me, "but rest assured, none of this you will forget. Come join us and see the light of his divinity."

"Over my dead body," I yelled before storming of the church.

"You'll be back," the priest reckoned.

"Really?" I shot back. "What makes you so sure?"

"Now that you've experienced it, you'll seek us out again."

"Bullshit," I yelled then exited.

I wrote up my report and handed it to my editor the following day. He called me up a few hours later and told me he'd pass on publishing it. I asked him why, he said it wasn't that believable. Believable? I had a hole in my hand I can shove a pencil through and my story was non believable? He told me the story was incomplete. It needed to be more compelling. I asked him if he wanted me to join the church, perhaps even attempt ascension. He said it sounded like a good idea.

That week, with no new assignments coming in, I gave some thought about going back to Lake Ketchum. I actually bought a video camera just in case I returned. I kept thinking about church, the priest, the blood, Melchiah, everything. Two months later, I was sitting with Serah and her kids at their long table eating lamb.

Strung Out

18 year old Simon, a teen so pale he's almost ghost-white, is zooming down a darkened Seattle street in the Central District as fast as his thin legs will take him. Paranoid and frightened, he keeps looking back as if the devil is at his heels. Pushing past two homeless men, the slender leather-jacketed teen inadvertently leaps over a woman sleeping near the curb, causing him to trip over a garbage can. Getting up, he crosses the street and continues running, then jumps to avoid stepping on a cat. This makes him fly into some overgrown hedges. Luckily, dawn is just breaking, so there's hardly anyone else on the block to see his embarrassment.

In a daze, he rises, runs his fingers through his dyed blood red hair, and limps down the block until he comes to the facade of a condemned five story building. To its right is an empty lot where another building used to be. The structure itself is protected by a high metal gate. On either side there is a high barbed wire fence.

Carefully, Simon pulls aside the base of the left fence, edges his way in, and treads down the litter-strewn alley towards the back where he sees a rusty fire escape already hanging down to the ground. Silently, he grabs the escape, ascends all five stories, arrives at a glass-less window, and pulls himself in on the fifth floor.

He walks over to a lamp sitting on the floor and flicks it on. Standing only about two feet tall, the lamp emits just enough light to walk around safely, but not enough to bring unwanted attention from outside. The poor lighting, no doubt, serves double duty in lessening the decrepit appearance of the room which serves as the apartment's kitchen. There are holes in every wall. The stove is so burnt and rusted that not even a junkyard would buy it for scrap metal.

Simon, attired from head to foot in gothic black garb, black eyeliner, lipstick, and fingernail polish, removes a small foil-wrapped packet from his pocket, places it on the rickety table and sits down on one of the four plastic chairs. Gently, he opens the packet to reveal a small amount of powdered speed about the size of an aspirin in it. His hands have a slight tremor.

He hears a scraping sound coming from one of the bedrooms. Closing the foil packet, he gets up, walks towards the bedroom, listens at the door, opens it, and enters. A table lamp, sitting low in one corner of the small room, is on but its light is subdued. The window shade is open, allowing the early morning luminescence to enter. Like the rest of the building, this room is on its last legs.

Decorated in eerie black and red, there are several old posters of goth rock and darkwave groups—Marilyn Manson, Skinny Puppy, KMFDM, GWAR, KISS, Psychotica, and Impotent Sea Snakes—on the walls.

Simon removes his heavily accessorized old leather jacket, drapes it over a chair, tiptoes over to the eighteen year old Spaniard sleeping on the floor mattress and whispers in his ear.

"Polo." The boy stirs, but doesn't wake up. Simon whispers a little louder. "Polo."

Polo remains asleep. Simon creeps over to the floor where a busted boombox rests, turns the volume knob all the way up, and presses play. Loud, screaming death metal shoots from the speakers.

"Ahhh," Polo yells.

Simon stops the CD.

"Jesus Christ!" Polo adds.

Simon laughs. Polo doesn't see the joke. "Do you know what time it is?"

"Hey," Simon apologizes, "I tried to wake you up the old fashioned way."

"By giving me a heart attack? What the hell is wrong with you, dude?"

"Easy, *mi Latino amigo*. I brought you a present." Simon sits next to his friend and opens the packet of foil. Polo sits up and studies it.

"Rolling powder?" he asks.

"Even better. GHB."

"What the fuck is that?"

Simon grabs a book from the floor, brings it onto the mattress, and makes two lines from the powder on it with his long pinky nail. "Twelve hour power," he brags.

"Man," Polo admits, "last time I tweaked I stayed up for a week and lost twenty pounds."

"Yeah, well that was Special K. This is different. I stole it from Rocky."

"Rocky who?"

"You don't know him. Just some greaseball dealer."

"You should be more careful."

"It's all right. He didn't see me, I think. It was dark. There was a couple of us there."

"You're crazy. Out all night, sleep all day like a fucking vampire. Look at you. You already look like a ghost."

"Which one? Casper?"

Polo groans.

"Gimme a dollar," Simon begs his friend.

"I look like I got money to you?"

Simon carefully rips out one of the pages from the book.

"I was reading that, dude," Polo protests.

"Bullshit, you fucking dropout. You can't recognize your own name in print."

"Fuck you."

"I'll make you a short line."

Simon rolls the page into a straw and inhales his line and half of Polo's while the young Latino studies him. Simon smiles and nods. Polo takes the "straw" and inhales his short line. The powder burns his nose. "Ouch."

"That's not enough for a burn, you wuss."

Simon wipes off the lingering bits of powder from Polo's nose then they kiss. Polo feels something inside Simon's mouth.

"What the ...?"

Simon sticks his tongue out and shows his boyfriend the silver stud poking through it.

"You did that last night?" Polo asks.

"Yeah. Some john bought it for me. I did contribute to it, though."

"Now I guess you're broke."

"So what? You're the angel Gabriel all of a sudden?"

"We've been in this place too long, Simon. Look at us. We're dying, man."

"Then we'll die together."

Polo shakes his head. Simon hugs him then licks his face with the stud. "Wanna see how this feels all over?"

***

In the living room of the same house, Rip, a nineteen year old white guy with blond dreadlocks, awakens next to his girlfriend, a pretty white-black mix with curly black hair named Janis. They've seen better days, and so has the room. And like the other rooms, there's only one source of light, a little lamp sitting on the floor which, at the moment, is off.

Rip, looking somewhat confused, turns the lamp on and studies the area almost as if he'd never seen it before. The meager decorations in the room reflect Rip's interest in reggae—red, gold and green paint with Marley posters—amidst a large wrinkled poster of Janis Joplin, Janis' heroine and namesake. On the makeshift door is a large sign which reads "One Love." Against a wall is a towering bookcase filled with old records.

On a small table near a window sits a fish tank with only one inhabitant, an angel fish the size of a fist. Like the kitchen, the walls show signs of wear and tear; the heavy curtain over the window is dry, crumbly, dusty, and full of holes. There's a crater the size of a bicycle wheel in the middle of the floor that looks down to the floor below. A black and white TV sits atop an old stereophonic system in a corner.

Getting up, Rip walks over to the TV and puts it on. Janis awakens.

"What time is it?" she asks.

"Almost seven. Why? You got someplace to be?"

"I was just asking." She notices he's busy searching the floor amidst the cornucopia of books, clothing, utensils and other items.

"Hey Rip, what are you looking for?" she asks.

He finally holds up a marijuana roach. "This. You got a lighter?"

She reaches under the torn mattress, produces a cheap lighter, and throws it to him.

"Thanks, Janis."

Several attempts at igniting its wick prove fruitless. "These sixty cent lighters suck," he moans.

Janis shrugs. Rip exits out to the kitchen to look for matches. Searching earnestly on the shelves and cupboards, he finds nothing. Then, he walks over to Polo's room and raps lightly on the door. Receiving no answer, he opens the door and peeks in. With his face in the slit of the door, he sees Polo and Simon sleeping under the covers in each other's arms.

Spying a lighter on an overturned box, he tiptoes into the room, steals the lighter, backs out quietly, and closes the door. Back in the living room, he lights the roach and takes a deep drag while Janis reaches for a near empty bottle of soda lying on the floor. Rip offers her a drag but she refuses.

"Not right now. My mouth's dry." After downing what's left of the warm pop, she flips the bottle across the room into the large hole.

"Two points," she says.

Rip plops down in front of the TV and changes the channel.

"What are you watching?" she asks.

"Wild Animal Rescues."

Janis looks at the program for a moment then winces. "Ewww. I know he ain't gonna do CPR on that deer."

"The mother's dead. How else they gonna save the baby?"

"Oh gross. I can't look at this shit so early in the morning. What I really need is a fix."

Rip grunts. Janis gets up. She's wearing a pair of black panties and an old tie-dyed T-shirt. "Where's my shirt?" she asks.

"I don't know. Take one of mine."

Janis puts on a lamp, searches the room momentarily, grabs a long sleeve shirt from the floor, shakes it, and sniffs the armpits. "Damn. This smell can trigger a spontaneous abortion." She removes her T-shirt and dons his shirt anyway.

"What are you doing today?" she queries.

"I don't know. What do you wanna do?"

"Oh, I don't know. I thought I'd complete my portfolio, maybe leave a resume at Prudential Securities."

"Sounds good. Don't forget to include your pre-afternoon $10 special on head."

"A bargain compared to what you offer."

"You're cute. You should be on the Tonight Show."

"Get me an application."

Rip turns the TV off and gets up. "I'm heading out."

"Where ya going?" she asks.

"To find gainful employment."

"You? Please. I'd be worm shit by then."

"Seriously."

"Your name on a pay stub? This I have to see."

"Why not? I'm tired of this Nowhere Man shit. It's fucking played out." Stepping over the crater, he walks to the glass-less window facing west, moves aside the blanket nailed in front of it, and gazes out.

"You're the one who wanted a Bohemian lifestyle," Janis berates him. "Sorry, Charlie. Welcome to Earth. Why don't you just sign up for The Army? Cut to the chase."

"Maybe I should. Ain't you tired of this fucking hellhole?"

"The rent's pretty reasonable. At least we got the best suite in the building. This one at *least* has a floor … most of it, anyway."

"I think you see my point, Janis. This ain't the kinda place to bring up my little brother."

"He ain't complaining."

He turns to face her. "He's only 14. He'll go where ever I go. I know I ain't doing right in his eyes."

"Here we go with that guilt trip shit again."

"Well, it's true, ain't it? I mean, who else is gonna look after him? The state? They'd just keep him medicated because of his condition. Turn him into a fuckin' zombie. Over my stinking corpse."

"How 'bout a shrink? He's nuttier than a fucking Almond Joy."

"Look at this. The pot calling the kettle black."

"You're both weird."

Rip ignores her comment and looks out the window.

"Your mother OD'd last year," she emphasizes, "and now you feel you gotta take care of Lucky? You don't have to."

"So what? He's my brother."

"You gotta get your own self together."

"That's why I've been thinking about Job Corps. They put you up in some kinda living environment, give you skills and shit."

"Skills? You're a garbage head, Rip."

"Fuck you."

"Admit it."

"And you're just a fucking whore."

"At least I know who I am. Who are you?"

Rip has no answer. Janis walks over to the large stereophonic and turns it on. Rip stares at her for a moment then climbs out of the window, walks along a ledge, and descends down the fire escape.

An alarm clock goes off in Lucky's room, or lab as he calls it, at 7 a.m. Its piercing noise is suddenly silenced by a baseball bat smashing it into pieces.

"Stupid noisemaker."

Laying the bat aside, 14 year old Lucky, Rip's brother, continues resting for about a minute, then rises from his mattress and staggers over to a window, rubbing his hands as he walks. He pulls the blinds open and stares out at the garbage-strewn lot where he sees Rip crossing it at a fast pace. He taps loudly on the sill. Rips stops, turns, looks up at his brother, and waves. Lucky returns the gesture, then goes back to his room.

Resembling a chem lab, his room contains an old light table fashioned from a discarded Formica top sitting horizontally near a corner with pens strewn all over. The green walls are bare except for a string tied high up from one end to the next on which dollar bills of varying values are clipped. Various glass jars and beakers of different sizes sit on the floor in random areas.

He walks over to the money wall, takes one of the bills down, and examines it in the light. Shaking his head, he rips the bill into pieces and throws it in a garbage can by the light table. He takes another bill off the string and, after examining it, also rips it into shreds and tosses it. He quickly goes through the rest of the bills. Like the first two, he is also dissatisfied with their appearance.

"I can't do nothing right," he grunts.

In a frenzy, he rips every single bill into shreds, yanks the thin string off the wall, then quickly races out of the lab and into the bathroom where he immediately washes his hands over and over with a bar of bacterial soap kept hidden on a shelf beneath the sink. He stops momentarily to stare at himself in the dusty mirror.

"You're a wuss."

***

A Pakistani greengrocer is laying apples in his outdoor stand as Rip stands by just down the block out of view. When the grocer goes inside his store, Rip slowly walks down the block towards the stand and grabs a bunch of bananas. The greengrocer reappears just in time to see the thievery.

"Hey!"

Without hesitating, Rip zips down the block. The greengrocer raises a fist.

"Damn American hoodlums. This whole country's going to hell."

***

Janis pulls open the door to the bathroom just as Lucky is leaving. "Up already?" she asks him.

"So what?"

"It's not like you're going to school or anything."

"Get off my case."

"You should get help for that hand washing problem."

"Kiss my slim anus."

He enters his lab and closes the door. Janis makes a face and goes into the bathroom.

Lucky, standing at his makeshift drafting table, is penning in details on a $20 counterfeit bill. His spanking new pen set, a Staedler-Mars collection, seems to be out of place on the busted table light and giant cracked magnifying glass.

Pasted at the very top of the table are enlarged photocopies of $20 bills. Turning the bill he's working on over, he studies it closely through the glass then adds a few more swirl lines to the garlands on either side of the White House. Stopping to look at his hands, he exits the lab and quietly sneaks into the steamy bathroom where Janis is in the midst of a shower behind an old curtain. Slowly, he puts the sink faucet on and washes his hands. Janis immediately feels her own water turning cold.

"Turn that fucking water off, Lucky."

"In a minute."

She sticks her head out. "Now, dammit."

Lucky opens both faucets all the way up and darts out of the room. Janis seethes.

"Fucking brat."

Minutes later Janis, seductively attired in tiny red vinyl shorts, shiny black pumps, and a thin blouse, is descending the old, dangerous looking fire escape. The heel of one pump lodges in the 2nd floor grating. "Damn it!" She tugs at the shoe until it's free—minus the heel. "Shoot." She takes off the other pump and hits its heel against the wall till it loosens and falls off.

Polo appears in his fifth floor window. "Hey, Janis," he yells. "Wait up."

She looks up at him. "Hurry up, man. I ain't got all day."

He hurriedly climbs out of the window, walks along a ledge, then onto the escape. Minutes later, they go casually strolling down towards Capitol Hill.

Polo is wearing Simon's black leather jacket, a red skull cap, blue cutoff jeans over black tights, gray baggy socks and a pair of old Dr. Marten's boots. His long brown hair is tied back in a pony tail. At times he'd make a come-on to the passing suits, much to Janis' displeasure.

"Don't do that shit near me," she scolds him.

"Everybody's gotta eat, honey."

The two stop at a busy corner.

"Why don't you go work down the block or something?" she suggests.

"Why don't *you*?"

"Your kind don't come around here, anyway."

"Capitol Hill? It's a gay Mecca. What are you talking about?"

"I meant the rich ones."

Polo ignores her. A man in a business suit walks by. "Spare any change today, Mister?" Janis asks him.

The man looks at her like she's pond scum and continues on his way.

"Go fuck yourself," she tells him, though not loud enough where he'd hear her.

"Honey," Polo advises her, "you need to work on your delivery."

"I'm starving like Marvin and you're talking about delivery?"

"Oh, no. You *didn't* just raise your voice to me."

"Sorry, Pole."

"Take it easy, girl. Don't start acting all crazy on me now. Wasn't it I who saved your ass from that crazy motherfucker with the watermelon fetish?"

"I remember."

"All right. You still owe me. Hey, let's go see what they got over at the soup kitchen."

They both think about that idea for a second.

"Nah," they proclaim.

"Last time I ate that shit," Polo remembers, "I threw up for hours."

Suddenly, they see a red Mazda RX-7 pull up to the curb down the block.

"Shit," Janis states, "there's Harry. Gotta go." She half-trots to the car and leans into the passenger side. Then, after a couple of seconds, gets in. The car screeches off. Polo shakes his head. "Lucky bitch."

***

Lucky is still putting the finishing touches on his "bill" in his lab when he hears a knock on his door.

"Go away," he utters.

Rip enters with the bunch of bananas and orange juice.

"Thought you might want this."

"Hell yeah. Thanks."

Rip takes a banana and drops the rest on an old couch sitting against a wall. "What are you working on now?" Rip asks.

"Same shit."

He picks up a blank sheet of paper and hands it to his big brother. "Feel that. It's 25% linen, 75% cotton pure Malaysian rag, acid free, cloth."

Rip studies it. "This is money paper?"

"With the right ink in the right light, yeah."

"Where did you get it?"

"It followed me home from the Office Depot downtown."

"I'm sorry I asked."

Lucky abandons the drafting table and heads for the door. Rip stands in his way. "Take a banana," he tells his little brother.

"I gotta wash up first."

Rip grabs Lucky's hands to examine them. Lucky pulls away.

"You can stop this thing, Lucky."

"Stop what? Just get outta my way." He tries pushing his big brother aside. It's a waste of time. Now, as nervous as a criminal awaiting verdict, he begins wringing his hands.

"I don't say nothing to you when you smoke all that shit," Lucky brags.

"I'm older. I can handle it."

"Bullshit. I've seen you OD."

"Just once, and that was a long time ago."

"Yeah. A whole year."

"You should be in school."

"Hello, we tried that, remember?"

"They're gonna catch you, Lucky. Mother Cabrini always has an empty bed."

"Freak Mother Cabrini."

"You wanna be like me? A loser?"

"I wanna be where ever you are, Rip, but not if you're acting like a jerk."

"I ain't going back to jail, little brother. I swore on Mama's grave to take care of you."

"I know. I was there."

Lucky softens his tone. "You wanna see what I'm working on?"

"Uh huh."

Rip walks over to the drafting table. Lucky uses the opportunity to dash out of the lab and into the bathroom. Rip shakes his head.

***

A ten year old boy, thin in frame and normal looking in every way, is sitting at his mother's dresser in her large ornate bedroom going through her make-up kits. First, a pair of large gold clip-on earrings captures his fancy. He puts them on and admires his new look.

Rifling through a rhinestone covered box of lipsticks, he settles for a red one which he applies gingerly while keeping an eye on the door for intruders.

Eye liner goes on next, then foundation and a little rouge. When he is through, he stands and models in front of the large mirror. Still not satisfied with his look, he walks over to a closet, removes a long flowery dress, removes his own clothes, and dons the dress.

Soon, he finishes accessorizing himself with a large feathery hat and a fluffy red stole. Suddenly, the door is pushed open. The angry, astonished man in the doorway screams out the boy's name in long embellished tones."Simon."

The young boy, frozen with fear, stands still, his face now a ghastly shade of white.

The brutish man slams the door shut, pulls his thick leather belt off his waist, stomps ominously towards the petrified boy who runs to a corner, and beats him with all the strength his six foot frame can muster.

Simon jettisons from his nightmare, grabs a nearby towel and sops up the beads of sweat on his brow. When he sees Polo is gone, he falls back into the mattress.

***

Polo, standing near the rear red door of a McDonald's, is tapping his fingers against the wall. Then, he paces back and forth a bit. An employee exits the rear door, looks around outside quickly, then hands Polo a bag of food.

"Thanks, Brian."

"Why don't you come back?" Brian urges him. "They always need somebody on the grill."

"Hell no. They abolished slavery hundreds of years ago. Somebody just forget to tell them."

"Hey, it's a living. Still, it is safer than that hustling shit you do. You're begging for food now."

"Maybe the perfect sugar daddy will come along soon. I believe in luck."

"You're crazy. With all those fucking nuts out there? Half of them are married anyway, right? You said so yourself."

"God, you always paint such a dark picture."

"Man, I gotta go. Catch you later. You be careful, huh?"

"Yeah. Thanks. Hey ..." Brian reenters and closes the door. "Are you a manager yet?"

Polo, realizing he's talking to himself, looks in the bag, pulls out a sausage McMuffin, and opens it. He shakes his head. "Forgot the damned ketchup again."

Minutes later, he is sitting on a bench out Seattle Central Community College eating his breakfast. Janis silently races up to him and yanks the bag from his hand.

"Hey," he yells.

"What you got in here?" she asks.

"The wrappers."

"What's the matter? You look down."

"I'm just tired."

"Life's not so bad."

"Pretty funny, coming from somebody with more lines on her wrists than a zebra."

Janis reaches into her pocket and shows Polo why she's so excited. A brand new leather wallet is in her hands.

"You boosted somebody?"

"Got it from a trick while he was zipping down his pants."

She opens the wallet, "Fuck," she curses. She pulls out the pieces of newspapers folded inside, all cut the size of money. Polo laughs.

"Girl, he saw you coming a mile away."

She flings the wallet away. "Stinking bastard."

"Thanks for cheering me up, though. You shoulda seen your face."

"It ain't funny, Polo. Damn. I had my hopes up, too."

"Well, if it makes you feel better, I ain't had no luck either."

He starts singing. "Someday, my prince will come—"

"Oh, shut up."

***

Rip is in the living room of his "suite" watching TV in a rocking chair. Both items are so old and worn that they look like they could crumble any minute. Lucky enters.

"Hey, bro. What are you watching?"

"Nothing much."

"I present to you ..." Lucky produces the bill he was holding behind his back, "my masterpiece."

"Let me see that."

Lucky hands his brother the bill. Rip examines it closely.

"Well?" Lucky asks.

Not bad. It seems real. I don't know if the green on the front is dark enough, though. You gonna try it out?"

"Not yet. I wanna make copies first."

"Do the copies later. You may as well try it out now to see if it works."

"Okay."

Lucky reaches for the bill, but Rip pulls it away.

"What are you doing?"

"You think I'm so crazy I'd let my only brother get caught with this shit in public?"

"So what. It's mine."

"You trying to be like me, Lucky?"

"Geez. Not this conversation again."

"That's it. You're going to Cabrini."

"Bullshit." Lucky darts out of the room. Rip stands looking at the bill, his mind a knot of confusing thoughts. Turning the TV off, he exits the room and knocks on Lucky's door. Receiving no answer, he opens the door, pokes his head and looks around.

"Lucky?" He pulls his head out of the door, walks down to the kitchen, and runs to the window to the fire escape. "Oh, shit," he groans. Looking down the escape then across the field, he sees Lucky racing towards the street. "Lucky," he screams, but his brother doesn't turn or answer. "Damn it."

As is his wont, Lucky stops at a standpipe near the edge of the field, quickly opens it, washes his hands a few times, and continues off.

Rip, rushing back into the musty living room, puts on his pants and shoes.

***

Janis and Polo are ambling aimlessly through Westlake Center smack in the middle of downtown. Typically busy for mid-morning, they walk past shoppers, tourists, sanitation workers, street entertainers, police officers, some on horseback, drug pushers, and a handful of people selling the end of the world t-shirts.

"So what's up with your man anyway?" Janis asks Polo.

"Who? Simon?"

"No. Brad Pitt."

"He's okay."

"I hardly ever see him."

"He's a night bird."

"He's a freak. Look at all this death shit."

She tugs Polo's leather jacket. "You're half and half. He don't say nothing about that."

"Well, I was born that way. It doesn't bother me."

"Bullshit. Those black girls in high school called you zebra and spit on you."

"Please."

"You couldn't relate to the white girls 'cause they had money. They were always cruising with their boyfriends while you were busy looking for yourself."

"You sound like Dr. Phil."

"Just like you, Simon had it rough with his old man. I know your stepfather hates you 'cause you're half black."

"What is this? This is your life?"

"All those times he was abusing you, I know you tried to put it out of your mind. You need to talk about it."

"You need to step back at least ten feet."

"You should talk about it. It's why you're so pissed all the damn time."

"And you should get a sex change and call yourself Joyce Brothers."

"Hey, I'm just looking out for a friend."

They arrive at the Abyssinia convenience store a few blocks away. "Well, just look out right here," Janis tells him. "I'll be right back."

She enters the store. A few seconds later, she casually strolls out with a handful of Twinkies and other goodies.

"Let's go," she yells.

They race up the block and turn a corner. Looking back, they see no one following and slow to a casual walk.

"Girl, you're good," Polo congratulates her. "With these bad habits, who needs a gym?"

"Yeah. I learned it from your mother."

"Oh no, she didn't. Your mama's so fat, I had to take a train and two buses just to get on her good side."

"Yeah, right. Your mama's so fat, the horse on her Polo shirt is real."

"Your mama's so fat when she gets in an elevator it *has* to go down."

"Oh, please. Your mama's so fat, she got two stomachs: one for meat and one for vegetables."

"That's weak. Your mama's so fat, when she gets on a bus she turns it into a low rider."

"Your mama's so fat, when she dances she makes the band skip."

"Your mama's so fat, the last time she saw 90210 she was on a scale."

"Well, I heard your mama's so fat, when she showers her feet stay dry."

***

Just a couple of blocks away, Rip is walking around the busy Gameworks arcade looking for Lucky. At times, he'd stop to press the flippers on a few pinball machines. When he doesn't see his brother, he exits. Three Mexican toughs walking past nearly knock him down.

"Hey," Rip yells.

One of the toughs turns around and gives Rip the finger. Rip continues down the block, looking all around for a glimpse of his brother amidst the sea of shoppers and tourists. He passes a stout man with sunglasses leaning against a wall.

"What's up, boo?" the man greets him.

"What's up."

"You looking?"

"Nah. I'm broke."

Walking on, he aimlessly goes through his pockets. Pulling out Lucky's counterfeit $20 bill, he walks back to the stout man. The man motions for Rip to follow him into a nearby alley.

The darkened alley is dead-ended by a construction wall. There are several barrels of sand sitting about. A few wooden skids, and empty or broken bottles, are strewn about everywhere.

"What d'ya got?" Rip asks.

"JB."

"What's that?"

The dealer displays a plastic bag about the size of a bottle cap with light brown powder in it. "Jungle Boy. Pure shit."

"Can I taste it?"

The dealer opens the baggie, dips his pinky in and brings out a minute sample. Rips takes it and puts it on his tongue. He nods and hands the dealer the fake $20 bill folded in four.

"That's all you got?" the dealer asks. "This costs fifty bucks."

"Yeah. I'm busted."

"Man, I don't take shorts."

"So just give me half."

"Tell you what. I'll front it, but you owe me."

"Yeah, okay. I'm always around."

The dealer sighs and hands Rip the package.

"Make sure you cut this shit good. It's butter."

The stranger exits. Rip studies the unusual packet which has the letters JB on it. He pockets it, exits the alley and runs right into Lucky.

"Hey," Rip greets him.

"Leave me alone." Lucky continues on down the block. Rip stays by his side.

"Everything I do is to make sure you get the best in life," he informs him, "but you keep pushing me away like a virus. Can't you see I'm trying my best?"

"You want me to disappear."

"I want you to have a better life than mine."

Lucky stops and faces his brother. "Then we can help each other."

"I really wish it was just that easy."

***

Janis and Polo are sitting on a bench in Cal Anderson Park in Capitol Hill watching the world go by. Besides the occasional squirrel and the plethora of soccer players and sun bathers, there are only a handful of "shopping cart" people either passed out beneath large shade trees or lying on scattered benches reading the early stock quotations.

The two see the three Mexican toughs Rip had run into earlier coming slowly towards them.

"Here comes trouble," Janis warns her friend. "Don't say anything. Just ignore 'em."

"Shit, you think I'm scared? The only thing that puts fear in my heart is a rubber with a hole in it."

The three toughs walk over and stand in front of Janis and Polo.

"Is this the one?" gang member Listo asks his pals, referring to Polo.

"I don't know," his partner in crime, Chiques, answers. "All these fags look the same to me."

"Whoever y'all looking for," Janis suggests, "he ain't the one."

"Shut up, bitch ass nigga," Listo advises her.

Chiques ogles Polo. "You ever been down to Othello?" he queries.

"I don't even know where that is," Polo answers.

"Fuck him," Chente, the third gang banger, speaks up. "He ain't the one."

"Yo," Listo explains, "I didn't come all the way up here for nothing. One of these fucking fairies ripped me off blind early this morning...somebody's got to pay."

"Hey, man," Janis tells the three, "we don't go anywhere near South Seattle."

Without provocation, Listo and Chiques sets upon Polo. Janis dives in to help her friend. "Get offa him," she yells.

She's pulled to the side by Chente. "Get the fuck off me," she yells. "Help."

She watches as Polo tries valiantly to protect himself amidst the barrage of kicks and punches flying his way.

A large homeless man comes running up with a stick.

"Hey," he screams. "Stop it."

The two toughs get off Polo and leave him disheveled on the ground. Chente pushes Janis away then all three take off. Janis finds a rock, hurls it at the retreating cowards, and strikes Chente in the back of the head. He whips around and glares at Janis, rubs his aching head and then takes off again.

Janis goes over to Polo sitting on the grass. "You okay?"

He's holding his bloody nose. "I think they broke my nose."

"Want me to call the cops?" the homeless man asks.

"Nah, that's okay," Polo tells him. "Folks get bashed every day. They're just gonna say it's my fault. They'll just turn their backs 'cause these thugs are doing their dirty work for 'em. No wonder they never get caught."

Painfully, he rises to his feet with Janis and the homeless man's help.

"They're all undercover fags anyway," Janis reckons.

"That's what I think," Polo agrees. "They just can't face the truth so they take it out on us. Ow, my ribs."

Janis and the stranger sit Polo on a park bench. "You should get to a hospital," the homeless man advises him.

"Nah. I'll be fine."

"He's always scared that if he goes to one," Janis reveals, "he'd never come back."

"I've been hospitalized several times," the man states. "I've been shot, stabbed, pushed in front of a car, ran over by cyclists, chased and bitten by dogs—you name it. I'm like the Energizer bunny of the homeless."

"You've been lucky," Polo nods.

A white van pulls up at the edge of the park a couple of yards away from them.

"Shoot," Janis groans. "Here comes Youth Outreach."

The driver, a social worker in her forties named Tracie, parks the van and walks over to the group. The homeless man lies down on the grass and tries to get in a few Z's.

"Hi, all," Tracie greets them.

"Hi, Tracie," Janis replies.

"Hey," Polo smiles.

Tracie notices how maligned Polo is. His nose has stopped bleeding, but already his left eye is beginning to puff up and change colors. His face is also swollen.

"What happened to you?"

"Just some punks."

"Wait right here," she tells him.

She returns to her van, rifles through a large strong box, takes out an ice pack, activates and shakes it till it is cold, and brings it over to Polo.

"Here."

Polo takes it and places it on his swollen face. "Thanks."

"Are both of you still homeless?" Tracie asks.

"Nah," Polo brags. "We have adjoining suites at the Marriott now."

Janis giggles.

"Both of you should return to the Youth Shelter," Tracie insists. "Don't y'all care how y'all will turn up?"

Polo eyes her. "Shit. The last time I was there a couple of delinquents tried to kill me."

"Who?" she asks. "What are their names?"

"I ain't no rat," Polo explains. "You stand a better chance of getting robbed in there than sleeping in the streets."

"They still got those daily meditation groups and shit?" Janis asks.

"They're to help you relax," Tracie answers. "You know, sort things out."

"And the curfew's too damn early," Polo adds.

"That's mandated by the state, Polo," she informs him.

"That's the problem," Polo grieves. "I like my freedom. That shelter's like a jail."

The homeless man suddenly speaks up. "Shit, I'll go. They feed you, right?"

"Sorry," Tracie tells him. "You're too old."

She takes Janis by the arm and whispers to her. "Can I talk to you for a minute?"

"Yeah. Okay."

They walk over to a quiet section beneath a tree at one edge of the park. "What's up?" Janis asks.

"How's your mother doing?"

"I don't know. Okay, I guess."

"You haven't seen her recently, have you?"

"It's been months."

"She was in the clinic recently.

"How come?"

"She didn't look so good. Kinda looked like your friend over there."

"What do you mean?"

"I know you've had some problems with your step father, Janis."

"Understatement of the year."

***

Janis, blood on her hands and legs, is staggering weakly in the rain from beneath the Redondo Beach boardwalk in Des Moines, just 25 miles south of Seattle. There's no one in the area. She falls to her knees on the beach. A bloody wire hanger is in her hand.

***

"I nearly killed myself pulling out his bastard child with a wire hanger," she reminisces.

"Maybe you should look in on your mother," Tracie suggests. "She won't admit it, but those bruises on her face didn't come from a fall."

"She's a grown woman. She knows when to ask for help."

"Do you?"

Janis, spotting Lucky and Rip walking in a far end of the park, shouts out. "Rip. Lucky."

The brothers see her and stroll in her direction.

"I haven't seen those two in a while," Tracie admits. "How've they been?"

"Okay," Janis answers. "Life's tough, you know?"

Seconds later, both parties connect.

"Hey," Rip greets them.

"Hi, Rip, Lucky," Tracie says.

"Polo's been hurt," Janis informs them. "He got jumped."

"That's nothing new," Lucky notices.

Janis points to the bench. "He's over there."

Rip and Lucky see Polo sitting on the bench a few yards away deep in conversation with the homeless man.

"If you kids need my help," Tracie requests, "you know where to find me."

She returns to her van. Rip turns to Janis. "What did she want?"

"The usual. Making her rounds to see who's still alive and kicking, I guess. Um, I gotta go check on something for a while. See y'all later."

"Where are you going?" Rip asks.

"My mother's house. I'll catch up with you guys later."

"Bye," the boys tell her, then walk over to Polo.

"Well," Polo greets them, "are you boys just gonna stare, or are you gonna help an old lady get home?"

Rip takes Polo's right arm, Lucky supports the left. Together, they get Polo up but he recoils from pain.

"What's broken?" Rip asks.

"Nothing," Polo answers. "Just my spirit."

"What happened?" Lucky asks.

"He got jumped by Rocky and some boys from Othello," the homeless man answers.

"*That* was Rocky?" Polo asks surprised.

"Yep," the homeless man answers. "The ugly one."

"Wait 'til I see Simon," Polo swears.

Minutes later, Rip and Lucky are escorting Polo down the block. Polo is using a stick to support himself.

"I should sign up with Job Corps, man," Rip tells his crew.

"Not with that pasta rasta hairdo, Chico," Lucky warns him.

"Marley rules, all right. He's iree."

"Go for it, man," Polo encourages him. "Ain't nothin' out here but these fucking hoodlums anyway."

"I'm trying to encourage Lucky to go back to school," Rip declares.

"I ain't going to Mother Cabrini, Rip. Get it out your mind."

"You should. They'd love you there."

"Fuck you, *maricon*."

"In your dreams."

"I know what I'm gonna do for a living."

"Honey, the only thing those fake bills are gonna get you is jail time."

"Yeah, right. I'm gonna be famous one day."

"Doing what?"

"Designs, commercials, IT websites, whatever."

"Please. Stick with the bills. Since you're going that route anyway, I suggest you at least practice at Cabrini's."

They see a man hosing down a parking lot across the street.

"Be right back," Lucky tells them.

"Where're you going?" Rip asks.

Lucky ignores his brother and races blindly across the street, getting nearly hit by a car. Seconds later, he's washing his hands under the stranger's stream of water.

"I'm sorry to say," Polo tells Rip, "but that boy has a problem."

"That's why he won't go to school. The teachers won't excuse him every time he wants to wash up."

"There's gotta be special schools for that sort of thing. He's a smart kid."

"Believe me, I tried. In order to get him to school, you need a recommendation from a shrink."

"Which Lucky won't see."

"And it's against the law to force him."

"What a shame."

***

Like a land surveyor, Janis is standing before a small one family house on a suburban street studying the façade as if she'd never seen it before. The blinds are closed. She walks up and knocks on the door. It opens. An unshaven pot-bellied white man in his forties steps out holding a can of beer. He is wearing long silk pajama bottoms and a stained white A-shirt.

"Hi, Ethan," she greets him. "Is mom home?"

He studies his stepdaughter momentarily. "She went to the supermarket."

"Okay. Tell her I came by."

She turns to leave. "Wait a minute. She was expecting you. Why don't you wait inside?"

"I'll just wait out here." Janis plants herself on the front steps.

"You want a beer or something?"

"No."

"Where are you staying now?"

"Barbra Streisand's guest house in Madrona."

"Your room's the same."

"What, you think I'm gonna come back here? In your dreams."

"What's past is past, Janis."

"I'm trying not to have a conversation with you right now. Anyway, you haven't changed."

Ethan pours the entire can of beer out on the ground. "Stopping's just that easy," he boasts.

"I ain't impressed. You have more inside."

Ethan knows Janis is right. He sees she's clearly too old to be fooled. Time to change the subject. "You look good."

Janis gets up. "I gotta use the bathroom. If mom ain't back soon, I'm history."

"Go ahead."

Janis enters the house. Crossing the mostly unkempt room, she stops at the mantle where she sees a picture of her, her mother, and Ethan. Ethan enters and closes the front door behind him.

"How come the place is so dirty?" she asks.

"Your mother's been pretty busy these days."

"I've never seen the place like this."

She exits to the bathroom and locks the door. Ethan reaches for another can of beer from the six pack in front of the TV. In the bathroom, Janis removes a towel hanging over the shower stall and hangs it over the doorknob.

Ethan, on his knees with his eyes in the keyhole, pulls back when Janis covers the hole.

"Shoot," he protests.

Janis, after using the toilet, washes her hands, smells her armpits, and makes a face. She opens up the medicine cabinet and sees nothing there but after shave, shaving cream, a canister of Old Spice deodorant, and a few bottles of cheap dollar store cologne. Closing the cabinet door, her curiosity is piqued when she sees there is only one toothbrush in the holder above the sink.

There is a knock on the door. "You fell in the toilet?" Ethan asks.

Janis opens the door and asks, "Where is all mom's stuff?"

"Right here."

He grabs her breasts. Shocked, Janis pulls away and slaps him. He slaps her back. She tries to run past him, but his large bulk blocks her path.

"Let me out," she screams.

He pushes her back in towards the tub and closes the door. Reaching blindly, she grabs a can of shaving cream from a shelf and throws it at him. It cuts his forehead. He touches it and sees the blood on his fingers. "You little whore."

"Help," she yells. "Help."

Ethan runs and slaps his palm around her mouth. She bites it.

"Ow," he bawls.

She kicks his knees. They wrestle into the tub with the torn shower curtain confusing both their movements. He grabs her thighs. "You're much firmer, I see."

Janis punches him in the temple. His head flies against the tiled wall. She gets up and runs for the door. While jiggling the lock, Ethan grabs her, pulls her backwards, and starts ripping her shirt. Naturally, she fights back.

"Get the fuck off me. Mom," she yells.

"You think she can hear you from the hospital?"

Janis is surprised to hear that bit of news. "You put her there, didn't you? Bastard."

They continue wrestling, making a complete sty of the bathroom. Finally, Janis knees him so hard in the groin that the intense pain causes him to drop to his knees in a corner. Janis grabs the heavy porcelain lid off the toilet's tank and hoists it ominously over Ethan's head. Looking up, he sees the weapon. Tears well in his eyes.

"Go ahead and hit me," he cries, his voice now subdued. "I deserve it."

Janis contemplates whether or not to smash him over the head. "Arrgghh," she screams.

Throwing the porcelain top in the tub, she stares at the downed Ethan.

"I know it's because of me your life is hell now," he admits.

"You're a pathetic asshole."

"I don't know what comes over me."

"You're sick."

She turns and exits. Just as she's about to open the front door, Ethan grabs her. "Come here."

She screams. He pulls her backwards into the house. Near the table, she grabs what's left of the six pack and hits his head with it. Letting her go, he staggers backwards, trips over a hassock, slams his head against a corner of the mantle, and passes out on the floor. She stares at him. "Fucking loser."

***

Back in the abandoned building, Simon's troubled sleep is interrupted when Rip and Polo enter.

"Hey," Polo greets him, "get up, lard ass."

Simon peeps out from tired eyelids. "Huh?"

Polo sits down on the mattress. Simon, making space for his boyfriend, sees the battered shape he's in. He touches his face. "What happened to you?"

"I got jumped over in the park."

"Which park?"

"The one with the trees and shit. I don't know what it's called. It's down by the Community College in Capitol Hill."

"Cal Anderson," Rip informs him. "Hey, you guys, I'm going over to the soup kitchen. Wanna come?"

"I'm okay," Polo states.

"You want a plate, Simon?" Rip asks.

"Yeah, if they'll let you. And bring lots of ketchup, too. I need it to drown out the taste."

"Go get your own," Polo nudges him. "You're so lazy."

"I don't mind," Rip explains. "He looks fried."

Simon nods.

"Thanks for the comp, Rip."

"Any time, *mon frere*. I'll bring two."

All this talk of soup kitchen food makes Polo nauseated. "Ugh. I can't eat that shit. I'd rather stir fry the roaches in this bitch."

Rip exits. Polo lies down with great difficulty.

"Listen, Mister," he tells Simon, "next time you rip Rocky off, make sure he gets a good look at you."

"I hardly know him. Why? That's who did this to you?"

"No. I fell down a rabbit hole."

"Whatever. Stop making a joke out of everything."

Simon gets up, grabs an already open container of OJ from a shelf and takes a sip. He makes a face.

"Ack. This shit's like battery acid." He sits in the large window and sips a little more.

"Where are we headed, Simon?"

"What d'ya mean?"

"You know what I mean."

"We're gonna get signed soon. A manager came down to our last practice."

"What are you talking about?"

"The band I'm in."

"Cathedral of Blood? I thought y'all broke up."

"Bands break up every day, but that don't mean nothing. We start practicing again today."

"I wish y'all luck. There are thousands of groups out there."

"Yeah, but we're special. We have a gimmick, you know?"

"What? Coffins and crosses and shit?"

Simon cracks a smile. "You forgot biting the heads off bats."

"I thought all that shit's been done."

"It has," Simon agrees, "but our show is gonna have real live corpses in the coffins, then they'll nail me to a cross at the end."

"A *live* corpse? That makes no sense."

Simon climbs out of the window and spreads his arms apart. Polo shakes his head. "Sick fuck."

"We're gonna be bigger than Manson," Simon brags.

"Who? The killer or the band?"

"Whichever. I don't care."

They hear a glass shatter in the kitchen. "What the ...?" Polo starts to say.

Simon reenters the bedroom and walks to the kitchen where Janis is having a meltdown.

"Arrgghh," she screams. "I hate this world."

"Take it easy, Jan," he advises her. "What's wrong?"

"I'm fucking sick of everything, that's what's wrong."

"Stop shouting, first of all. You're gonna wake the dead."

"I *am* the dead. I'm so fucking confused."

She grabs a plate and, screaming, smashes it against a wall.

"Well," Simon bellows, "I'm mad as hell myself!"

He grabs a porcelain pitcher, screams, and crashes it against another wall. Janis overturns the old gnarly kitchen table. Simon flips the ancient, near empty refrigerator to the ground. Janis bashes a chair against a wall then bangs it on the stove. Simon yanks some cabinet doors off, punches holes in others, and karate kicks the shelves off the walls. The canned goods sitting on them go flying about everywhere. Janis picks up a large can of flour and shakes it all over the kitchen. Simon grabs a jar of peanut butter, opens it and, using his hand as a paintbrush, starts drawing shapes on the walls. Both start jumping up and down on the floor as if purposefully trying to create a hole in it.

The duo finally stop and stare at an angry Polo who's standing in the entrance with his arms folded.

"That was exhilarating," Simon smiles. He licks the peanut butter on his fingers and offers some to Polo who adamantly remains steadfast staring at them.

***

Over in the soup kitchen, Rip and Lucky are just leaving. Rip is toting one plate of food wrapped in foil. There are several other homeless people milling about. Lucky is picking his teeth.

"Not bad for warmed-over cardboard."

"Actually, it's cat food," his brother corrects him. "I feel like an alien's gonna come busting out of my chest."

Walking down the street, Rip, seeing an old acquaintance approaching, hands the plate to his brother. "Here, take this to Simon."

"Where're you going?"

"I got company."

"But, Rip—"

"Just go already, okay? He's starving."

"Man, you got an attitude problem."

Reluctantly, Lucky turns and leaves, then stands down the street a distance so he can see who Rip had met up with. He sees his brother shake hands with the older, rail-like stranger just before they walk off.

Minutes later, Rip and his Southern-fried friend, a forty year old dark skinned ex-tobacco sharecropper from Mississippi named Rodney, are sitting on boxes in the rear of an alley passing a joint back and forth.

"So, Rodney" Rip asks, "when did they let you out?"

"Last *naht*."

"That was early."

"Good behavior helped. You should know."

Rip nods. "You still seeing that mulatto chick?" Rodney continues. "What's her name?"

"Janis. Yeah, we're still hanging out."

"Ah know that's *raht!*"

Rip sucks the last drag from the roach and flings it away.

"She was the biggest Janis Joplin freak ah ever seen," Rodney admits. "Even used to sing like her. What a trip. She coulda been a star."

"The good old days, huh?"

Rodney suddenly grabs Rip and tries kissing him on the mouth, but Rip immediately pushes him off. He stares angrily at his Southern friend. "What the fuck?" he yells.

"What's the matter with you?" Rodney states. "You used to like that."

"I ain't that way no more, Rodney."

"Bullshit. People don't change."

"I did. You need to know that."

"You? Used to be every trick in town had yer number memorized."

"I think you stayed inside too long."

Rodney rises with his fists balled up. "Oh, all of a sudden, yer holier than thou?"

From Rip's defensive position, Rodney suddenly seems ten times taller and five times as wide.

"Take it easy, Rod."

"No. Ah don't like when ah gets out and everybody suddenly gets all distant on yer ass, like they don't wanna know you or wanna kin with you."

"Who said that?"

Rip suddenly remembers the dope he'd scored earlier. "Look," he explains, "I got something this morning that'll ease your mind." Reaching into his pant's fob, he brings out the packet of JB.

Rodney smiles. "Now, that's more like it."

Suddenly, they hear a police siren. "Oh shit," Rip exclaims.

"Fuck," Rodney spews.

They look around quickly, but there is no egress from the blocked off alley. Rip stashes the JB under a slab of stone. A police car rolls into the alley. The siren stops. Rip and Rodney scale a wall using boxes and barrels for support. The two police officers abandon their car and give chase, cornering the two up on a fire escape where they try opening adjacent windows but none budges.

"Come down with your hands where we can see 'em," the first cop yells.

Rodney finds a bucket on the escape and flings it at the cops. He misses. The police train their pistols on the fleeing duo."Y'all coming down right now, one way or another," the first cop yells again. He fires a warning shot which startles Rip.

"All right," he shouts. "Don't shoot." Compliant, he descends the escape, jumps off, and puts his hands up.

The second cop puts him in cuffs, leans him with his palms up against a wall, frisks him and removes his wallet.

Rodney, finding himself trapped, also climbs down. When he hits the ground, he takes off running towards the exit just beyond the squad car and promptly collides with a passing bicyclist.

Within seconds, the second officer slaps cuffs on him while he's on the ground. The bicyclist gets up.

"Are you okay?" the officer asks him.

"Yeah. I'll be fine." Shaken but unharmed, he rides off.

"Lemme go," Rodney yells. "You ain't got nothin' on me."

The second officer goes through Rodney's pockets and comes up only with an ID card.

Rip and Rodney are ordered to sit in the alley with their backs to a wall and their feet outstretched. The first officer goes back into the car and runs a background check on the two. About one minute later, he reemerges and walks straight over to Rodney.

"Where were you last night?" he asks him.

"Ah slept right here in this alley," Rodney answers. "Right on them boxes."

"Where did you sleep the night before?" Rodney doesn't answer. He remains as quiet as a Scandinavian hamlet in winter.

"Your friend here escaped from jail last night," the officer tells Rip.

Rip is taken aback. "He did?"

"They're still trying to figure out how," the second officers adds. "The clever devil must've had outside help."

Both officers stare at Rip. "Hey, wait a minute," Rip protests. "I have people who can vouch for my whereabouts last night."

"Nobody helped me," Rodney asserts.

One of the officers stands him up, places him in the back seat of the squad car, and returns to Rip. The two officers stand him up and one removes his cuffs.

"Do you know why we're letting you go today?" he asks.

"I didn't do anything?"

"Rodney acted alone," the first officer stated, "but we were just testing *him*. Don't you go too far."

"Where am I gonna go?" Rip asks rhetorically.

"You need to be more careful who you hang out with," the first officer warns him. "Your pal Rodney assaulted a clerk with a bat last night. Could've been you."

The cops return to their car and one yells out, "And get a haircut."

Rip gives the cop the finger secretly by stroking his dreadlocks with it.

The officers reverse out of the alley and take off. Rip goes to the stone slab, lifts it, removes the JB, re-pockets it, and ambles out of the alley.

***

Polo, Janis, and Simon are sitting around in their living room watching the tiny TV. Simon is unpacking his foil-wrapped plate of food. Janis, in a deep blue funk, is more casually attired. Polo notices she's nervous and biting her nails.

"Why you so nervous, girl?" he asks her.

Janis, not in the mood for small talk, answers with a shrug.

"Wait till Rip sees that mess y'all made," Polo warns.

"What's he gonna do?" she asks angrily. "Beat me?"

Lucky enters shaking water from his hands.

"Your brother forgot the ketchup," Simon tells him.

"Sorry," Lucky explains. "He's only human."

"I can't eat this shit," Simon complains.

Lucky has a suggestion. "Give it to the dogs."

"How could he forget?" Simon bawls, "One. Lousy. Pack. Of. Ketchup."

"What the hell?" Lucky shouts. "Scratch his skin, all right? If anything other than blood comes out, call the FBI."

"Damn," Polo notices. "Everybody's all tense and shit. Y'all need to chill."

Lucky plops down on the floor against a wall. Simon nibbles his food like a mouse. "The service here sucks," Simon laments. "I want my money back."

Janis shrugs. "Why don't you check in at the Westin downtown? I heard they have a goth special."

"God, I was only joking," Simon groans. "You're always so pissed."

"You don't know the hell I'm going through."

"Can't be no worse than us," Lucky observes.

"You don't know half the story," she says, then stands up.

"Where're you going?" Polo asks.

"I don't know. I just gotta do something. I don't know."

Polo shakes his head. "Poor thing's going through some serious changes."

Lucky gets up and follows her. Out on the fire escape, Janis is sitting in a fetal position crying. When Lucky climbs onto the landing, she stops crying.

"What's up?" he asks. "I saw you crying."

"No, I wasn't."

"Just wringing out your tear ducts, huh?"

"I'll cry if I feel like it, okay?"

"Geez, can I have my head back now?"

"Sorry, Lucky. I just wish everything was hunky-dory and shit. I saw Ethan today. He'll be an asshole his whole fucking life."

"Did you see your mother?"

"I stopped by the hospital. She's in the ICU. They won't let me see her right now because she's in bad shape."

"What happened to her?"

"Ethan, but she's protecting him and I don't know why."

"Battered woman's syndrome. I saw that on TV."

"I guess. I don't know. Whatever I do in life, it always gets screwed up. You'd think I was born under a bad sign or something. Look at me. Poor excuse for a human being. Hey, Lucky, do you think I'm pretty?"

"Yeah."

"You're just saying that. I know I'm a fuck up."

"You're not so bad. I know if I was your boyfriend I'd take better care of you than Rip."

"Thanks, Lucky, but I'm an ugly duckling. I know it. My body's total shit. Toxic."

"No it ain't. I've seen you in the shower."

She pinches him softly. "Pervert."

He face turns as red as a Tennessee sunset.

"You're a good kid," she adds. "You shouldn't be hanging out with us. We ain't going nowhere. You're a good artist. You could get a scholarship one day."

"Yeah, right."

Simon sticks his head out the fifth floor window and looks at them. "Can one of y'all help me get Polo back to bed? I think he's getting a fever. He looks weak."

Lucky stands up. "I'll go." He climbs into the window.

Simon looks at Janis. "Can you go boost some pills somewhere, like Advils or something?"

"Come on, Simon," she moans, "luck's like toilet paper, it's gotta run out some time."

"He's really sick, Jan. Please?"

"Jesus Christ! All right, but just this once."

"What if they only have Tylenols?"

"Whatever's clever."

Janis begins climbing down the escape's rickety metal stairs. "Y'all owe me," she shouts.

Strutting down the street towards the pharmacy, a squad car rolls alongside her. She sees it and continues walking. Officer Trent McDougal, a cop who she's familiar with, is alone in the car. He stays with her. She glances at him again.

"Problem, Officer?"

"Not yet, Janis," he answers.

As she steps off the sidewalk to cross the street, the car rolls in front of her. She sighs and assumes an arrest position on his hood. McDougal steps out.

"You're not under arrest."

"I know this is how you really want me, Trent."

"Get off the car."

Janis removes herself from the hood. "Why are you stopping me?"

"You haven't been to see your parole officer."

"I'm sorry I forgot the appointment. Geez. I'm only human."

"You're buying yourself a one way ticket to the state pen."

"Me? Up there? Over my breathless corpse. I'll go see her tomorrow."

"Jan, for your own good, I'd suggest you clean up your act and get a decent job."

"I'm looking, Trent. I'm looking. You can see I ain't working the streets no more."

"Oh yeah?" The officer grabs her left arm, rolls her sleeve up, and looks at the track marks in her arms. "So how do you pay for all this? Charity?"

Janis pulls her arm away and rolls her sleeve back down. "You got no right."

"Don't think we're not keeping an eye on you, Janis. You just be careful." He returns to his car.

"Yeah, you too," she whispers under her breath.

He overhears her and walks back over. "I can bust you right now for public indecency or resisting arrest."

She stares at him with flames in her eyes.

"You need help," he advises her. He goes into his car and squeals off, burning rubber and spitting smoke. Janis flips him off.

"Asshole."

***

Polo is lying on the mattress in his bedroom with a damp rag across his forehead. Simon is sitting by his side holding his hand. There's a knock on the door.

"Come in," Simon says.

Janis, wearing a long face, enters. "How is he?" she asks.

"Worse."

She hands Simon two packets of aspirin. He ogles them. "That's it?"

"I had to move fast. They're watching me now."

"Thanks." Simon helps Polo sit up. He then tears open one of the packets, gives him the two brown pills and a sip of water.

"Maybe he should go to a hospital," Janis suggests.

Polo shakes his head.

"He won't go," Simon attests.

"Then knock him out and drag him there."

"Forget it, girl," Polo states. "I ain't going out like that."

"You queens are giving me a headache. Polo, you're stupid. Hard-headed."

"I had two friends who went to the hospital with some dumb ass stomach problems," Polo testifies. "Simple shit. Now, where are they? Potter's field. There's not even a fucking headstone to mark where they are. They go too far in those hospitals. Always gotta find something new in you, then they treat that, but it creates something new, then they have to treat *that,* and on and on. Uh, uh. Forget it."

Janis shakes her head. "You're a fool."

Simon turns to Polo. "She's right, you know."

"Oh, she got to you, too?"

Janis sticks her head back in the door. "You know, I must be stupid. I just remembered I have an appointment over at the clinic this afternoon."

"Why?" Simon asks. "What's the matter with you?"

"Nothing. Just a checkup. They might have pills for him there."

"You mean like antibiotics?"

"Maybe."

"Why y'all talking about me like I'm dead?" Polo protests. "Hello. I'm still here."

Simon gets up and walks over to Janis. "Let's go."

"It's too early," she informs him.

"I have band practice in a few hours," Simon affirms. "Maybe they'll see you now?"

Janis grunts like a Pamplona bull. "Okay."

Smiling, Simon says, "Let me get my shoes."

As he looks for his footwear, Lucky walks into the doorway and asks, "What's going on?"

***

"They're going to the clinic to bring me back a tall, dark, and handsome doctor," Polo wishes aloud.

"More like antibiotics," Simon corrects him.

"Can I come?" Lucky asks.

"No," Janis explains. "Stay here and keep Polo company."

Polo winks at Lucky. "Hell no, he'll try to rape me."

"I'm sick, remember?" Polo states.

Lucky puts his foot down. "I'm going to the clinic."

Polo shakes his head and utters, "Kids today."

***

A group of teenage kids are playing hacky sack on the lawn in the shadow of the water tower in Capitol Hill's Volunteer Park. Reggae music is playing on their boom box. Rip strolls by and says, "Nice music."

They stop playing and look at him. "You like reggae?" one of the kids asks.

Rip points to his own long dreadlocked hair. "I guess so," the kid notices. "Wanna play?"

Rip nods and gets into the hacky sack circle.

***

Lucky, Simon, and Janis are strolling down Western Avenue near Pike Place Market. All three are wearing sunglasses. They look cool. Simon has tidied himself up and is wearing skin tight black pants and a black t-shirt. His sunglasses have white plastic rims. Although his clothes are dirty, they seem to be holding up despite the obvious wear and tear in the seams. He's also wearing spiked wrist bands, a spiked collar, and several earrings in each ear.

Janis, ever the retro, is wearing a long flower dress over black lace leggings and black boots. Flowers have been painted on her face. On her head is a straw hat with a peace sign in the middle. Lucky, looking like Joe Average, is wearing jeans and a T-shirt which reads, "Mo' Money, Mo' Problems." He's carrying a folder of his artwork.

They see a yellow Mustang pull up down the block. Simon stops. The others stop with him. "Y'all go to the clinic without me," he informs his pals.

"Why?" Janis asks. "Where're you going?"

Simon ignores her and walks quickly ahead towards the waiting car.

"Simon," she yells.

"Tell Polo I'll be back later," he shoots back.

They watch as Simon gets into the car.

"Who's that?" Lucky asks.

Janis shrugs. "I don't know. Some trick, I guess."

"Maybe it's a manager," Lucky guesses, "you know, for his band."

"Please," Janis bewails. "You never heard his band?"

"They're okay."

"They suck. Just a bunch of noisemakers jerking off."

"That's what they're buying today."

"Waste of vinyl."

"Vinyl? CD's are aluminum."

"Whatever. Everybody downloads now anyway or just look at YouTube."

"What are you? A commercial?"

"Just saying."

Minutes later, Janis and Lucky enter the Clinic. Among the rows of mostly empty chairs is a pregnant girl awaiting service and a young man who looks pretty burned out. A guard is standing in a corner reading a magazine. There are posters on every wall, mainly warnings about STDs, smoking, drugs and sexual abuse, and the National Suicide Prevention Lifeline. At the far end of the room, posted above a copier, is an anti-meth ad with pictures of people with the worst skin and teeth imaginable.

Janis and Lucky walk to the desk where a girl with multi-colored hair and a nose ring is sitting making notes in a ledger. Janis appears happier than usual. “Hi,” Janis greets her.

“Hi,” the receptionist replies.

“I have an appointment with Mr. Schecter.”

“And your name is?”

“Janis.”

The receptionist leafs through the ledger and finds what she’s looking for.“Okay, you’re early nut you can go on back.”

“Room 3?”

“Uh huh.”

“Thanks.”

She turns to Lucky and says, “Sit right here. Don't touch anything.”

“What are you? My mom?”

Janis shakes her head, removes her sunglasses, and exits towards the back of the Clinic. Lucky looks at the receptionist. “Does that hurt?” he asks her.

“Does what hurt?”

He points to his nose referring to her piercing.

“Nah. You get used to it.”

She pulls a needle out from a spool of thread and holds it to view. “You want one?” she asks.

“Maybe some other time. Hey, do you have a color copier?”

“That one in the corner over there prints color.”

“Can I use it?”

“I think it's out of paper.”

Lucky opens his folder and pulls out sheets of blank paper. “That's okay. I have some.”

“Then go ahead. There’s a copy limit, though, because the toner runs out quickly. You know how to use it?”

“Piece of cake.”

***

Across town, Simon is sitting in a comfortable sofa soaking in the john's fancy apartment. Large original oils decorate the walls. The ceiling fan has a classic, rich look to it. Even the shag carpeting seems like treasure could be found deep within it. Practically dust-free, the room is immaculate in every way. The john, Oscar Peteroff, is at a polished oak bar fixing two drinks.

"This looks like something out of House Beautiful," Simon remarks.

"You like?"

"It's nice. This is actually my first time in Broadmoor. Nice view of Lake Washington."

Oscar brings the drinks over, sits next to Simon, and offers him a glass. "Why are you hiding your beautiful eyes?"

Simon removes his sunglasses and lays it on the center table.

"That's better," Oscar nods. "So where are you staying now?"

"Oh," Simon answers. "Here and there."

He sips his drink and coughs a little. "What is this?"

"A diamond margarita. Three types of tequila with lime juice and orange liqueur. How is it?"

"Strong."

"Why don't you stay here with me?"

"What about your wife?"

"Oh, forget about her."

"Why? What do you want a poor boy like me for?"

"Take one guess. Anyway, poverty is a state of mind. You're only as rich as you think you are."

"Yeah. Whatever."

"You're very tense today."

"It's the high pollen count, you know."

"Would you like to shower?"

"Shower?"

"You know, water, soap."

Oscar touches Simon's leg. Simon gets up. "What's the matter?" the john asks. "Did I upset you?"

"This is a mistake. I shouldn't have come here."

"Nonsense. Last time you were here you didn't want to leave."

"I have band practice."

"Oh? Fabulous. What do you play? Trumpet? Trombone? Tuba?"

"Not that kind of band. I sing in a rock group."

"Sounds wonderful. Music is such a wonderful creation, don't you think?"

Simon shrugs.

"Maybe that's what's missing," Oscar posits.

Laying his drink down on a coaster on the center table, he gets up, walks over to the stereo, and puts in on. Unknowingly, his wallet had fallen out of his pocket by the couch. He opens a CD folder, goes through its collection page by page, finds the classical disk he's looking for, and puts it in the player. The strings of a symphony start playing.

"You like?" he asks Simon with his back still turned. Receiving no answer, he twirls around. "You like?"

His jaw drops when he realizes Simon is gone. The front door is wide open. He searches his pockets and soon discovers his wallet is history. He stomps his feet.

"Simon, you motherfucker."

***

Simon, happy as a meadowlark with the morning's first worm in its tiny beak, practically dances down a quiet street in the Central District counting the money in his hands. Carelessly, he blindly runs into Rocky and his two friends from Othello Avenue. Immediately, they surround him.

"Aw shit," Simon blurts out.

"You're hard to find, motherfucker," Rocky states.

"You didn't have to beat up my friend like that."

"Just be glad it wasn't you."

"I was looking for you, Rock. I was gonna pay you back."

Rocky grabs the money from Simon's hand.

"Hey!"

"Shut up, man, before I rip your throat out." Rocky counts the bills.

"I need that money, Rock," Simon pleads. "It's important."

"Okay. I'll make a deal with you. I'm a pretty easy guy. Either I take this money," he says as he whips out a switchblade and points it at Simon's face. "Or I take an eye."

Some choice, he thinks. Simon's decision was easy, in any case. "Take the flow, Rock. We're squared now, right?"

Rocky cuts Simon's face anyway.

"Ow," Simon yells, recoiling in pain.

"Now we are," Rocky agrees.

Simon presses his wound. "My face."

"Don't you fucking ever think about ripping me off again," Rocky warns him.

One of Rocky's friends punches Simon in the stomach so hard that the anorexic teen cowers to the sidewalk and falls on his side.

"Pussy," Rocky remarks.

The three thugs leave. Simon coughs and spits. He shakes his head when he sees blood, not sputum, fly from his mouth. An old Ethiopian man with a cane comes by seconds later.

"Can you help me?" Simon asks.

The old man looks him over. "I don't want any trouble."

"They're gone."

"In that case, you need a doctor."

"Just help me get up. Please."

The suspicious émigré studies the downed youth for a moment then helps him to stand.

"Thanks," Simon acknowledges.

"You should call 911."

"No. I'll be fine. Can you help me out with a dollar? I just need something to drink."

"Sorry, my friend. I don't have any money."

"Thanks, anyway."

The old man turns to walk away then stops, goes through his pockets, pulls out a business card, and returns to Simon. "Here. There's a restaurant on Jefferson called Mesob. I know the owner. Tell them you got this from Kebede. They'll help you."

"Thanks, but why would they help me?"

"It's our nature, even if you're not Ethiopian." The old man turns and shuffles off down the street.

***

Lucky is at the copier making two-sided copies of his counterfeit bills. Deftly manipulating the papers, he's carefully keeping one eye affixed on the guard.

He sees Janis emerge from the back. Clearly, she's a different person from the one who'd entered only minutes ago. She has a look of someone who'd just witnessed a bad accident.

Lucky puts all his papers together in his folder and walks towards his friend. "Are you okay?" he asks.

She hands Lucky a clear plastic bag containing a vial of pills, some gauze, antibiotic ointment, hypoallergenic tape, a small bottle of saline, alcohol and iodine pads

"These are for Polo. Let's go."

"What happened in there? You look different."

"Let's just fucking go before I start tripping."

Lucky eyes her with worry as they exit the Clinic. Walking up a downtown street minutes later, they spot Simon getting off a bus carrying a paper bag.

"Here comes Interview With A Vampire," Lucky smiles.

As he nears, they see his face is bleeding and he's clutching his stomach.

"What happened to you?" Janis asks.

"Rocky."

"Fucking punk," she cusses. "That's twice today."

"What does he look like?" Lucky asks.

"You don't want to know, Luck," Simon attests. "He's just some asshole not worth thinking about."

"One of these days I'm gonna cap his ass," Janis promises.

Lucky stares at Simon's paper bag. "What do you have there?"

"Some food from an Ethiopian restaurant."

"You have money?" Janis asks.

"Nah, they're just helpful."

Lucky takes the bag, opens it, lifts up the foil covering the dish, takes a piece of meat, and eats it.

"Wow," he complains. "It's hot."

"I'm going in the clinic," Simon tells the two. "Maybe they can do something for this pain."

"You don't have to," Lucky explains, holding up the medicine bag. "We got the whole pharmacy right here."

***

Simon is sitting on a bench in tiny and ultra-populated Victor Steinbrueck Park near Pike Place Market. Known locally as Native Park, it's a gathering spot for many Native Americans. Lucky, his sunglasses off, is busy cleaning and bandaging the gash on Simon's face. Janis is off to one side brooding.

"What's with her?" Simon notices.

"Beats me," Lucky answers. "She went in to the clinic all gung-ho and came out like that."

They hear reggae music coming from a boom box on the field where several natives are relaxing.

"Sounds like a party," Simon says.

Just behind the natives, they see a group of kids playing hacky sack. Among them is Rip.

"I didn't know your brother hacked," Simon muses.

"Me neither." Lucky puts away the supplies, then he and Simon walk towards the group. Lucky turns to Janis. "Are you coming?"

"No. I'm gonna stay here and take root."

The two boys walk over to the hacky sack group. Lucky points back in Janis' direction which Rip observes. Simon waves goodbye to his pals and exits the park. Rip walks over to Janis as Lucky joins the hacky sack group.

"Hi," Rip greets her. "They say something's up with you."

"I got HIV, Rip."

The news stuns Rip. It's like someone just reached into his chest and ripped his heart out.

"How do you know?"

"I just found out in the clinic."

"They make mistakes."

Janis walks up to Rip and stares in his eyes. "I have HIV, Rip."

"So? What are you gonna do now? Lay down and die?"

"Is that all you can say?"

"What do you want me to say?"

"I don't know."

"Maybe I have it, too."

"You must."

"Why? Why do you say that?"

"Cause I've been careful with everybody else except you."

"Bullshit. You've been with so many tricks you lost count."

"I was always protected with them."

"Yeah, right."

"You know I don't go all the way with them."

"How the hell should I know that? You think I got a spy camera following you around to every basement and back alley?"

"Fuck you, Rip. I can see you're the last person to ask for sympathy."

"Oh, no you don't. Don't start playing all helpless angel now. Ain't nobody holding a gun to your head telling you to turn tricks."

"This ain't how it's supposed to be. Can't you fucking hear me?" She starts crying.

He punches a pole. "Damn." Then hugs her.

"I'm sorry, Janis. How can I know what to do? It's not like I hear this shit every day."

"I ain't going out like a skeleton, Rip," she affirms.

"You'll be all right," he promises. "Consider it a wakeup call."

They continue hugging though the look on Janis' face betrays her hopeless feeling.

***

A rock band is tuning up and testing the PA system at a rehearsal studio. As the guitarist fiddles with his rack of pedals, the bassist fine tunes his amp's eq, the drummer practices a few paradiddles on the snare, and the keyboardist auditions different string sounds.

Simon arrives and asks, "What's up, guys?"

They all glance at him, say nothing, and continue whatever they were doing. Simon walks over to the guitarist. "What's going on, Mike?"

Mike casts his eyes downward. Simon, thinking his friend's behavior odd, walks over to the female bassist. "Vicky?" he calls to her. "What's going on?" She looks away.

Suddenly, a teen with black shoes, black pants, a black 'Bauhaus' sweater and hair dyed blue, enters the studio carrying a microphone. "I hope I'm not too late," the kid apologizes. "There was a problem with the bus."

"Who the fuck are you?" Simon asks.

"That's our new singer," the drummer, Domenico, answers.

"What?" Simon shouts. "What the hell are you talking about?"

"It's true, Sy," Vicky swears.

Simon looks at his pals. "You mean I'm out?"

No one says a word. The new singer tries his best to blend into the woodwork. "I can't believe this shit," Simon yells. "*I* fucking put this band together. It was me and you, Mike. This was our dream."

"Sorry, man," Mike apologizes. "We just think you're losing it. Look at how you look now. Gets worse every day."

"I got mugged. So what?"

"You always miss practice. When you do show up you're loaded on something."

"What the fuck? This is a rock band. This ain't the fucking Boys' Choir of Harlem."

"Who's saying we are?" Domenico asserts. "You just don't know when to turn it off."

"Okay, okay," Simon states. "Are y'all at least gonna give me another chance?"

A collective silence befalls the group. Simon turns to the new singer. "What's your name?"

"A.J."

"Well, A.J. I hope you enjoy your short stay with these fuckin' back stabbers."

"Don't say that, Simon," Vicky berates him.

"Let him get it out, Vicky," Mike insists.

Simon stomps towards the thick, insulated door. "Y'all can't use any of my songs," he warns them.

"Bye, Simon," Mike waves as Simon storms out.

"He seems like a loser," A.J. blurts out.

"Be careful, A.J.," Mike explains. "That's my cousin."

***

Simon, still stinging from his band's rejection of him, is so deep in thought that he doesn't see the cars whizzing past as he crosses a busy street. Luckily making it across unscathed, he stops by a car wash where dance music is emanating from a horn high up on a pole.

Touching Lucky's bandage on his face, he cringes from the pain but, getting into the beat, he starts dancing. He twirls around slowly, seductively, waving his arms like an Egyptian belly dancer. Running to a pole, he whirls around it gingerly like Gene Kelly in 'Singin' in the Rain', then leaps back to the street and sways his hips. A man in a taxi cruises by. Simon's makes "come and get it" signals with his hand and body. The man drives off.

Still in motion to the music, Simon raises his shirt and rubs his chest while keeping pace with the rhythm. At times he'd throw kisses at the passing male motorists. Eventually, a cop car pulls over.

Red with embarrassment, Simon quickly pulls himself together. One of the cops is not amused. The other has a grin the size of the Atlantic. When the angry cop turns around to admonish his gawking partner, Simon takes off.

***

Nearly an hour later, back in the living room, Janis, Polo, and Rip are lying around on cloud nine. There's a knock on the door. None raise a finger to open it. Another knock follows, much heavier that the first. This time a voice on a megaphone is heard behind the door.

"Open up. This is the police."

With the speed of cheetahs, Janis, Polo, and Rip get up and stash every bit of paraphernalia in sight. Janis shoves the pipe beneath the carpet. Rip pushes some small silver spoons under the sofa's seat while Polo uses a pillow to wave away any distinguishing scent that may have accumulated.

There's another thunderous knock on the door, like the devil himself is standing there. "This is our last warning!"

"Coming, officer," Rip shouts.

Trying his best to look normal, he pulls open the door. Simon, standing at the entrance with the megaphone, starts laughing so hard it seemed like he would die.

Rip groans and clenches his fists.

"You ain't so fucking funny," Janis yells.

"Look at you," Polo observes, "with that big ol' bandage on your face playin' stupid."

"Nasty trick, dude," Rip agrees.

"I couldn't help it," Simon apologizes. "I found this old thing down by the field. The thought just came to me out of the blue."

"Freaking retard," Janis yells. "I'm having the worse day of my fucking life and Tinker-fucking-bell here wants to play cops."

"Chill, Jan," Simon explains. "I didn't mean nothing. You think I'm having the time of my life, too? Ain't no sense moping around like it's the end of the world."

"I want everybody out of here now," she orders. "I'm going to sleep."

"Geez," Polo whispers.

Polo, Rip, and Simon walk into the kitchen where they set the overturned table and refrigerator back upright. After sitting down in chairs around the table, Simon produces a six pack of beer.

"Where'd you get this?" Polo asks.

"I ran into somebody I know on 23rd. He hooked me up."

"Cool," Rip nods, taking a beer. The others follow suit.

Polo raises his beer and says, "Here's to…forever." They clink their bottles.

"What's up with Jan?" Simon asks. "Been snotty, like, all day."

"She found out she's got HIV," Rip informs them.

"Really?" Simon queries. "I'm sorry. I didn't know." He absentmindedly plays with the bandage on his face.

"Stop touching that," Polo warns him. "You'll get an infection."

Simon sits on his hands.

"Anyway," Polo continues, "I'm not surprised Jan turned out positive. I need to go get tested myself. But, why bother? I already know what they'll find."

"What?" Simon speaks out. "You're positive, too?"

"Maybe you should get tested," Polo guesses.

"I'm probably positive, for all I know," Rip states.

Simon folds his arms and looks away. "I'd better not be."

"Let's face it," Polo explains. "It's our destiny and shit. We're, like, doomed. Some must die so others may live."

"Please," Simon protests. "Don't give me that Jerry Springer psychobabble bullshit. If my band don't want me, I'll just form another one."

"What happened?" Polo asks. "They kicked you out?"

Simon looks at his boyfriend. "Fuck 'em!"

Polo shrugs and adds, "I don't see how you can sing that death shit anyway. It's depressing."

"Oh," Simon retorts, placing his hands on his hips, "like that rave shit you listen to is so special?"

"Some of it's okay," Polo says.

"Same beat over and over," Simon rants.

"At least," Polo lets on, "they ain't singing about dismembering babies and shit."

"Listen, y'all," Rip interrupts, "we're gonna have to start making some drastic moves."

"Tell me about it," Polo agrees.

"What d'ya mean?" Simon asks.

"Like robbing a bank," Rip answers.

Polo stares at him. "I used to think you're crazy, now I *know* for sure."

"I'm serious. Between the three of us we can do this."

A voice from the doorway speaks up. "You mean the four of us." The three turn to see Lucky standing there.

"Sorry, kid," Rip tells him. "You're out of the running."

"Why?"

"We're just joking around, Lucky," Polo smiles.

The youngster doesn't believe it. "Yeah, right. I know what you guys are planning."

"We ain't planning shit," Rip reveals.

"Besides," Lucky adds, "none of y'all have a getaway car. How do you think you'll make it?"

"The kid has a point," Simon states.

Rip shoots Simon a sharp look. Simon uses an imaginary zipper to close his lips.

"Well," Polo admits, "shit is getting kinda hectic. I, for one, know I gotta leave town soon."

"Why?" Simon asks.

"Because I can't stay here no more. Ain't nothing here. This is a fucking dead end."

"I agree," Rip says.

Simon gets up and walks to a window. "I don't know. I think we fit in right here. Where are we gonna go? To the fucking suburbs and light jack o' lanterns on the porch all night, with mom's warm apple pie sitting in the window, next to shiny new Mariners baseball caps? I don't think so. We need money, honey. And lots of it."

"I know where to get it," Lucky confesses.

"You do?" his brother asks. "Where?"

***

As the sun begins to set, some of the streets around Seattle's Central District become somewhat emptier, almost devoid of life and personality. The main thoroughfare, where crime is sometimes present, is necessarily avoided. The familiar odor of Ethiopian *injera*, Somali *halal* meats, and world class friend chicken is soon replaced by the repulsive stench of unclouded fear.

Simon, Polo, Rip, and Lucky are ambling down a quiet block near the edge of the district close to Swedish Hospital's Cherry Hill branch. The tree-lined street would be perfect save for the unpredictable element of danger always close behind. Simon is the first to break the quartet's silence.

"Are you sure he lives down here?"

"Where else?" Lucky answers. "Just look at the place."

They study the newly-developed condos, pristine homes, and perfect hedges on the block.

"You'd better be right," Simon sighs.

"Who is this guy anyway?" Polo asks.

"Mr. Frick," Lucky answers. "He used to teach math in Garfield High School."

"I remember him," Rip muses. "It's been a long time since I heard that name."

"Frick," Polo adds, "sounds like German for deviant sex."

"Nobody liked him," Lucky states. "Never smiled, never gave anybody an 'A', nothing. When his wife died, he retired. They say he snuffed her with a pillow for insurance money. Made it look like natural death."

Simon stares at the little informant. "How do you know all this shit?"

"'Cause he was our teacher. They used to talk about him all the time. His wife was planning to use her money for an orphanage, but the stingy bastard kept it all to himself."

"How much further?" Polo asks. "My legs are beginning to give out."

"Just up ahead. It'll be worth it."

"I hope you're right," Rip warns his brother. "I'm telling you, I ain't going back to jail, especially on some bullshit loitering charge."

"We're almost there," Lucky insists.

"What time is it anyway?" Polo asks.

Lucky glances at his watch. "Around nine o'clock."

Polo looks at the darkening sky."Maybe we should wait till it gets darker."

Lucky points to a small white and yellow house a few yards away and says, "There it is."

They come to the front of the house. A lamp and TV are on inside.

"Are you sure this is the house?" Simon asks.

The house's front door suddenly opens. The four boys jump backwards and hide behind a large tree on the curb. Kebede, the old Ethiopian, emerges from the yellow cottage with a cat in his arms. He places the feline on the porch and strokes its fur.

Simon recognizes the old man. "I know him."

"What?" Lucky asks. "That's not the school teacher."

"I know."

"From where?" Polo asks.

"From today," Simon believes. "He helped me out right after that fight I had with Rocky. His name's Kebede."

They watch as the old man looks up and down the street, stops petting his cat, and turns to go back inside. "He's leaving," Simon whispers.

Rip and Polo quickly don black stocking masks and pounce onto the porch. The startled cat shrieks and darts off. Lucky and Simon wait behind the tree.

Kebede jumps back when the two youths approach him.

"Ahh, don't hurt me," he shouts.

"Who's inside?" Rip asks.

"Just me," Kebede explains. "I don't have anything."

"I hope you're not lying," Polo yells.

The old man suddenly clutches his chest, gasps deeply, falls to his knees then falls flat on his face on the porch.

"Oh shit," Polo screams.

Lucky and Simon race over. "What the hell!" Simon explodes. "This is a good guy."

He kneels down and check's Kebede's pulse in his neck but doesn't find any. "Damn."

Polo and Rip remove their masks. "We didn't do anything!" Polo shouts.

"Honest, Simon," Rip adds. "This guy was on borrowed time to begin with."

"It ain't what y'all said," Lucky intervenes, "it's how y'all said it. You scared him to death."

"So what do we do now?" Simon asks. "Just leave him here?"

"Let's take him inside," Polo suggests.

"I'll deal with this," Rip explains. "It's my fault. I dragged everybody into this."

"Are you sure?" Simon asks.

"Yeah. You guys go."

Luck, Polo and Simon nod in agreement. Rip opens the front door and starts dragging Kebede in while the others take off.

In the neatly arranged one bedroom home, Rip places Kebede flat on the floor. He gets up, looks around the sparse living room, and decides to leave. Walking to the door, he stops and looks back at Kebede. Shaking his head, he kneels down next to the old man and commences CPR. With every breath and compression, Rip grows more tired. About two minutes later, the old codger comes to.

"Are you okay?" Rip asks.

"Where am I?" the confused old man asks.

"You're in your house. You had a heart attack out in the street." Rip helps Kebede sit up on a couch. "You'll be okay." He then turns to leave.

"Wait!" Kebede yells. "I know you. You tried to rob me."

"It wasn't me."

"What? You think I couldn't see through that mask? I've been robbed before."

"I'm sorry, mister. I'll see you later."

"Why do you boys go out doing things like that? Don't you know nothing good comes out of it?"

"Listen, old man. I didn't have to save your ass tonight."

"But, you did. That's the honorable thing. You know something, you look familiar."

"Yeah. See ya around."

Rip reaches for the front door's handle.

"Hold up," Kebede mentions. "I have a special reward for you."

"Oh yeah? What?"

"How about...," He reaches beneath the sofa's seat and whips out a pistol and adds, "a shot in your ass."

"Shit," Rip yells. Opening the door, he goes flying out like The Flash.

An hour later, Rip, in a somber mood, is sitting on a platform in Waterfront Park just off Alaskan Way downtown. Just a few feet above the Puget Sound water, he's dangling his feet in the cool moist air. Night has descended. The lights from the nearby restaurants and bright full moon are all the beacons the handful of passersby need to see their way around.

Rip, closing his eyes and nodding off, has a dream of a land where food is plentiful and troubles non-existent. Suddenly, his reverie is interrupted by a familiar voice.

"Mind if ah join you?" Rodney asks.

Waking up, Rip sees his Southern friend who'd been arrested only several hours earlier.

"What the fuck?" Rip shouts. "You escaped again?"

Rodney sits near Rip. "It's hard to keep a good man down, you hear?" he answers.

"How'd you get out?"

"They thought it was me who banged up that clerk, but they caught the *raht* guy."

"But you escaped from jail."

"Rip, you of all people should know about *mah* twin brother."

"So you didn't escape?"

"From jail? That's impossible, man."

"I was about to say, if it was you, then you should be selling that escape act in Vegas. You'd make a fortune."

"What are you doing out here anyway?" Rodney asks. "Getting some fresh air?"

"Just passing the time. Got anything on you?"

"Nah. Ah was hoping you did."

Rip checks his pockets. "I'm busted."

Rodney stares at the ripples in the water. "You know, *ah've* done some crazy shit in *mah lahf*, Rip."

"Probably not more than me."

"Oh, yeah?" Rodney yells suddenly. "You don't know the half of it. If you did you'd have me committed."

"Okay, okay. Calm down. You win. Whatever you did, I don't wanna know."

"My uncle used to yell at me for bullshit. You know what ah did one day?"

Rip shrugs.

"We went to an Observatory. He was up against the railing by a cliff? I pushed him off."

"Just like that? Why?"

"Ah don't know what came over me. When people piss me off, ah lose control."

Rip stares down at the moon and stars reflecting off the water below. Suddenly, he's a little uncomfortable with Rodney. "Well, Rod," he admits, "I gotta go now."

"What's the rush?"

"No rush. I just got things to do."

"You're abandoning me?"

"Abandoning you? You got it all wrong, Rod."

"That's what they all do. Use you for shit then dump you like coon sludge."

"That ain't me."

"No," Rodney admits. "You're *raht*." He grabs Rip. "But fuck you, anyway." He flings him off the bridge.

Rip screams, then he wakes up. Still sitting alone on the pier, Rip realizes it was just a dream. Nervously, he gets up and trots away.

***

In no great rush, Lucky is taking his sweet time returning to the abandoned house that night. With his hands in his pockets and his head lowered, he looks like the national poster child for Sad Sacks Anonymous.

He passes by a large fenced in house and sees three boys his age practicing tricks with their skateboards in the well lit driveway. Stopping momentarily, he stares at the youths. They also stop and stare at the stranger. There is longing in Lucky's eyes. Desperately, he wishes the boys would call him to play; instead, they simply resume their practice leaving him to covet their fun.

About a block later, Lucky sees a sprinkler is on in another fenced in yard. Unable to resist the urge, he tiptoes quietly into the yard and, as he's about to stick his hands in the cool shower, a German shepherd comes barking, charging from the rear.

Immediately, Lucky darts towards the gate. Because the lawn is wet, he slips and falls. Quickly getting up, he hobbles towards the gate with the watchdog only inches behind. Then, pushing through the gate, he quickly closes it behind him, narrowly escaping while the dog stops at the closed entrance.

He runs up the block as quickly as his legs would take him. Stopping at a corner to catch his breath, he looks down the road and sees nothing but rows of houses, most of them sitting behind well-manicured hedges. Against the trees, shrubs, and beautifully quiet houses, he suddenly looks like the smallest, loneliest person on Earth.

At the gas station on the corner, he walks over to the phone booth attached to the side of the building. Checking his pockets, he comes up empty handed. Eyeing a woman at one of the pumps, he walks over and asks for some change. He points in the direction of the phone booth and she gives him fifty cents. After thanking her, he walks over to the booth, flips through the Community Pages, sees a 1-800 number, and dials it. Seconds later, a woman's voice answers.

"Hello."

"Hello," Lucky begins, "can I—"

"... you've reached the Suicide Prevention Hotline. No one is available right now. If you'll please stay on the line, someone will be with you shortly. If you're having a life threatening emergency, please hang up and dial 911."

Lucky sighs and holds. Elevator music comes on. A yellow Mustang cruises by slowly on the street. Lucky pays only minimal attention to it till it turns a corner up ahead. Rubbing his hands, Lucky starts shuffling his feet uneasily.

Looking down, he sees a flyer on the sidewalk and picks it up. It is an ad for a reggae concert and it contains a picture of a smiling Bob Marley. Shaking his head, Lucky hangs up the phone, leaves the flyer on the telephone, puts his hands in his pockets, and walks on with his head bowed.

Moseying back to the five story hovel, Lucky doesn't notice the yellow Mustang trailing him with its headlight off a few yards back. Instead of going straight to the escape, Lucky walks on the field towards the standpipe. He opens the pipe, lets the rusty water run out then starts washing his hands.

The john from the yellow Mustang, Oscar Peteroff, suddenly grabs him around the neck and puts his hand around his mouth. "Don't move," he warns him. "Don't you twitch a muscle. If you scream I'll make you regret it, you hear me?"

Lucky nods.

The john removes his hand from around Lucky's mouth.

"Who the hell are you?" Lucky demands.

"Oscar. Is this where Simon stays? This dump?"

"Simon who?"

"Don't play games with me, boy. I've seen you hanging around with him all over town.

"Where exactly?"

"Don't test me, kid. He stole something from me today."

"Let me go, man, or I'll scream."

"You truant little bastard. How'd you like to spend the next few years at the juvenile farm in Yakima? You think this city's gonna miss one more street rat?"

Less than a minute later, Lucky, followed closely by the john, are ascending the creaky flight of metal stairs. Lucky makes a bold attempt at running down past him, but Oscar, despite his bulkiness, is surprisingly quick. Easily preventing Lucky from passing, he forces him back up the stairs.

Lucky climbs into the kitchen and turns on the lamp sitting on the floor. Oscar climbs in soon after and takes a gander at the site. Though poorly lit, it's still apparent the room seems uninhabitable.

"You boys live in this filthy dump?"

"At least there ain't nobody to tell us what to do or how to live."

"Lucky," Janis yells from the living room, "who are you talking to out there?"

"Be careful, now," Oscar warns him. "Tell her it's a friend."

"He said it's a friend," Lucky shouts.

The john slaps the back of his head.

They walk to the living room door. Constructed by the group from found parts, it doesn't sit perfectly in place. Still, it's effective in creating a third bedroom in this large two bedroom apartment.

"Knock on the door," Oscar whispers to Lucky. "And be careful."

Lucky knocks on the door.

"It's open!" Janis shouts.

Lucky and Oscar enter the dimly lit living room. Janis is sitting alone watching the TV. She looks up and sees the stranger.

"Who the hell are you?" she asks.

"Oscar Peteroff. Where's Simon?"

"Simon? Ain't no Simon living here. Just me and my little brother."

"Don't lie to me."

"What?"

Suddenly, like two stealth bombers, Simon and Polo fly through the air and ram right into Oscar. His toupee flies off his head. Polo butts him in the stomach. Oscar punches Simon in the face, sending him sprawling halfway across the room towards the west window facing the lot. Lucky kicks the john's shin. Janis grabs a broom and whacks the man so hard that the stick breaks. Polo throws an ashtray at him.

Grabbing the TV, Oscar raises it above his head and runs toward Simon. Accidentally, his left leg falls in the carpet covering the crater. In a panic, he drops the TV and bangs his chest against the opening while catching himself from falling through the hole. Hanging by his arms, he looks at the group.

"Help me," he begs. He tries getting out, but he's too awkwardly positioned in the hole.

Simon walks over to him. "I should stomp on your head right now, fucker."

"Please, Simon," he cries.

"Bullshit. You prey on little boys, pervert."

"What are we gonna do?" Janis asks, putting the TV back in place.

"Just let me go," Oscar begs. "I've learned from this." He slips a little further in the hole.

"Hurry up. I'm falling."

Simon, Polo, Lucky and Janis look at each other for a moment, then turn to the man.

"No tricks," Janis warns him.

He nods. Together, they pull him out of the hole.

"Remember," Simon cautions him, "I know where you live, and I know what you've done."

"Keep the wallet," Oscar insists. "I don't care."

He leaves. All four watch him closely as he climbs out of the kitchen window and down the escape. They also watch him lose his footing, slip off a broken section of the escape near the second floor, and fall to the yard below. Even in the relative darkness they could see his body, twisted in the weeds, is not moving.

"I think he's dead," Lucky muses.

"That's all we need," Janis laments.

She turns to Lucky. "Why'd you bring him here?"

"He forced me, all right? What was I supposed to do?"

"Did he have a gun?"

"Who cares if he had a gun? It's Simon's fucking friend."

"He's not my friend," Simon protests.

"Well, you need to handle your business," Janis tells him.

"Look who's talking."

They look down the street and see a police car cruising past the house.

"Oh, shit," Janis remarks. "Simon, go turn off the lights and the TV."

The car stops down the block, reverses back towards the field, and shines its light in it. Eventually, the spotlight illuminates the fallen Peteroff.

"*Puñeta,*" Polo moans, "This is it. This is the end."

The cop leaves his car, walks over to the fence, shines his flashlight Oscar and then up at the buildings windows. The teens back in quickly.

"I knew this shit was gonna get outta hand one day," Polo rants.

Simon returns from killing the lights. "We gotta get outta here, dudes."

"Right," Janis asserts. "We'll just walk past that cop as if nothing happened."

"We should wait for Rip," Lucky offers.

Janis looks at him and asks, "How is that gonna help?"

"He'll think of something."

"Like how to plead guilty in three easy lessons? He's probably on the run now that y'all fucking scared that old man to death. Geez, you guys are bad news."

"How were we supposed to know he's sick?" Lucky asks.

"Hell-fucking-lo," Polo answers. "There's a man, probably dead, out in the lot and y'all want to play Truth or Consequences and shit?"

Janis walks hurriedly to the living room, quickly puts her shoes and a jacket on in the darkness, and returns to the group.

"Where're you going?" Simon asks.

"Out of my mind," she answers.

They hear a siren and look out the window.

"Fucking backup," Simon yells.

They notice two squad cars coming their way.

"And something told me not to get up today, too," Polo moans.

"Rip told me that there's a shaft on the roof that goes straight down to the cellar," Lucky maintains. "He said it connects to a grate down by the old A/C unit in the back yard."

"How does he know that?" Janis asks.

"From that summer maintenance job he had last year."

"So there's some kinda air vent up there?" Simon asks pointing to the roof.

"I guess," Lucky answers. "He said it's part of the structure that holds this apartment up."

They watch the squad cars converge in front of the building.

"So what are we gonna do?" Janis ponders. "Slide down, like, five stories? We may as well leap out this fucking window."

"In buildings this size," Lucky informs her, "the vents usually have steps. Not really steps, more like partitions and dips."

Janis' face lights up like a star on a Christmas tree. "What are we waiting for?"

"How are we gonna get on the roof?" Lucky asks. "Climb the walls like Spiderman?"

"How do they usually get up there, then?"

"Through the emergency exit to the roof."

"Where is it?"

"Out in the hall, you know, down at the end."

"Won't it set off an alarm?"

"Probably not. Most of the electricity here was turned off."

"The hall," Janis remembers, "ain't *got* no floor."

"It does," Lucky admits, "but it's so eaten away it can't support anybody's weight."

"I bet if I can get up there," he continues, "there might be a rope or something I can drop down to you guys.

"That's crazy," Polo assumes. "Sounds dangerous."

"Or we can climb over each other using the drainpipe for support," Lucky says.

Simon nods. "That's a good idea."

"That's the most ridiculous thing I've ever heard," Polo asserts. "Suppose a strong wind hits us? Ain't nothing down there but the hard concrete. We'd be screwed."

They hear an officer speak over a megaphone. "This is the Seattle police. If there's anyone inside, come out with your hands up."

"Seems like we're screwed anyway," Janis reckons. "We gonna do the drainpipe thing?"

"It might still be too risky," Lucky guesses. "Listen, *this* will work. All y'all have to do is throw me across the hall to the railings."

"What railings?" Simon asks.

Lucky exits the apartment to the hallway and the others follow. Lit solely by the moonlight shining in through a few broken windows, the walls look just as bad as all the others. The floor is mostly absent and the other five apartments are boarded up. At the far end, across the chasm, are railings for a partially destroyed staircase that leads to a heavy metal door. Polo shakes his head.

"You're as loony as your brother."

"If I miss," Lucky hopes, "I'll only fall about one flight to the next floor."

"I say we do it," Simon utters.

Polo's not so sure. "This is sick. You're both freakin' crazy." He looks out the distant window in the hall at the full moon illuminating the sky.

"And I can see why." Janis nervously taps her thighs.

Lucky asks, "What d'ya say, Pole?"

"If you get me high enough till I don't know left from right, maybe I'll think about it."

"So then, what else do you suggest, Einstein?"

Polo thinks hard for a second or three. Lucky taps his watch and says, "Time isn't on our side."

They hear the officer with the megaphone repeat his message. "This is the Seattle police. If there's anyone inside come out peacefully with your hands up."

"Okay," Polo agrees. "I'll do it, but I won't like it."

They stare at the chasm between them and the metal rungs attached to the wall some twelve, maybe fifteen feet away.

How do we do this?" Janis asks.

"All you gotta do is tie a rope to my waste," Lucky suggests, "and hold it tight. If you want we can tie a couple of sheets together."

Polo shakes his head. "This is insane."

Lucky looks at him and says, "Do you have any better ideas?"

After quickly tying a few sheets together, the group attaches one end to a radiator in the hall and the other around Lucky's waist.

They hear the Officer speak again with his megaphone. "This is your third and final warning. Come out with your hands up."

"We'd better hurry," Simon insists.

Polo, Janis, and Simon follow Lucky to the edge of the huge crater in the hall. Suddenly, Lucky nearly slips into the hole, but the other three are quick to react and pull him backwards. Polo holds his stomach. "I think I'm gonna be sick."

Simon says, "Just don't look down."

"I'm not scared of heights," Lucky boasts.

"Good," Janis nods.

"But I gotta wash my hands first."

"What?" Polo shouts.

"Now?" Janis asks.

"I gotta wash my hands," Lucky begs.

"Do it later," Janis tells him.

"Y'all don't understand. I gotta go." He turns to go back to their apartment, but they don't let him out of their grasp. As a result, he goes into a screaming fit of rage. "Let me go. Let me go."

Polo cuffs his mouth telling him, "Be quiet."

"Let him go," Janis whispers. "He's gonna bring the damn police up here."

They let him go. Instead of going to the apartment, he runs to the door, stops, then stands sobbing like a baby. "Why can't I help it?" he cries.

Janis walks over and hugs him. "It's okay."

"I wanna be normal, Janis."

"I know, baby. I know."

Polo and Simon walk over and pat him on the back. "It's all right, Lucky," Simon tells him. "It's okay."

"I don't understand it myself, Lucky," Polo admits, "but then again, there's millions of things I don't even understand about myself. Maybe that's why you're one of us."

"So, Lucky," Janis congratulates him, "now you're part of the gang. Misfits forever."

Lucky cracks a smile and says, "Thanks. Let's do this like Brutus."

Down below, Rip is standing behind a lamp post watching the police cars that have converged around the abandoned building. There is also an ambulance parked in the street. The front fence, he notices, has been cut wide open.

He sees someone being carried to the ambulance on a stretcher by two paramedics. He notices the man is still alive because he is fighting against his restraints. Rip quickly dashes behind a bush when an officer shines a light in his direction. Accidentally, he hits his left knee on an old stone planter which is completely shrouded by vines and leaves.

Back in the building, Lucky is getting prepared for his space flight across the hall's chasm. His friends pick him up.

"It's a good thing you're light," Polo notices.

"Here we go," Simon begins. "One ... two ..."

"Wait," Polo interrupts. "Do we throw him on three, or wait just 'til after three?"

"What is this?" Simon whispers, "Lethal Weapon? We toss him on three. One ... two ... three."

They toss him with such force that he actually flies past the metal rungs, hits the wall, then recoils and grasps the railings.

"Whoa," Janis claps.

"Sorry, Lucky," Simon apologizes.

"I'm okay," Lucky says.

"Can you open the door?" Simon asks.

"I'll try." He carefully pushes the door's emergency exit lever. The door opens and there's no alarm.

"Sweet," Polo remarks.

Simon bites his nails. "I'm as nervous as a turkey at Thanksgiving."

Lucky turns to his friend. "Untie the sheets."

They untie it from the radiator. Lucky pulls the makeshift sheet rope towards him then opens the door and climbs out onto the roof.

Polo, Janis, and Simon climb back out to the fifth floor landing and watch as Lucky drops the "rope" over the roof near the structure's dark side.

Janis tugs at it. "Is it secure?"

"Shh," Lucky warns her. "Yeah."

Quietly, but quickly, Janis climbs up the dangling bed sheet rope, followed by Polo, then Simon. Up on the roof, they pull up the rope then try their best to avoid detection by crouching and speaking in hushed tones.

"Where's the air shaft?" Simon asks.

Lucky point to a distal section of the roof. "I think it's over here."

They follow Lucky over to a large aluminum shaft and realize the handle for the cover is missing.

"How do we get in now?" Janis asks.

"I don't know?" Lucky answers. "Maybe the handle's around here somewhere. Let's look for it."

"Shit. It's so dark," Polo groans, "I can barely see my hand in front of my face."

"It must be on the inside," Lucky says.

"What?" Janis asks.

"It's an internal opening shaft."

"Are you sure?"

"Yeah. I think so."

"This is unbelievable," Polo whispers.

"If my cousin could see me now," Simon utters, "he'd wrap his guitar strings around my neck and dangle me from this roof."

They hear another siren blaring down the street towards them. "What the fuck?" Polo asks. "They're bringing out the whole troop tonight?"

They creep to the front side of the building and see a fire engine with a cherry picker parking out front.

"They're gonna come up here," Janis says.

Simon shakes his head. "Oh, man."

"This shit bites," Polo emphasizes.

Lucky agrees. "You're telling me."

"I'm not going in alive," Simon promises.

Polo stares at him. "What? What are you saying?"

"You don't mean that, Simon," Janis states.

Simon has a distant glazed look in his eyes. "I ain't going to prison."

"Oh, whatever," Polo says. "You're such a drama queen."

Simon creeps over to a distant end of the roof. Polo follows him. Simon, sitting with his back against an exhaust pipe, takes out a cigarette and lights it. Polo flops down near him.

"Can I have one?" he asks.

Simon hands him the rest. "Take the pack."

"I don't like how you're sounding tonight, Simon."

"Then go back with the rest, Polo. This is how I feel, all right?"

"You're scaring me."

Simon looks at Polo's face then takes his hand. "I'm sorry, Pole. I don't know what to do."

At the front end of the roof, Janis is sitting with Lucky, both of them silent as if awaiting the Armageddon. She looks at Lucky. "Stay right here for a minute. I'll be right back."

"Where are you going?"

"I just want to talk to the boys in private for a second."

She gets up and creeps over to Polo and Simon. Both silent, they appear to be deep in thought.

"Hey," she says.

"What's up?" Polo asks.

Janis looks at Simon. "You didn't mean what you said a while ago, did you?"

Simon shrugs. Janis reaches into her pocket and brings out the small brown packet of 'JB'.

"What's that?" Polo asks.

"I found it under our mattress. Rip probably had it stashed for later."

Simon stares at it. "What is it? Blow?"

"It looks like dope," Polo says.

"It is," Janis agrees. "I tasted it. Might be uncut, too."

Polo is doubtful that it's really uncut. "Ain't no pure primo shit around here."

"Y'all want some?" she asks them.

Polo smiles broadly. "Hells yeah."

Simon nods. "What kinda question is that?"

Janis looks at Polo and tells him, "Hold out your hand."

He does and she opens the JB and pours about half of it into his hand.

"Thanks."

"See you boys later."

She moves back towards Lucky. The boys study the fine powdery substance, totally entranced by its presence.

"You wanna go first?" Polo asks his boyfriend.

"Why don't we do it together?"

"Like old times."

Using his long pinky nail, Polo makes two powder lines in his hands. Simon creeps closer to his pal.

"You ready?" Polo asks.

"Yeah. Wait a minute." Simon gently removes the bandage from his face and throws it away. "Okay," he says.

Down in the yard, Rip creeps unseen through the bushes behind the abandoned building towards the large old A/C unit next to the structure. From where he stands, he can see two officers entering the cherry picker. The rest of the officers mobilize themselves behind their car doors with teargas rifles and lights aimed up at the building. Two firefighters are attaching their hose to a hydrant nearby while a third is manipulating the lift.

Quietly pulling the rusty grate off the large duct, Rip lays it in the grass, clears the old cobwebs off the entrance, and creeps in as silently as a jaguar stalking its prey in the Serengeti. At the front end of the roof, Janis is sitting with Lucky who seems to be going into a panic.

"Are you okay?" she asks him.

"Where's Rip?"

"I don't know. We need to try getting down that vent."

"You think they caught him?"

"I don't know."

"He said they'd never let them take him."

"It's hard losing these guys, Lucky. They have these satellites that can see the tracks in your underwear and shit.

Janis takes out the rest of the JB. Lucky stares at it. "What's that?"

"You wanna know what heaven's like, Lucky?" He shrugs. "It's a place you go where no one can hurt you," she explains. "You're invisible there. Invulnerable. You can dream all day and not have to worry about food or shelter or love because all those things don't matter. In your case, think of it as a place where the faucets are made of gold, the handles are sterling silver with mother of pearl inlays, the sinks are polished Italian marble, and the cool clear water runs forever like a mountain spring. You want me to take you there?"

Lucky stares at the JB then sneaks a peek over the roof where he sees the cherry picker's two inhabitants carefully checking the building floor by floor.

"Yeah," he agrees. "I wanna go."

Janis pours a little in her hand and brings it close to Lucky's face. He's hesitant. "Don't be scared," she whispers, "I'll meet you there."

Lucky nods. Gently, she once again brings her powdered palm to his face. He inhales some of it and immediately goes into convulsions. Janis holds him tightly and grabs a sheet to mop up the spittle now flowing from his mouth. She starts humming a tune. Then, after a few terse moments, his body stiffens and falls limp. Crying, Janis closes his eyes, kisses his head, and takes out the last of the JB while he's still cradled in her arms.

A scraping sound is heard coming from the vent. There is a slight tapping, then a rusty handle is heard turning. Seconds later, the square aluminum door opens and Rip creeps out. Closing the door behind him, he sees Polo and Simon in the distant end of the roof and creep towards them.

Like two star-crossed lovers, Polo is lying still in Simon's arms. Even by the light of the moon, he could see they're gone. Rip, putting his fingers on their necks, receives no pulses. He clenches his teeth. Tears well in his eyes. "Fuck!" he whispers. "What did you fucking guys do? I hope this wasn't about the old man 'cause I saved him."

Hugging the boys, he leaves them and sneaks to the front edge where he sees Lucky and Janis huddled together in a deathly embrace. "Oh, fuck." He checks their pulses then hug them tightly.

"No," he shouts.

The two officers in the cherry picker swing up to the side of the roof. An officer his gun.

"You kids got me doing overtime," he states. "Stand up slowly and put your hands in the air."

Rip, torn by the death of his brother and friends, pays no attention to the officer. "Lucky ... Janis ..." he cries. He sees the empty packet of JB on the roof. "Oh shit. Fuck!"

The officer holsters his weapon. "I want you to listen carefully," he tells Rip. "Stand up and move slowly towards me."

Rip stands up slowly, looks at the cops, looks at Janis and Lucky, then backs away from the officer.

"Stay where you are!" the cop orders.

Rip squeezes his temples in anguish. "No." He backs up a little more till he's a few feet from one of the edges.

"Don't move anymore," the cop tells him. "Everything's gonna be okay."

"No. It's not fucking okay. Nothing is okay."

"Just come down, man," the second officer pleads. "We'll sort it all out. This building isn't safe. It can collapse any time."

"I don't know," Rip bawls. "My brother's dead. I was fucking careless, now I have to pay."

"Listen to me," the first cop says. "Sometimes you get your back against the wall and think there's no way out. I know it's hard, but this can be worked out."

Rip backs up a little more. "You don't have a clue."

"You gotta remember what you want out of life and go for it, you know what I mean? You gotta think about the future, man."

"The future?" Rip shoots back.

"Yeah. That's right. You have a future beyond this tragedy."

Rip looks at his quivering hands and takes a few steps forward.

"That's it," the officer tells him. "Take it easy."

Rip gazes at his brother, Janis, Polo and Simon. Then, looking at the cops, he sees the officer slowly remove a set of handcuffs and dangle them below his belt.

Suddenly, Rip turns.

"Wait," the first cop yells.

He runs towards the far edge and off, shouting, "There is no future."

"No," the officers yell.

Belltown

Lil Jeep woke up that morning with a monster truck sized headache. It wasn't the weeklong heat wave that spurned it, but his decision not tell his "posse." Even though he was the youngest of the five, he already began to think gang life just wasn't his cup of tea.

He'd seen a lot for his fifteen years—rape, murder, poverty, destitution, homelessness, juvenile detention—but he just couldn't get out of his mind the tragedy he'd witnessed one day. A Chicago bloods gang with ties to Seattle tried to assassinate his best friend in a drive by but, instead, wiped out a totally innocent family whose beautiful daughter he had eyes for.

His posse, comprising of Yung Prez, Dru'wan, The Future, and Run E. Gunz, called themselves the Rainier Boyz. Not really a true gang, they did adopt some of its survival mechanisms, including dope peddling and burglary. They weren't able to retaliate against the Chicago affiliated group because their numbers were too small and lacked the firepower. That's when Lil Jeep thought about leaving "the life." He was done, had it up to here. He just had to work out the minor details of when.

The Seattle clubs were beginning to fill up that Friday night with revelers. That means it was time to let the games begin. Soon, the Belltown section would overflow with party goers, hot dog carts, the ubiquitous sound of car horns crashing against each other like a cacophonous symphony awash over the masses, and the occasional drug dealer.

Marnie and her new boyfriend, Alden, was club hopping when it happened. Alden only smoked herb when he'd been out drinking, and tonight was no exception. Before continuing to their next dance hall, he had to obtain some bud come rain or high water.

With Marnie in tow, they walked to a seedy, darkened area in the nooks of Belltown. She was a little scared and protested outright, but since there was a slight bump in police presence, she decided to just go along with him. All of the unsavory characters he ran into were selling crack, a drug he had no interest in.

"Come on," she pleaded. "We're wasting time."

"It's around here somewhere," he promised. "I've never been unlucky."

"Well, there must be a dry spell."

Alden, himself, was beginning to give up hope until they passed an alley. The distinctive whiff of marijuana emanated from the narrow passageway. Looking over, they noticed five youths standing between dumpsters. Puffs of smoke hovered above their heads like mist on a lake.

"What d'ya think?" Alden asked Marnie rhetorically. "Should I go ask them?"

"It's kinda dark down there," she answered. "Just signal 'em or something."

"It'll be all right," he hoped as he walked towards the smokers.

The five young black men, the Rainier Boyz, didn't pay them much attention. They were too brazen to care if anyone approaching was with the police. Marnie could feel the lump in her throat get bigger.

"What y'all want?" Yung Prez turned and asked.

"Bud," Alden answered.

"Like this?" Dru'wan wondered, holding up a fist-sized baggie half-filled with herb.

"What you looking to spend?" Yung Prez queried.

"Fifty."

Alden removed a crumpled $50 bill from his pocket. Yung Prez took it and put it in his pocket. All five young men then turned to walk back down the alley.

"Hey," Alden yelled. "That's a fifty."

The Future turned around. "Get lost, punk," he shouted.

Alden, however, was already seething with fury from the slight. "You motherfucker," he shouted at Yung Prez.

Like a pack of feral wolves, the boys turned and set upon the couple. Marnie screamed as punches and kicks flew. Alden got in a few licks of his own, but the youths were just too strong, too powerful, and too angry. Lil Jeep, still in the planning stages of exiting the gang, pretended to join in the fight. With two of his posse struggling with Alden, and the other two attacking Marnie, he kept a lookout for the police.

The beatings lasted about a minute. Though no metal weapons were used, Marnie and Alden sustained contusions, black eyes, bruises, broken ribs, torn ear lobes from earrings being yanked out, fat lips, bloody gums, scratches and several spots of hematoma throughout their bodies. And they were still out of $50. The paramedics thought the two were lucky to be alive. It could've been a lot worse.

About one hour later, the thugs were walking around Yesler Way near downtown Seattle when a squad car came rolling up the street. The young men kept walking, acting as casual as possible. When the car's lights finally came on, they scattered. One officer jumped out and chased after Yung Prez, the other after Dru'wan. Run E. Gunz and The

Future disappeared between the buildings. Lil Jeep ran down a nearby flight of stairs, cut through a park, and hopped over a railing. On his way over, his shoe laces got caught on some nettles from a spindly bush. When he fell, the audible "crack" of his right arm could be heard for a block.

Screaming, he carefully took off his jacket. Rolling up his sweater's right sleeve, he moaned when he saw his broken right ulna protruding through his skin near the wrist. Painfully, he got to his feet and also soon realized his left ankle was sprained. Carefully, he limped towards a friend's house. No one was home. Still in pain, he walked the few blocks to Harborview Medical Center.

Two hours later, he was lying in a recovery room with a splint on his right arm, a bandage around his left ankle, and an IV stuck in his left forearm. Although he'd been sedated, he could still overhear the hospital staff talking among themselves.

"What is this city coming to?" one asked.

"It's time to get that gun permit I've been putting off," added another.

"Where are their fathers?" a third asked. "There's no discipline, no love, no guidance."

Unable to sleep, Lil Jeep got up, stood near the entrance of his room and looked down the hall. He saw a crying little girl sitting in a wheelchair near the nurse's station. A CNA was comforting her. Just then, a woman in her fifties came walking around the corner.

"Mommy," the girl shouted, hugging the woman.

"It's okay, Marianne," her mother said. "Your sister and her boyfriend are fine. They're in surgery now."

"But she promised this city was safe," the girl bawled.

"It is, dear," the woman reassured her.

"So why did they do that? Why did they beat them up like that?"

"I don't know, Marianne," she sighed. "They love it here. They think it's vibrant, full of energy, but some people just don't see it that way."

"It's not fair."

"Yes, dear, I know. Let's wait inside."

The woman and the little girl went down the hall and walked into a room where a police officer was sitting just outside. Lil Jeep tried getting the image of the crying Marianne, and the potential girlfriend he'd lost, out of his mind. He started to walk back to bed then shook his head and limped towards the nursing station.

"You should be resting," a nurse cautioned him. "You lost a lot of blood tonight."

"I'll go lie down," he admitted then looked down the hall at the officer, "but first, I have to make a confession."

About the Author

Robin Ray was born in Trinidad & Tobago and went to the U.S. when he was 12. He minored in English at Iowa State University then later studied nursing at Elizabeth Seton College in NY, all the while pursuing his dream of becoming a recording artist. Later, leaving the music field behind, he went back to his first love – writing fiction. His short stories and fairy tales have been published in magazines such as *Enchanted Conversation, Darkest Before the Dawn, Free Flash Fiction, Powder Burn Flash & Red Fez*. Wetland & Other Stories is his first book.

ALL THINGS THAT MATTER PRESS, Inc. ™

FOR MORE INFORMATION ON TITLES AVAILABLE FROM
ALL THINGS THAT MATTER PRESS, GO TO
http://allthingsthatmatterpress.com
or contact us at

www.ingramcontent.com/pod-product-compliance
Lightning Source LLC
Chambersburg PA
CBHW072104020726
47501CB00003B/705